The Vermilion Bird

A FIVE DIRECTIONS PRESS BOOK

The Vermilion Bird

A NOVEL

C. P. LESLEY

ISBN-13 978-1947044104
ISBN-10 1947044109

Published in the United States of America.

A Five Directions Press book

Cover photographs: Horseman at sunset © dtopal/Shutterstock; phoenix © DVARG/Shutterstock; Grand Kremlin Palace interior © 2007 politkleit, CC 3.0 via Wikimedia Commons. Map on page ii based on data from Google Maps © 2017.

Book and cover design by Five Directions Press
Five Directions Press logo designed by Colleen Kelley

FIVE DIRECTIONS PRESS

CONTENTS

The Campaign to Capture Prince Andrei of Staritsa, May 1537

Map Data © 2017 Google.

Muscovite Forces ——

Koshkin ••••••

Battleground 𝍐

Prince Andrei ------

Prince Andrei's Men ══

Cast of Characters

(in alphabetical order by first name)

FICTIONAL CHARACTERS

Alexei Bulatovich: Formerly Tulpar, Bulat's eldest son by the concubine Sania, cast out at the age of sixteen by his father; Maria's husband and hero of *The Vermilion Bird*.

Bulat: Tatar khan in Russian service; fictional older half-brother of the historical Shah-Ali Khan, ruler of the subordinate Russian principality of Kasimov; father of Alexei, Nasan, and Ogodai; husband of Sumbeka.

Daniil Nikolaevich Kolychev: Bulat's son-in-law, a Russian nobleman; husband of Nasan.

Firuza: Ogodai's wife and Nasan's sister-in-law; mother of the twins Altan-Alia and Irek.

Fyodor Mikhailovich Koshkin: Maria's father; an enemy of the Kolychev clan since his plans for an alliance with them failed to yield the desired results.

Gleb Glebovich Bogdanov: Andrei of Staritsa's chamberlain.

Grigory Osipovich Kolychev: cousin of Daniil; has a brother named Denis.

Grusha: Slave who escaped from the Kolychev household and has taken up residence in Ogodai's horde.

Guzel: Alexei's lover, 1527–1534; mother of Timur.

Ilya Petrovich Shuisky: Junior member of a princely clan, fictional nephew of the historical Prince Vasily Shuisky.

Father Job: The Kolychevs' chaplain. Married, like all Orthodox priests (except monastic priests), and father of a large family.

Lyuba Fyodorovna Koshkina: Maria's six-year-old sister.

Maria Fyodorovna Koshkina/Kolycheva: Heroine of *The Vermilion Bird*; widow of Daniil's older brother, Boris Kolychev; wife to Alexei Bulatovich and thus doubly sister-in-law to Nasan. She is the eldest of seven; her siblings, by order of age, are Varvara, Mikhail, Foma, Timofei, David, and Lyuba.

Nadezhda Shuiskaya: Wife of Prince Ilya Shuisky; part of Grand Princess Elena's inner circle.

Nasan (Irina) Bulatovna Kolycheva: Daughter of Bulat Khan, Ogodai's sister, Alexei's half-sister, and wife of Daniil Kolychev; Maria's sister-in-law.

Natalya Vasilyevna Kolycheva: Daniil's mother, Nasan's mother-in-law, and Maria's former mother-in-law.

Nikolai Borisovich Kolychev: Daniil's father, a high-ranking Russian nobleman (boyar).

Ogodai: Son of Bulat, older brother of Nasan, half-brother of Alexei; married to Firuza and khan of her deceased father's horde; father of Firuza's twins, Irek and Altan-Alia.

Roxelana: Wife to Fyodor Koshkin; Alexei's former concubine; originally a Christian slave from the area that is now northwest Afghanistan.

Ruslan: Alexei's close friend and ally; another sultan from Crimea.

Sania: Bulat's concubine, 1507–1515; mother of Alexei.

Solomonida Sheremeteva: Daughter of the Kolychevs' next-door neighbor and related to them through her marriage, now ended, to Daniil's cousin Semyon.

Father Spiridon: The Koshkins' chaplain.

Sumbeka: Bulat's chief wife, mother of Nasan and Ogodai, Alexei's stepmother; the daughter of a Crimean sultan.

Theodosia Zakharina-Koshkina: Maria's aunt and the wife of one of the young princes' official guardians, hence within the inner circle of the court. Both the guardian and his wife were historical personages, but so little is known about Theodosia that she is best considered a fictional character.

Timur: Alexei's son by a previous nonmarital relationship with Guzel.

HISTORICAL CHARACTERS

As often happens with medieval and early modern people, we have limited information about Russians and Tatars, even royalty, who lived in the sixteenth century. To the extent possible, I have ensured that details about real people included in the Legends novels match the historical record, but often these details do not extend much beyond dates of marriages, deaths, and sometimes births. Therefore, these characters' appearance, personalities, words, and motivations are just as much my invention as those of their fictional counterparts.

Andrei Ivanovich: Youngest brother of Vasily III; uncle to Ivan IV; prince of Staritsa.

Elena Glinskaya: Grand princess and regent of Russia; mother of Ivan IV, known to posterity as Ivan the Terrible, and his younger brother, Yuri Vasilyevich; widow of Grand Prince Vasily III, whose death in 1533 led to much uncertainty and aggression at home and abroad.

Islam-Girei of Crimea: Nephew, rival, and heir of Sahib-Girei and his predecessor; Alexei's chosen overlord since his exile in 1524. After a decade of strife Islam-Girei again rebelled against his uncle in 1536, unleashing a new round of hostilities that ended with his assassination in August 1537. The Girei dynasty ruled Crimea for centuries; the name is often spelled Giray.

Ivan IV Vasilyevich: Grand Prince of Russia (1530–1584, r. 1533–1584); crowned tsar 1547; known as "the Terrible" (meaning "terror-inducing," not "bad").

Ivan Fyodorovich Ovchina Telepnev Obolensky: Boyar, prince, military commander; favorite of Elena Glinskaya and a prominent court figure during her reign. His cousin Nikita also makes a brief appearance in the novel, as does Prince Yuri Obolensky, Andrei of Staritsa's majordomo.

Safa-Girei Khan: Ruler of Kazan, nephew to Sahib-Girei Khan of Crimea; an enemy of Bulat's family.

Sahib-Girei Khan: Ruler of Crimea, 1532–1551, despite the periodic attempts of his nephew Islam-Girei to unseat him.

Vasily III Ivanovich: Grand Prince of Russia (r. 1505–1533), father of Ivan IV and Yuri Vasilyevich.

Vasily Vasilyevich Shuisky: Boyar, prince, leader of the Shuisky clan; a prominent member of the government, especially in foreign affairs.

Yuri Ivanovich: Younger brother of Vasily III, uncle to Ivan IV, prince of Dmitrov; died in captivity, reportedly of starvation, 3 August 1536.

Yuri Vasilyevich: Younger brother of Ivan IV.

Firebird

REBORN FROM HER OWN ASHES, THE EMPRESS OF BIRDS *shakes her fiery wings and calls to her natural mate, Lord of Water and Weather. Where phoenix unites with dragon, the forces of nature achieve balance, and marriages and kingdoms prosper.*

But fire sparks desires for both passion and power. And in the fertile lands of the south, where the Vermilion Bird resides, the embers of love and insurrection burn bright. Borne on winds of fear, they enflame the kingdom to the north.

Chapter 1

"IT'S A SCANDAL, I TELL YOU. FYODOR HAS GONE MAD." Over the plink-plink of psalteries, the chatter of fifty women, the murmurs of servants in corners, and the noise from the courtyard below, Aunt Theodosia's voice soared like a song. "Marrying a hussy two years older than his own daughter? Then wedding his own girl to his new wife's former lover? Abominable! Where is his honor?"

"Auntie! How can you?" Maria, tempted to shrink into herself like a tortoise into its shell, instead gripped the hand of the hated Roxelana, whose fingers returned the favor with equal strength. "Stop squeezing me," she hissed at her stepmother, who narrowed her eyes and hissed wordlessly back.

But Roxelana, although a general irritant, bore no responsibility for Maria's present agony. On the contrary, she shared it. *Must* Auntie announce their predicament to the world? Thanks to her, every woman here knew—now, if she hadn't before—that Roxelana had lived for years with the man destined to become Maria's husband tomorrow, only to abandon him for Maria's father and the respectability he offered.

A hint of sandalwood and cinnamon released into the air as Roxelana shifted in her seat. Among the many perfumes wafting around the room, hers stood out: seductive, elusive, foreign.

Respectability? Roxelana? As if that's not a contradiction in terms!

Aunt Theodosia was still talking—bellowing, rather, with the blissful unconcern of the hard of hearing. "Twenty-two years old, and him a ripe thirty-seven. What does he want with a lovely nincompoop to warm his bed? After wearing my dearest sister to the bone, bearing and raising his children. Thirteen she gave him. Thirteen. And seven who lived!"

"We know, Auntie. We can count." This voice, young and sweet, belonged to Maria's sister Varvara, second of the seven living offspring. She spoke in softer tones than Theodosia.

"Don't mumble like that, girl," Theodosia snapped. "Speak up."

"Hush now." Varvara raised her voice as commanded. "The whole room can hear you." She gestured with her right hand. "Including our stepmother."

"Don't be absurd. I'm whispering, just as you are," Theodosia said at top volume. "Stepmother, indeed. Harlot, more like."

Roxelana hissed again, louder this time, and Varvara pressed her lips together, as if trying not to giggle. In response Theodosia fixed Roxelana with her basilisk glare. "Ridiculous. Just ridiculous."

"You're being rude, Auntie," Maria said. Anything to deflect the discussion to another channel, although she agreed with Theodosia. Watching Papa glow like a schoolboy while her stepmother flirted and cooed left her two steps short of disgust. Parents were *not* supposed to act like that.

As for this new match with her stepmother's discarded lover, Theodosia was right: Papa had lost his mind. A man nine years older than Maria, and a Tatar—what would they talk about?

"I am not being rude," Theodosia said, no quieter than before. "I speak the truth, as anyone here can see for herself. And don't try to convince me that marriage to a man without morals, an outsider, is other than a disgrace. Although he did have enough sense not to marry the hussy."

"I *am* your hostess," Roxelana announced in a voice as piercing as Theodosia's. "If you have no respect for me, your brother-in-law, or your niece here, please do not let us delay your departure." The guests drew closer, drawn by the conflict, their faces avid with curiosity.

"He's a *tsarevich*, Auntie," Varvara said in soothing tones. "The son of Bulat Khan. A descendant of Genghis. No doubt Papa thought him a great catch. He raises the standing of our entire lineage."

Theodosia harrumphed, visibly unimpressed. "I don't care if he's the son of St. Andrew. It's indecent, that's what it is. Worse than marrying that strumpet." She jerked her head in Roxelana's direction, leaving no doubt whom she had in mind.

"That does it," Roxelana snapped. "Either stop insulting me or leave." Her hazel eyes flashed, and she pressed her lips together.

Theodosia snorted. "I came to attend my niece's wedding, shameful as it is, in my sister's house. I do not care if I offend you, and you do *not* order me to leave."

"Auntie, please stop." Maria fought an unexpected lump in her throat. "I know you're defending me, and I appreciate it, but causing a scandal at my bride's party is not helping me." She sent Varvara a pleading glance.

"Come, Auntie." Varvara put a hand under Theodosia's elbow. "Let me find you a seat and some food. You can listen to the musicians. Watch the dancing." She grinned over her shoulder at Maria as they moved away, Theodosia still grumbling about her brother-in-law's shocking behavior while Varvara made clucking noises like a chicken.

The grip of Roxelana's fingers drew Maria's attention to her hand, where linen wrappings protected a concoction of henna paste, overlaid with rare, precious lemon juice to enhance the color. The wrappings pulled taut, like a bandage tied too tight. Roxelana scowled at Theodosia's back, then bent her head and tugged at the knot binding Maria's left wrist as if nothing had happened.

Because she had some plot up her sleeve? Studying her bandaged hands as if she could pierce their secret by will alone, Maria bit her lip and shivered. Her sister-in-law, Irina, had hidden the design as Roxelana painted it, insisting it must remain a surprise. A mark of good fortune, Irina said.

She made it sound innocuous, but Maria trusted neither of them. Roxelana had near-magical powers. How else could one explain her ability to captivate men: her former lover, the beys who preceded him—and Papa, who seldom allowed his heart sway over his head? Exactly where she came from, Maria did not know. Chorasan, Papa said. But where was that? Somewhere in the south, where they had Christians—heretic ones familiar with the dark arts of Hindustan and Persia.

As for Irina, where to start? A Tatar by birth, wife to Maria's brother-in-law by her first marriage, and half-sister to the new bridegroom, Irina was in her own way more alien than Roxelana. At times she wore boys' clothes. She practiced archery and swordsmanship with her husband. Maria had seen her shoot a fleeing man from horseback. In the last year alone she had saved Maria's life twice. Maria had learned to respect her—even to like her—but understand her? That would not happen within the Ages of Ages.

Look at this heathen version of a maiden's party, which Irina and Roxelana had organized. At first it seemed ordinary, even expected. Cousins and aunts and friends arrived in droves, bearing jewelry and cosmetics, scents and good wishes, ready to adorn the bride. A party of women to celebrate a wedding: what could be more natural? Maria welcomed their petting and their praise, showered effusive thanks on Irina and Roxelana, and chided herself for her sharp tongue. Why did she so often assume the worst?

But that was before finely honed shells shaved every bit of hair from her body, leaving only her eyebrows and the double braids secured with ties atop her head. Before the henna paste started its slow drip-drip against her skin. Hours passed while she sat helpless as patterns formed in cool, moist lines she could sense but not see. She strove to turn the sensations into drawings in her mind, but Roxelana moved too swiftly, the lines she formed complex and overlapping. Irina encouraged and suggested, plied Maria with turnovers and cider, coaxed the others to preserve the secret. Now she perched on a stool nearby, quietly observing, a state unusual for her.

Varvara returned, without their aunt, oohing as Roxelana unwrapped Maria's left hand. Maria craned forward. What would she see?

Not much. The unwrapping revealed only her fingernails, encircled by tiny swirls. A few more turns, and the swirls extended into long sweeping lines down the back of each finger. As Roxelana rubbed off the dried paste with a damp cloth, the ocher gel turned a rich reddish brown. Five swirls, five sets of lines.

Maria leaned against the wall behind her and released the breath she'd been holding. Nothing scary. A vine, most likely, like the ones Roxelana had worn for her wedding. Irina had painted them.

Odd how she'd forgotten that until just now. She should have guessed they would do the same for her. Why hadn't she?

Because she was Russian, and Christian, and they knew that. Their pagan customs had no place in her life.

Although Roxelana declared herself Christian too.

Maria's stomach tightened. Roxelana. Everything came back to Roxelana. The sorceress who had lured Maria's new bridegroom, then Papa. Who missed no opportunity to remind Maria who ruled the household. So what if Irina had drawn pretty flowers for Roxelana? Irina had her flaws, but she was not vindictive. Whereas Roxelana …

Auntie Theodosia was right, and the whole arrangement a disgrace.

"Don't listen to Auntie, Maria," Varvara said. Maria, startled, jerked her head toward her sister. Had she spoken her random thoughts aloud?

She checked her sister's face, but Varvara had turned to peer at the design. A corner of her headdress swung between them, and Roxelana batted it away. "Such a handsome husband," Varvara went on. "I wish Papa had picked him for me! Young, distinguished, a warrior, of royal blood—"

"And so good between the sheets," Roxelana drawled.

A ripple of laughter ran around the room. The musicians stopped mid-note, and Aunt Theodosia hove back into view, pursed lips signaling her willingness to resume battle. Varvara's cheeks turned the color of a ripe apple. Even the maids clustered in corners, poking one another in the ribs and giggling.

"Oh look, Maria's blushing," someone said from the crowd. "Isn't that sweet?"

Solomonida Sheremeteva. Another long-time foe— blonde, beautiful, and depraved. Well, not truly depraved, but a terrible flirt. Trust her to find Roxelana's jab funny.

"Shouldn't you be in a convent?" Maria asked Solomonida. A divorced woman *should* be in a convent, not donning gorgeous silks to celebrate the wedding of a cousin by marriage she didn't even like.

Solomonida laughed. "Don't you wish I were. But I wouldn't miss this for the world. Your second wedding. How many women get that chance? Are you ready to weep 'the tears of the harlot'?"

Maria bristled. Quoting the ceremony for a second wedding, considered a concession to human weakness by the Church, struck her as a low blow. "Well, you won't, will you? Not with a six-year-old daughter in tow!"

Solomonida laughed. "Thank the Lord for Anna. Who wants another husband? The first one was more than enough for me."

A tart voice interrupted. "Why not stay with him, then?" Another aunt pushed herself forward and stood at Theodosia's side—Paraskeva, the nun, serene in her black robes. "You could have wallowed in sin together."

Maria gave a quick shake of her head. How could Solomonida stay with her husband? She hadn't *chosen* the divorce. That's why she was refusing to enter a convent. And although her husband had been a pig of the first order, living with him could not be considered wallowing in sin.

Then she realized Paraskeva was talking to Roxelana, responding to that earlier comment about Maria's bridegroom being skilled between the sheets. And was that *envy* in Paraskeva's voice?

Maria stared openmouthed at her aunt. A nun, yearning for a life of wicked pleasure?

"He left Crimea," Roxelana said with a shrug. "He needed a new alliance, and so did I. We will continue to see each other, but not in the same way."

Continue to see each other? Has their affair not ended?

Maria searched the guests' faces for evidence that others shared her suspicions. Women lined the room, craning their necks to watch the unwrapping ceremony. Some encouraged her with a nod, a lifted hand. Others leaned forward, eager not to miss a word. Maria suspected more than a few of enjoying the tension in the room.

Solomonida, for example. And those cousins snickering in the back. They lived to upset her.

Well, let them snicker. She didn't need their approval.

Roxelana could not have meant what Maria thought she'd heard. The aunts would have leaped on so outlandish a statement. Yet why assume that a sensual older man from a land where most khans and princes had as many women as they desired would abandon a lover like Roxelana, married or not?

What have I let myself in for?

"Varvara is right. I am lucky." She raised her chin, daring them to contradict her. "I want children, and here I have a second chance. And by a man of high standing at that."

Roxelana's lips tightened. She disliked reminders that Maria would soon outrank her. A small glow of triumph warmed Maria's chest, only to vanish as Roxelana retaliated. "A *faithless* man of high standing," she said. "He'll get you with child, then move on. It's his way. So enjoy the time you have with him, darling, and hope he leaves you a son to remember him by."

"Behave yourself, hussy," Aunt Theodosia said. "And stop upsetting the bride. What kind of heathen celebration is this?"

But Varvara murmured, "Enjoy it. What must that be like?" She glanced at Roxelana, as if seeking further confidences, and Roxelana smiled, a sensuous curve of the lips that hinted at indescribable bliss.

Maria wanted to shake them both. *Stop encouraging her, Varvara!*

"Is your husband so dreadful?" she asked. Varvara had married three years ago, at fifteen and a half. "I thought you liked him."

"He does well enough," Varvara said with a sigh. "But I don't know: if it's such a sin when you break the rules, shouldn't it be more fun when you don't?"

The rustling and giggling among the women increased. Warmth bathed Maria's cheeks. Her first husband had ignored her after the wedding night, and thank the Most Pure Mother for that. She shivered, pushing the memory away.

Children, rank, status, Maria. Remember the prize. Not so many children as Mama, please Holy Mother, but a son or two to secure my position in my husband's household.

Varvara sent her a sympathetic glance. Maria held out her bandaged right hand, then withdrew it. She couldn't speak her fears aloud here. If she and Varvara were alone …

If only Roxelana would finish!

But Roxelana was still unwrapping. To distract herself from thoughts of tomorrow's ceremony, Maria concentrated on the emerging design. At the base of her fingers, the five vines joined in wave-like spirals. She fought a yearning to pull her hand away, to tear off the wrappings, to see what these foreign women had done to her, to *know*.

She had agreed to this, hadn't she? She could not wriggle like a baby. She could not sneeze—definitely not that. A bad omen for a wedding.

The women chattered and giggled, shifting places as one person after another wriggled to the front, only to be pushed back again by the next eager observer. The musicians resumed their play, singing about raspberries and rivers. Solomonida danced in the center of a circle, her cerise skirts swishing around her as she swayed, waving an embroidered kerchief, a group of women cheering her on.

Maria heard whispering and muffled laughter, snatches of conversation. Her silk robe was lovely. No, Roxelana's was lovelier. Would *you* marry a Tatar, however highborn? Oh, of course you would. Anyone would! But poor Maria, saddled with a stepmother her own age. And such a wicked stepmother, at that! Did you hear what she *said*?

Some of the chatter involved the royal court. Most of the time Maria liked to hear about the wider world, but today the speculation drained and confused her. Have you heard, my dear, we may have peace after all? The negotiations with the Lithuanians will end any day. Prince Andrei had better watch out then. Grand Princess Elena and her advisers don't care to bring him to heel now, with the foreigners reporting on everything they do. But the moment the ambassadors leave for Vilnius, Elena will go after Andrei. He's the only remaining thorn in her side—and honestly, the nerve of the man, faking illness for months. Oh, but can you blame him: why risk ending up in a Kremlin dungeon like Elena's other brother-in-law? Poor Prince Yuri, starved to death in his cell! Maria's head ached as she disentangled the overlapping threads.

Irina clapped in time with the music, letting the conversation flow past her without joining in. Pregnancy rounded her porcelain features and slender figure, softening her exquisite foreignness with a maternal glow. The heat generated by the stove and the assembled company caused black wisps to curl at the edges of her headdress. Even impending motherhood could not alter her deceptive air of fragility.

On her left sat Maria's six-year-old sister, Lyuba, so intent on the unwrapping ceremony that even her flyaway copper hair seemed stilled. As Solomonida ended her dance to cries of acclaim, Irina pointed to Maria and murmured something in Lyuba's ear. Lyuba nodded. A gurgle of laughter escaped them.

Is Irina making fun of me? Maria glowered at her hand, where the spirals veered off on both sides into shells and rosettes, then continued in a long looping curve. Flowers and vines? But then why the spirals and shells?

"What is it?" she asked Roxelana, hoping for but not expecting an answer. So far her queries had provoked no more than grunts.

Roxelana raised her head and again produced that mysterious smile. Maria swore her stepmother must practice in the privacy of her chambers. Hazel eyes held Maria's own. "Can't you guess?" Roxelana said. Her silky tone implied that only a creature of sublime ignorance would need an explanation.

Maria fought to keep her voice level. "You know I can't. Isn't that why you chose it?"

Roxelana unfurled another strip of cloth. "What do *you* think it is?"

"Don't tease." Irina, her amusement audible, broke the tension. "Why should our legends be familiar to her?"

Our legends. Tatar legends, Irina meant. Maria froze.

The design drew her, repelled her. No, she could not guess. Five vines, waves, a pair of shells, a looping curve? It was a game for children.

This was the world her father wished her to enter, a place filled with images she did not understand, tales spoken in unfamiliar languages, expectations she could not meet—or even identify. This very morning her soon-to-be husband had sent her a horse, although no woman in her family learned to ride. An icon, a dress, an ivory comb—these were suitable gifts from a bridegroom. Not a horse.

Roxelana bent again to her work. On the left of the curve another shell drooped overlapping ovals. Scales or feathers. And above that a curved neck ending in a rounded head.

A snake? A symbol of Satan?

About to leap to her feet, Maria forced herself into stillness. The large eye connected to what looked like a beak, and more feather lines decorated the head. As the last wrapping peeled off, a second set of feathered curves, larger than the one on the left and more obviously a wing, helped calm her rapid heartbeat.

Not a snake. A bird.

The waves marked the body, the shells and dots and leaves formed a tail. But what sort of bird had a tail longer than itself? Suppose it was a demon, a div, a creature of Tatar magic?

They wouldn't do that to me, would they?

Irina tolerated her, Roxelana lived to humiliate her, but they wouldn't set up this whole elaborate party so they could play some horrible trick. And if they tried, at least some of Maria's relatives would step in. Aunt Paraskeva, Aunt Theodosia—they wouldn't stand by while Roxelana drew demons on their niece's hands.

But of course, they knew no more about Tatar magic than she did. No more about Tatars, period.

"Lyuba." Irina tucked her left arm around the child's waist. "What did your stepmama paint? Do you remember what I said before?"

Lyuba squinted, rubbed her nose, and squirmed. Aunts and cousins and sisters turned, ready to shush the little girl the moment she opened her mouth. Maria again extended her right hand, still wrapped in linen, in reassurance. "Tell us, Lyuba."

"You spoil her, both of you." Roxelana frowned at the six-year-old, who responded by burying her face in Irina's silk-clad shoulder.

Irina sighed. "Must you, Roxelana? She's been quiet as a baby mouse all day."

Without answering, Roxelana twisted back into place and reached for Maria's right hand.

"It's a firebird, Maria. A kumai. See the flames?" Irina pointed at the flowerlike shells. "It means happiness in marriage. Roxelana has drawn a dragon on your other hand to symbolize the perfect union."

The assembled women gasped. Maria dragged her right hand free and leaped to her feet, tugging at the knot, then shaking her wrist to release the rolled linen. It piled at her feet as an elaborate fire-breathing beast greeted her horrified gaze. Still covered with mounds of dried, tawny henna, it stood out against the back of her hand, an ominous symbol written in paste. A serpent with clawed feet and wings—not the snake on the icons of St. George but a larger, fiercer relative.

"A dragon? Oh, you have cursed me. Wash it off at once!" Maria grabbed for the damp cloth and scrubbed at her hand, revealing the rich brown design beneath. "Why did I trust you? You are wicked, wicked. You imperil my immortal soul!"

Irina started to laugh, and for an instant Maria would have sworn she saw imps of fire dancing in her sister-in-law's dark eyes. Why had she not realized how much they hated her, these women of the south? Only a fool would have expected kindness from them, even on this special day!

Roxelana reached across the table, picked up the small brush she had used to apply the henna, cleaned the tip, and tucked it into a vermilion case. Maria shuddered at the sight of it. The demon bird and its evil dragon adorned that too.

"Such an absurd to-do." Roxelana rose, ever graceful, to her feet. "And for no purpose whatsoever. Henna does not last for life, but neither does it vanish in a day. You must wait for it to fade." She tucked the case in her sash and strolled away. As she reached Irina's side, she said over her shoulder, "It seems, my dear stepdaughter, that you are doomed to accept our good wishes whether you like it or not."

Maria watched her stepmother glide from the room, glared at her sister-in-law—still convulsed in laughter—then studied the brands of Satan they had duped her into bearing on her person.

If only they were not so beautiful. But then demonic things often were.

Chapter 2

"WELL, WELL. TULPAR. ABOUT TIME YOU SHOWED YOUR face. And here I thought you'd decided to make a run for it." Bulat Khan, richly dressed for the afternoon's ceremony, sat in the room's one armchair. Brow creased, voice cutting, he greeted his eldest son with an autocratic disdain better suited for a raw recruit on the eve of battle.

Which was, indeed, Bulat's usual style of greeting his sons, especially his firstborn, who today stood before him in the uncomfortable position of petitioner. Tsarevich Alexei Bulatovich—or, as he still thought of himself, Tulpar Sultan— ran a finger under the collar of his scarlet brocade robe. It hadn't felt this tight an hour ago.

Given a choice, he would have skipped this meeting altogether. Alas, he was due to marry tomorrow. For reasons known only to Bulat himself, he had declared his intention to support the match by playing his assigned part as father of the groom, an offer generous enough to send Fyodor Koshkin, Alexei's prospective father-in-law, into a state of ecstasy. Alexei's insistence that he had no desire for even a temporary reconciliation with his father had, as a result, fallen on deaf ears.

In truth, Alexei would have preferred to avoid the marriage too. But the hand of Koshkin's widowed daughter was the price for Koshkin's support, which would not only secure Alexei's position in the Russian court and guarantee him a powerful and knowledgeable ally but, with luck, ensure that he could ignore future summons from his father.

Or so he hoped. One could never predict what Bulat might take into his head.

So here they were. Today Bulat would negotiate the marriage contract for his son, according to Russian custom, and Alexei would keep his antagonism in check.

Bulat's opening roar did not bode well for that effort. Thirteen years ago Alexei would have roared back, ensuring an instant conflagration and his own dismissal, but he had learned a few things since then.

He crossed the threshold and bowed. "A pleasure to see you, *Ata*," he said, keeping his voice steady. Bulat grunted in response.

"I can't say the same for you." This new voice was young, familiar, hard-edged—and a surprise, as Bulat's roar could never be. Alexei's half-brother Ogodai, last seen nine months ago aiming an arrow at Alexei's head as he and his men fled toward Moscow. Ogodai had missed, but not by much.

Alexei searched the room for the source of his brother's voice. His eyes slid over heavy furniture, ornate gold patterns against dark green walls, a book propped open on a wooden stand. In a shaded spot next to the window he found his half-brother, arms crossed over his chest. "What brings you here, Tulpar?" Ogodai asked.

"Alexei," he said. Not that it mattered, except to score a small point. "I've joined the Christians. Didn't *Ata* tell you?"

Ogodai jerked one shoulder as if he couldn't care less. "Alexei, then. What brings you here, *Alexei*?"

"*Ata* summoned me, not that it's your business." Alexei forced his clenched hands to open. "What are *you* doing here?

Horde get too hot for you? I'm sure you didn't ride from the Urals to bless my marriage."

"Of course not." Ogodai continued to scowl. "*Ata* requested my presence. But I meant, what brings you to Moscow? Have you thrown your Crimean lord to the wolves?"

That stung. Alexei heard the message, loud and clear. *You don't belong here.*

"I'm surviving." He moved forward until he stood toe to toe with his brother, then crossed his arms, mimicking Ogodai's aggressive stance. "My lord has lost his mind. He suspects everyone, even those of us who have backed him for years. I left because I heard he sought my death. But why should you care? You have your own camp, and this is good news for you. I won't be getting in your way. Your horde would not accept a Christian khan."

"Empty words." Ogodai smacked the windowsill. "Conversions can be reversed. You broke your last promise to leave me and my horde alone. Or have you forgotten that?"

Oh. No wonder Ogodai was fuming. Breaking his oath had seemed necessary at the time. He'd forgotten his brother might bear a grudge.

Alexei opened his mouth to explain, but Bulat cut him off. "We're taking nothing for granted," he snapped. "You have to prove yourself, son. My support for you depends on your good behavior."

Alexei's half-formed apology died stillborn. Good behavior—was he an infant? But he heard that message too. Ogodai and Bulat stood together against him—the unwanted son of a runaway mother. They always had. They always would.

So be it. He didn't need their approval.

Except that he did. Not Ogodai's, but Bulat's. His father stood high in the Moscow court and had done so for decades. Alexei could not afford to antagonize his father.

If only his collar were not so tight.

"Starting with this wedding," Bulat went on. "I expect you to honor our lineage. To act in a manner appropriate to your station."

"I just turned twenty-nine, *Ata*," Alexei said through gritted teeth. "I am familiar with the Crimean court, the Ottoman court, and the rules of matrimony. I will not disgrace you."

"The Russians do things differently," Bulat announced. "Today I act on your behalf. Your father-in-law dowers your bride, and you manage her property during your lifetime. Then it reverts to her—unless she dies childless, in which case it goes to her father. He will ask for an accounting when that happens, so you must keep one. They will not expect the bride gift customary among us, but they will assume you have the resources to support her and any children God chooses to send you. Do you?"

"Sufficient for our needs," Alexei said. "And I intend to make provision for her, whatever their custom. I already gave her a horse."

Ogodai choked, then put one hand over his mouth and waved the other at him. Bulat glowered. "Sorry," Ogodai said. "Continue. You gave her a horse."

What's that about? Alexei glared at his brother, who was still laughing, although what Ogodai found funny remained a mystery. "Why shouldn't I give her a horse?"

"I'm waiting," Bulat interjected. "You plan to make provision for her. That will take more than a horse."

"I know that." Apparently he would die before his father granted him the benefit of the doubt. "I brought jewels from Crimea, satins and silks, perfume, furs, gold. I had to leave the herds and the grazing lands, so I took whatever I could carry."

"You've some sense then," Bulat said.

Alexei bit his tongue and ran his finger under his collar once more, wishing the inquisition would end. What he wouldn't give for a flask of koumiss!

Bulat spoke again. "Where will you live?"

"With her father, until I can secure an estate of my own."

"And with your former woman? A mess that, isn't it?" Bulat paused—long enough to let the point sink in, Alexei assumed—then added as if the suggestion pained him, "This house is big enough. Bring her here."

Live under his father's roof again? As a man grown with a wife, wanted or otherwise? No, that was one thing he could not accept.

Alexei shook his head. "Koshkin has offered us a section of his house. I won't see Roxelana. I'll make sure I don't see her. Once I receive a service assignment, I can request land. Then I will support my wife in her own home as the Law decrees."

"Our Law," Bulat said. "Not theirs."

"I still consider myself bound by it." Alexei strove to keep his voice level, although each blunt statement and unjustified assumption made that more difficult. Hostility hung in the air like steam from the furnace.

"There's my estate," Ogodai said. Alexei turned, hastily shutting a mouth that had dropped open at assistance from that unexpected quarter. Ogodai did not smile, but he raised both eyebrows in a silent challenge. "The one Uncle Shah-Ali gave me. I don't need a house in Moscow, and it's just a few streets away. You'll have to hire people to clean it up, but it was in decent condition the last time I saw it."

"Perfect." Bulat pushed himself to his feet. "You will live there, in a separate house owned by our family, with your wife and her attendants, and I will assign lands to you commensurate with your station. It is settled." He walked to the window and clapped Ogodai on the shoulder. "Thank you, son." Without missing a beat, he turned to Alexei. "Let's get this over with."

Settled. Whether he liked the arrangement or not.

In fact, he owed his brother a debt for his solution—but still. Did his opinion count for nothing? Too dumbstruck even to protest, Alexei watched his father stalk with measured tread, thumbs tucked into his sash, toward the door. Ogodai sprang forward to open it, then stood aside.

Bulat sailed through. As he stepped into the hallway, he said over his shoulder, "Stop dawdling, son. This isn't a coronation. We're going to sign a few documents and leave. If you have no interest in marrying this girl, you shouldn't have accepted Koshkin's offer."

He charged out of the room and down the stairs. Ogodai gestured with turned-up palm. "After you, *aby*." His mouth quirked in a wry smile, as if the title "elder brother" was somehow a joke. "Father, groom, best man—that's the protocol."

So Ogodai had not only responded to their father's summons but agreed to fill the role of groom's best man. Were there other wedding arrangements that the family had neglected to mention?

Yet Ogodai had done Alexei a huge favor. No need to share a house with Koshkin and Roxelana—or worse, his own father and stepmother. A chance to retain the independence he had enjoyed for thirteen years. And support at his wedding, superficial or not. "Thank you, *ené*," Alexei said as he drew level with his younger brother.

Ogodai stared straight ahead, his expression unreadable, his lips pressed together. Even the stray wisps of black hair that so often fell across his forehead today remained tucked under the sable cap. He produced a small, ironic bow. "It was nothing. I never stay there, so you may as well use it. Houses need someone to live in them, but when we visit, *Ana* wants her grandchildren near at hand."

"I appreciate it, nonetheless." Alexei left the room, and Ogodai fell into place behind him. As they approached the courtyard, he saw his stepmother Sumbeka and Ogodai's wife, Firuza, heading for a closed horse-drawn carriage. On their way to pay their respects to his unknown bride, perhaps.

And to Roxelana, his former lover, representing the mother of the bride. A mess, indeed.

Alexei lifted a hand in greeting, but the women ducked into their conveyance without acknowledging him, although both knew him by sight.

His horse waited at the bottom of the steps. Alexei adjusted his collar one more time and swung into the saddle.

It was going to be a long afternoon.

Koshkin slipped behind a screen in the room he shared with his new wife. He hadn't much time before his guests arrived, and he had yet to change his robe for one more suitable to the occasion, but he could not resist the opportunity to spy on Roxelana undressed. She was so beautiful, so sensuous, and her agreement—even in exchange for a promise of marriage—to give up the Tatar sultan who had supported her for two years amazed Koshkin even now, months after the fact.

True, she claimed she had yielded to Alexei out of necessity. And Alexei had surrendered her without a fight and for political gain. Perhaps he had indeed never appreciated the extraordinary blessing conferred on him, as Roxelana insisted whenever her new husband expressed doubts.

No matter. Koshkin had her loyalty now—and, more important, her body. No more servant girls and army whores for him. He peered through the crack in the screen, where Roxelana bent and stretched as the servant passed a cloth dipped in scented water over those luscious curves. Her creamy brown skin flushed with pink, the rounded breasts, the silken hair that fell to her waist without a single wave or curl. Ah!

She turned her head, glanced at the screen, and laughed. In his ardor he had given himself away. He stepped into the room and dismissed the servant, then patted Roxelana dry and took her in his arms. She pressed against him with a moan of pleasure, welcoming his attentions as she always did.

Not much time before his guests arrived. He had best make the most of it.

"Firuza! When did you get here? Did you bring the babies?" Nasan, known to the Russians as Irina, ducked past Roxelana and Maria and hurtled toward her sister-in-law as fast as a pregnant lady could hurtle.

Firuza grabbed her. "Look at you! What is it—six months? Seven?"

"Six." Nasan pulled back enough to put her hands on Firuza's shoulders and study her. "I'm due in May. We think. Mid-May at the earliest, because Daniil didn't get back from Lithuania until last August." She released Firuza's shoulders, tucked an arm through hers, and moved toward the window seat. "You must tell me everything. It's been ages, and I feared you and Ogodai would miss the wedding. Say you brought the twins!"

Firuza freed her arm. "Every detail, sister, I swear. We brought the twins. And Tulpar's—sorry, Alexei's—son. Timur. You remember him? He can't miss his father's wedding. We even brought that Russian woman you sent us and *her* son."

Nasan nodded. She did remember Timur—a bit. She had met him at Ogodai and Firuza's wedding two years ago. "How old is he now? Eight?"

"Nine," Firuza said. "The children are at your mother's house. But we also brought gifts for the bride, and that's why we're here. So we will chat later, yes?"

"Oh dear," Nasan said. "You're right, of course. What a scatterbrain I am." She stepped away from Firuza and bowed to Sumbeka, who shook her head (but she was smiling, Nasan could not fail to note).

"Greetings, *Ana*," she said. "Forgive my impetuosity." She switched from Tatar to Russian, for Maria's sake, and spoke slowly enough for Firuza to follow. She hoped it would work: mixed-language situations easily became awkward. With outstretched hand, she drew the other two women forward. "You met Maria at my wedding. I think you do not know her stepmother, Roxelana?" Out of courtesy, she did not mention Roxelana's past relationship with her half-brother Tulpar, whom Sumbeka knew well.

Sumbeka—ever composed, ever gracious—acknowledged both introductions with warmth and compliments, then snapped her fingers at the servants who, Nasan now realized, had trailed her into the room. They came forward, arms laden with furs and rich fabrics, then stopped at a sign from their mistress. Sumbeka inclined her head, first to Maria, then to Roxelana. "To the bride and"—she hesitated for the briefest instant—"the mother of the bride, congratulations. Please accept these tokens of our delight in welcoming you into our family."

She reached into her sash and extended her palm, on which lay an exquisite ring, gold surrounding a faceted ruby that glowed from within, and a medallion depicting the Mother and Child in the style of a Persian miniature—a dark-haired, moon-eyed Mary holding on her lap an equally dark-haired son, his head encircled by flames and adorned with a Tatar-style hat.

One day, Nasan thought, *God willing, I will have a tenth of her style. The Queen of Sheba couldn't have done it better.*

Chapter 3

KOSHKIN DID NOT RECOVER FROM HIS DISTRACTION AS quickly as planned. He had just belted his caftan when the sound of hooves in the courtyard alerted him to the arrival of the eagerly awaited guests.

Damnation. I should not have given into passion like a heedless recruit. When did I last show such a lapse of judgment?

His self-reproach lacked conviction, even to his own ears. Memories of Roxelana's fragrant skin would undermine any man's resolve. She had left the bed before he had, completed her preparations, and departed to welcome the mother—or, in this case, stepmother—of the groom.

But he must hurry. Today's meeting marked a crucial stage in his plans to advance the fortunes of his lineage. He dare not risk offending Bulat and his son; their alliance would raise his status at court.

His daughter, a tsarevna! Who would have imagined he could achieve so much?

As fast as possible he pushed his feet into his boots, assumed his outer robe, and placed a tall hat of black fox fur on his head. He could explain his lateness by citing the vagueness of time passing, but to appear without the appropriate display of riches would insult both himself and his honored guests.

At last he was ready. His two adult sons awaited him on the other side of the door, one dressed in green velvet, the other in blue: Mikhail, seventeen, and Foma, a month or so past his fifteenth birthday. They were a disappointing pair, but their presence ensured that the other side did not outnumber his. Bulat had declared his intention of bringing both Alexei and another son, Ogodai, whom Koshkin had met once before. A hothead, Koshkin recalled, although Bulat seemed to think otherwise.

Ogodai had not yet arrived, adding lateness to his sins and imperiling the negotiations. He might miss the wedding, although Bulat had appointed him the groom's best man and insisted that his son would reach Moscow before tomorrow.

There was no excuse for a father's blindness. Koshkin did not permit such laxity with *his* sons.

The two boys trailed him as he descended the staircase. So long as they kept their mouths shut, he would have no complaints.

Father Spiridon, the house chaplain, met them in the main hallway. As expected, he wore full ceremonial regalia: stiff white cap with a cross, white robes embroidered and trimmed in gold. He carried a jeweled and enameled crucifix in one hand and a book in the other.

His bearded face relaxed as they came into view. "Your guests have arrived, Lord. I greeted them in the courtyard," he said, "and asked the servants to bring refreshments to the sitting room."

"You did well." Koshkin ignored the implicit reproach, deserved as it was. "You're a good man. How many are there?"

"Three," the priest said. "Bulat Khan, your bridegroom, and another man. Younger than the bridegroom. If I had to guess, Alexei Bulatovich doesn't much like the other two, or they him."

"Yes, Alexei has long been estranged from his family. I don't know the details. It appears that his brother got here in time after all. Shall we go and see what we're dealing with?" When the priest nodded, Koshkin turned to his sons. "Stay quiet and watch. We have a powder keg here."

The boys drew closer together and hunched in on themselves. Satisfied that he had cowed them, Koshkin opened the door and walked in.

Three men, as the priest had said. Two young, one old, the resemblance among them visible when they sat side by side. Bulat had aged since he and Koshkin last met—hardly surprising, except that the khan had been so vigorous, so energetic, that it looked odd to see his hair and mustache grayed. Ogodai had changed, too, growing into adulthood as his father approached his fifties. Taller, stronger, more filled-out, Ogodai looked every bit the khan. And perhaps no longer a hothead, although the grim set to his mouth suggested that Father Spiridon had read the relationship between Bulat's sons correctly. Alexei, too, looked far from comfortable.

Good. On principle, Koshkin preferred conflict to a united front. On this occasion he foresaw few difficulties; the two sides had worked out the terms and even the guest lists in advance, and both benefited from a lavish display that revealed their wealth and prestige to society. Bulat had proven himself more than generous, and Maria's previous in-laws had returned her dowry as required, allowing Koshkin to reuse it for this new match. In deference to his daughter's soon-to-be-higher status, he had added icons and furs and a small rural estate, but that imposed only a minor drain on his resources. The arrangement pleased him. With four sons and one daughter still to wed, a little economy here would serve him well later.

He greeted the three visitors. Ogodai stood and gave a small bow. Alexei did the same. Bulat, as the senior and highest-ranking among them, did not rise but inclined his head and said, "*Salaam aleikhum*, Fyodor Mikhailovich. And congratulations on your recent nuptials. I trust you are well?"

Koshkin did not respond in kind to the Tatar greeting. Instead, he placed both palms on his chest and bowed from the waist. "Welcome to my home, khans and sultan. I thank you for your felicitations. I apologize for not greeting you at the doorway."

"It is of no importance, Fyodor Mikhailovich," Bulat said with ponderous courtesy. "My son was also delayed"—he indicated Ogodai—"on the road, in his case. Otherwise we could have completed this business two days ago. But we are here now. Shall we begin?"

Koshkin gestured to the priest, who blessed the assembled company at length before ushering everyone to benches on either side of a wooden table unadorned by anything except a tray holding cups and a brass ewer, flanked by piles of paper. The guest lists for bride and groom were exchanged and approved. Father Spiridon handed over the document describing the contents of Maria's dowry: household goods, religious objects, clothing, furs, the lands and nearby village.

"If you are satisfied," he said, "let us sign."

"You speak too soon." The groom rose to his feet, a folded piece of paper in his hand. "The bride must also receive her due."

The bride? Her due? What nonsense is this?

Koshkin blinked as Bulat, with the air of a traveling magician, produced a scroll from his sash and gave it to Alexei. Bulat snapped his fingers, and two manservants appeared, heavily laden. They deposited their piles on Koshkin's desk.

Alexei unrolled the document, added the page he carried at the front, and read off the entries, one by one. As he named each object, the servant in charge lifted it for inspection.

Brocade and satin, velvet and cloth of gold, an entire casket of jewels, another of perfume, a pair of books bound in fabric, boots of rich soft leather, a saddle, stirrups, a bridle, reins, a pointed and veiled Tatar hat. All this for Maria?

This will be her life now. This is what I wanted for her. For our lineage. For myself.

As the priest recorded item after item, his eyes grew rounder and rounder. One of Koshkin's boys could not suppress a gasp, and Koshkin spared a moment to glare at the miscreant. "You understand," Alexei said as he reached what appeared to be the end. "These goods go to the bride, not to her family. It is her property from this moment on. Neither you nor I have any right to it."

"*Her* property?" Father Spiridon asked, his voice a squeak. "But why? She will have her dowry if, God forfend, you pass away—as well as anything you set aside for her in your will. And your sons, if you have them, must provide for her support."

"It is the Law," Alexei said, as if stating the obvious. Facing three implacable Tatar faces, Koshkin refrained from pointing out that Alexei was in principle no longer governed by Muslim law. "*I* provide for her," Alexei said, "so long as she pleases me. But these goods belong to her, and to her alone."

He returned to the scroll. "And one more thing. My brother"—he cleared his throat, as if the acknowledgment of their relationship stuck in his craw—"has kindly yielded the Moscow estate that he holds of our uncle Shah-Ali to me. Please advise my wife that we will live there after the wedding."

"Unnecessary," Koshkin said. "My gratitude to the khan, but we have plenty of space here, and my wife counts on Maria for assistance with my youngest child. Lyuba suffers from the loss of her mother. She and Roxelana have not had time to ..." He stopped, unable to find a descriptive phrase that did not implicitly accuse Roxelana of insensitivity.

Alexei snorted, raising Koshkin's hackles. Who could blame Roxelana for preferring her husband to an awkward and unappealing child? When she had babes of her own, her motherly streak would emerge.

"It *is* necessary," Bulat announced in a voice that brooked no argument. "A man should live with his wife under his own roof. My son may have come propertyless from Crimea, but since I have revoked the edict of banishment against him, he is again a member of my lineage and will live in the style to which his descent from Genghis entitles him. You may visit your daughter whenever you like. This estate lies nearby."

"Your younger daughter may live with us, if you wish it," Alexei said. "She will be my wife's responsibility, so she must consent. But if they prefer not to be parted, I do not mind." His mouth quirked. "I feel certain that Roxelana will not mind either."

Forcibly reminded of Alexei's past familiarity with Roxelana, Koshkin felt his hands clench. The desire to argue left him. Not only was his wife likely to rejoice at the departure of both Maria and Lyuba, but separating Roxelana from Alexei struck Koshkin at that moment as an excellent idea.

He pushed a quill pen and ink pot toward Bulat. "Then I thank you on Maria's behalf. Let us sign the contract, Khan, so that Father Spiridon can bless our children's union once more while we drink a toast to their happiness."

He gloated as Bulat signed the documents, followed by Ogodai and Alexei. At last the deal was done. Today the contract, tomorrow the betrothal and wedding. No more fears that his plans would fall through. Bulat and his sons were now kin.

Koshkin, allied with descendants of Genghis. After eighteen months of fighting to reestablish himself and his family at court, success warmed his heart better than the red wine that would seal the bargain.

When his turn came, Koshkin picked up the pen and signed—not a mark or initials but his full three-part name with a flourish. That surprised the Tatars, he saw. Not many Russian noblemen bothered to learn to read and write. His sons had failed miserably, despite his efforts to convince them that a smart leader should not depend on others to decipher the content of messages that could mean the difference between life and death. Even regular beatings had not sufficed to get the shapes of letters into their cloth-filled heads.

He did not share that information with his guests. Instead he handed the pen to Father Spiridon, to sign as witness, and called to the servants. "A toast to tomorrow's newlyweds, then let us visit the mother of the bride!"

Maria returned Sumbeka's bow with as much grace as she could muster. Pressing her palms together in front of her chest, she observed Sumbeka through her eyelashes, comparing what she saw with her memories of her first mother-in-law, Natalya. Sumbeka was more slender, more stylish, more regal, and certainly more beautiful—even in middle age. She bore a distinct resemblance to her daughter, Irina. Maria had noticed the likeness the first time she met them, at Irina's wedding to Daniil Kolychev, the younger brother of Maria's first husband. It was becoming more pronounced as Irina matured.

As befitted her station as the lady of the house, Roxelana took the lead in inviting the visitors to sit and supervising the disposition of the gifts—except for the ring and the medallion, which Sumbeka handed to Maria. Irina captured the young woman she had called Firuza—and who was Firuza, exactly?— and dragged her over to the window seat, chattering in Tatar, only to be called to account once more by her mother.

"Daughters," Sumbeka chided. "Delay your reunion for the space of a breath, if you please."

Firuza, flushing, returned to Sumbeka's side. "Maria, Roxelana," Sumbeka said. "Permit me to present Firuza, the chief wife of my son Ogodai, the mother of his children and *khatun* of his horde." She tut-tutted at Irina. "As you see, she and my birth daughter are good friends. I hope one day the three of you will get along so well."

Maria murmured polite nothings. A lovely thought, but unlikely. She looked at the three Tatars, hair and eyes as black as those of the woman on the medallion (and who ever heard of a dark-haired Mother of God?), skin tones ranging from ivory to tan—one stately and distinguished, one flush with the beauty of youth, and the third with a strong, determined countenance but pretty even so. What had she in common with any of them?

And what had Firuza said that involved Alexei's name?

She glanced at Roxelana, sensuous and mysterious as ever. Experience suggested that her courteous exterior concealed boredom; Roxelana preferred the company of men. Left to her own devices, she would pinch and snipe, alleviating her ennui by causing trouble. Maria could already see the signs: her stepmother tapped a finger against her lips to cover a yawn, and a disturbing gleam entered those hazel eyes.

Maria stepped into the breach, asking her father's housekeeper to see the visitors' servants entertained in the kitchens while their own maids fed the guests. She took a cup of apple juice from a tray and offered it to Sumbeka, who touched the henna painting as she accepted the drink with thanks.

"Extraordinary," Sumbeka said. "Firuza, Nasan, do you see this? A firebird. And painted with such skill." She traced a remembered pattern against the back of her hand. "I had flowers and lace, as I recall. With leaves here, near my thumb, and down this little finger. Mirrored patterns, left and right. How long ago that seems."

Maria frowned, puzzled. Who was Nasan? Only when Irina stepped forward in response to her mother's call did Maria realize that must be her sister-in-law's childhood name. Her sense of traversing, blindfolded, an alien land increased.

Firuza caught Maria's fingers in hers and examined the painting. "I had rosettes. Starting in the center and radiating out, with matching patterns under each fingernail. But this is beautiful. For marital felicity." She lifted Maria's other hand. "And a dragon, for harmony. He looks so fierce. A true lord of the sky!"

"Roxelana did them," Irina/Nasan volunteered. "Amazing, isn't it? She's very talented."

Roxelana preened, not unlike a bird herself. "My pleasure. And I'm glad you like the dragon. You wouldn't believe the fit *someone* had when she saw it." She widened her eyes at Maria, underlining the identity of the uncooperative someone.

"Dragons are evil," Maria said, provoking a chorus of denials from the three Tatars. Roxelana smirked, sparking a new fear in Maria's mind.

Will these foreign women combine against me?

Instead, Firuza intervened, her words clear despite her strong accent and the occasional mistake. "Tell me, Nasan," she said. "How does your mother-in-law? Natalya Vasilyevna—is that her name? She was ailing, according to my husband."

It was a good diversion. Maria watched Roxelana's mouth tighten and sent Firuza silent thanks.

Irina/Nasan answered. "She is still ailing. Her heart fails her, and there is no cure. She will see her first grandchild, I think—out of pure determination, if naught else. But if she lasts the year, I will be astonished." Sadness tinged her voice, and Maria wondered at it. More often than not, Natalya took a hard line with her daughters-in-law, especially Irina. Yet Irina seemed to feel a genuine affection for her.

"I grieve to hear it," Firuza said. "And your husband?"

Irina laughed then. "He is well, almost indecently so. His right arm still troubles him, but he is learning to shoot with his left. And to use a firearm, which he detests. But it is too much to hope that he will remain forever assigned to Moscow, so he must be able to defend himself in battle."

"A blessing," Sumbeka put in, "that he has been at your side these six months."

"Indeed." Irina touched the region above her left breast. "May he stay as long as possible." She gestured at the door. "You will see him later. He said he would stop by to fetch me, and I told him to meet me at your house. He fusses over me, although Mama-in-law and I tell him every day that I won't lose the baby now. Besides, I'm healthy as a horse."

"But he worries," Firuza said. "It is natural. My husband nearly drove me mad when I was carrying the twins. It means he cares for you." As if the last sentence recalled her to her surroundings, she raised the cup a servant had handed her while she was talking and added, "May your bridegroom love you as wholeheartedly, Maria."

"Touching." Roxelana rose. "And on that note, Maria, I think you had best retire. I hear booted feet. The men are about to join us, and your groom must not see you before the ceremony." She bowed to Sumbeka, Firuza, and Irina, who had risen when she did. "You ladies are welcome to stay, if you wish. We are part of one family now, so there can be no impropriety."

"We will go," Sumbeka said. "Nasan, are you ready?"

"Quite ready." She pressed one cheek, then the other, against Maria's before bowing to Roxelana. "Until tomorrow."

"Wait," Maria said as the reality of their leaving sank in. "You will see Alexei Bulatovich this afternoon, will you not, Irina?" Irina nodded. "Then please give him this." Maria pulled the gift she had made for her bridegroom from the drawer where she had hidden it earlier and held it out to her sister-in-law.

Irina accepted the gift, turning it over in her hands, touching the scarlet embroidery, the thickly strewn pearls. "A sash. How lovely. Why, it must have taken you months!"

Maria nodded. The praise warmed her heart. Irina showed the belt to Firuza and Sumbeka, who oohed with delight, then tucked it into the cloth purse she carried. "I will be happy to deliver it for you, sister," Irina said. "Such a work of art. It casts shade even on your phoenix and dragon."

"Another to-do about nothing," Roxelana snapped. "Any servant could have carried it for you. Why, I could hand it to Alexei Bulatovich myself."

Which was exactly what Maria did not want. Why else had she gone to so much effort to ensure that her gift reached its intended recipient without assistance from either Roxelana or her servants? If she'd thought of Irina sooner, she could have arranged the transfer in a less ostentatious way. Too late for that now.

"No need," Irina said cheerfully. "I will see him soon."

Male voices sounded outside the door. The three Tatars donned their veils, and Firuza and Sumbeka stepped forward to repeat Irina's farewell.

"Until tomorrow then," Sumbeka said.

"Until tomorrow," Maria replied. She watched the women go, then slipped out the other door before the men could enter. As she left, she heard them exchanging greetings with Sumbeka and her daughters. The women's parting words echoed in her head. *Until tomorrow.*

Tomorrow, when her life would change once more. She could only pray that this marriage would prove more satisfying than her first.

🐎

"Maria, you *have* to see this!"

"See what, Varvara?" Maria crossed the threshold of her room, which her sisters would share for tonight, since the house was filled with guests and Varvara's husband remained stationed in his southern fortress in case Safa-Girei Khan of Kazan launched another lightning attack on one of the border towns.

Lyuba skipped about the room, her natural vivacity reasserting itself in the absence of her stepmother's quelling frown. From somewhere she had acquired a length of scarlet silk embroidered in gold, which she had wrapped around her shoulders like a shawl.

"Give that to me," Varvara scolded. "Before you dirty it."

Lyuba retreated, clutching the cloth with both hands. "Won't. You're not my mama. You can't tell me what to do."

"Where did you get it, Lyuba?" Maria held out a hand. "Let me see."

The little girl pointed to a chest in the far corner of the room. Maria glanced that way, and her mouth fell open. It was piled high with fabrics and furs, although the servants had not yet brought Sumbeka's gifts from Roxelana's sitting room. The pile spilled over onto the small table where she kept her brushes and cosmetics. A black lacquer box trimmed in gold lay open, revealing glittering stones. A second, smaller box sat beside it, and next to that a pair of books, bound in a way that reminded her of the ones Irina had received as a gift from her brother last year.

"What is this?" she asked Varvara, who was gazing at her with a smug expression on her face. "Where did these things come from?"

"Your bridegroom," Varvara said. "There is more, according to Papa. Including a house. You don't have to live with Roxelana after all."

"A *house?*" Her prayers had been answered. No stepmother! "Where? Why?"

Varvara laughed. "Right here in Moscow. Your own house. As to why, he told Papa it is their custom. You are a tsarevna now—or you will be tomorrow."

Lyuba tugged the length of fabric free and thrust it into Maria's hands. "She left out the best part. Papa says I may come and live with you, if you don't mind."

Maria shook her head to clear it, only to see her younger sister's lips tremble. "You don't want me?"

She knelt and put an arm around Lyuba's shoulders. "Of course I want you, little dove. I was just surprised. No one mentioned any of this to me." The child wiped her wet cheeks on her sleeve.

Maria chided her softly, then stood. "Let's see what you have here," she said in a rallying tone.

"It's the drawings on your hands," Lyuba said. "That's why I liked it."

Maria spread the red silk on the bed. Lyuba was right. The gold thread formed a firebird and a dragon. The animal and bird circled each other, emitting waves of flame. It was beautiful, just as the henna paintings were beautiful.

She sighed. Wherever she went today, she tripped over firebirds and dragons. The heavenly powers must be trying to tell her something. If she could only figure out what.

Chapter 4

"YOU WILL JOIN ME AND MY FAMILY FOR DINNER?" KOSH-kin, perhaps unconsciously, rubbed his hands together as he issued the invitation. He reminded Alexei of a sleek, well-fed cat contemplating his prey.

"It is customary," the priest added. "A declaration of solidarity to bless the union."

"And would confer great honor on my clan," Koshkin said.

"Then I wish we had managed to complete the contract sooner." Bulat tipped his chin, as if the mark of respect could soften the blow to come. "My fault, I fear. But we cannot stay this evening. I have a horde of relatives on my doorstep, and I must host them. You and your sons are welcome to attend."

"Alas," Koshkin said. "I too have a house bursting at the seams with guests. Until the morning, in that case." He bowed, serenely self-satisfied on the surface, but the hands clutching his sleeves told a different story.

"Until tomorrow." Bulat ignored the signs of anger and beckoned to his sons, who echoed his farewell before following him into the courtyard.

Back to his father's estate then. Alexei tried to invent an excuse for staying behind and failed. There was something to be said for celebrating with someone else's family—no old scores to settle, no grudges ready to explode in unpredictable fashion. Expectations to fill, perhaps, but he had reached an age when he no longer paid much attention to the expectations of others.

His father would no doubt say that Alexei never had cared what others thought, but *Ata* was wrong. Alexei once ached to impress the old man, in fact. And where had that led him? To more than a decade as a wandering exile tied to a lord who in the end stabbed his loyal servants in the back. A lord he missed, sentimental idiot that he was, as he missed the steppe and the mosque.

Surrounded by Tatar warriors, beset by memories of those lost years and the childhood that preceded them, Alexei rode in silence as the group traveled the short distance from Koshkin's estate to Bulat's. With his father in the lead and his half-brother behind him, conversation was impossible, but in any event he had nothing to say to them. Their very presence unsettled him—the support that came without acceptance, the judgment that lay behind their words and showed on their faces. "You have to prove yourself," Bulat had said. But what would satisfy them? And if he knew, could he provide it? Did he want to? What, in the end, did his family mean to him after so much time apart?

Ahead of him a pair of wooden gates, twice the height of a man, stood open. Above the gates flew his father's standard, the nine horse tails swaying in the chill wind of late afternoon. Next to them a winged horse, gold-embroidered in the sweeping abstract lines typical of steppe art, rippled against its white silk background. Ogodai's banner, which should have been Alexei's, as evident in his birth name—Tulpar, the winged horse.

The sight provoked memories that still rankled. As Alexei followed his father through the gate, where massed ranks of warriors greeted them with bowed heads, his determination to succeed in this new Russian world hardened.

One day he would have a banner of his own.

Inside the gates, cacophony. In addition to the warriors, released from their obeisance as soon as the khan entered, relatives filled the space with their retinues. Shouts of greeting mingled with orders to go here and do this. Servants dodged horses and noble guests; dogs raced about the yard as if demented; veiled women embraced; men hugged and slapped shoulders. Alexei shook his head, struggling to separate one face from another, dragging names from the depths of his mind.

He had yet to identify a single aunt or uncle when two small bodies toddled out from the crowd, shrieking "*Ata*" at top volume. A harried-looking Russian woman in the drab clothing of a servant, with light brown hair and the usual pasty complexion, pushed through the throng and hurled herself forward, arms stretched toward the children, but succeeded only in falling flat on her face. Ogodai's horse, moments ago brought up to Alexei's side in preparation for dismounting, emitted a shrill scream and reared. The fallen woman shrieked, and the two children howled.

For an instant, thrashing front hooves hung over the threesome. The pandemonium stopped, as if the entire courtyard held its breath. Then Ogodai brought his mount down, angling to the right. His leg brushed Alexei's. Alexei reached for his brother's reins, intending to steady the beast, then pulled back. Ogodai had matters well in hand. The woman rolled to her feet and made another, more effective grab for the toddlers. The crisis was over.

Ogodai, his face strained, swore in Russian and threw his leg over the caparisoned chestnut gelding. Once on the ground, he gripped the woman by the shoulders and shook her. "Hell and damnation, Grusha! They might have been killed!" The children's howls rose in concert, and Ogodai released the woman and patted their heads. "There, there," he said without looking at them.

Tears flooded the woman's cheeks. "It wasn't me, Khan. One of your aunts was playing with them. She sent me to fetch a kerchief for Tsarevna Altan-Alia, and I was halfway across the courtyard when I heard someone call Tsarevich Irek's name. I turned around to check and saw both twins disappearing into the crowd. I ran after them, but it took time to find them. I spotted them right when you did." Her words came out in long gasping sobs.

Ogodai swore again, in Tatar this time. "Very well. I see how it happened. Give them to me. I'll take them to their mother. It's a madhouse out here."

When Grusha, still sobbing, released the children, he swung them into his saddle and held them there. "Your niece and nephew," he said to Alexei. "Altan-Alia, Irek, greet your uncle."

Alexei repeated their names. The toddlers stared at him, their eyes round as owls'. He judged them to be about eighteen months old. Irek reminded him of his own son, Timur, abandoned of necessity more than two years before. And where *was* Timur? He searched the courtyard, but it was impossible to distinguish one nine-year-old boy amid the throng.

He returned his attention to the toddlers. Only the clothes—and Altan-Alia's messy pigtails—made it possible to tell the children apart. Round cheeks and chubby bodies, hands pressed against pink lips—it seemed no more than yesterday that Timur had been that young. Alexei reached out a finger and caressed Altan-Alia's silken skin, bent forward in his saddle to inhale Irek's baby smell. The toddlers continued to stare in silence, but they did not pull away.

"Congratulations," he told Ogodai. "And my son?"

"He's here somewhere." Ogodai swiveled his head. "By the ancestors, have you ever seen such a mob?" He swung into the saddle behind the twins and roared Timur's name at a pitch suitable for a battleground. Irek, startled, nearly tumbled from the horse, but Ogodai held him firm.

Timur, however, did not appear. Bulat, still in the lead, turned his mount to face them. "We'll go inside," he said. "The boy's probably with your mother, and if not, we'll send for him." He patted his grandchildren on the head. "A fine pair, aren't they? Fearless."

"Too much so," Ogodai replied. "We'd best get them to my wife before she has a fit wondering where they went." He scowled at the toddlers, giggling into their hands. "Bad children. Never run in front of a horse." They sobered at once, and he glanced at Grusha, who shuddered. "Get inside, Grusha. You're not to blame. But next time don't bring them out into such a crowd. It's a miracle you found them, and another that they escaped trampling."

When she nodded, he kneed the gelding into motion and pushed his way through the throng, leaving Alexei and Bulat to follow him to the house.

It wasn't easy to reach the outer stairs. Aunts, uncles, cousins Alexei hadn't seen for years surrounded him. Some pressed forward to greet him; others kept their distance, neutral—perhaps hostile. After the first onslaught, he dismounted and turned his horse over to the nearest servant he saw with a hand free to take the reins. The sensation of being welcomed back into the family he had lost threatened to overwhelm his defenses. He fought his instinctive response by concentrating his attention on the skeptics. He had three days to separate those who withheld judgment from those who had long since tried and condemned him in absentia. Then most of them would go home, leaving him in this Russian world he barely understood.

It did not surprise him that no one mentioned the breach between him and his father or remarked on the years when Bulat had falsely declared his oldest son dead. But the truth hung there, between him and his relatives, like mist on the steppe. He could almost hear the unasked questions. He could not afford to relax his guard.

At last they entered the house. Bulat led him, not to the room he and Ogodai had occupied earlier but to a more feminine chamber claimed by Sumbeka. Unlike her husband, she had already replaced much of the Russian decoration with lighter colors and geometric designs, giving the room a familiar feel. Brass jugs and elegant pottery adorned wooden tables carved to resemble leaves, vines, and trees, some adorned with dragons and birds. Embroidered, tasseled cushions lay piled on the benches that lined the walls, and iron filigree lamps cast both light and shadows.

Sumbeka came forward. Her hands felt light on his shoulders as she stood on tiptoe to press her powdered cheek against his. "I am glad you returned to us, son," she said. Her warm, melodious voice recalled the years she had cared for him, the comfort she offered after his mother left without warning.

Alexei returned her hug. Ever gracious, she stepped back and swept her arm in a semicircle. "As you see, the immediate family is here. I think you need no introductions."

He did not. Across from the entrance Ogodai's wife, Firuza, sat with a young woman who could only be his half-sister Nasan. The rescued twins perched near them, Irek on his mother's lap and Altan-Alia at Nasan's side. His half-sister smiled shyly at him, but Firuza restricted herself to a curt nod. Apparently she hadn't forgiven him for stealing her away two years ago. He couldn't blame her for that.

Behind her, near the window, Alexei saw his half-brother in conversation with a tawny-haired Russian about Ogodai's age. Daniil, Nasan's husband and Ogodai's sworn brother, his *qarïndash*. Another person ready to assume the worst based on Alexei's past actions, another curt nod. Alexei responded in kind. He'd have to talk to Daniil before the evening ended, but for the moment he had other people to greet. His son, in particular.

As if conjured by the thought, Timur appeared in a flurry of robes and pounding feet, a head taller than the last time Alexei had seen him but not a whit less enthusiastic. He laughed and embraced the boy, relishing Timur's well-remembered scent—equal parts horses, honey, and mares' milk—then led him to a small sofa.

"Tell me how you've fared." He ruffled Timur's short, straight hair. "I missed you. You've grown!"

It was like unfastening a corral. Timur launched into a long and complicated account involving his pony and his bow and the training—not only military—he received. The twins, Auntie Firuza, his mother, the other boys, his tutor. And his uncle Ogodai, whom he clearly adored.

Alexei tried not to take that as a personal reproach. Two years' absence was a long time in the mind of a child. It was his own fault, too. He could have refused Ogodai's offer to take charge of the boy. He hadn't—well, because it would have meant dragging Timur away from his mother, and he didn't want his son to suffer as he had. He'd gone off with Roxelana, and it took no shaman to predict that Guzel would refuse to leave her home and family to live under another woman's thumb. That decision had ended seven years of intermittent but rewarding contact, destroyed by his misplaced fit of passion.

Another act of poor judgment for him to rue. Guzel had never strayed, whereas Roxelana had revealed her true nature in less than a month. The first time he saw the calculation in her eyes as she beckoned to him, he understood what a fool he'd been.

Watching Timur, Alexei realized his circumstances had changed. He had agreed that his bride could bring her sister, so why not a second child? At nine Timur must already spend most of his time among men. Life with his own father would do the boy good. He should stay in Moscow. It was fitting.

While Alexei listened to his son, Nasan passed her niece to her mother, who summoned the Russian nurse and called to Timur. Alexei bid him a reluctant goodbye, promised to talk again soon, and watched his son cross the room. Firuza handed over Irek, who wrapped chubby arms around Timur's neck. The nurse took Altan-Alia, and the four of them departed, the babies watching the guests over their carriers' shoulders with the same round-eyed stare they had bestowed on Alexei in the courtyard. They seemed unaffected by their near-escape from death. The advantage of extreme youth, he supposed.

Firuza sat, twisting her hands, her eyes fixed on the departing babies. She had no doubts, he saw, of how close she had come to losing them.

Nasan stayed in her corner, patting Firuza's hand and murmuring. But when the door closed behind the children and their nurse, she excused herself and headed his way, the first person other than Sumbeka and his son to approach him. Alexei admired her as she glided toward him. Who would have guessed that the wild child he'd loved would grow into such a beauty?

"May I speak with you, *aby*?" She stopped at arms' length, and he sighed. Even his little sister kept her distance.

"Of course, *sengel*." He indicated a covered bench nearby. "You should not stand about in your condition. Let us sit and talk. Tell me of your life. You were six when last we met!" He bent forward to rub her nose with his in the greeting between siblings. She tensed but did not withdraw. The fragrance of jasmine filled his nostrils.

As he straightened and took her elbow, she glanced at Daniil and Ogodai, then walked to the bench he had chosen. Her hands, palms up in her lap, suggested a certain openness. "I am as you see me, the wife of a Moscow nobleman—bearing his child, managing his parents' household. Like every other woman."

"Are you?" Alexei reached for her hand and clasped it briefly before releasing it. "Like every other woman? What happened to the girl who chased boys on her pony and shot blunt arrows at their feet? The girl who demanded I teach her how to use a sword? Tell me she is not stitching altar cloths and doling out flour to servants!"

Nasan's constraint dissolved in laughter. "Oh dear, you know me too well, *aby*. How could I resist when the women worked so hard to reform me? *Ana*, my mother-in-law—I drove them distracted. But altar cloths? No fear of that. I sew abominably. It's your Maria who has a gift with a needle." She reached into the purse she carried, pulled out a folded length of silver cloth, and handed it to him. "She gave me this, for you. To celebrate the wedding. It took her months to work it."

Alexei accepted the cloth but, distracted by the unexpectedness of this opportunity, did not look at it. "You know her? How so?"

Her eyes widened, as if she couldn't believe she had to explain. "Her father didn't tell you? She was married to Daniil's older brother. Before I joined the family. *Ata* killed him in a raid. It's a long story, but in the end she stayed with us for two and a half years, until her father called her home in October."

"He said she was a widow. Nothing about her prior husband. A raid?"

She shrugged. "A long story, as I said. You will hear it someday. From Maria, perhaps."

The urge to press her gnawed at him, but she was the friendliest face he had so far encountered within his family. He decided to leave the raid aside for the moment. "You had another brother, as I recall. He was so young when I left, I doubt I'd recognize him or he me, but I've met everyone in the room, and he's not here. Is he off with a tutor?"

It seemed a neutral enough topic, but Nasan shuddered. Her mouth trembled, and he caught her hand and squeezed it. "What did I say?"

"He died." She sounded as if he had grabbed her throat instead of her hand. "That was the cause of the raid. *Ata* and Ogodai thought Maria's husband killed him."

"Had he?" The years of his absence yawned like an abyss. A brother less than four years old when he left, already dead in a raid. Killed by the first husband of the woman he would marry in the morning, and himself unaware of the whole. What else had he missed that he did not even know to ask about?

"No, a cousin did it. They looked much alike." She brushed a tear away with her free hand. "He was only fourteen. Girei, I mean, not the cousin."

"I'm sorry, *sengel*." He touched her cheek, catching a second tear in mid-flow. "How terrible for you." When she shuddered again, he considered releasing her to join her husband, whom he could see studying them with a frown. Having completed her errand, she might prefer to go. But no one else so far had told him much about his bride-to-be. So once Nasan recovered her composure, he switched back to what seemed like a safer topic. "So this Maria is good with a needle. What else?"

Nasan hesitated. When she did speak, the words came slowly, as if she selected each one with care. "Her appearance is striking—hair the color of copper, brown eyes, skin like fresh cream. Quite beautiful, if not in the Tatar style. She has intelligence, I think, but no one has ever asked her—or permitted her—to use it. She believes what the priests tell her, that women should not learn from books. So she can't read or write. She has never learned to ride, and she has little interest in or knowledge of the world outside Moscow. Our mother-in-law trained us well in household management, so Maria will have no trouble with that. She loves to sew and does it well. Her embroidery is exquisite, like stitched art." She indicated the gift he held. "As you will see. The gift is important. It means that she intends to be a good wife to you."

Listening to his sister's every word and nuance evoked a flash of memory: his half-brother this morning, madder than a wet wildcat at the time but incapable of controlling his laughter when he heard about Alexei's gift of a horse. At last he understood why. "You're joking me. She can't read or *ride*? What kind of ignoramus is she? That can't be typical. I've seen Russian women on horseback." The humor of it struck him too, and he chortled. "Oh, ancestors, and I gave her that gorgeous mare."

"I saw her. She's a treasure." A wicked expression he could not interpret crossed Nasan's face. It reminded him of the six-year-old sister he had loved—and missed. "You could teach her. I'm sure it would do her good to learn."

"I'll have to, won't I? To read and write, as well. And she must learn to speak Tatar, of course. She and her sister can study together."

Nasan laughed. "She'll love that." But when he asked why, she shook her head and refused to answer.

He flicked her cheek. "You're hiding something, Nasan. You don't lie any better than you ever did. Spit it out. Why did her father keep her unmarried for three years? You say she's ignorant but not ugly. No squint, no disability that explains why she doesn't ride?"

She shook her head again. "No disability. She has all her limbs. No crooked spine or anything like that. Her father was disgraced and exiled, then her mother died. That's why she couldn't remarry. So she said. And as soon as he returned to Moscow, he did arrange the match with you. So I guess she spoke the truth."

He examined her through narrowed eyes. "Disgraced?" Koshkin had not mentioned that detail.

"Another long story."

"I have time," Alexei said.

"But I don't." She perched on the edge of her seat, ready for flight. "Ask one of the men. Daniil, Ogodai. Daniil, especially. He was there."

As if they would tell him. But Alexei didn't want to scare her off. He switched subjects. "You're still hiding something. If no disfigurement, then what? Is she bad-tempered?"

Nasan wriggled in her seat. Aha. He'd touched a nerve. She glanced over her shoulder at Daniil, as if seeking support, and he said something to Ogodai and got to his feet.

"Is she?" Alexei rushed his words. It wouldn't take Daniil long to cross the room. "If you don't tell me, I'll assume the answer's yes. There has to be some reason her father was so eager to foist her on the first candidate he found who'd have difficulty saying no."

"Not bad-tempered, exactly." Nasan studied her fingers, avoiding his gaze. "Not to everyone. She didn't like staying with my in-laws after her husband died, but she coped well enough with my mother-in-law most of the time. She and Daniil don't see eye to eye, so they spat whenever they meet. I think she deflected some of that to me. But her main gripe was that I had usurped her place." She looked up then. "I didn't want to, but I had no choice. When her husband died, I became the wife of the oldest son. Only son. So she took it out on me.

Until last summer, when things changed. Another long story. These days we get along, more often than not."

The surge of protectiveness took Alexei by surprise. How dare this unknown Maria sharpen her claws on his little sister?

To hide his unwanted reaction, he shrugged and said with an air of elaborate unconcern, "Women's fusses." Those he could deal with. "Well, tell her not to try that nonsense on me. I've no patience with serpents' tongues."

Daniil arrived. He stretched out his right hand to his wife and offered a smile that did not reach his eyes. "Haven't you?" he asked. "You should have chosen a different wife, in that case."

Alexei had endured a great deal today and retaliated not even once. Watching Nasan accept her husband's hand and rise, a sense of mischief filled him, a payback for the slights his male relatives had dealt him. "Stay true to yourself, *sengel*," he told her. "Don't let the women obliterate you. Or is your Russian husband to blame?"

Daniil's fake smile turned to a scowl, but Nasan burst out laughing again. "Quite the contrary," she said. "In fact, didn't I mention that he could tell you some tales?" And she walked off with her husband.

Alone once more in the crowded room, Alexei leaned back against the wall and swore to himself. What *was* it between him and his family that he inevitably did and said the wrong thing?

Again seeking to mask his discomfort, he unfolded the cloth of silver and pretended to study it. A sash inlaid with pearls amid swooping lines of vermilion thread in patterns so intricate it seemed unlikely any human hand could create them, flowers and tiny birds brilliant as a henna painting but more permanent.

Nasan had not exaggerated his bride's skill with a needle. He would wear the sash tomorrow, to honor the giver while acknowledging her gift. Like it or not, he was committed. He had signed the contract. He could not draw back now.

And thanks to Nasan, he had an idea of what to expect from his marriage. Koshkin had grabbed the chance to rid himself of an ignorant vixen.

Too bad. But Alexei needed the alliance, not the wife. He'd do his duty by this Maria, then move on. No doubt by then she'd be glad to see him go.

Chapter 5

SOMEONE BOUNCED ON THE BED SHOUTING, "MARIA, WAKE up. They're putting the bed on the sleigh. And Varvara looks like a queen. You should see her. Plus it's a beautiful day!"

Identifying the voice, Maria rubbed scratchy eyelids, scrunched up her nose, ran a hand along the back of her neck to loosen it. Her head ached. "*Oi*, Lyuba, stop." She dimly recalled dreaming—before the nightmare of a bouncing sister began—so she must have fallen asleep after all. Somewhere around the time when the church bells rang for matins, she'd been convinced she never would.

"And weren't you a joy to be with?" Varvara grumbled. "If you kicked me once, you kicked me a dozen times. Your poor bridegroom will awaken tomorrow black and blue."

Groaning, Maria forced her eyes open and herself to a sitting position. Lyuba, red hair wild around her face like a forest demon, stopped bouncing and pointed to the window, where some uncaring soul had already thrown back the shutters. "Look. Sunshine!"

"Lovely." Maria dragged herself out of bed, staggered to the window, and peered out. The sight outside lifted her spirits. Lyuba was right. It *was* a beautiful day. Sunlight shot through the icicles, causing them to glitter like rainbow-hued diamonds, and fresh snow imparted a fairytale air to the swept courtyard and banked drifts. The air shimmered as winter's chill battled with the warming sun for supremacy. A perfect day to bind oneself for life to a complete stranger out of his mind with desire for one's stepmother—who clearly had not forgotten him, despite her recent wedding vows. How could weather be both beautiful and cruel?

And freezing. She pulled the shutters closed and dashed for the bed.

"Sorry about kicking you," she mumbled. "I didn't sleep well."

Varvara patted her shoulder. "I understand," she said. "But how bad can it be? He's just a man—and a good-looking man at that. Let's get you dressed. The sun's up, and the ceremony will begin before you've donned your tunic if you dawdle like this."

Maria squinted at her sister, who did indeed look fine: every wisp of hair tucked under her sable hood, more sable trimming her high collar and turned-back sleeves, the turned-up toes of scarlet boots peeking from beneath her yellow robe.

She took heart from Varvara's words, revisiting the many advantages of the match in her head. A rank, a *title*, a handsome husband—years older than she but still this side of thirty. The prospect of children, a household of her own, a comfortable life. Lyuba to stay with her, freedom from Roxelana. If only she'd slept—truly slept, not whatever poor excuse for a nap she had managed—the future would look brighter.

"The drawings on your hands are darker today," Lyuba said, bouncing again. Unlike Varvara, fully attired for her procession to the groom's house in the wake of the marital bed (Maria shuddered at the significance of that), Lyuba wore her long-sleeved linen chemise and nothing more. The tiled stove put out plenty of heat, but even with the shutters closed, winter drafts slipped through the slats.

"You need to dress too, Lyuba," Maria said.

"The dragon looks angry. Maybe he'll eat Stepmama." Lyuba grabbed Maria's right hand. "Nom, nom, nom. Very tasty."

"Naughty child." Maria dragged her hand loose and rubbed Lyuba's chin with it. "Maybe he'll eat you—nom, nom, nom." As Lyuba shrieked with laughter, Maria tickled her. "No. He says you are young and tender, but you have too much sauce for a girl your age. You will give him a bellyache." Lyuba laughed harder at that, and Varvara joined in.

Maria shook her head at them both. "Send a maid for some water, sisters, and let's get started. You're due in the courtyard soon, Varvara." She tipped her head toward the window, where the distinctive jingle of horse tack sounded. "Our brothers are already mounted. And it will take half the morning to comb Lyuba's hair so she doesn't look as if someone pulled her backward through a thicket."

Lyuba groaned. While Maria chivvied her youngest sister into her clothes and waited for the maid to appear with a bowl of warm water, she wondered what her bridegroom was doing. Would he wear her sash? That would bode well for their life together, would it not?

Maria spun in a slow circle, admiring the swirl of her brocade caftan. The heavy silk glowed in the winter sun, its rich turquoise background interspersed with flowers the size of her palm in soft shades of green and yellow. The lightest shades matched her primrose tunic, its wrists bound in the same brocade, highlights picked out in pearls surrounding a single amber oval as big as her thumbnail. More pearls edged the cuffs at top and bottom. Her pointed ceremonial headdress replicated the style of the cuffs. At moments this wedding seemed like a dream, at others a nightmare, but either way she would go to it looking her best.

A creaking sound from outside drew her attention, and she ran to the window, throwing open the shutters in time to see the bed lurch out of the courtyard. Her brother Mikhail led the way, with Foma right behind him. An elderly servant braced himself against the headboard, one hand outstretched for balance, the other holding aloft the icon blessed by Father Spiridon. Varvara, her golden robe hidden in part by a knee-length coat of black fox, rode behind in a sleigh. Maria recognized her sister by her clothing; a leather canopy and light veil hid Varvara's face from the curious populace. The maid who brought the water had reported a stiff breeze, so of those in the procession Varvara traveled in the most comfort.

A few years ago Maria herself had ridden in that sleigh, wearing similar clothes, as the same servants delivered the marital bed to the home of Varvara's husband-to-be. Memories flooded in: the way people in the streets had stopped to stare, to shout crude jokes and words of encouragement. Such a spectacle. It had seemed funny at the time, heartening even, to imagine complete strangers rejoicing unasked at a ceremony that had nothing to do with them. Now, recalling her first, disastrous wedding night, she could not bear to follow the bed on its journey, to imagine it dismantled and reassembled, awaiting the consummation of her contract with her husband-to-be.

Although ... Roxelana's words from the day before haunted her. Was this unknown Alexei in fact "so good between the sheets"? What did that even mean? And how wicked to want to find out!

Maria glared at the dragon on her right hand. As Lyuba had said, the henna had darkened overnight, and the dragon looked fierce enough to devour an unwanted bridegroom. Not to mention a foolish bride.

And where *was* Lyuba? The maid, declaring the flyaway hair ungovernable, had taken the child off with her, muttering that a stronger comb and a touch of oil might permit some headway against the tangles.

It seemed unlikely that even Lyuba could get herself into trouble in the care of a maid armed with a comb. Maria left to join the female relatives gathering in the room where she and Roxelana had received the three Tatar women yesterday before dinner.

Like it or not, her wedding day had arrived.

Throughout the morning horses came and went. An endless procession of jangling chains and stamping hooves, the runners of sleighs scraping against the ice-covered planks that in warmer months kept mud from miring boots, fetlocks, and vehicles alike. Maria caught a glimpse of the groom's best man— Ogodai, whom she recognized because of his past visits to Irina, his younger sister. He was also her bridegroom's half-brother, but Papa had hinted that Ogodai and Alexei did not get along.

Good news. Maria had clashed with Ogodai more than once. Arrogant and impossible to understand, he had made it clear he had no use for her. In fact, half her fears of marrying a Tatar came from him. Who wanted to face supercilious rejection for the rest of her life?

Ogodai greeted her father on Bulat Khan's behalf and announced his brother's readiness to set out. Maria, dragged behind a screen by her stepmother, only half-heard her father's assurance that they too were ready, but she had attended enough weddings to supply the ceremonial phrase. Soon Ogodai left.

So the half-brothers must have established some kind of truce, or Ogodai would not have agreed to play so important a part in today's wedding. The groom's best man supported the bridegroom at every stage of the ritual. Even the thousandman, the nominal master of ceremonies, contributed less to the success of the day's festivities. It seemed an odd place to find a man whom the bridegroom disliked.

A long pause followed, broken by intermittent sniping between Aunt Theodosia and Roxelana. More cousins arrived; Solomonida's rose-scented cheek pressed against Maria's own. Each entry came accompanied by the same collection of sounds—the stamping hooves and jingling tack, the clack of heels against wood, the shushing of silk robes, hearty shouts of greeting from the men and soft laughter from the women. As the morning rolled on, inexorable as Mother Volga, Maria lost track of which stage they had reached. Boredom weighed heavy on her scratchy eyelids, and her head drooped under the pull from her headdress. To conquer fatigue, she replayed the sequence of events in her mind: Varvara and Mikhail accompanying the bed to Bulat Khan's estate; Ogodai here to pay his father's respects, led by Varvara and Mikhail; Ogodai leaving to fetch his half-brother. The next visitor would be Irina, Varvara's counterpart on the groom's side. Then, and only then, could she expect the arrival that mattered most: the bridegroom, with his thousandman and his retainers. Which meant that if the latest set of clicking heels and swishing skirts belonged to Irina, the appearance of the bridegroom could not be long delayed.

Maria clasped her hands, eyes glued to the spot where dragon and phoenix embraced amid white-knuckled circles. Her stomach roiled like the tendrils of flame the mythical beasts blew at each other. Time stretched and contracted. The day would never end; it would end too soon. Her happiness hung by a feather.

A woman's voice, lightly accented, sounded in the room beyond. Irina indeed, greeting Roxelana, who cooed a response. Varvara chattered nonstop, addressing Irina, Solomonida, and various noblewomen arrayed to welcome the newcomers. Maria peeked around the edge of her screen to see her sister-in-law bowing to one female relative after another, names and compliments tripping off her tongue as if she did this every day. Her dress exceeded even Varvara's in splendor: a flowing outer robe of crimson velvet, embroidered with gilt phoenixes hovering over pearl-encrusted flowers. A white gauze veil wafted from the tip of Irina's spiked headdress, gold studded with precious stones, and her loose tunic of white silk ended in a broad hem of twisted cord that gleamed in the winter sunlight. A crimson sash embroidered with white flowers fell from her left shoulder to her right hip, beneath the outer robe, and pearls ringed her neck.

The garb of a tsarevna, which Maria too would soon wear. Had not her bridegroom bestowed fabrics and jewels as magnificent as these on her, sight unseen? Her troubled spirit revived, shook its wings, and trilled at the thought.

Her greetings finished, Irina stepped around the screen and kissed Maria on both cheeks. "It is time to receive your lord," she said, giving the ritual phrase a lilt that made it seem like normal conversation, then lifted Maria's hands and examined the henna.

"It's darkening well," she told Roxelana, who smirked at the implicit praise.

Aunt Theodosia pushed her way to the front and banished the smirk with one sharp tap on Roxelana's cheek. "Absurdity that it is," Theodosia snapped, "you're standing in for my sister.

Bless your 'daughter,' so she can get to her singing before we expire from hunger."

Maria groaned. More sniping. Roxelana had won the last round, sending Aunt Theodosia into huffy retreat. Yet here Auntie was, sailing back into the fray, drawn by the perceived slight through which Roxelana assumed the role of bride's mother. Resentment hardened the lines in Theodosia's face until she resembled an ancient idol. Fueled by past defeats, her annoyance with Roxelana knew no bounds.

Other than Roxelana's own refusal to give in or give up, that is. "You'll be eating the rest of the day, you old witch," she retorted. "And could stand to miss a meal or two at that. So don't tell me what to do. My husband explained my duties to me long ago."

"Hah," Theodosia said. "Long ago, indeed. When you've been married four months? Don't make me laugh."

Battle was joined. Maria, searching the room for support, caught Irina's eye. The Tatar raised both slim dark brows and, lips curved in a conspiratorial smile, approached the combatants. Maria experienced a fleeting sense of connection with her sister-in-law.

Tempted to intervene, she forced her tongue to stillness. Irina might do something outrageous—or not. It depended on her mood. At the moment she looked more mischievous than angry. Either way, better that any rebuke come from a person other than the bride, who could only inflame those present by appearing to choose sides.

"If your husband had the sense of a mouse, *I'd* be mothering the bride," Theodosia grumbled. "Anyway, what does a man know about the duties of women?"

Irina physically separated the two women with a well-directed shoulder and a conveniently placed knee. "Hush, ladies, please. For better or worse, Maria's father has ordered his wife to act as bride's mother, and we cannot gainsay him. You must fight that battle another day."

Theodosia retreated, silenced but not subdued. Her eyes flashed disdain as she stalked toward the center of the assembled crowd.

Roxelana, however, stepped forward. Anger gave her cheeks a becoming flush; tension showed in the hands that gripped her sleeves. She appeared more irritated than mollified by Irina's swift routing of the enemy. "Not bad," she said. "I suppose I should thank you."

"So you should," Irina said. "And stop causing trouble. You are as guilty as she is. Why ruin this joyous occasion?"

"Well spoken, girl." Theodosia, reinvigorated, spun on her heel. "Hussy, bless the bride, so she may sing before your former lover appears on the doorstep."

Irina muttered in Tatar, Roxelana hissed, and Maria clutched her forehead as the full horror of her situation broke over her head once more. Her father had given her to a man she had no chance of winning. Roxelana need only snap her fingers to bring Alexei back to her side. For one terrible moment Maria wanted to tear off her headdress and race from the room as fast as her emerald slippers could carry her.

Then Lyuba darted in. Hair neat, eyes wide, mouth open, she ran to Irina and clasped the Tatar's hand. "I didn't miss the singing, did I?" Maria heard the child whisper. "Maria looks so beautiful—like an angel."

"She does," Irina agreed. Amusement tinged her voice.

"You too," Lyuba added, as if in afterthought. Her free hand caressed Irina's crimson velvet and brushed her white gauze veil. She appeared mesmerized by the way it lifted as each person walked by.

"Hush." Roxelana tugged Lyuba's plait as she passed. "You talk too much. Always babbling. Listen and learn." Lyuba's small, straight nose crinkled, but she did not argue. Instead she put a hand over her mouth, as if holding the unruly words inside by sheer effort of will.

Roxelana approached Maria, who placed her hands together and studied her feet. To sing these songs in this context struck her as a travesty. She did not honor Roxelana as she had her own mother, despite the myriad disappointments that had marred that relationship. She did not want to stay in Roxelana's house, married to Roxelana's former lover—who might not be "former" at all. Even Papa, besotted with Roxelana, no longer seemed like the father she remembered. Would he miss her once she left? The whole experience seemed humiliating, like the situation that spawned it.

Yet tradition must be served. Her father's prestige, her mother's memory—her songs served to preserve their reputation, and therefore her own. The words she had practiced sounded clear in her mind, and she reviewed them as Roxelana tied the medallion of the dark-haired Madonna around her neck. Her stepmother pressed a soft, fragrant cheek to hers—right, then left—and murmured a blessing over Maria's bowed head.

Roxelana retreated as the other women pushed forward, humming with expectation. This was Maria's moment—the last act she would perform alone, as an unmarried woman, before her bridegroom arrived. And although her mother no longer lived and an unwelcome near-stranger had usurped Mama's place, Maria sang not to those present but to the girl she had once been and the mother who cried to see her eldest daughter go. It had been one of the few times Maria had felt her mother's love, and she cherished the memory.

> *Oh, my mother and my father,*
> *Do not send me to live among strangers.*

Who will not weep for your white quail?
Who will comfort her in her sorrow?
For I will work all day and all night,
Without even a crust of bread to call my own.

The same words she had sung then, before marrying Boris Kolychev, while Mama sobbed in a corner and Maria worked to keep each sound clear despite the lump in her throat. How strange was time, looping in circles. Boris was dead, and Mama too, yet Maria remained—singing her wedding songs, suspended between hope and despair.

And at that she wept, as the ritual required.

After a short but tumultuous journey the bridegroom's procession had at last reached its destination. A crowd of men on horseback, with two well-dressed servants running alongside each stirrup, cheered through the streets by passersby eager for a spectacle—the procession appeared to Alexei as a cross between a military parade and an invasion force. The party seemed better equipped to capture the bride than to celebrate the union of a consenting if unacquainted couple.

Ogodai led the way, with the two boys Alexei had met at the contract signing yesterday—his bride's brothers, he gathered, although neither looked old enough to serve, let alone to guard their sister's interests. He supposed her father did that. No fly or flea had the nerve to settle on Koshkin's canny hide.

A host of warriors and servants followed Ogodai and the two boys. Alexei rode at the back, his thousandman to his right.

And that was a pleasant surprise. Until yesterday evening, Alexei had expected to be saddled with one of his disapproving uncles. Instead Ruslan Sultan, his closest friend, had arrived from Crimea in time for dinner and in defiance of expectations—a fellow exile from the undeserved wrath of Islam-Girei, Ruslan's nephew as well as Alexei's former lord.

How good it felt to welcome a man who brought news from home, who faced the same challenges, who understood how it felt to fall from inner circle to supplicant. He and Ruslan would fight together, as they had since they met at sixteen. Although of different generations, they were the same age.

The procession entered a courtyard filled with servants and guests, dotted with tables bearing food and barrels of ale. Alexei dismounted and followed his taciturn half-brother up the wooden staircase. Ruslan marched behind him. As they reached the top step, Ogodai dropped back to stand at his right, and Ruslan took his place in front of them. Unfamiliar Russian noblemen clustered in the entryway. They offered greetings, then retreated toward an open double door through which light gleamed. As Alexei drew closer, he saw a panoply of color and fabric, men and women intermingling in a way he had not previously encountered in Moscow except within his own family. Search as he might, he detected no veiled bride.

Then he heard a woman's voice. Exceptional in its purity, the voice soared in melancholy solitude, singing of mistreatment its owner would never receive at his hands. Feed her on crumbs and beat her? Had her last husband behaved so badly as that? The barbarity of these Russians left Alexei speechless.

But what a voice. It drew him as the fabled golden apples drew the firebird of legend. When it broke into sobbing, he reached out a comforting hand before realizing the singer remained hidden from view. Behind that corner screen, he guessed. He withdrew his hand and tucked the thumb into the sash his bride had stitched. With luck no one had noticed his flash of compassion. Men who openly doted on their wives earned nothing but ridicule.

Still, it seemed his new wife could do more than sew. And if her looks equaled her voice, as his half-sister Nasan had indicated, today might not be the disaster he'd anticipated. Positioned between Ogodai and Ruslan, Alexei searched the hall once more. Surely his bride would emerge from her hiding place soon.

Koshkin came to greet them. Alexei bowed his head, spoke the sonorous phrases Russians loved, then introduced Ruslan. The addition of another sultan to his gathering cast Koshkin into such a babble of delighted exclamation that Alexei feared for a moment that his father-in-law-to-be would explode from sheer joy.

The sobbing stopped, and for a short time nothing happened. Then Roxelana stepped from behind the screen at the far end of the room, followed by Nasan and another young woman whom Ogodai had earlier identified as the bride's sister Varvara. Nasan and Varvara supported a fourth woman dressed in turquoise brocade and primrose, a sparkling gold veil obscuring her features. Slender and tall, she moved with grace. Yesterday's priest, dressed in crisp white robes embroidered in red and gold, blessed the bride and flicked water over the seating area, then stood back as she settled onto one of two identical tasseled pillows covered in copper satin.

Exquisite, impersonal, and silent, his bride gazed at him from across the room. If the sobbing had come from her, her veil concealed the evidence.

A small girl darted out from behind the screen and poked the ribs of a boy about Timur's age. From the looks of him, the boy could only be Koshkin's son, although the girl's identity was harder to determine. His sister, perhaps, for who but a sister would act so impetuously? The child Alexei had accepted into his household, maybe. Her darting movements and her energy reminded him of Nasan at that age.

The boy said something that caused the girl to put both hands on her hips and scowl. Words led to shoving, and Varvara intervened. A smack from her sent the boy slouching toward the second pillow, where the bride grabbed his elbow, pulled him down beside her, and whispered in his ear. The small girl ran off, and the boy glowered at the assembled company as if a storm cloud floated right above his head.

The bride poked his arm and whispered again. This time her words had an effect. The boy straightened in his seat, his sulky expression yielding to curiosity.

Ogodai had explained the ritual yesterday. Everyone had taken his or her place for the betrothal ceremony.

Alexei took a deep breath, stiffened his spine, and hoped for the best.

Chapter 6

FROM BEHIND HER VEIL MARIA ASSESSED THE MAN DESтined to become her husband within the hour. Tall, although not as tall as his half-brother, with muscular shoulders and a slim waist, wavy dark hair, a small mustache but no beard, warm brown eyes, and strong features—he was as handsome as Varvara and the other women had said.

And he had worn her gift. A good sign, suggesting he too wanted their marriage to succeed. Against the background of his scarlet and gold robe, the sash stood out, the vermilion flowers and birds a perfect match for the fabric.

He watched her as if he sought to pierce the veil with his eyes. Gauze, it obscured her features but did not conceal them. Once he came closer, he would get a sense of her face. Her friends and relatives told her she was pretty. Would he agree?

Her youngest brother, David, squirmed on the wedding pillow. "Not long now," she whispered. "See, Ogodai Khan is approaching."

David pulled a face but straightened once more, his clasped hands resting on his crossed ankles. Ogodai strolled toward them, a purse dangling from his fingers. "There's a horse for you in the Horde," he said, as if the ritual words amused him. "The Golden Ones are beyond the Ugra."

David, forgetting his manners again, leaped from the pillow, snatched the purse from Ogodai's hand, and dashed into the crowd. Maria shook her head and sighed. No fewer than a dozen promises to behave, and the first thing he did was offend a khan.

But Ogodai was laughing, and the other men joined him. In response to a murmured instruction from Father Spiridon, the bridegroom sat on the pillow David had vacated and took her right hand in his. Warm, firm, smooth, his touch first startled her, then reassured and supported her. She turned her head, studying him as she could sense him studying her. A flick of his finger pushed her veil away. He released it immediately, murmuring an apology, but she could tell from his smile that he had done it on purpose.

And he was not displeased. The smile told her that too.

Father Spiridon began the betrothal ceremony. Alexei's fingers tightened around hers, then loosened as he spread out her hand and traced the line of the dragon's spine. The ritual required her not to speak most of the time, but she touched her thumb to his. He leaned toward her and whispered, "Greetings, bride."

It would be rude not to answer, whatever the rule. "Greetings, husband," she said as softly as she could.

His thumb traced a lazy pattern against her palm. Maria forced herself not to react. The rite required them, strangers or not, to hold hands throughout the service. The whole ceremony emphasized their oneness as a couple. They would walk together, enter the church together, stand together to make their vows, then—crowned, hands still joined—follow the priest around the table as one. After that came their physical union, of which this slow circling of her palm was the smallest precursor. How could she pull away like a frightened child? Doing so would dishonor her father and herself.

Her stomach churned. Her muscles tensed with the urge to flee. Thoughts plagued her: Boris's assault on her cringing flesh, Ogodai's scornful dismissal of her talents, elegant Sumbeka and tempestuous Irina and the strange world they called home.

Alexei must have sensed her turmoil, because he abandoned his gentle caress and placed his left arm around her waist. "Relax," he murmured. "Am I a monster, eager to eat you up?"

His words echoed her thoughts with uncanny precision. At a loss for words, she took refuge in the silence required by ritual. But as his left hand pressed against her back and his right continued to clasp hers, desire flooded in. This was like nothing she had imagined—as if she stood at the edge of a cliff, ready to fall or to soar.

Father Spiridon ended his exhortation and turned to address prayers to the icons arranged in the corner. Behind his back, a body clad in fine silks the color of leaves in springtime, silver-gilt trim glittering with emeralds and rubies, swayed invitingly as Roxelana passed the wedding pillows. As she reached the midpoint between the bridal couple and her husband, she glanced over her shoulder and treated Alexei to a slow, sultry curve of the lips. If Maria had harbored doubts as to where her stepmother's passions lay, those doubts would have melted in the burning gaze of Roxelana's hazel eyes.

Alexei's grip crushed Maria's fingers, wringing a sharply indrawn breath from her. He muttered another apology and rubbed his thumb across the painted dragon. To his credit, he did not respond in kind to Roxelana's provocation, and by the time Maria turned her attention back to her stepmother, Roxelana had already resumed her sashay across the hall.

Maria glanced at her father, who was beaming at his wife as if her shocking behavior had escaped his notice, then looked once more to the right. Alexei stared straight ahead, his lips compressed at the corners, his face impossible to decipher. She lowered her gaze to their loosely clasped hands and tried to take comfort from the sight. Whatever Roxelana did, she could not stop the wedding. Whether driven by passion or spite, she would have to accept, sooner or later, that Maria held pride of place in Alexei's house, if not his heart.

True statements, but they didn't restore the glow to her morning.

Nasan sat near the center of the room with Natalya, her mother-in-law, who despite her heart condition had chosen to bless the betrothal with her presence. If women attended the church ceremony, no doubt Natalya would insist on doing that too: she had a formidable sense of duty. But since women did not, she could sit through this initial rite and leave before the wedding feast.

After a small hiccup caused by the women's delayed entrance, the ceremony had returned to its familiar track. Nasan gave a soft, nostalgic sigh as Ogodai lured Maria's brother away with a purse filled with gold. His words reminded her of her own wedding: her fear of losing her family and of the unknown enemy who had won her heart, starting with the moment when Daniil sat next to her and clasped her hand, as her brother Alexei now held Maria's.

"I have never seen Maria so subdued," Natalya said in a quiet voice. "What troubles her, I wonder? It is past time she had a husband and a home. And children. A woman must have children to fulfill her purpose in this world."

Nasan did not argue. She rejoiced in her pregnancy, although she could imagine other purposes that would make her life worthwhile, even as a woman. Instead she said, "She wanted a Russian husband. My half-brother must seem as strange to her as your family did to me when I joined it three years ago. She need not convert, as I did, and we speak Russian. But she has much to learn. I suspect the prospect frightens her."

"Will he be good to her?"

"I think so, Mama-in-law. If not, my mother will ensure he reforms." But of course, neither Sumbeka nor Nasan could guarantee that her half-brother would not seek out other women. Natalya must know that too.

The ceremony rolled on like a horde moving across the steppe, slowly but inexorably heading for its intended destination. Some events that Nasan recalled from her own wedding did not take place: no one combed Maria's hair to symbolize her transition from maiden to wife, because she was already a widow. And the betrothal seemed shorter, with much talk of repentance and people being unable to bear the desires of the flesh—an odd topic to bring up at a wedding. But the priest's exhortation, the ritual kiss, the toasts in red wine, the sprinkling of hops and coins over the bride and groom— each of these stages in the ritual occupied its allotted space of time and passed by, until at last the couple left for the church.

With the other women—except Natalya, who remained seated—Nasan ran to the outside staircase to watch Maria depart in her closed-in sleigh, Alexei riding at her side, surrounded by his retinue and the male wedding guests, Koshkin in the lead. As they vanished around the corner, Roxelana led the noblewomen to the side room where she had received Firuza and Sumbeka the day before. Servants piled into the main room as the women withdrew, pushing tables and benches into place in preparation for the feast to come.

Firuza, Sumbeka—Nasan couldn't wait for them to arrive. They would adore discussing Roxelana and her sensuous ploys.

Within the church, life returned to the familiar. When Papa had wed Roxelana, that had been a second marriage, too, so Maria should have known what to expect from the betrothal ceremony. Yet prayers about resisting the hot desires of the flesh—so appropriate for her besotted father and sultry step-mother—seemed out of place when applied to herself. Whatever hot desires Alexei nurtured, it seemed unlikely that he had married to satisfy them, whereas she ... The quiver in her belly stopped that thought half-formed.

Careful not to disturb the taper she held in her left hand, she extended her pinkie and touched the silver ring that adorned the fourth finger of her right. A crowd of male friends and family pressed bride and groom close together, so close that the long line of Alexei's thigh touched hers. Papa had removed her veil when she entered the church; otherwise she would have feared for the proximity of the candles. When she twisted her head to the side, she found Alexei observing her. Now that he had a full view of her face, what did he make of her?

The priest—not Father Spiridon here but the archpriest of the cathedral—finished addressing the altar and turned to face them. Another exhortation about the duties and responsibilities of marriage. Maria watched her bridegroom. She had heard the speech before. But what of him, raised in such different traditions? What did he think, standing in a darkened church amid a fog of incense, holding a lighted taper as a Russian priest told him how to behave with a wife he had met this very afternoon? His shuttered face gave nothing away, but once he glanced at her and smiled. She looked away then, embarrassed and hopeful at the same time.

Behind Alexei someone shuffled his feet. The archpriest interrupted his sermon to cast a stern look in the direction of the offender. Daniil Kolychev, no doubt. As if fate had not played the fool enough this year, her former brother-in-law had agreed to sponsor her wedding, since as Muslims Ogodai and Bulat could not enter the church. Nasan must have urged Daniil to agree, because he disliked Maria as much as she disliked him. If she weren't the center of attention, the temptation to kick Daniil from under her robes would be near-impossible to resist.

The archpriest ended his exhortation with another prayer. Maria's mouth dried, and her throat closed up. She had been awaiting this moment for months, since Papa first told her of his plans for her. And here it was: the future, promise and threat flowing together in one glittering stream.

"Have you, Alexei," the archpriest asked, "a good, free, and unconstrained will and a firm intention to take to wife this woman, Maria, whom you see before you?"

Maria held her breath. "I have, Reverend Father," Alexei said, and she released it.

"You have not pledged yourself to any other bride?" the priest said.

Not counting Roxelana?

But Alexei's answer was firm. "I have not pledged myself, Reverend Father."

The archpriest faced Maria. She stated her vows in turn. The taper wavered in her hand, and Daniil reached from behind her shoulder to steady it.

Alexei bent his head and whispered in her ear. "Trust me," he said.

More prayers drowned any need to reply. As the priests droned on, the taper weighed on Maria's wrist and the cloying aroma from the censers made her want to sneeze. At last Daniil removed the candles and returned with a pair of matching crowns, tied together with a long white ribbon. He placed hers on her right shoulder, indicating that this was her second wedding, and held Alexei's a hand's breadth above his head.

Crowns came in many shapes and sizes: these were crimson velvet bands embroidered in gold thread and pearls. Maria had stitched them herself—for Varvara, three years ago.

More prayers, more incense, responses from the crowd; Daniil's fingers against her shoulder to balance the crown. One of the serving priests brought a jeweled cup, and the archpriest blessed it. He held it before Alexei, who sipped it. Maria did the same. Even this single swallow of wine alleviated her dry throat. Alexei again, then herself, and once more for them both.

The priest removed the cup, and the archpriest extended his hand, covered in a gold cloth. Alexei and Maria placed their joined hands on his and followed the archpriest three times around the table. "Rejoice, O Isaiah!" he sang. "A Virgin is with child, and shall bear a Son, Emmanuel, both God and man."

When the procession ended, Daniil removed the crowns. A final set of prayers, and the crowd pressed in to congratulate them. An unwary guest, perhaps tipsy from the red wine liberally poured at the betrothal ceremony, bumped into her. Alexei reached out an arm to steady her, and she looked at him, her eyes at the level of his cleft chin. For a wild moment she thought he might kiss her. It was the custom, and he had brushed her lips with his earlier, to seal the betrothal.

He did not kiss her. Instead he rubbed his thumb across her cheek.

"Greetings, wife," he said, as he had when he first entered the hall at her father's house. It seemed like ages ago.

"Greetings, husband," she said, as she had then, hiding her disappointment. Did he not know the custom?

She didn't believe it. He had been word-perfect throughout the ceremony. Someone had coached him, most likely Papa. And her father would not have left out that part. Papa's passionate kissing of Roxelana had set every tongue in Moscow wagging. No, the explanation was obvious.

He does not want me. Oh, Papa, how could you do this to me?

Too late. For the rest of their lives, they were husband and wife.

Chapter 7

"WHERE IS THE CARRIAGE?" ALEXEI'S VOICE, CLEAR AND carrying, turned heads among his retinue, and Maria blushed behind her veil for his ignorance.

"They expect us to walk," she explained. A cold blast swept past them, and she shivered. Ahead of them the planked street extended, cleared of last night's dusting of snow, although chunks of ice clustered against the houses. "It's tradition."

He said something harsh in Tatar. When she winced at the sound, he caught her hand. "Not you." He beckoned to the closest servant. "My horse, Dimka, and quickly, before my tsarevna perishes in this wind."

"At once, Tsarevich," the man said. He ran off, returning with a saddled, fully caparisoned horse before Maria had a chance to protest. Alexei put both hands around her waist and without a word of warning hoisted her onto the horse, so that she sat sideways in front of his saddle.

She gulped. From where she sat, the ground looked far away. The white mare he had given her was big, its massive teeth frightening, but this horse seemed a giant by comparison. She clung to the saddle lest she slide off.

Alexei mounted, wrapped his right arm around her, and took the reins in his left. She gasped as the veil pulled tight around her face. He released the reins to help her, leaving just enough gauze to hide her features from the crowd. "Better?" he asked. A hint of laughter warmed his voice. "Never walk when you have a horse. It's the Tatar way. I've known men ride from tent to tent in the same camp."

She couldn't tell him she would rather walk the width of the city than ride with him. Still less would she confess that his arm around her waist made her breathless. "Truly?" she managed. "You're right about the cold. This wind is brutal."

"You can speak," Alexei said, his amusement still audible. "And you're trembling. Is it your first time on a horse?"

"More or less," Maria admitted. "I have ridden pillion once in a while, but not like this." She stopped. Could she say what had to be said in a way that sounded sincere? If she wanted to win her husband, she could not spurn his gift. "On which, thank you for the beautiful mare, although I don't know what to do with her."

There. She had got it out. Not a hint of distaste. Maria released a long breath. What next?

"And you, for the sash. You have an extraordinary gift," he said.

His casual tone made the compliment sound perfunctory, as if her handiwork of five months meant no more to him than the mare did to her. Maria bit her lip, uncertain how to respond. Tempted to snap a quick retort, she forced herself to find a courteous response. "It was nothing," she said, although a half year's work was in fact a great deal.

"As for the horse, I'll teach you to ride her, and the servants will take care of her." He issued this promise as if learning to ride were the most natural thing in the world. "Nasan will help, I'm sure, once her child is born. I'm sorry: you call her Irina. But you should switch. She'll prefer it, and everyone in the family uses it—even her husband. They're having enough trouble with my new name. And I don't know who decided to call my sister 'peace,' but none of us who love her can imagine a less appropriate choice."

Maria had to laugh at that, for it was true. "The family chaplain picked it, I think. To honor the truce between clans. What is your original name?"

"Tulpar." The horse took exception to a passing cart, and Alexei's arm tightened around her. "It's the name of the Winged Horse—of all winged horses. A legend, of course."

Maria clung to the facing of his coat. Soft black lambs' fleece curled around her fingers. "Should I call you Tulpar?" She rolled the name around on her tongue, mimicking his pronunciation.

He gave a quick shake of his head. "I don't mind Alexei. I chose it for myself, unlike Nasan. My family has not cared so much for my welfare in recent years that I need cater to its preferences."

And there it was, an open wound, bitter as the note in his voice. But how to respond?

Beneath her the horse trotted steadily, jostling her when it did not terrify her by turning its massive head to snap at passersby who, drawn by the unaccustomed sight of a bride and groom riding together, came too close. Alexei clearly had the upper hand with his equine monster, but his tight grip on her waist disturbed as well as reassured her. And they had not much time.

She settled for the simplest question. "Do you wish to tell me about that?"

"Later," he said. "And what of you? Will you miss your childhood home, your loving stepmother?"

His mouth had that hard set to it again. Maria puzzled over the reason, but it wasn't the right time to probe. "If Lyuba comes with me, we will both be content," she said. "Which reminds me, I owe you gratitude there too. She has been so happy since she found out she need no longer live with Stepmama."

Oh dear, she should not have said that. "Sorry. My wretched tongue. It slipped out."

But he was laughing again. "Don't apologize. Roxelana hasn't a maternal bone in that glorious body. I'm sure she's said hosannas every day herself." He tapped her nose with the hand that held the reins. "In any event, I'm relieved to hear you talk. For a while I thought I had married a woman without a voice."

"I'm not supposed to, until the dinner is over. But no one can hear us." The wretched horse jerked again, causing her brocade skirts to slip in an unsettling way.

Alexei pulled her closer. Her chest pressed against his, and her palms lay flat against the tanned lambskin of his coat. "Indeed, no one can. What happens if you break the rule? Do they feed you on bread and water for a week?"

"I wish they would. Much better than starving for hours. But no, it's supposed to be bad luck. Isn't it the same among Tatars? Your sister said so." She laughed, remembering. "Although she didn't stay quiet at hers, and she and Daniil adore each other. So it must be an old crone's rule."

Alexei rubbed her nose with his, as if inhaling her scent, and Maria squirmed and pulled away, only to feel herself tugged closer again as the shying horse caused her skirts to slip once more. "Hold still," Alexei said. "I don't want my wife trampled by a horse. And do speak to me. I want to know all about you, but we haven't time for that now. Before we reach your father's house and they silence you again, can you tell me quickly who these people are?"

He wanted to know all about her. It was the nicest thing he'd said yet, and Maria's mercurial spirits took to the air once more. Papa's house lay at the end of the street. She could already see the open gates and a crowd of well-wishers—servants, for the most part, because of the cold.

She looked around. Men surrounded them, most on horseback. If the groom could ride, it seemed, so could they. Lots of Tatars—more than she could count—but at least twice as many Russians. Alexei must recognize his own people, so she sorted out the rest. "Uncles and cousins—too many to keep straight. You'll meet them at the banquet and forget their names by its end."

"You think so?" Alexei produced an unexpectedly boyish grin. "I doubt it. My father will have my head if I do."

"Why should he care?" Maria asked, astonished. "They're my relatives."

"It's a matter of training," he said. "You'll see."

Not sure what to make of that, she took refuge in her identifications. "That big man with the gray beard"—she pointed to a massive nobleman dressed in cloth of gold trimmed with sable—"is Prince Vasily Shuisky, with his nephew Prince Ilya at his left." She pulled a face. Prince Ilya had pawed her more than once during ceremonies like this, although surely even he would not assault the bride. "Prince Vasily handles most of the diplomatic visits to Moscow. Papa was happy as a cow in clover to see him. It's a real honor. In fact, with three khans, two sultans, and everyone but the grand prince and princess themselves attending, Papa may collapse from joy before morning."

"I had that very thought myself," he said, surprising her. When the smile lit his eyes as it did now and he dropped the guard he seemed to maintain against the world, he was devastatingly attractive. She couldn't help returning the smile.

He flicked her cheek with his finger. "I know Shuisky," he said. "Who's that?" He indicated another man, riding ahead of Shuisky and arrayed in dark blue velvet trimmed with ermine.

Younger than Shuisky, his curly dark hair remained brown and his beard was trimmed rather than shaggy.

"Prince Ivan Telepnev," she said. "Grand Princess Elena's favorite. I was surprised to see him, because he has not always supported Papa."

"Has he not?" Alexei gently squeezed her waist. "What brings him here, then?"

"Your father, most likely. They have been allies for years." She twisted her head to face Alexei and placed a hand on his shoulder to steady herself. "That's Nikolai Kolychev riding with them. He is your sister's father-in-law, the father of my first husband, and an old friend of both Telepnev and Shuisky."

Alexei stared past her, a slight frown between his brows. "I had the impression your father disliked the Kolychevs."

"Oh, he does. But Irina—Nasan—is part of their clan. And by inviting them, he can emphasize that he has a descendant of Genghis in his lineage too—and a male, at that."

"How observant of you." Alexei returned his attention to her, gazing deep into her eyes. "So not every guest is a friend?"

Maria heard an odd note in the question—as if he tested her. "That's right," she said. "But one must keep up appearances, because in the battle for power friends become enemies, and enemies friends. Is that not true where you come from?"

He bent his head. His kiss found a path behind the veil, landing at the very edge of her jawline, sending a ripple of pleasure straight to her toes. "Very much so," he said, in a voice not quite steady.

As she opened her mouth to ask which enemy had driven him from Crimea, they rode into the courtyard. Alexei dismounted, and his hands closed around her waist, lifting her down. As a servant led the horse away, she climbed the stairs to the house, Alexei at her side. The return to silence weighed on her.

Who could have predicted that I would not want that ride to end?

Nasan's family arrived not long before Maria and Alexei returned from the church. When the bride and bridegroom appeared in the doorway, Sumbeka and Firuza still circled the room, greeting one noblewoman after another, beginning with Roxelana. Nasan took advantage of the distraction caused by the newlywed couple's appearance to capture Firuza and pull her onto a bench near the head table. Natalya had gone home as expected as soon as the betrothal ended.

Firuza accepted the seat without complaint, but she did not take her eyes off Maria, now freed of her veil by Roxelana. Alexei escorted his wife to greet Bulat, then Sumbeka, before bowing and leaving to join his father-in-law. Sumbeka drew Maria away from the men. Maria did not resist, but her gaze followed her husband until Aunt Theodosia swept in and embraced the bride.

"Look at that," Firuza said. "Our brother has made another conquest, I think."

"Maybe." Nasan watched Roxelana, who had managed to insert herself between her husband and her new stepson-in-law. A hand on Koshkin's arm declared her allegiance, as did her proprietary air, but her position also placed her firmly in front of Alexei, ensuring that he did not miss a single wiggle or wink. "Too bad he has yet to lose the last one. She will cause trouble for Maria if she can."

"That would bother you?" Firuza looked incredulous at the thought.

Nasan shrugged. "I wish her well. And I can guess what she's thinking. I've had times when I worried that Daniil lusted after other women, although I turned out to be wrong. Maria doesn't know our brother yet, and there's Roxelana standing there, luring him. I'd hate that."

"*We* don't know him," Firuza said. "He abandoned Maria fast enough when he entered the room. Maybe Roxelana has reason to believe he wants her."

"He let her go, though," Nasan pointed out. "I think she's taunting him. She wants him to yearn for what he gave up. Maybe she's taunting her husband too, to keep his attention fixed on her. Why else would she flirt like that right in front of him?"

"Gossip, gossip, gossip." Sumbeka swirled into place beside them, Maria no longer at her side. Queried, she said, "I left her with her aunt. I gather the aunt and that 'hussy,' as she puts it, don't see eye to eye."

Nasan laughed. "Not in the lifetime of mountains! You should have heard how rude Theodosia has been since the moment she stepped out of her palanquin. Why, watching her almost makes me sympathize with Roxelana."

Sumbeka's eyes twinkled. "A feat, indeed. And what do you make of our bride?"

Nasan repeated what she had said to Firuza, who murmured and excused herself, saying that the three of them could not cluster in a corner while the guests fended for themselves. "I will join you shortly," Sumbeka told Firuza. "But this is important too." Firuza nodded and left.

"What do *you* make of her, *Ana?*" Nasan flicked an upturned palm in Maria's direction. "Can you train her to act like a tsarevna? She has intelligence, but she lacks an education. Alexei wants her to learn. He told me so yesterday."

"Oh yes," Sumbeka said with her usual calm assurance. "If she is capable, I will teach her. But let her enjoy her wedding first. If she can. She looks scared. I bet she's imagining the worst, and that stepmother of hers is not helping."

As if summoned by the mention of her adversary, Aunt Theodosia loomed behind them. "Helping? The hussy's too busy throwing herself at the bridegroom to help." Her piercing tones carried across the room, and Koshkin and his wife swiveled their heads toward the sound. Alexei doubled up laughing, and Ogodai and Daniil dragged him into a corner, where the three of them leaned chortling against the wall.

"You *bitch*. Stop calling me names!" Roxelana ran toward Theodosia, but Koshkin grabbed his wife round the waist and pulled her into his arms, patting her back in a soothing manner.

Maria stamped her foot and said, loud enough for even Theodosia to hear, "Auntie, for shame! You're ruining my wedding!" Varvara descended on their aunt, hauling a protesting Theodosia to the far end of the room, where a group of younger women led by Solomonida Sheremeteva surrounded them. Sumbeka dropped her forehead onto her hand with a sigh, but Nasan could not take her eyes off Maria, standing alone in the center of the room. Her outburst over, Maria stared in their direction, her cheeks blazing, her lower lip caught between her teeth. She brushed her fingers across her face.

"I'd better go to her," Nasan told her mother. "I think she's on the brink of tears. And who can blame her?"

Sumbeka stood. "I'll come with you," she said.

Damn Aunt Theodosia. Damn her, damn her, damn her. Would it kill her to whisper?

Irina—no, Nasan—and her mother arrived without delay, whisking Maria away from the startled company and behind the screen where she had sung her wedding songs. With a flourish Nasan pulled a handkerchief from the sleeve of her tunic and patted Maria's cheeks with it. "Don't listen to her," she said. "Your aunt is jealous, and Roxelana is more jealous. My brother gave her up. She wants him to smart for it."

"He yearns for her," Maria said. Tears massed in her throat and behind her eyes, like an army preparing for battle. "Why wouldn't he?"

Sumbeka hugged her. "Because, *kilen*, he is not a complete idiot. I swear I taught him better than to lose his heart to a slut. If she held his interest once, I doubt she still does. If she did, he would leap to her defense, not laugh like a jackal when your aunt insults her."

The tears retreated. "I suppose."

"Has he made no attempt to woo you?" Sumbeka took the cloth from her daughter and patted Maria's cheeks again. "What a muttonhead!"

That provoked a watery chuckle. "On the way home we talked." Maria's neck tingled with the memory of his kiss, too precious to share. "About who was who, mostly. And about horses. There wasn't time for much else."

Nasan regarded her with a sparkle in her eyes. "My goodness," she said. "*Ana* has it right. He *is* a muttonhead. Did he kiss you after the ceremony?"

Maria shook her head.

"Hopeless." Sumbeka dropped the cloth on a nearby table and patted Maria's shoulder. "How did he earn his reputation, I wonder? But muttonhead or not, my stepson must be capable of making love to a beautiful woman, and once he has done that, I will teach you ways to keep him focused on you, whatever games Roxelana chooses to play."

Maria's lips parted as every word in her vocabulary raced out of her head. Not a single woman she knew—not her mother, not her aunts, not even her sister—would have promised to teach her how to attract her husband. She mumbled her thanks.

Nasan caught her hands and held them up, displaying the images. "Phoenix and dragon," she said. "There's no room for a snake."

Phoenix and dragon. Marital harmony. "Thank you, Nasan," she said. When she saw her sister-in-law's eyes widen, she added, "Alexei says you prefer it."

"Oh, I do," Nasan said. "It will please me to hear the name from your lips."

"Let us return, daughters." Sumbeka moved to the edge of the screen. "We are needed at the high table."

Maria glanced around the room. Too bad she could not hide here until the banquet ended. But without her the ritual could not continue, so she trailed Sumbeka and Nasan into the main room.

Alexei came to her at once, murmuring something in Tatar to his stepmother and sister as he took Maria's arm and ushered her toward the high table. He did not so much as glance at Roxelana as they took their seats, Bulat on his right and Sumbeka on Maria's left. Koshkin and Roxelana anchored the two ends of the table, with Nasan, Varvara, and Firuza arrayed on the women's side and Ogodai, Daniil, Ruslan, and Alexei's uncle Shah-Ali Khan on the men's.

Father Spiridon arrived to bless her and Alexei, the food, and the company, in that order. The toasts began, and the speeches. Every so often, shouts of "Bitter, bitter," arose from the hall, but Alexei must not have understood that he was supposed to sweeten the bitterness by kissing her, because he kept his attention trained on the company, listening but not speaking. Each missed opportunity brightened Roxelana's smile.

Maria—short on sleep, deprived of food, and exhausted by the day's emotional whirlwind—found herself obsessing over Alexei's disinterest. Bride and groom occupied the center of everyone's attention. Every guest could attest to her husband's rejection of her. The gossips would spread the tale for weeks. And thanks to Aunt Theodosia, Roxelana's role in Maria's humiliation would not go unnoticed. The overlapping family ties were the best part of the story.

Then Alexei bent his head and whispered in her ear. "Too many toasts, too many boring speeches. How long must we wait?" He brushed her neck with his lips, as he had during the ride, although for once none of the guests were shouting.

She released her breath in a soft, ecstatic sigh. "Not long," she whispered.

Please, God, let that be true. Because one more push of the swing, and she would fly to pieces. It wouldn't be as bad as with Boris. It couldn't be. *Could it?*

Chapter 8

ALEXEI SAT AT THE CENTER OF THE HIGH TABLE, A SILENT bride on his left and a taciturn father on his right. Maria seemed tense, unhappy. Perhaps that business with her aunt still bothered her—and what possessed the old biddy to make such a scene? Couldn't she tell she was upsetting her niece and delighting her adversary at the same time? Anything that guaranteed Roxelana a spot in the sunlight pleased her, and the chance to outshine a bride must send her over the moon. Her husband would rue the day he fell for those hazel eyes, but he would not learn the truth from Alexei. Let Koshkin wallow in his misbegotten joy for as long as his ancestors permitted.

In the hall chatter and laughter resounded, interspersed with toasts and demands that Alexei kiss the bride, which he ignored. That the Russians, who limited themselves to one wife and imposed an insane number of restrictions on what they could do with that wife and when, should take such an interest in his relationship with a woman he'd known for less than a day amazed him. He had no intention of satisfying their prurient curiosity, although out of their sight he kept a reassuring hand on his wife's waist and at times murmured in her ear. Once or twice, she murmured back.

As the toasts continued, a long line of servants delivered a profusion of dishes until the tables creaked under the strain.

The absence of conversation gave Alexei a chance to assess the room. Maria had not told him much about the guests during their short ride, but what she'd said impressed him. A wife capable of equaling his stepmother and half-sister in ability exceeded his expectations. In the past he had not picked his women for their political acumen, but a wife was different. A wife should not be only a bedmate like Roxelana. Sumbeka had drummed that dictum into his head since the day his mother left.

An old hurt, best left in the deeps of time. He pushed the memory down. More than twenty years gone, and the pain never lessened. He had decided long ago not to let it rule his life.

He turned to his father and spoke quietly. "Can we get my wife into Grand Princess Elena's court? Everywhere I go, I hear rumors of trouble brewing between her and her brother-in-law Andrei. It would benefit us to have a woman within the inner circle. Maria has the right connections."

Bulat grunted. "You consider her capable?"

Alexei glanced at Maria. From the tilt of her head, he guessed she was listening. He pinched her hip and, when she turned a startled face toward him, winked at her. "I do," he told Bulat. "Elena will entertain a tsarevna at her court, I assume."

"She should feel honored," Bulat said in the lofty tone he reserved for such declarations. He jerked his chin at Aunt Theodosia, sitting at a table facing the bridal party. "Let that troublemaking aunt earn her keep. You wouldn't think it to look at her, but her husband holds one of the highest ranks at court. He's ill, or he'd be there beside her. She can present the bride. I'll speak with Telepnev tonight. You come with me, once they stop loading us down with food. This conflict between Elena and Andrei looks to become a great bother."

"Which," Alexei whispered to his bride, "may be the understatement of the decade." She did not reply, but her lips parted as if she wanted to.

Seeing the glint of tears in her eyes, he decided to indulge the shouting Russians for once and kissed her. She gave a soft gasp, but her parted lips softened under his and her palms pressed against his robe. The company exploded in roars of approval.

Alexei released her, then caught her hand and raised it to his mouth. "Until later," he said. The crowd, as if invigorated by his concession, resumed its chant of "bitter, bitter."

"Ignore them," he murmured. She swallowed, then nodded. The tense muscles of her back relaxed. He could hardly wait for this infernal feast to end.

The banquet did eventually draw to a close. Soon the bridal couple—so Koshkin said—would depart for Bulat's estate and the bedding ceremony that finalized the marriage. But Bulat wanted first to tackle Telepnev, as he reminded Alexei as soon as the last dish left the table, carried high by servants wending their way through the crowded room.

Alexei bent to whisper a reassurance in his bride's ear. "I'll be with my cousins," she whispered back. With a pat on her shoulder he rose and joined his father, heading for the man in dark blue whom Maria had pointed out earlier.

Reaching Telepnev took some time, as each person they passed stopped to congratulate the bridegroom. Alexei stored every name, although he admitted halfway across the room that Maria had been right: the flow of similar patronymics and sobriquets was enough to stress the most competent memory system.

When he and Bulat at last reached their destination, Alexei regarded Grand Princess Elena's favorite with curiosity. He liked what he saw: Telepnev had a strong, pleasant face; he looked honest and intelligent. A long exchange of pleasantries gradually shifted into more pointed queries from Bulat about the state of the realm, the negotiations ending the recent conflict between Russia and Lithuania, the grand princess's current concerns, the possibility of inviting Maria to court, and—most important—the rumors that Elena intended to send an ultimatum to her sole surviving brother-in-law, Prince Andrei of Staritsa, who had twice refused her demands to present himself in Moscow and swear fealty to her son, the six-year-old Grand Prince Ivan.

"She can't let his defiance go unchallenged," Bulat said. "It sets a bad precedent."

"Agreed." Telepnev, for reasons Alexei could not determine, stared not at Bulat but past him. Turning his head, Alexei saw his father-in-law, chatting with one of the guests.

"Koshkin took part in that visit to Staritsa last autumn," Bulat said. "To verify Andrei's claim that he was too weak to travel. The evidence was mixed, as I recall."

Telepnev returned his attention to Bulat and Alexei. A frown creased his brow, and he hesitated before speaking in a low voice. "Don't trust Koshkin. Do you know why we exiled him three years ago? Because he supported Andrei's brother Yuri, even after we imprisoned Yuri for trying to take his nephew's throne. During that mission in the fall Koshkin had at least one private meeting with Andrei's majordomo. I suspect your father-in-law secretly sympathizes with Andrei, Tsarevich. It would fit, given his stated belief that an adult prince of the blood makes a better ruler than a child and his mother."

Alexei clenched his hands. His new father-in-law, a traitor to the crown? If Telepnev spoke the truth ... He couldn't finish the thought. The consequences of allying with a man who might bring down his entire clan through misplaced allegiance to a doomed prince were too dreadful to contemplate.

"Treason," Bulat said. "Why have you not arrested Koshkin, then?"

Telepnev shrugged. "Grand Princess Elena once favored him. She questioned the evidence, so we exiled him instead. For the moment we watch, to see what we can learn from him. But when Elena gives the word, we will take him into custody. I warn you for the sake of our long friendship, Khan: keep your son out of it." With a long-fingered hand Telepnev tapped Alexei on the arm. "And you, Tsarevich, look after your wife."

Another noble interrupted their conversation, and Telepnev walked away. Bulat shook Alexei's arm and snarled. In Tatar he said, "*Stupid* boy. Why didn't you come to me for help instead of Koshkin? Now you're in worse shape than before, with only yourself to blame. And you'll drag me down with you, damn your ungrateful hide."

Both hands curled into fists, Alexei glared at his father from the advantage of his own greater height. "Why would I come to you? You declared me dead," he said, matching Bulat's tone. "How do you even know these accusations are true?"

"I don't care," Bulat snapped. "If Elena and Telepnev suspect Koshkin, that's enough to damn him—and us."

The conversation deteriorated from there.

Koshkin surveyed the banquet hall with satisfaction. Other than the brouhaha caused by that harpy Theodosia, the day had gone well. He would have done better not to invite her, but he dared not slight the wife of his most powerful relative, one of young Grand Prince Ivan's official guardians. Too bad her husband had fallen ill at the most inconvenient moment; he might have been able to keep her in hand.

Even so, Koshkin had a house full to bursting with khans and sultans, princes and boyars and high-ranking courtiers of every description. His daughter looked like a queen in her gorgeous brocade, declaring his worth in every stitched pearl; he had a beauteous wife to act as his hostess; and his children had so far refrained from embarrassing him. Life was good.

With the conclusion of the meal the men gathered in tight knots about the room, the women congregating in small groups of their own. Maria stood with her cousins; the pregnant Kolychev girl sat with her mother and sister-in-law; his daughter Varvara rode herd on the abominable aunt. He'd compliment Varvara tomorrow; she'd done more than anyone to keep Theodosia away from Roxelana, who occupied the center of another circle at the far end of the room.

But where was his son-in-law? Not with Maria, a defection Koshkin found mildly disturbing. Bad enough that Alexei had failed to kiss the bride in church, then ignored her throughout the banquet, despite the guests' urging. He could pretend, couldn't he, even if he had no interest in the girl? And running off the moment the feast ended also didn't bode well for their future as a couple. Suppose Alexei failed to do his duty tonight? All this expense and preparation wasted. It did not bear thinking of.

Koshkin glanced again at his daughter. Prince Ilya Shuisky passed by, and Maria gave an odd little jump, raised her hand as if to hit him, then lowered it before she could cause yet another fracas. What was that about? Koshkin couldn't guess.

Prince Ilya stopped midway, salivating as he caught sight of Roxelana. Triumph surged in Koshkin's chest. That *he* should have captured the heart of such a woman. Let other men gaze, filled with longing and desire, knowing that when night fell she would lie in Koshkin's arms. His first wife, although the honorable bearer of his children and keeper of his house, had never caused so much as a flutter in a male heart—including his own. Still less had possession of her ever raised his status among his peers. His new wife drew every eye—even the bridegroom's.

After an extended period of imitating a bull struck by lightning, Ilya tore himself away from gazing at Roxelana and resumed his stroll across the room. He passed his wife, standing next to Solomonida Sheremeteva. Solomonida jumped as Maria had done, and Shuisky yelped as Solomonida's foot connected with his shin. He muttered words Koshkin could not hear before catching the elbow of a medium-height, medium-weight nobleman of undistinguished coloring and clothes. Grigory Kolychev. With Shuisky, Grigory had accompanied Koshkin on his unsuccessful mission to Staritsa last autumn.

Shuisky and Kolychev sought refuge in a corner. They gave no sign of noticing when Solomonida slipped behind a screen, an action that put her within earshot of their conversation. Koshkin briefly puzzled over her motives before resuming the hunt for his son-in-law.

Ah, there he was, with his father and Telepnev. Koshkin strolled toward them, relishing the role of gracious host. It pleased him that Telepnev had chosen to attend. The favorite's presence implied that Elena, ruling in her son's name, approved of the match. The grand prince and grand princess never attended the wedding of a subject, but they had sent their emissary. A gesture that Koshkin appreciated.

He had come within earshot of his quarry when another guest pulled him aside. "Yes, yes," he said to the rambling congratulations poured into his left ear. "You are too kind, Prince. Far too kind. Your presence honors us." As the maundering guest at last subsided into silence, Koshkin caught the sound of his name.

What is Telepnev telling Alexei and his father about me?

As he sidled closer to the trio, Telepnev walked away. Bulat and Alexei faced each other, eyes locked, arguing (Koshkin assumed from their pugnacious stance) in Tatar. Koshkin had taken a step toward them when Ogodai Khan brushed past him. Ogodai interrupted his father and half-brother without ceremony, switched into Russian, and urged them toward the high table, where Ruslan Sultan, the thousandman, awaited them.

"What was that about?" Koshkin asked his son-in-law as the two of them took their seats at the table.

"Nothing of importance," Alexei said, his voice curt.

Tempted to press, Koshkin decided not to bother. Whatever kept Alexei and his father at loggerheads concerned only themselves. And Ogodai had launched into his prescribed speech, delivering Bulat's invitation for the entire company to dine at his estate on the morrow, then asking Koshkin to bless the bride and groom before their departure. Koshkin dipped his head and accepted.

As he finished delivering the blessing, Roxelana came to beg for permission to accompany Maria to her new home. He kissed her and sent Mikhail to watch over her and escort her home. "I will take care of our relatives and guests," he said, rubbing her cheek, soft and fragrant, with his thumb. "Enjoy yourself, my darling. Maria is lucky to have you at her side."

A muffled snicker sounded behind him. For a wild moment he thought it came from his daughter. But when he turned his head to study her, her face was bland, controlled.

He must have imagined the snicker. Roxelana was a pearl beyond price, and he felt blessed to have her at his side.

Packed into a sleigh with Varvara and Nasan, Roxelana perched opposite, Maria fought butterflies fierce as dragons as they traversed the short distance to Bulat Khan's estate. As they passed through the gates and she saw the men ahead of her dismounting, the open doors of a chamber with two armed men standing at either side, tufted lances pointing at the darkened sky, her hands trembled.

Veiled once more, she stepped from the sleigh. Varvara caught her elbow, steadying her, then led the way to the open door. Alexei joined her halfway, tucking her hand into the crook of his arm, then ushered her into the room.

Maria stepped across the threshold, and her mouth fell open. She had never seen a wedding chamber like this one. Scarlet silk fell in curves from an iron ring at the center of the ceiling, pinned against the wooden walls with a long embroidered strip to resemble a nomadic tent. A square, raised platform at the far side of the room—elaborately carved and trimmed with gold paint, covered in an intricately patterned rug, and displaying tasseled brocade bolsters around three sides—held plates and goblets, a covered basket that oozed steam, and a brass pitcher with a long spout. The only familiar object in the room was the bed sent this morning from her father's house. The servants had reconstructed it, although the icon had not made its way onto the wall above the headboard. In this alien environment the bed looked out of place.

The veil hid her shock from the assembled company, who pushed her toward a screen that stretched behind the platform. Maria submitted to the hands that stripped off her clothes, unfastened her jewelry, and tugged loose the pins and ties that confined her braids. Soon she stood, shivering despite the warmth of the chamber, feeling naked in her simple chemise, her hair long and heavy against her back. Most of the women left then, piling out from behind the screen and swarming in a giggling mass toward the door. Varvara and Nasan remained, with Sumbeka and, alas, Roxelana.

Nasan peeked into the room and pronounced it safe for the bride to emerge. Maria heard Alexei's voice, saying something in Tatar that provoked laughter from Nasan and a reply that Maria understood no better than the comment that preceded it. The fears that had swirled in her stomach since this morning like so many bats swooped together into a gnawing pain that made her want to bend double and sob. Could she do this? Did she want to? Really—even for children?

Thoughts of Boris lunging at her, her pain and confusion, that odd ache of dissatisfaction mixed with relief that he was done—the memories assailed her as if an evil spirit had shoved her back in time to that other evening, greeted with shy expectation that soon dissolved into raw despair. Could it be three and a half years ago? It felt like the present.

And that had been a man of her own kind. A Russian, a *Christian* who had fallen on her as a wolf might grab a deer, not a wild Tatar whose unpredictable tastes had caused his sister and his former lover to shave his bride's body, paint her hands with heathen symbols, and bathe her in warm scented water for his carnal delight.

Sumbeka placed both hands on Maria's shoulders and squeezed them gently. "Breathe, *kilen*, breathe. My stepson will not bite you."

"Not hard, anyway," Roxelana said in a throaty purr that provoked a slap from Sumbeka.

"Behave yourself," Sumbeka said in a voice guaranteed to chill milk. "He is no longer yours. Remember that. And stop trying to unsettle my daughter-in-law." She waved at the edge of the screen. "Be gone with you. You have no business here."

"I am the mother of the bride," Roxelana said. But her attempt at hauteur could not withstand Sumbeka's implacable glare, and after a moment she kissed Maria on the brow, wished her well, and glided around the screen. A murmured conversation, again unintelligible, sounded from the other side.

Nasan poked her head past the screen and snapped something in her alien tongue. More laughter sounded, and Nasan hissed. Then a door slammed, and Maria allowed air into her lungs. How could she have forgotten, even for an instant, that her stepmother had known Alexei intimately for years?

Sumbeka touched her nose to Maria's, then released her. "Come, child, it will soon be over. And it is not your first time. You have nothing to fear." Maria, her throat tight, did not reply.

"Don't worry," Nasan whispered in her ear. "He has lots of experience. He must know how to make it right for you." Maria tried to take comfort from those words, but she could manage no more than a nod.

Nasan placed a hand under her left elbow, and Sumbeka did the same on the right. Together they walked her into the room, embraced her and Alexei, and continued toward the door. Varvara, whispering good wishes, hugged Maria before following the other women. As Nasan raised the latch, Alexei spoke to his stepmother, who shook her head. "I will tell them," she said in Russian. "Although I think Ogodai already has. No challenges. A foolish custom at the best of times, and quite unnecessary here."

"Thank you." He switched languages, as if reminded that not everyone in the room understood his native tongue, and bowed. "You are incomparable, as always."

"Silly boy," Sumbeka said. "Most of the guests are our own people. They know better than to demand a report on whether you're done. I think we can trust them to keep the Russians in line." She gestured at Maria. "May you find happiness together." She swept from the room, driving Nasan and Varvara before her. The latch dropped back into place, and Maria was alone with her husband.

While she watched tongue-tied, he crossed the room. He had not permitted his attendants to do more than remove his outer robe and his boots; he remained fully covered in shirt and trousers. He scanned her in an assessing way that heightened her sensation of nakedness under his gaze. Her thoughts danced in odd jerking patterns.

Perhaps he realized the effect he was having on her, because after one comprehensive survey he sat cross-legged on the platform, reached for the covered basket, pulled back the towel, and held it out to her. "Sit," he said. "Eat. You had nothing during the banquet, and you look ready to faint."

Her knees threatened to give way. Maria dropped onto the platform before they could disgrace her, only to find herself at a loss. Did he expect her to cross her legs as well? It seemed so improper!

She settled for curling her feet under her and pulling a bolster between her and the wooden frame. He shook the basket, his lips curved in a smile. She blushed under his gaze but didn't reach for the basket, even though her mouth watered at the sight of glistening brown semicircles emitting a rich aroma of meat and onions. Clearing her throat relieved some of her fear, but she hesitated to trust her body to accept food.

Alexei placed one of the turnovers on a plate decorated with blue ducks and put it in front of her, then filled a second plate for himself. A small gold knife lay between them. Maria cut the turnover in half and essayed a bite. "Tasty," she said. "Like fried *pirozhki*. What do you call it?" Her voice sounded strangled to her ears, but the words had made it past the lump in her throat. A start.

He touched her cheek with a careless finger. "Good girl," he said, somewhat obscurely. "It's a *cheburek*. Not too different from your Russian pies, indeed. Have some more." He picked up his own turnover.

Maria, watching strong white teeth cut through golden brown dough, had a vivid memory of her stepmother's purring malice. What had she meant, that Alexei would not bite hard, and why had Sumbeka reacted so strongly? She shook the question off and ate a quarter of the turnover. When she raised her head, Alexei was watching her.

He lifted her right hand to his mouth and kissed the dragon's fiery head. "Beautiful," he said. She assumed he meant the dragon, although he fixed his gaze on her face.

"Roxelana," she replied, then silently cursed herself. Of all the people to bring up! "She did the paintings." She held out her left hand to show him the phoenix.

One side of his mustache rose, as if he appreciated the irony of discussing his former lover with his wife. "Impressive. I'd have sworn Roxelana had no talents she could exercise standing."

Maria gasped. His bluntness shocked her. At the same time, she couldn't suppress a flicker of joy. He didn't *sound* like a man devastated by lost love. "You lived with her for two years," she said as a test, although in truth Roxelana's artistic talent had surprised her too. "Did she never draw around you?"

He released her hand and leaned back. The lanterns placed about the room cast glints in his dark brown hair. "Is that what she told you?"

"It's not true?"

He emitted a rueful sound, halfway between a laugh and a grunt. "It's true in a sense. She lived in my house, therefore under my protection, for two years. But after the first month I went back to my lord on the steppe. She wished to stay in the city, told me she'd had enough of tents. I expected her to find someone else. You could have knocked me off my horse with a feather the day she announced she would accompany me to Moscow. I'd gone to say farewell, out of courtesy—to warn her she'd need another patron. I still don't know why she decided to come along."

Maria stared at him. When she realized what she was doing, she released the finger she was holding between her teeth and reached for the knife, cutting the uneaten *cheburek* into quarters, then eighths. "You don't like her," she said.

"Well, you're a surprise, aren't you?" He tipped his head and leaned forward, his eyes intent. "You're right. I don't. I doubt she likes me either. She only pretends to care for people, you know. She uses men's desire to get what she wants, then dumps them for the next pathetic soul who pants after her."

"Like Papa." The *cheburek* was in shreds now. She set the knife down. Alexei poured a stream of dark red liquid from the pitcher into one of the goblets and handed it to her. When she sipped, the sweet-tart taste of red wine slid over her tongue.

"Like Papa," he agreed. "But Papa married her, which makes Papa hard to replace." He reached for a second goblet and filled it. "Don't let her fool you. As you see, she's not ashamed to lie if it serves her purpose." He raised the goblet to her. "To us. Let's forget Roxelana, my sweet. This is our wedding night, not hers. If you're finished destroying that harmless *cheburek*, let us celebrate our union."

"We usually eat later," Maria told him, her words spilling out as she strove not to offend him just as things were going well. "After the ... you know. I didn't expect food yet." She stumbled to a halt as she realized how tactless it would be to reveal how nervous he made her.

"I asked for it. So we could take our time." His moment of warmth had vanished, as if he'd heard something she hadn't meant to say. Maria suppressed a sigh. Then he relaxed once more, and the half-smile returned. "I don't like interruptions. If your brothers dare pound on that door, I'll have their heads."

"Oh," Maria said, for lack of anything better.

"Come." He drained his goblet, flipped the towel over the basket, stood, and extended his hand to her. "If you're finished eating for now, let's get to the main event, shall we?"

She hung back. The moment she dreaded had arrived, and memories of the disaster with Boris clustered thick as ravens around her head. Her mouth felt dry, and the food she had so recently enjoyed threatened to surge back into view. The wine did not help, and she left the goblet almost full beside the ruined *cheburek*. She stood, clutching at the side of the platform for support, and saw confusion in his eyes.

"Are you still worried about Roxelana?" he asked. "Don't let her trouble you. I never think of her. And I wouldn't put much stock in anything she says, if I were you—especially if it involves me."

He'd misunderstood. At least he hadn't guessed how the thought of bedding him tied knots in her stomach. Striving for lightness, Maria said, "She praises your skills as a lover."

He burst out laughing and swept her into his arms. "Well, *that* you can believe, my sweet."

Only it was not so easy. They lay together on the bed, Maria's head on her husband's shoulder, his arm around her waist. "Tell me what you like," he said.

She shuddered and pressed her face against his shirt. He had not lunged at her. Yet. But that must be only a matter of time. And how could she tell him something she didn't know herself?

He rolled toward her, placed a finger under her chin, and tipped her face up. She could not meet his eyes. *Stop shaking!*

"You're scared," he said. "No, terrified. Why? We're strangers, I know, but it's a pleasant thing, on the whole. And you're a widow, not a virgin. That's what your father told me."

When she didn't respond, he pinched her chin. "Look at me." She raised her lashes. "*Are* you a virgin?"

"I don't know." Admitting the truth was almost worse than reliving it, but what good would it do to lie? "I don't think so. I did bleed. Only it was so horrible and unpleasant and over so fast that I can't be sure. And I didn't like any of it, so I can't answer your question. I felt like a lamb led to the slaughter." Her cheeks burned, but she forced the words out. "And when Boris asked if I was all right because I was crying so hard, I lost control and shouted at him that he was a monster. I told him never to come near me again. And he never did."

Alexei listened, his eyebrows drawn slightly together—more thoughtful than angry. His good looks struck her anew. She wanted him to like her. Suppose the truth disgusted him?

But the hand that held her chin moved to caress her cheek. "Poor beauty," he said. "Why do they marry pretty girls to boys with no more sense than sheep? But if he caused you to bleed, I doubt you're still a virgin. We'll take it slow. You can tell me if I make you uncomfortable. And it won't hurt this time. Trust me on that."

And whether it was the assurance in his voice or her own desperate desire to believe, Maria found to her surprise that she did trust him. As he pulled her against him, murmuring words she didn't understand, her head filled with tangled images of Nasan, blissful in her pregnancy, mingled with a disturbing memory of Boris's face, teeth clamped against his lower lip as he strained against her.

Alexei captured her mouth with his. His hands roamed over her body; he traced the line of her ear with his tongue. Her head buzzed with muddled words. Unable to talk, she stroked his face. His skin, smoother than she would have expected from a man who spent so much time on horseback, gave off a subtle aroma of musk. Hope stirred. Perhaps her marriage to

Boris *had* been an anomaly, and it did not have to be like that, even with a near-stranger.

"Show me," she said. But who had produced that husky growl?

"I can't wait." He bent his head and kissed her neck, where the artery throbbed, and Maria emitted a low moan.

He laughed, tickling her ear as he whispered, "You're a natural at this, my sweet."

In the end she had to admit he kept his promise. With him there was no pain, only pleasure—which in its way disturbed her most of all.

Chapter 9

THE HOUSE WAS BEAUTIFUL BUT STRANGE. MORE THAN strange—unlike anything in Maria's experience, even the chamber from the bedding ceremony with its obvious resemblance to a nomadic tent. As Alexei led her through mosaic-tiled rooms in colors that reminded her of her wedding clothes, their walls lined with low padded benches in contrasting shades, floors and benches covered with ornately woven carpets, light falling from intricately cut grill work and sparkling mica of extraordinary clarity in the windows, she alternated between staring in awe and shuddering at the unfamiliarity of it.

How could a house look so Russian on the outside and so different within? Even the inlaid wood tables, the stuffed and tasseled pillows, the brass jugs, the hanging lamps, and the round braziers that decorated each room had an air of fairy tales and folklore. Yet the rooms were beautiful in their grace and proportion. The patterns resembled her embroidery, looping curves and perfect squares that interlocked to form more complex shapes.

Lyuba dashed from room to room, emitting a steady stream of exclamations intermixed with squeals. Alexei's son, Timur, chased after her, no more restrained despite his additional three years of age. As Maria watched, he grabbed Lyuba's hand and pressed it to the surface of a padded bench. Lyuba produced her loudest squeal yet and jumped back, staring at her palm as if it belonged to someone else. Timur broke out laughing, and Lyuba tested the bench again.

"It's warm," she said. "How is that? Maria, come and feel it. It's warm."

"I heard you," Maria told her, but she stepped forward. To her surprise Lyuba was right. The bench gave off a noticeable heat. She turned to Alexei, who observed the three of them with a twinkle in his eyes.

"Don't tease, son," he said. "You know I explained it to you the last time we came here." To Maria he added, "He was just as surprised as Lyuba, so don't let him fool you."

"Is there a furnace inside?" She hadn't seen one since they entered the house, and the absence puzzled her. The rooms were indeed comfortably warm, and the small braziers in their enclosed hearths seemed incapable of supplying so much heat, even if lit—which most were not.

"In a sense," Alexei said. "But the furnace is elsewhere. How does the heat get here, Timur? Do you remember?"

Timur stood straight, like a soldier, and said, "Pipes."

"Pipes?" Maria and Lyuba chorused.

"Huge ones." The boy held out his arms to form a circle, fingertips touching. "Like this. Under the sofas, filled with hot water. They bring water to the bathing room too. And the kitchens. We'll see them later." He tapped Lyuba's nose. "But you can't touch the pipes, or you'll burn your hands. That's what *Ata* told me."

"Who's *Ata*?" Lyuba stared at Timur, her gray-green eyes round at the wisdom of this superior being.

Timur pointed at Alexei. "Him. What do you call your father?"

"Papa," Lyuba said, as if no other answer were possible. "But how can he be your father if he just married Maria?

Babies don't come out *that* fast. Even I know that. And they aren't as big as you when they do come out, either."

Maria blushed, and Alexei gave a choking sound. Timur adopted a worldly-wise expression, which only made it harder not to laugh. "Because she's not my mother, you goose. My mother lives in Uncle Ogodai's horde." He added with a lordly air, "I call her *Ana.*"

"Goose yourself." Lyuba, blessed with four older brothers, had learned the hard way to give as good as she got. "It's rude to call people names, isn't it, Maria?"

"Apologize, Timur," Alexei said. "How would Lyuba know who your mother is? And if you're both going to live here from now on, you will be like sister and brother. I expect you to treat each other with respect."

"Sorry," Timur mumbled. He held out a hand to Lyuba. "Do you want to see the bathing room? The water comes out in a gush. It's exciting."

"Yes! May I, Maria?" Lyuba caught Timur's outstretched hand. On tiptoe, she looked like a bird ready to take flight. The phoenix, perhaps, which had yet to fade.

Maria nodded, and the two children darted away. "Remember not to touch the pipes," Alexei called after them. A double yell that might have been acknowledgment resounded like an echo.

"*Is* Timur going to live with us?" Maria strove to keep the annoyance from her voice, but the sudden tightening of her husband's brows told her she had not succeeded. "I don't mind," she added. "Although I would have liked to know. You asked me about bringing Lyuba."

He clasped her hand and drew her closer. "I found out only this morning that my brother had agreed. The boy is mine, so Ogodai has no right to object, but he and Firuza looked after Timur for two years while I returned to Crimea. I hoped you would accept him. He will not be a child much longer, and living in Moscow will do him good." His mouth curved. "I think he will make life more fun for your sister too."

"Well, it's done now, isn't it? Your brother has left." She saw his eyes darken. "Of course I accept him," she said, to head off the approaching storm. "You took in Lyuba, and I am grateful. But you can talk to me even without a definite answer. 'Would you mind if my son lived with us, assuming my brother agrees?' Not so difficult, is it?"

He dropped her hands and turned his back to her. "I make my own decisions."

Did he think she was questioning his *right* to make a decision, even though husbands always made the important decisions? She strove to explain. "But we're married now. I run your household. I don't expect you to consult me on everything you do, but if you ask people to stay, then I need to make arrangements for them. You will take care of your son's education, I assume, but a child that age needs food, a bed, clothes, shoes. Especially clothes and shoes. My younger brothers grow like weeds, and what they don't grow out of they rip to shreds. The seamstresses will have to start work right away." She waited for a reply.

None came. Alexei stared at the patterned window as if she didn't exist. What on earth was wrong with the man? Clearly he knew nothing about children—or wives.

As the silence continued, her impatience to resolve the situation grew. This was ridiculous. Eager to mend a break she couldn't imagine how she'd caused, she caught his left hand and tugged. "Won't you show me this marvel of flowing water before those two children scald themselves?"

His resistance was a physical thing, a matter of muscle and sinew, a refusal to return her grip. But as her shoulders slumped, he let out a sigh and tightened his fingers around hers. "You will like the bathing room. It is a great convenience. It amazes me whenever I enter a Russian house that you have not adopted our heating and our pipes. So yes, let us fulfill our responsibilities."

But as they walked hand in hand from room to room in pursuit of Lyuba and Timur, Maria could not help dwelling on her husband's last sentence.

Is that all I mean to you: a responsibility to fulfill? What of those magic nights that have transformed my life? Do they not touch you too?

She got no answers to her questions in the days that followed. Alexei spent much time out of the house, drifting in as evening approached—sometimes warm and engaging, sometimes taciturn. His brief admission, if one could call it that, of wanting to see more of his son did not at first keep him at home. Timur moped in corners, emerging only to tease and impress Lyuba, who seemed to regard him as a cross between an authority and a demon. The rest of the time she trailed at Maria's heels, which suited Maria just fine. A household that had long lacked a mistress required as much attention as she could spare, and Lyuba needed to learn such skills as well.

Or so Maria thought until, five days after the wedding ceremony, Sumbeka appeared in a swirl of jasmine-scented silk. When she arrived, Maria was demonstrating the intricacies of yeast dough to a young Tatar servant. The girl spoke little Russian, and Lyuba was hopping about, trying to help by spouting whatever Tatar words she had picked up from Timur, with results that could only be considered comical. Maria had flour up to her elbows, and her small sister, despite an apron folded almost in half with strings tied three times round her waist, had acquired a strip of white across the bridge of her turned-up nose. Commands to wash it off had produced no more than giggles, and with her arms encased in flour and water paste Maria saw no way to intervene until she had a chance to clean herself.

Sumbeka took one look at the kitchen and threw up her hands. "Darling, what *are* you doing? Don't you have a steward? My son must hire one for you at once!" She snapped her fingers at the attendant who had followed her into the room. "Go back to the house and send Jamil here. Tell him to hurry."

Maria stared at her. "I don't understand." She grabbed Lyuba by the apron, ignoring the fall of flour that caused. "Make your bow to Tsaritsa Sumbeka, and stop hopping like a frog. Have you no manners? Then go wash that mark off your nose like I told you before."

Lyuba cast her a sulky glance, but she put her palms together and bowed. Her chestnut hair, so neat when Maria led her to the kitchens this morning, had escaped from its bounds and formed a fuzzy circle around her head. Maria looked at her and sighed before returning her attention to her new mother-in-law. "I apologize, Tsaritsa. I did not mean to receive you in this state."

"It does not matter." Sumbeka waved a gracious hand. "And you must call me *kaenana*. It is 'mother-in-law' in our tongue, which my son desires you to master. I came to discuss your education." She nodded at Lyuba, who by a miracle stood still, awed by this great lady. "And yours. You are now my niece and may call me *apa*. It means 'aunt.' But go and wash, as your sister tells you, while I talk to her." She gestured to the Tatar servant whose incompetence had set off this entire exchange. "Take care of the child. Comb her hair and see that she washes. And when she is clean, entertain her until I call for her." When the servant stared at her blankly, she switched to Tatar.

The servant held out a hand. Lyuba gulped, but she did not lack courage. Maria silently applauded her little sister as Lyuba bowed again and said, "Yes, *Apa*," before leaving with the servant. Wishing she could duck out as well, Maria moved to the kitchen sink—which, marvel upon marvels, also drew water from the magical pipes—and washed the flour from her arms. She untied her apron, draped it over a stool, and spoke to the cook. "Bring refreshments to the blue room with the yellow cushions." Then she too bowed, still struggling to understand what bothered Sumbeka but determined not to yield until she did. "If you would join me, *Kaenana*." The word twisted on her tongue, but she got it out. "We can discuss this under more pleasurable circumstances."

Sumbeka turned, beckoning Maria to follow. "I know the room. Yes, let us discuss these matters there."

Maria quickened her pace as they approached the room she had chosen. Of the many areas of the house she liked this one the best; although here, as elsewhere, screens and grillwork covered the street-level openings, a second level of tall pointed windows shaped like church doors permitted the entry of the bright light her embroidery required. By the time she caught up with her mother-in-law, Sumbeka was standing in front of the wooden frame that displayed Maria's latest project: a blanket for the infant that would soon grow in her womb.

"You have an extraordinary gift, *kilen*." Sumbeka caressed the gold flowers at the edge of the quilt with one long finger, then looked at Maria and smiled. "And yes, so you need not ask, *kilen* means 'daughter-in-law.'"

Maria sat on the closer of the two sofas. A servant scuttled in with a brass tray and placed it on the octagonal wooden table in front of her. Tea, she guessed based on the steam emerging from the spouted pitcher. Something for which she had yet to acquire a taste, but perhaps Sumbeka liked it. Next to the pitcher lay a plate of round honeyed sweets that Lyuba loved.

But they were not here to talk about food, were they? "Tell me please," she said to Sumbeka, "what I did to dismay you. Lady Natalya always said, 'Do it yourself. If you don't know how a task is performed, how can you ensure it's done correctly?' The girl could not understand me, and I could not understand her, so I showed her. Is that wrong?"

"Not for Lady Natalya." Sumbeka sat next to Maria and lifted her hand, red from its recent scrubbing. "But you are one of us now, a tsarevna. We will appoint a steward to manage the household. You have more important duties. You are your husband's most important asset—his eyes and ears, his guiding light. Anyone can make pastry; you will rule a kingdom. Alexei does not have one at present, it's true, but I have faith in his ambition and his skills. So you must prepare yourself for the likelihood that you will one day occupy the position I do. And we are sending you to represent us at court."

Attend court instead of supervising the household? It sounds too good to be true!

"Wouldn't I have to live in the fortress to serve the grand princess? But I should pay my respects to her as a married lady. We sent the kerchiefs and taffeta, as is the custom, but my Aunt Theodosia has promised to present me next week."

"You will not live in the fortress. Nor act as a formal attendant. What we need is information about what goes on inside the royal court, so that we can anticipate trouble and protect our family from harm. General information: who enjoys the grand princess's favor and whose loyalties she doubts. The moves she plans to make in this worrisome conflict with her brother-in-law. But also specific information that may affect the men in our clan—the women too, of course, but the men's fate is more likely to determine that of the women than the reverse."

Maria did not challenge that last, which struck her as obvious. More important to understand what exactly Sumbeka expected of her—and whether she could fulfill a task so different from any of those demanded of her by her mother, her former mother-in-law, and the Church.

Yet the prospect called to her. She had always hoped to escape the restrictions that consigned her exhausted, unresponsive mother to a premature old age. A childhood spent as her mother's arms and legs, followed by marriage and widowhood under Lady Natalya's conventional thumb, had convinced Maria that no alternative future existed for her. Why else had she so resented her Tatar sister-in-law? Sumbeka's command opened a door.

"You think I can find out so much?" she asked. "Who is in and who out, yes. I will see evidence of that even on a first visit. And the women will talk, although based on speculation more than knowledge. But specifics about our men? I suspect those decisions come down from outside the women's quarters, whatever elevated role the grand princess may have secured for herself."

"Do your best," Sumbeka said firmly. "Your husband, your father, my daughter—you and I too—depend on what you can discover. Whether you learn it from your aunt or from others or from Grand Princess Elena does not matter, but if you can establish yourself with the grand princess, so much the better. We have little time. My husband tells me that the talks with Lithuania are nearing completion. Then Elena will make her move."

Maria clasped her hands together and leaned toward Sumbeka. A tea-scented wisp of steam wafted past, reminding her that she was the hostess here. Swiftly she poured tea into one of the fragile ceramic cups and passed it to her mother-in-law. Sumbeka accepted the tea and sipped it but shook her head at the plate of sweets.

"What must I know to succeed?" Maria heard the mixed apprehension and excitement in her own voice and strove to steady it. "My aunt can teach me the court protocol."

"Yes, and you have ties with the other noblewomen. That will be useful." Sumbeka tapped a fingernail against her cup, a thoughtful expression on her face. "You have much to learn: to read and write, to speak Tatar, to ride that lovely mare my son says he gave you. The last can wait until spring. The Tatar can wait too, since your steward will deal with the servants. I will find you a man who speaks Russian."

Maria released a silent breath. No stinky horse for a while and no language study. Reading and writing, though? She opened her mouth to tell Sumbeka that women did not need such knowledge, then shut it again. Sumbeka would no doubt reiterate that such views, although fine for Lady Natalya, did not suit a tsarevna.

Meanwhile, her mother-in-law continued without a pause. "But the reading and writing are crucial. I will have our imam's wife—oh, no, for you we need a priest, so you can learn in your own language first. Perhaps Nasan can spare their family chaplain for the task. He taught her husband, she said, and you know him. He can work with your sister and Timur at the same time. A little book learning will do them both good."

A statement so outrageous that a retort hovered at the tip of Maria's tongue. What benefit could book learning offer a child?

Again she did not speak the thought aloud. Sumbeka, despite her graciousness, was proving rather intimidating. That calm confidence brooked no disagreement.

"Don't look at me like that, *kilen*." Sumbeka laughed—a light, girlish sound that contrasted with her authoritative stance. "My daughter told me that Russian girls—and even Russian men—seldom learn to read. But as my son's wife you must keep him apprised of everything from gossip to political moves against him. Right now Tulpar—I mean, Alexei—is here in Moscow. But when he receives his first service assignment, how will you fulfill your responsibilities if you cannot write regular letters?"

"We send messengers," Maria said, more sharply than she intended. She was not irresponsible, whatever Sumbeka thought!

"Messengers talk." Sumbeka clapped her hands together as if closing a book. "When they don't forget. This Russian dislike of reading gives you a great advantage. You will be able to write what others cannot read. I expect you to learn quickly. Once Tulpar—*ai*, Alexei—leaves, you must write to him once a week, more often in case of trouble."

Maria had yet to craft an answer to that when the door opened to reveal a slender dark-haired man of medium height with light brown skin and black eyes.

"Ah, Jamil." Sumbeka waved him in. "This is my daughter-in-law, Tsarevna Maria. Her household needs a steward. A man who speaks Russian. I wish you to set things to rights, but can you also recommend one of my servants for the position?"

"Not a man, *Khatun*." Jamil bowed to Sumbeka. "But Tanya, who used to serve as maid to your daughter, would do excellently here."

Sumbeka clapped her hands again. A delighted smile lit her face. "Of course! I should have thought of her myself. Send her as soon as you return to our estate." To Maria she added, "You will like Tanya, and she will serve you well."

It sounded more like a command than a recommendation, but Maria, overwhelmed by this rapid-fire decision making, had no energy left to protest. Even Sumbeka couldn't compel her to like Tanya. In fact, perhaps she would *not* like her, if that's what it took to maintain some independence in this voluble and domineering family.

Jamil departed in a flurry of bows, and Sumbeka returned her attention to Maria. "So what else must we settle? Have you clothes appropriate to your station?" She wrinkled her nose at Maria's everyday dress: a soft green caftan over a cream tunic. "Not that, certainly. Your wedding clothes are adequate."

"Not this," Maria said. This time she did not try to hide her irritation. "I wore this to the kitchens. Naturally I will choose something else for my visit to court. Something better." But a flash of doubt assailed her. Her wedding clothes were the best she had. If they were only adequate, what else could she wear?

"Hmm." Sumbeka frowned. "I will ask Tanya to check. Probably you need new robes. And you must wear the jewelry my son gave you. It is good that he was generous. Tanya will instruct you on what goes with what. You represent our lineage now, not your father's."

Am I not even to pick my own jewelry?

Sumbeka stood. Roiling with resentment, Maria endured the pressure of her mother-in-law's scented cheek against her own.

"Well, I must be off," Sumbeka said. "If Nasan's priest cooperates—and why should he not?—expect to begin your lessons tomorrow morning. Tell your sister and Timur, if you please. And Tanya will have the sewing maids start work in the afternoon. With only a week to get you ready, we can't afford to waste a moment."

With that she left the room, exuding jasmine and determination.

"Can't you *stop* her?" Maria, red-faced and raging, pounced on her husband as he came through the door.

He jerked away from her, startled. Nasan had warned him that his new wife had a temper, but since the wedding he'd seen little evidence of it. The occasional rash comment, a sharp tone to her voice the day he revealed that his son would stay with them, but nothing like the virago who faced him now. "Stop whom?" he asked, in part to buy time and in part out of genuine confusion. The only "she" who came to mind was his six-year-old sister-in-law, whose high spirits might become galling under the wrong circumstances but who otherwise struck him as biddable enough. Unless Roxelana had paid a surprise visit, of course.

"*Ka-en-a-na,*" Maria said, emphasizing each syllable. "Your stepmother. She arrived unannounced this morning, and by the time she left she'd informed me that I'm to spy for the family at court, I'm to start learning to read tomorrow, I should forget about managing the household because someone named Tanya will take over for me, and—as if that weren't enough—my clothes are fit for a peasant and my jewelry is acceptable only because you gave it to me."

She picked up an ivory thimble and tossed it at the big yellow pillow lining the back of the sofa. "If it were spring, I would also be learning to ride that big-headed, wall-eyed monster with the giant teeth. But given that it's February, she will permit me to wait until the snows melt before I give it a chance to kill me." She paced back and forth across the room, kicking her skirts as she walked.

He bit his tongue. Laughing would not help. "She tried your patience sorely, I see," he managed after a while. "But do you want to spend your days ordering servants about? And by big-headed, wall-eyed monster, do you mean the mare? She won't kill you. Timur could ride her sitting backwards without a saddle. She's an absolute lamb."

"A *huge* one." Maria stopped her pacing to glare at him. In her simple dress, with her hands planted on her hips, she did look more like a peasant than a khan's daughter-in-law.

He knew better than to point that out. Thirteen years of unfettered living conflicted with five days of matrimony in many ways, but he had enough experience of women to guess how his wife would react.

Her face softened as he watched her. "The mare is your gift to me. I'm sorry I misspoke. And I *will* learn to ride her, because you wish it. Even before the spring, if you like. I'm just tired of being told what to do, as if I were a child instead of a woman grown. Three years of Lady Natalya moaning on for hours every day about mushrooms this and washing that and never let a servant perform a task I can't perform myself, then your stepmother charges in here and acts as if I grew up in a barn because she catches me showing some stupid girl how to knead dough. It's more than any reasonable person could stand."

He put his arms around her then, allowing his laughter to emerge. "Alas, sweetheart, welcome to my family. Compared to my father, my stepmother is even more of a lamb than the horse. Why, I had no say in where we would live, and I'm older than you!"

"I bet she's nicer to you because you're a man," she said, surprising him anew with her insight. "Irina—sorry, Nasan—might tell a different tale."

"Perhaps." He kissed the tip of her nose and, when she did not resist, her mouth. "They are two of a kind, and I remember them as partners in crime. But that was a long time ago, and Nasan did say she drove her mother distracted, so I suspect you have the right of it." When she did not argue, he pulled her closer. "I'll show you how a mare is ridden, shall I?"

At first he thought she took the suggestion at face value, but then she gasped and pushed at his chest. "Alexei! For shame! In the middle of the day?"

Instead of releasing her, he picked her up and whispered in her ear. "I'm your husband, remember? And I wish it. The question is, will you enjoy it too?"

"Put me down!"

He lowered her feet by a hand's breadth.

"Oh, very well," she said. "Do as you will."

He decided to take that as a yes. "You won't regret it. The middle of the day is especially fine."

And in the end he convinced her to admit that it was.

Maria hushed Lyuba and Timur long enough to greet Father Job, dispatched bearing good wishes from the Kolychev household. A warm and kindly man, he had won Maria's respect in the years she'd known him, and she took pleasure in introducing the two children to him.

"I hear that my mother-in-law gave you instructions," she said when the greetings ended. "But could you not teach Lyuba and Timur together, and me on my own?" A tiny spark of rebellion, but surely she need not compete with two children. How embarrassing if they mastered the lessons faster than she did!

"I planned to suggest that myself," he responded. "Children learn differently from their elders, and so I must teach them differently. You will grasp the principles more quickly and, I trust, apply yourself more diligently than they will." With one hand he caught Lyuba, already dancing with impatience, by the shoulder. "Sit you here, child."

Lyuba sat, picked up the quill pen lying on the paper before her, and stuck it behind one ear. "Look, Maria, a feather!"

Timur dragged it from her hair, provoking a wail of anger. He sat next to her and plunged the quill into the ink pot. "You write with it, goose. You don't wear it."

"Don't call me goose!" Lyuba snatched at the quill, but he held it over his head, out of her reach, while fending her off with his free hand. Maria leaned forward, intending to intervene, but Father Job touched her arm and she withdrew.

"Then don't act like a goose." Timur unwrapped Lyuba's clenched fist, hovering dangerously close to his chin, pushed the quill between her fingers, and cupped them around the feather. "Look." Holding her hand in his, he drew a series of sweeping curves, added some strategic dots and a final flourish, then released her.

"What does it say?" Lyuba leaned over the table, her nose almost touching the paper, as if she could read the curves by smell.

Timur clasped her index finger and drew it across the curves. "It's your name. Lyuba."

Father Job patted the boy on the head. "Very good. Now let's learn to write it in Russian." He smiled at Maria. "They are like dry cloths at this age. They absorb whatever comes near them. You see, they will do fine. Will you return at the next ringing of the bells? I'm sure you have many other tasks to occupy your time."

"I will." Maria laughed and saluted him with a bow. "Until then, Father. And thank you."

Chapter 10

"THE TROUBLE WITH SWITCHING SIDES," ALEXEI SAID TO Ruslan, "is that in Crimea I would have many people I could ask for information. Here there's only my father and Koshkin—and Daniil Kolychev, who dislikes me as much as I dislike him—so my head's in a noose. *Ata* says he doesn't care what my father-in-law has done or not done; I should shun him based on Telepnev's suspicions alone. But I can't do that. Maria loves her father; she won't condemn him without proof. And I don't want to either. Not after barely escaping death myself due to the baseless suspicions of a madman in power."

"Nor would I," Ruslan said. "And for the same reason. You can't stand back and let him pitch the whole family into the political sea, though, can you?"

They were meeting in a side wing of the house assigned to Alexei on his wedding. Ruslan's unannounced arrival in Moscow had not left time to arrange accommodations, so Alexei had offered his friend a place in his home. Today, a week after Sumbeka's invasion of the household, Ruslan had moved in, and he and Alexei had a chance to talk.

"No." Frustrated, Alexei pounded one fist into the opposite palm. "I have to find out the truth, so I can stop Koshkin if he has joined a conspiracy and support him if he hasn't. *Ata* convinced me on one point: because I married

Maria, Telepnev and Elena will blame us, too, if Koshkin does something stupid. It's infuriating."

"Have you found out anything?" Ruslan stood and paced, threatening the safety of a small inlaid table that barred his path.

"Not much," Alexei said. "Ogodai confirmed Telepnev's story regarding the events three years ago, also that Koshkin did spend two years in exile before Prince Vasily Shuisky summoned him back to Moscow. But neither Ogodai nor *Ata* has any direct information about Koshkin's mission to Staritsa last fall. Nor about his current political sympathies, if any. Which stands to reason, doesn't it? If he does favor Andrei, he won't want it to become common knowledge."

"Telepnev didn't say who reported your father-in-law's meeting with Andrei's majordomo?" Ruslan's robes knocked the table as he turned, and he bent to steady it.

"Not a word. Someone who traveled with him, I assume." Alexei rubbed his forehead, where a line of not-quite-pain stretched between his brows. "Daniil Kolychev may know who went with Koshkin to Staritsa. He's adjutant to Telepnev."

"Well, the only way to find out is to ask," Ruslan said.

"True," Alexei said. "And come to think of it, he should want to know, if he doesn't already. He married my sister. Koshkin's actions affect him, too. Let's pay him a visit."

Maria lifted her veil—not enough to reveal her face to passersby—and peered through the small window of her enclosed sleigh. Screams split the air on her left, and she shuddered to see a debtor pinned down while bailiffs beat his shins with rods. She turned her head to the right, where market stalls clustered around the edge of the moat and extended onto the ice. Boys on bone skates tested their powers against one another. In the bitter cold, skinned cows and sheep stood straight up, as if alive. The throng of purchasers and vendors pushed past the frozen carcasses, oblivious, once in a while sending one toppling to the ground. Shouts then broke out while sellers rushed to right the rigid beast.

Maria had no view of what lay straight ahead, but the stalls meant that her destination must be close. Soon enough, a crenellated wall appeared on both sides. Another crenellation, a brief stop, and her sleigh passed through St. Frol's Gate and continued along the wooden street, past noble estates on one side and the Ascension Convent on the other. She was inside the Kremlin.

Although she had entered the fortress before—to visit her father, mostly—this time was different. A tsarevna traveling to an audience with the grand princess—and the first of many, Sumbeka had said. Maria had never dared aim so high.

But there lay the heart of her problem. Sumbeka assumed that Maria could win the confidence of the grand princess or her closest ladies. How to accomplish that task, though, remained a secret. Sumbeka's assurances that her daughter-in-law would find a way rang hollow so close to the palace.

More noble estates, a church or two, and the Miracles Monastery replaced the Ascension Convent on her right. Then the square opened up, and the wooden buildings gave way to cathedrals, their onion-shaped domes gleaming in the morning sun. On Maria's left a two-storied building with stuccoed walls hummed with activity as clerks and scribes bustled about their work. She returned her gaze to the cathedrals. Yes, that was the great Dormition on her right and the Archangel Michael, which housed the royal princes' tombs, on her left. Beyond that, she saw the jewel box that was the Cathedral of the Annunciation, its nine gold cupolas impossible to mistake. She had arrived.

On the thought her sleigh stopped, and the coachman came to open the door. Ahead of her a fence marked the entrance to the royal quarters, where no vehicle could pass. Beyond that, rounded arches marked the opening to the Red Staircase, the entry to the Faceted Palace and the grand prince's apartments beyond. She took a path to the right of the palace, heading for the Cathedral of the Virgin's Nativity, which marked the end of the women's quarters. A long low building in white stucco with a green-tiled roof, it took some time to negotiate in long skirts. By the time she reached the end, the bitter wind had scraped her cheeks raw despite her hooded cloak, and her teeth chattered until she wondered if she would be able to identify herself, never mind converse.

When at last she mounted the right staircase, she straightened her veil and shook out Sumbeka's remade robe, a knee-length cream-colored marvel embroidered with mystical animals in rose, green, and pale blue over a full-skirted taffeta tunic the soft green of leaves in springtime. Gold thread trimmed the opening, sleeves, hem, and neckline of the outer robe, and a wide pearl collar encircled Maria's throat.

The clothes bolstered her confidence. Even her distant yet passionate husband had stopped his discussion with his friend Ruslan in mid-sentence to stare at her. And when the servant approached with her cloak, Alexei took it and draped the fur around her shoulders himself. "Lovely," he whispered in her ear. "Quite lovely."

Maria hugged the memory to her as she faced the noble guards who guarded the women's quarters. Large and brown-haired, they resembled Daniil too much for Maria's taste, and their ankle-length white robes, tall hats, and crossed spears intimidated her. "The grand princess has summoned me." She raised her chin and dared them to contradict her. "I am Maria, wife to Tsarevich Alexei Bulatovich."

They expected her, she guessed, for they uncrossed their spears and ushered her in. In the doorway Maria turned and spoke to her coachman, who had followed her up the stairs. "Take the horses to the stables. Someone will fetch you when it is time to leave."

"Yes, Tsarevna." He ducked his head and left.

"This way." One of the interchangeable guards indicated a passageway to their right. "The grand princess is receiving petitions this morning."

Maria followed him, silenced by the majesty of the decor and the enormity of today's event. Grand Princess Elena's favorite had attended her wedding (although she had had no more interaction with him than a congratulatory kiss), but the grand princess herself remained an unknown entity. She rubbed the ruby ring that her mother-in-law had given her to welcome her into the family, as if doing so would confer on her Sumbeka's self-assurance.

The excitement of the sleigh ride gave way to fear. People described Elena as cold, power-hungry, ambitious. They complained that she did not keep a widow's place but instead meddled in the affairs of men. They blamed her for the death of her brother-in-law and her uncle, charged her with wanting to eliminate her one remaining brother-in-law. Some whispered of Lithuanian sorcery. What risk did even nobles run by trying to gather information about such a woman?

Sumbeka's lectures of the last week echoed in Maria's mind. Perhaps Elena *was* everything that people said of her. Or perhaps she was like Sumbeka, set on defending her husband and children, and the fault lay with those who defined womanhood too narrowly.

Another doorway, flanked by lanterns and carved with gold birds and vines against a scarlet background, loomed ahead. Maria breathed deeply, only to shy away as a large and ungainly shape rose from a covered bench next to the door jamb. "Maria," the shape said in familiar piercing tones. "It's about time you got here. What kept you, child? Not that hussy, I hope."

Maria released her breath in a rush. "Auntie Theodosia! Have you been waiting long? I promise, I arrived on time. The messenger said noon, but I wanted to take no chances. I'm glad to see you."

It was true. She *was* glad. Despite Auntie's outrageous behavior at the wedding, at heart she was a good person. And her familiarity with the court was a godsend. Maria was determined to learn as much from her aunt as possible. She removed her cloak and handed it to the guard.

The guardsman, seeing her settled, withdrew. Maria caught her aunt by the elbow. "Tell me, Auntie. What must I know before my presentation to the grand princess?"

"Just be yourself, dear. You're no threat to Elena, so you've no need to worry." Theodosia looked her over. "You're well turned out, I must say."

"My mother-in-law saw to that." Maria rubbed her leaf-green taffeta sleeve in illustration. "She has half the maids in Moscow working on gowns for me." Gorgeous gowns, unlike anything she had owned before. Even this altered one made her look like a queen.

Or so she thought until Theodosia ushered her into the audience hall where Grand Princess Elena held court. With icy blue eyes set off by high cheekbones, tight lips, and a long, straight nose, Elena looked every bit the autocrat. As required of wives and widows, she had hidden her hair behind a peaked headdress fringed with gold, but Maria knew from her aunt that it was the pale blonde that bards compared to winter sunlight. Forbidding in her beauty, the grand princess held the eye by the force of her spirit. The magnificence of her robes cast even Maria's into the shade.

I'd better not tell Sumbeka. She won't like that at all.

Tempted to laugh, Maria refrained. It would be hard enough to explain the joke to her aunt. Justifying it to the grand princess was unthinkable. Hands clasped, a demure expression on her face, Maria studied the room while she stood next to Theodosia and waited for a signal to move forward.

The chamber was exquisitely painted—its low, curved ceilings covered in brightly colored medallions and flowers against a pale blue background. Noblewomen of all ages sat in massed ranks to either side of the central chair; Maria recognized many of them from weddings and family gatherings.

The smell of beeswax filled the room, generated by hundreds of candles. A tile stove in the corner gave heat. From the snatches of speech she managed to catch, the current petitioner, a young man she did not recognize, wanted permission to marry one of Elena's ladies. As he finished, the grand princess beckoned to a girl standing nearby, who came forward and bowed.

"Does he please you?" Elena asked. "Have your parents consented?"

Who asks a girl whom she wants as her husband?

But the young noblewoman responded, "He does, Lady, and they have."

Would I have said yes if Papa had asked me? How would I have known what to say, when I had not met either of them?

But that was not true. She would have refused Alexei rather than marry a Tatar, although this match seemed promising. And agreed to wed Boris, the marriage that failed. Wasn't that lack of foresight the reason a girl's parents selected her husband instead of the girl herself?

"We grant permission," Elena said. "May you live happily together."

The young man backed out of the room. The noblewoman returned to her bench, giving a skip as she passed from the grand princess's line of sight. Another girl caught her by the hand and pulled her to sit next to her, whispering in her ear.

Aunt Theodosia pushed Maria forward, and she made her obeisance. Her forehead touched the colored tiles. Through a haze of apprehension and excitement she heard her aunt introduce her, the cool edge of Elena's acknowledgment, the command to rise. Maria's knees shook as she reached a standing position, and she kept her eyes lowered.

"You are Fyodor Koshkin's daughter," the grand princess said. "The girl who married the Tatar tsarevich—what is his name? He has joined our service. From Crimea. You will both demonstrate greater loyalty than your father has, I hope."

"How can you—" A jab in Maria's ribs stopped her in mid-sentence. Her aunt was right. To snap a retort would be unwise. She watched Elena through narrowed eyes, assessing her, then forced herself to keep her voice neutral as she answered the questions one by one. "Yes, My Lady, Alexei Bulatovich and I married last week. That is the reason for my visit: to inform you of the change in my status. And of course we are loyal to you and your son, as is my father."

"And as your husband was when he abandoned his lord in Crimea?" Elena looked down her long nose and waved a languid hand at a woman who stood at her left shoulder, behind a dais, wielding a pen. The woman scratched with her quill, as if recording both question and answer. "What do you think of that decision, Tsarevna?"

The hostility in Elena's voice was unmistakable. Winning the grand princess's confidence would be impossible if she could not allay Elena's suspicions. But how?

Again Maria strove for a neutral tone. "He has not shared his reasoning with me, Grand Princess." She suppressed a flicker of irritation. So far Alexei, despite his promise on their wedding day, had skillfully dodged her attempts to learn more about his past. "But I believe he left only in response to a direct threat to his life. And surely service to the grand prince of Moscow confers greater prestige than allegiance to a would-be khan whose deeds seldom match his ambitions."

"*Should* he share his reasoning with you?" Elena swept a hand to the right, indicating the ranks of giggling girls. "Do wives warrant their husbands' trust? In your opinion."

Aunt Theodosia gave a small snort, hastily converted into a cough. Elena broke off her interrogation long enough to glare, giving Maria a precious moment to run potential responses through her head. Elena's obvious antagonism threw her off-balance. The grand princess had no qualms about laying Papa's sins at his daughter's door. What would command Elena's respect?

Elena's head again turned toward Maria. "Well?"

What does a woman who seized power from her boyars want to hear?

Maria could only guess. She had much to lose from a wrong answer, much to gain from a right one, and no way to tell the difference. Yet Elena's actions made it likely that she endorsed views of a woman's place closer to Sumbeka's than to those drilled into Maria's head since childhood. So she pressed her hands tightly together, said a silent prayer, and took a risk.

"My mother-in-law tells me a wife is her husband's greatest asset," she said. "She protects their children and defends his interests. To do that, I must prove myself worthy of his trust, and he must express confidence in me. So yes, I think a husband should share information with his wife, if he sees that she is capable."

"Clever." Elena did not smile, but she nodded at the ranks of young women. "You may join the other boyars' wives. Dine with us."

Maria released a soft breath as she bowed and obeyed. She had crossed a threshold, it seemed, although she still had a long way to travel. The fumes of the grand princess's distrust swirled around her as she followed Aunt Theodosia to the benches behind Elena's left shoulder. Once settled, she looked around, taking care not to pay attention to any one person for long but checking to see whom she knew, which relatives other than Aunt Theodosia she might converse with, but most of all who sat close to the grand princess and who stayed farther away. Sumbeka had asked who occupied the inner circle, and the seating arrangement expressed the court hierarchy. Many of the seats reflected no more than the prestige of the clans whose names the women bore, by birth or by marriage, but that only highlighted the exceptions. Those Cheliadnin princesses, for example, clustered at Elena's right—every one of them a relative of her favorite, Telepnev. And Princess Nadezhda Shuiskaya—despite the low position her husband, the obnoxious Prince Ilya, enjoyed within his clan—benefited from her connection to Ilya's uncle, who stood close to Telepnev in the court hierarchy.

The church bells rang one hour, then another. Maria sat quietly at the back of the reception room. The grand princess continued to hear petitions, and Maria continued her silent observation. Behind her the massed ranks of women at times broke into murmuring conversation, but Maria learned little she had not already heard at her bride's party. Prince Andrei's fate appeared to offer a topic of endless fascination, although the tales grew wilder with each retelling, as if based on rumor rather than fact. The prince did have defenders as well as accusers, though. Maria recorded whatever she learned in her mental notebook.

As supplicants appeared, made their case, and departed—satisfied or otherwise—Maria watched the woman who stood, pen in hand, recording each decision as it issued from Grand Princess Elena's mouth. What did the book say about *her*? Did it contain information Sumbeka could use?

Perhaps learning to read was not a waste of time after all.

As midday approached, the young grand prince joined them, and the group moved to the dining room, the hum of quiet conversation continued. Surrounded by a bevy of cousins, Maria strained to hear. Did they speak so low because they were talking about her, the newcomer, or because they wanted to avoid a scolding from the grand princess?

At first she could not make out words. Then she heard something about a cat. Cat = *koshka* = Koshkin? She inched closer, covering her movement by pretending she needed to stretch her neck.

Stealthy or not, she couldn't get close enough for certainty. But she thought she heard the girl next to her say, "capture the cat."

She didn't know what that meant. But it didn't sound good—for the cat.

Alexei and Ruslan went first to the Kolychev household, where Nasan kept them waiting a considerable time before sweeping into the reception area trailed by a servant bearing refreshments.

"Greetings, *aby*." She stood on tiptoe to rub her nose across his, and he steadied her with an arm around her waist. She dropped back onto her heels and dipped her head.

"And to you, Ruslan Sultan. Forgive me. My mother-in-law's condition worsened overnight, and you arrived in the middle of my examination. Please be seated." She indicated the closest bench with her outstretched hand. "May I offer juice and fruit tarts?"

Alexei took the seat but waved away the refreshments. "It's Ramadan, sister," he reminded her gently. "Ruslan keeps the fast, as do my men. So I do also."

She flushed. "I had forgotten. Here we have Lent, so we can eat but not certain foods, and I have not seen *Ana* since the holy month began."

"You would not fast this year in any case, I hope." He indicated her rounded belly with his hand. "You might harm the child."

"I would not, but it troubles me that I forgot. I am losing my links to the past."

He nodded, understanding. It might happen to him too, one day. Then he changed the subject. "I will not keep you from your tasks, *sengel*. I am looking for your husband."

"Daniil?" Her voice rose in what sounded like astonishment.

"Unless you have another hidden away." He smiled, and she responded in kind. "You needn't say it. We're not friends. But I'm trying to discover how much trouble my father-in-law is in. Prince Telepnev warned me at the wedding that he considers Koshkin disloyal. I'd like to know whether his suspicions have any basis in fact. Daniil seems like the obvious person to ask. Is he here?"

"He's not at home. You'll find him at the Kremlin, in the stables, serving the master of horse." She lifted a black lacquer cup from the tray and sipped it. "But why not ask your wife? Maria is close to her father."

"I ..." He twisted his hands, searching for the right phrase. "It seems like a business best handled by men."

As soon as the words left his mouth, he wanted to call them back. Nasan sent him a scathing look so like her mother's that he would have sworn Sumbeka herself sat there. "Best handled by men," she purred. "And why is that? Because Maria will melt when faced with the possibility of danger? She has her faults like everyone else, but you can't truly believe that Daniil—lovable, straightforward soul that he is—has a better grasp of what gets whispered in corners than she does."

The heat rose in his cheeks. "I deserved that," he admitted. "I have no reason to doubt her. But the truth is, I barely know her."

"You know Daniil even less," she pointed out. When he didn't reply, she glared at him again. "Oh, but he's a *man.*"

Ruslan, curse him, was laughing. "It's easy for you," Alexei told him. "What am I supposed to say to her?"

When his friend did not reply, Alexei raised his hands in surrender. "You know I didn't mean that, *sengel.* I have every respect for your skills—and your mother's."

Nasan gave an irritated sigh, like a horse blowing through its nostrils. "Trust me on this, *aby.* Your wife understands better than any of us the kind of trouble her father can get into. But by all means ask Daniil as well." She pushed herself off the bench. "You will find him in the Kremlin, as I said. If you will excuse me." Without waiting for a response, she tipped her chin in the tiniest bow Alexei had ever seen and left the room.

"I swear," Alexei told the closing door. "That girl gets more like her mother every day." He scowled at Ruslan, still chortling. "Some help you are."

"Serves you right. And here you're supposed to be so good with women." Ruslan jumped to his feet and slapped his friend on the shoulder. "Let's go find Daniil Kolychev."

"I suppose we may as well," Alexei said. "What do we have to lose?"

Chapter 11

A LOT, AS IT TURNED OUT. MORE ACCURATELY, THE POTEN-
tial gains seemed hardly worth the effort as Alexei, Ruslan at
his side, waited on horseback while the captain of their escort
explained to one fractious guard after another that they were
Tatar sultans in Russian service who, as Christians (a falsehood
in Ruslan's case), did not have to enter the royal palace by a
separate stairway and in any case had no plans to enter the
palace, since their business lay with the master of horse (that
is, his adjutant—a justifiable exaggeration, in Alexei's view). By
the time his group had made its way through the massive gates
and—on foot, because the grand prince did not permit riders
anywhere near his residence!—around the horseshoe-shaped
building to the stables beyond, Alexei wished he had decided
to consult anyone in Moscow other than Daniil Kolychev.

Nor did Daniil prove easy to find even after they reached
the stables. One could not mistake the home of hundreds of
horses, but the very size of the complex inhibited the discovery
of a single person—even if the dress worn by most of those
present clearly distinguished them from a young man of noble
birth. Repeated inquiries yielded unsatisfactory results until at
last Alexei caught sight of his quarry in earnest discussion with
another nobleman—older, shorter, and stouter, with reddish
hair that struck him as a pale reflection of his own wife's

glorious copper. As he approached the pair, he heard Daniil say, "Next week at this time. Prepare. But tell no one of our destination. Understood?" The redheaded man nodded. Alexei stopped mid-stride, determined to eavesdrop if possible, but the redhead moved away.

Tempted to kick the nearest stable door (or the redhead), Alexei refrained. "Daniil Nikolaevich," he said.

Daniil turned, and his eyebrows shot upward. "Alexei Bulatovich." He emphasized the first name, as if he still regarded it as fraudulent. "What brings you here?"

The antagonism in his voice raised Alexei's hackles. "My sister told me where to find you." He would not give in to this stripling's jibes. "I have questions for you. Questions better not asked in so public a place." He swept his hand in a circle, indicating the wooden ceiling and walls. "If you have a moment to spare?"

Daniil leaned his back against the closest stable door and crossed his arms over his chest. Although not dressed in full military garb, he wore a high-collared quilted coat, a fur-trimmed hat, trousers, and knee-high boots, giving him a warlike appearance enhanced by his forbidding stare. "I don't, in fact," he said. "I'm on duty for the next two days. Can your questions not wait?"

"Because you have a journey to undertake?" Alexei asked. Startle him, and he might reveal the meaning behind that cryptic command.

But Daniil only laughed, a hostile sound that included no genuine amusement. "So you did hear me. If that's your question, forget it. My future assignments are no concern of yours."

Oh well, he had not expected to fool Daniil so easily. "No, I came to ask about my father-in-law. I've heard rumors that cast him in a bad light, but having been in Moscow such a short time, I don't know whether to trust them. Given the ties between our families, I thought they might interest you too. Now you see why I wished to talk with you in private."

"I do see." Daniil stood straight, and his grim expression lightened. "Alas, I have nothing to tell you at the moment, but we should discuss the possibilities. I will call on you Friday afternoon, or you may visit me if you wish to include my father in the conversation. Something I highly recommend, by the way. He has court connections you and I can only dream of."

"Until Friday then. I will visit you after the midday meal." But as Alexei left, he could not help wondering where Daniil's secret journey would take him—and for what purpose.

As Maria rounded the corner of the Faceted Palace, the Dormition Cathedral on her right and the bell tower straight ahead, a group of horsemen on the far side of the square caught her eye. To one side, tucked behind the Cathedral of the Archangel Michael, she saw her coachman, waiting in response to the message Aunt Theodosia's servant had delivered a short time before. But the horsemen, some of whom had not yet mounted, did not look at him or notice her. Most of them were Tatars, warmly dressed in sheepskin hats and belted coats, but the leaders stood out in their velvet-covered outer garments, sable visible in the turned-back sleeves and high collars and rimming their jeweled hats. One of them wore her embroidered sash.

Alexei and Ruslan. What brought them to the Kremlin? And why had her husband not told her he had business here too?

She didn't expect him to ask for permission. Still, while she was recounting every detail, from the help offered by Aunt Theodosia to Sumbeka's demand that she learn more about potential threats to their family, surely it would have been natural to mention that she might see him there.

But no. Whatever Sumbeka said about wives being their husbands' greatest assets, Alexei clung to the idea that women belonged in the bedroom and the kitchen.

And she wanted to be a good wife, a good mother, as her own mother had tried but failed to be. Still, she had come here to help *him*. Didn't he understand that?

The Tatar horsemen left. Maria crossed the square and entered her closed sleigh. "To Tsaritsa Sumbeka's house," she told the coachman.

Although dinner at the palace had ended not long before, the winter sun was setting when Maria arrived at her mother-in-law's house. Her entrance coincided with cries of delight and a rush of servants bearing trays of cups and plates of what looked like dried fruit. Sumbeka, directing the scene with clapped hands and the air of an elegant silk-clad general, stopped long enough to pluck a cup from the nearest tray, then made her way through the crowd to offer it to Maria. "To break the fast," Sumbeka said. "I know you don't observe it, but it is our custom to greet guests in this way when they arrive after sunset."

"Oh, I have chosen a bad time." Maria took the cup and swallowed. A tart, milky flavor not unlike thin sour cream spread over her tongue. She decided not to mention the Lenten ban on dairy foods. Instead she handed the cup back, still half-full. "Thank you, but I ate an indecently huge meal in the grand princess's apartments. Would it be better to return tomorrow morning?"

"When you have news?" Sumbeka passed the cup to a servant crossing the hall and took Maria by the elbow. "Come and tell me the whole. First we break the fast, then we say prayers, and the meal follows sometime after that. Right away, in midsummer, but here it is three of the clock. There is no rush." She led Maria to a room that combined Russian-style windows and tiled stove with tasseled pillows and elegant inlaid wood tables. The whole looked like what might happen if Alexei's house and Papa's married and started a family.

Perched on a carpet-covered bench, Maria asked, "Nasan is not here?"

"A crisis with Lady Natalya. She is recovering, but my daughter doesn't want to leave the estate until she feels confident there will be no relapse." Sumbeka crossed the room and sat next to Maria.

"I should visit her," Maria said. "Lady Natalya, that is. I had no chance to talk with her at the wedding, and the preparations took so much time. I haven't gone to her house since the beginning of the Christmas feast. It's good she has Nasan, but I wouldn't like to fall behind in my attentions to her. Although she can be stern, she has a kind heart." The phrasing struck her then, and she wrinkled her nose. "An ailing one, alas."

"Nasan will appreciate that too," Sumbeka said. "She works so hard, between caring for her mother-in-law and managing the household. I worry about her. I offered her a competent steward as well, but she insists that the man they have has done the work for years and the family doesn't like to replace him."

"I know him," Maria said. "It's true. But perhaps Nasan will accept a housekeeper. Even before we became friends, I knew she hated domestic tasks."

"Ask her, please." Sumbeka patted Maria's hand. "It may come better from you. Not so much 'Mother demands.' And tell me how she responds."

"I will visit her tomorrow," Maria promised.

"So how did your day go with the grand princess?" A servant entered with a tray, which he placed on the largest of the inlaid tables, at Sumbeka's left. "Are you sure you won't have some tea? It settles the digestion after one of those heavy Russian meals."

"Yes, please," Maria said. The fragrant steam, when Sumbeka handed her the round porcelain cup wrapped in a linen cloth, did offset the memory of garlic and onions—although an experimental sip still tasted of grass. She took a second sip, then placed the cup nearby. "Grand Princess Elena distrusts me. Because of Papa. He disappointed her, and she challenged me to prove my loyalty."

"And how did you respond?"

"I quoted you. It seemed to calm her. Even so, I think it will be difficult to find out any information from her directly."

"We will see," Sumbeka said. "If you continue to visit, she may lower her guard, especially if your aunt puts in a good word for you. If not, there must be others who will talk."

Maria risked another sip of the grassy tea. "I have relatives among the ladies-in-waiting, and my mother was friends with Agrafena Cheliadnina, the princes' nanny, once upon a time. I have heard too that Solomonida Sheremeteva, who is a cousin by my first marriage, has been attending the grand princess. She will know everything—it's her nature—but we dislike each other, so she may not tell me."

Sumbeka's haughty expression, so reminiscent of Grand Princess Elena's, returned. "Befriend her," she ordered. "When you curb that temper of yours, you can be quite charming. So curb it. It will benefit you in general, and here especially. Your family needs you."

Maria bit her tongue before replying. "Yes, *Kaenana.*"

"Good. I count on you. Now tell me the whole. What happened after you calmed Elena?"

Maria summarized her observations on the court hierarchy, relayed the essence of the rumors as well as the cryptic phrase she had overheard, described the uneventful if filling dinner, and ended with her unexpected identification of Ruslan and Alexei in the courtyard. Sumbeka listened, nodding from time to time but not interrupting. As the narrative continued, her imperious air became one of quiet contemplation.

"I am so frustrated with him, *Kaenana*," Maria finished.

She stopped. Those last words had slipped out. *Kaenana* was right. She must learn to control her tongue! "I'm sorry. I shouldn't have said that."

But Sumbeka sent her an encouraging glance. "Tell me, *kilen*. I won't gossip. Husbands are by nature frustrating creatures. What has he done?"

"He can be so charming and so kind that he convinces me he cares about me." Thinking of how he most often demonstrated that caring, she felt her cheeks warm. Her face must have the hue of a robin's breast. "But I no sooner feel comfortable than he traipses off on his own as if I don't exist—inviting friends to stay, giving me no clue where he's going or when to expect him home, telling me it's not a woman's business what he does. And in a sense it isn't, but I do run his household. I need to know how many rooms or meals or baths or clothes the servants must prepare, if only to tell Tanya. Honestly, I could smack him sometimes."

Halfway through this recital of woes Sumbeka started to laugh, a rueful sound that Maria found oddly reassuring. "Oh, my dear." Sumbeka patted her cheek. "How like a man. Here you are working on his behalf, and he leaves you in the cold. No wonder you want to smack him. I would myself."

Maria giggled, her frustration dissipating. No lectures to turn the other cheek, no demands that she pray for obedience and forbearance—Sumbeka's ready acceptance of anger constituted a considerable part of her charm.

"But I think you must consider the life he's led," her mother-in-law went on. "He was only sixteen, you know, when my husband cast him out. I didn't approve, but Bulat refused to listen to me. Since then Tulpar—sorry, Alexei—has survived on his own. I'm sure he's had lovers aplenty, but Roxelana and her ilk are not the kind of women one trusts with information, still less one's private self. Passion he understands, but partnership? I doubt it. With Timur's mother maybe. But I sense they spent much time apart."

"That's another thing," Maria said. "He avoids talking about his past. Right after the wedding he promised he would, but whenever I ask him, he tells me it's not the right time. I can't imagine *what* he's feeling, because he doesn't share it. Why did your husband cast him out? Nasan said something about an argument during a battle, but I could see she didn't believe that was the real reason."

"Ah." Sumbeka walked to the side of the room, where she reached up to adjust a decorative bowl that did not appear to need adjusting. "My daughter's right, and so are you. That was not the reason. It was the excuse."

She turned and came back, resuming her seat to Maria's left, lifted the teacup and returned it to its place without drinking.

"Should I tell you the truth, I wonder? Yes, I think I must. Because your husband doesn't know the whole, and if mine does, he has not shared his understanding with me. And as"— she paused, then continued as if forcing herself to get the name right—"*Alexei's* wife, you have a right that transcends my daughter's or even my son's. Ogodai, I mean, since the story concerns him too."

It felt like an acknowledgment that she and Sumbeka were equals. Touched, Maria reached for her mother-in-law's hand.

"Do tell me, please," she said. "I want to understand him better, and I need your help."

Sumbeka squeezed her fingers, then released them, pressing her back against cushions covered in gold velvet and drawing her feet up to rest on the carpeted seat.

"Very well," she said. "It began when I came from Crimea. I was seventeen, and your Alexei was four. A quarter-century ago. It's hard to believe so much time has passed."

Maria dared relax as well. The hard bench pressed against her ankles, but if she kicked off her slippers and rested her feet on the bench, the cushions permitted her to sit in comfort. "What was he like at four?"

"A charmer." Sumbeka gave a soft, reminiscent chuckle. "Imagine Timur at his most effervescent, a handsome boy with bright eyes and a ready smile, quick to respond to everything that went on around him. He was so open and trusting when I first met him, you wouldn't believe it. His mother, Sania, adored him—that never changed—but she hated being set aside when Bulat married. She was a concubine, and I think she expected to become chief wife. She had produced a healthy son, so we can't blame her for that. But Bulat married for political reasons, like everyone else. He wanted an alliance with my uncle, and Sania had no connections to speak of."

Maria thought of Alexei—so warm at some moments, so guarded at others—and of Timur, who displayed an exuberance she found it difficult to envision in her husband. "What happened?"

Sumbeka shivered, despite the heat radiating from the furnace. "She turned Alexei against us. Poisoned him with her resentment. Bulat wanted to send her away, keep his son with him, and I, idiot that I was, told him it would be cruel to separate them. By then I had a son of my own. Five months after his birth he died one night in his crib." Her voice broke, and Maria again reached out a hand to clasp hers. This time Sumbeka did not pull away.

"How terrible for you." Maria pressed her free hand against her belly. It was too soon to be certain, but her last monthlies had brought no more than light spotting, and her breasts ached. A certain queasiness that afflicted her in the mornings pointed in the same direction. Suppose she bore Alexei's child only to have him die before he teethed?

Sumbeka must have seen the gesture, because she said, "Yes, you can guess how it felt. At the time, horrible as it was, I blamed it on fate. God's will. But it didn't stop there. After Ogodai was born, before he even learned to smile, his nurse caught Sania looming over his cradle with a pillow in her hands."

Maria gasped. "Such wickedness! Did she kill the other child, then?"

"She did." Sumbeka pulled away and twisted her hands together in her lap. "Bulat questioned her, and she admitted it. He could not let her live, but Alexei was only seven. We didn't want to tell him that his father had executed his mother for the murder of his half-brother, so we said she had gone away and left him in our care."

"And he believed you?"

"He did. He still does, so far as I know."

"Such a tragic story." Maria wrapped her arms around her knees, putting herself in the place of that seven-year-old boy. Her own mother had disappointed her more times than she could count, but however frail, she had been present. How must it feel to believe that your mother had walked away and left you?

Yet Sumbeka was right. The truth would have hurt Alexei worse than the lie. "I still don't understand why his father cast him off. Didn't he need your family even more after losing his mother?"

Sumbeka nodded. She stared at her feet, avoiding Maria's gaze. "During the argument—not the first argument between my husband and yours, I should add—Alexei threatened my son. I don't think he meant to act on the threat. He was furious, seething. He believed Bulat loved Ogodai more, which was true in the sense that Ogodai, being younger, didn't challenge his father the way Alexei did. He said something stupid, as reckless boys will, about how Bulat couldn't protect Ogodai every moment. But Bulat remembered Sania, and how she had exploited the chance he gave her because *I* pled with him to relent. He ignored whatever I said."

"And banished his eldest son." Maria shuddered. It was so clear, so stark, so hideous—and in its own ugly way so comprehensible. What *should* Bulat have done under the circumstances? But the effect on Alexei—abandoned by his mother, then exiled by his father—she couldn't imagine what that had done to him.

A long, ululating call sounded from the courtyard, sung in a rhythm and a pitch clearly distinct from Russian. Maria didn't understand the words, but she recognized the sound. She heard it at her own estate five times a day.

"It is the call to sunset prayers," Sumbeka said. "I must let you go."

"I will." Maria stood and bowed. "Thank you so much for telling me. I need to think about what you've said. May we talk again soon? Tomorrow I go to Lady Natalya's, so perhaps the next day?"

Sumbeka rose and pressed her jasmine-scented cheek to Maria's. "Of course, *kilen*. You are always welcome in my house."

Chapter 12

ALEXEI RETURNED FROM HIS VISIT TO THE KREMLIN IN TIME to break the fast with his and Ruslan's men. A brief consultation followed, but as the call sounded for sunset prayers, Alexei withdrew.

What have I achieved by converting, other than to make myself even more of an outsider than before?

He gave a rueful sigh. In the past he had honored his religion mostly in the breach, obeying the laws and performing the rites as required but no more. He'd thought one faith much like another—a tag around the neck, a way of separating friend from foe. But now he missed the familiarity of the ritual, the sense of belonging to something bred into him since birth.

Timur darted past and raced for the building set aside for religious observances since Shah-Ali Khan first took possession of the estate. The boy's hands still dripped water from a too-hasty washing, and he scuffed off his shoes as he crossed the threshold. Alexei returned to the enclosed porch attached to the hut and, following the prayers in his mind, waited for his son to finish.

Another decision he must make before long: would it serve the boy best to let him keep the religion into which he'd been born or to help him adjust to this new, ascendant Russian principality, knowing that accepting service here would bar him from leading a khanate of his own? And father or not, did he have the right to decide?

The nomads would say yes—among them a father's word was law. But religion inscribed a person in a particular community, opening doors as well as closing them. Russia offered Alexei more than the certainty of disgrace and death in Crimea. But Timur would have different opportunities, and who knew which state would have moved up and which down a decade from now?

As Alexei reached this point in his deliberations, Timur emerged from the prayer hall and grasped his hand. "Auntie has food for us," he said.

"Auntie? My sister is here?" Alexei frowned. Nasan had seemed preoccupied with her mother-in-law when he'd seen her a short time ago. Nor had she even remembered it was Ramadan. Why bring food when they had plenty here?

"No, Auntie Maria," Timur said, using the Russian word for "auntie." "She told me I could call her that if I like. It's confusing: so many stepmothers and mothers and mothers-in-law—that's what she said."

"Ah, I understand. Let's see what the cooks have prepared, shall we?" As Timur, a solemn expression on his face, led the way, Alexei smiled. His wife had found a way to reach his son while convincing him she did not seek to displace his mother in his heart. Not bad for a young woman everyone characterized as a shrew.

They found Maria in the room she had adopted as her own. A rectangle of cream-colored wool spread across a robe the color of chestnut leaves in autumn, and she was picking out a delicate pattern at one edge in sky blue, aqua, and forest green.

Lyuba sat cross-legged next to a large bronze disk on short wooden legs, where she was arranging chess pieces on a board with an intent expression on her face. A long trestle table near the window held a bowl of Tatar stew and a plate holding Russian turnovers, even a basket or two wrapped in towels, from one of which peeked the edge of a golden-brown *cheburek*. Timur leaped for joy at the sight and dashed forward, stopping only when Alexei caught the back of his son's jacket. "Greet your stepmother and sister," he told the boy in Tatar, then repeated the phrase in Russian. Timur needed practice.

His son stopped in mid-rush long enough to bow. "Greetings, Auntie, sister. I am so hungry. May I eat?"

Alexei shook his head. "'May I bring you something to eat?' Say it, Timur. You are a prince, not a wild animal. You must learn manners."

Timur repeated the phrase, looking and sounding rather sulky. Maria put down her sewing and came toward them, kissing her husband and patting her stepson on the head. "I am not hungry," she said. "Please feed yourselves. Lyuba has already eaten."

She touched Alexei's shoulder. "Tanya tells me you have been fasting with your men. I didn't know to ask until I visited your stepmother this afternoon. You should have said something. We can serve dinner later. In fact, Tanya tells me the staff would prefer it, as so many of them are fasting too. So long as we serve Lenten food when we do eat, everyone will be happy."

He pointed at the *cheburek* disappearing into Timur's mouth. "That's not Lenten food."

"It is, actually. I asked the cooks to use fish and fry them in oil, and they did." Maria resumed her seat and picked up the embroidery once more. "I'm not hungry because I ate with the grand princess and her ladies. I don't think I've ever seen so much food in one place at one time, except at weddings."

Lyuba waved the carved ivory queen from the chess set. "Here is a wedding. Look, Alexei! She is marrying the wooden king."

Timur heaved a sigh appropriate to a centenarian with the gout. "I've tried to explain the game to her, *Ata*, but she won't listen. The bishop is marrying them"—he rolled his eyes— "and the knights and pawns are the guests."

He looked so gloomy at this desecration of a game he had yet to master that Alexei could not help laughing. "Let her enjoy herself, son." He clapped a hand on Timur's shoulder. "You and I can play chess when she's finished. Meanwhile, let's eat. I want to talk with my wife before starting a game, anyway."

A short while later Maria made room for her husband as he returned, plate in hand, to sit next to her. He touched the edge of the cream wool where it fell onto the sofa. "Exquisite. What is it?"

Maria's cheeks warmed. "A baby blanket," she said. "As with bride goods, it works best to have everything ready before you need it."

He studied her, his dark eyes alight—could it be with affection? "And do you expect to need it soon?"

"I can't tell," she said. "Not enough time has passed since the wedding."

She didn't think she'd given herself away, but she must have, because his eyebrows quirked. "But you suspect you may?"

"Perhaps." She didn't want to talk about the signals she'd detected in her body in front of the children, especially when they might mean no more than anxiety over her wedding. "I should know in a month—or two."

His face relaxed, and basking in his smile, she would have sworn that it *was* affection that softened the defenses he appeared to keep perennially raised against the world. "Well, don't decide too soon." He caressed her cheek with his thumb. "I'm supposed to stay away from you if you're with child, and I've enjoyed our nights together."

Maria stared at the embroidered links snaking their interconnected way among the golden flowers that lined the edge of the blanket. His caressing thumb sparked a trail of fire that spread throughout her vitals, but it was the hint of some deeper desire for connection that brought the laughter to her throat. "In that case I may not be certain until the summer, or longer."

"That's my girl." Alexei brushed a kiss across her neck. "Now tell me what you discovered today. At the grand princess's table."

"I'm invited back next week." She repeated what she'd told Sumbeka, adding her assessment of Grand Princess Elena. "And I remembered, as I was watching her, how flattered I felt when Papa explained politics to me. My mother insisted women should manage their households and leave government to their husbands, whom God has ordained to handle it. Lady Natalya agrees. But your stepmother tells me otherwise, and there's Grand Princess Elena, ruling the country for her son. So who's right?"

"Elena rules because she must." Alexei had been regarding her with a thoughtful expression on his face, as if seeing her for the first time. She couldn't guess what went through his mind. "Oh, perhaps she enjoys it. But if she sat in her tower spinning, what would happen to her boys? No one else has as compelling a reason as she does to keep those children alive. The favorite and his sister, maybe, but even they—"

A shriek from Lyuba cut him off mid-sentence. "Holy Mother," Maria cried. Her needle jabbed into her palm; she tugged it out and sucked the wound. When she checked the cloth, she saw no blood, but she set the blanket aside and placed the needle in its holder. She'd have to rethread it tomorrow. No more stitching today.

When she looked up again, she saw her husband on his feet, wresting a chess knight away from Timur. "If she can play weddings, why can't I play war?" Timur demanded.

"He's the thousandman," Lyuba announced at top volume. "He was giving a speech, and Timur grabbed him right out of my hand." She scrunched up her face at him. "Bully!"

Alexei shook his head. "Timur, fetch your toy warriors." He tapped Lyuba on the crown of her head. "And you, miss, no name calling." He handed her the knight and spoke to Maria. "Unless you'd rather send them both to bed?"

A concerted howl greeted that suggestion. "Soon," Maria said. "But play well together—or at least side by side—and you can stay up for a while."

Lyuba settled down with her chess pieces right away, although she made another face at Timur's back as he went off, grumbling under his breath, to fetch his toys. Alexei called for the servants to remove the food and to bring him a cloth dipped in water, which in due course he applied to his wife's hand. The blood was already drying.

By then Timur had stomped back in with a leather bag. He spread the contents out on the half-empty trestle table and glared at Lyuba. "Don't touch them. They aren't wedding guests."

"Don't need them," Lyuba said, her nose in the air. "I have lots here, now that you've stopped *stealing* them."

"Children." Maria infused her voice with as much sternness as she could muster.

"Last chance, you two." Alexei's warning, delivered in those deeper male tones, sounded more threatening. Which was unfair, but Maria decided to overlook the unfairness if it kept the children quiet.

"Leave the table for now," Alexei told Tanya, who was supervising the removal of bowls and plates. "The men can collect it later." He handed her his own cleared plate, and soon only the four of them remained in the room.

Maria laid her needlework out on its stand and let her husband lead her to the farthest point of the room, where they could keep an eye on the children without being distracted by their play.

"Before that brouhaha started, you mentioned your father. I'm sorry—I was paying attention at the time, but ..." He left the sentence unfinished.

Maria laughed. "You can't remember every word? After so much fuss I'm impressed you even know what we were talking about."

"It sounded important," he said with a dismissive shrug that irritated her anew. "Help me understand. You told me he explained politics to you. Does he do that often?"

"Hardly ever." Maria wrinkled her nose, considering, then straightened it. The gesture probably made her look no older than Lyuba. "Before I married Boris, he probably considered me too young. But since his return from Vologda he has discussed things with me a few times. Why he arranged our marriage, for example."

"Nothing else?" Alexei's willingness to listen to her without interruption drew her. "He's never spoken to you of Prince Andrei? His mission to Staritsa last fall? His opinion of the grand princess?"

He sounded as if he had something specific in mind. "Not the mission," she said slowly, trying to follow his train of thought. "Nor Prince Andrei. Papa hates Grand Princess Elena, and he always believed one of the adult uncles should take the throne. He's not alone there. Many men disapprove of a woman ruler."

"So they do," Alexei said. "But then your father should support Andrei, the only one of the grand prince's uncles left."

"He should, but he hasn't said that he does. He served Andrei's older brother Yuri for several years and developed a great respect for him. And for Grand Prince Vasily, the oldest brother. But Andrei has kept to himself since Vasily died. I'm not sure Papa knows him well enough to have an opinion."

Another childish outburst cut off any potential reply. Alexei sprang to his feet with a warrior's grace and advanced on his son. Lyuba jumped up, overturning the bronze disk and the chessboard and sending men flying in every direction. "My wedding," she shouted as she dove after the pieces.

"I didn't touch a thing," Timur protested. "I looked at her and she started to yell."

Maria joined them, stopping on her way to collect the box that stored the chess pieces. "Come, Lyuba, it's bedtime." She knelt beside her sister and held out the box, its lid raised. "Let's see if we can match every piece to its proper place."

When Lyuba nodded, Maria beckoned to Timur. "Can you help us figure out where each one goes? Pick up the men that are missing?"

Alexei bent to collect a handful of those nearest. "Good idea." He held out his find to Timur, who carried them to the box and showed Lyuba where each one went.

Watching her husband with his son, Maria recalled the story Sumbeka had told her about Alexei's past. She'd had no time since returning home to think about what she'd learned. Should she tell Alexei what she'd heard?

But Sumbeka had not shared the story herself—with Alexei or Nasan. Maria decided for the moment to respect her mother-in-law's confidence. Twelve days after her marriage seemed too soon to relate a truth that must overturn her husband's whole understanding of his past.

With the chess men restored to their wooden home, Alexei chivvied Timur into putting away his toy warriors, then chased the children from the room. They laughed and shrieked as he turned himself into a pretend wolf, growling and holding his hands like claws over their heads before capturing them both at the doorway and pressing his cheek against Timur's, then Lyuba's. "Off you go, dreadful children."

Maria went to hug them. "Good night. Pleasant dreams," she said.

They dashed out the door, Timur swinging his bag of toys like a catapult. Lyuba danced behind him, her grievances forgotten.

"What a pair," she said. "They act like brother and sister in truth. What will they be like after a month, never mind a year?"

Alexei wrapped an arm around her waist and nuzzled her neck. "More mischievous than ever, I expect." He patted her stomach. "Like this one of whom we cannot be certain until the summer." He treated her to that devastating smile that always made her weak at the knees. "You've had a long day, my dear. Do you wish to sleep alone?"

She leaned against him, breathing in his characteristic scent of leather and sandalwood oil. For the first time in her life she understood why the steppe peoples placed so much emphasis on each person's unique combination of aromas. "No," she said after a while. "Stay with me. Please."

Alexei studied the tiled ceiling, its patterns dimly visible thanks to a lantern hanging from a sconce in the washroom beyond. Maria curled at his side, fast asleep. Although pleasurably re-laxed, he did not feel drowsy. He considered getting up and moving to another room to read. But that would wake his wife,

most likely, and she needed to rest. Especially if, as she'd hinted, he had already fathered a child on her.

She hadn't said why she thought that and probably
would not now that he had turned it into a joke. But if it
hadn't happened yet, it would soon enough. However little
time they had spent together since the wedding, *that* part
of their marriage had worked well from the first night. More
than well: his wife's unsuspected capacity for passion had
proven a delight. Despite Roxelana's surface charms, Maria's
innocent ardor touched him in ways her sultry but calculating
predecessor never had. Since the day his father kicked him out,
Alexei had refused to place his life in anyone's hands. And he'd
survived against the odds, proving the wisdom of that choice.

But Maria, with her quicksilver temper and insightful mind,
might undermine his defenses. If he were not careful, that is.

He still didn't know how much Koshkin confided in her.
But tonight her grasp of the essentials had impressed him.

Alexei owed his wife protection, no matter what. But in
this evening's conversation he glimpsed the possibility that
she might become more than a means to secure his place in
Russian society, more than a delightful bedmate, more than the
mother of his children.

She might become an ally. If he lowered his guard enough
to let her in. If he dared take that risk.

Chapter 13

Moscow, March 1537

FROM A WINDOW SEAT IN THE ROOM WHERE HE HAD SIGNED the wedding contracts with Bulat Khan, Koshkin glowered at the grand princess's departing messenger, the man's rotund form blurred by the pale gold of the mica panes. He would gladly have put his fist through the window, but the results would no doubt be unpleasant. Still, the urge to violence nagged at him.

What saint had he offended that his ruler must drop him into the same snare twice? Had he not bowed as low as the rest, flattered with the same assiduous charm, practiced the protocol until he could say each ponderous phrase without missing a single jot or tittle? Had he not reported every detail from his previous mission? Hang Prince Andrei of Staritsa and his intransigence. Koshkin wanted none of him and his troubles!

"Bad news, dearest?" Roxelana's sultry tones sounded behind him, and he swung about to face her.

"Why do you think that?" He strove to keep his voice calm, eager to spare her the slightest worry. She was a prize to cherish in soft furs and perfumed silks.

An image of Roxelana at Maria's wedding assailed him— his wife's hand on Tsarevich Alexei's, her soulful gaze fixed on his face, her luscious body a prize few men could resist. He had reveled in her allure at the time, but the certainty that he must soon leave her cast a different light on her behavior. Young, beautiful, desirable—she could have any man she wanted. He had known he would find it difficult to hold her interest. Why else had he rushed to put the ring on her finger?

He couldn't confide in a woman whose loyalty he questioned. Koshkin sighed. As ever, he walked his path alone, caring for his ungrateful lineage at great cost to himself.

"You seem troubled," Roxelana said. "And the grand prince's messenger has just left. Am I to believe there is no connection between these things?"

Trapped, he sought the most neutral answer possible. As the mistress of his household, she had a right to hear about his comings and goings. If only he did not wonder whom she might invite to fill his place while he was gone. "I am to leave on a journey," he said. "A week from Monday. To Staritsa."

Roxelana plopped onto a covered bench near the window, her usual grace quite abandoned. "Staritsa again." While he gazed at her, too stunned to speak, she frowned. "I don't like this, Fyodor. Better to stay invisible in the family feuds of royalty."

Her concern appeared genuine. He was a beast for suspecting her. Worse than a beast. Had she not agreed to marry him, although it meant abandoning Alexei?

Filled with remorse, he sat next to her and took her hand. "I don't like it either, my love. But I can't refuse. That would raise questions about my allegiance. My recent exile was based on a false accusation, and I must tread carefully."

"Yes, you must go." Her fingers gripped his. "But dearest, take care. Without you, what will become of me?"

The tears in her eyes restored his faith in her, and he kissed her. Worse than a beast, indeed, to give way to jealousy on such shaky grounds. "Have no fear. I'll be back in your arms before long. Exactly when depends on how much persuasion Prince Andrei requires. In the meantime, my sons will keep you safe."

She watched him, her eyes soft and moist.

"Nothing bad will happen." He patted her cheek and stood. The trouble in her face told him he had not convinced her. Hell, he didn't even believe himself.

When Alexei left his escort in the courtyard of the Kolychev estate on Friday afternoon, a steward ushered him into a room that combined ornate Chinese silk on the walls and elaborate ironwork on the windows with a square wooden desk holding a pen stand and simple brass candlesticks. Behind the desk sat Nikolai Kolychev, imposing in velvet and fur, his bushy gray beard touching the neckline of his outer robe. A leather belt struggled to contain his girth, and next to the desk he had propped the long walking stick that senior members of the Muscovite court seemed to consider an essential part of their wardrobe.

Daniil rose and greeted Alexei with a nod. "You remember my father?" He extended his hand, indicating the man behind the desk.

"Nikolai Borisovich." Alexei inclined his head. "Thank you for receiving me today."

Nikolai hauled his bulk out of the chair long enough to return the greeting, then pointed to a wooden settle on the side of the desk opposite Daniil. "Please be seated."

Alexei sat at one end of the settle. Daniil returned to the bench. Unlike his father he wore riding gear; he could not have long returned from the Kremlin, because the whiff of horseflesh clung to him. "I didn't have time to change. Sorry," he said.

"It's of no importance." Alexei raised a hand, accepting the apology.

With the three of them seated, Nikolai took the lead. "My son tells me you have doubts about Fyodor Koshkin, Tsarevich." He plucked a long white quill from the stand and twirled it between his fingers. "What do you wish to know?"

Alexei, accustomed to wasting hours in idle courtesies before a real conversation could begin, spared a moment to appreciate this straightforward approach. "At the wedding Prince Ivan Telepnev warned my father and me away from Koshkin," he said.

Next to the pen stand a small bound book lay. He touched the leather, treasuring its familiar blend of smooth and rough—not unlike his life these days. "He mentioned an incident some years ago where Koshkin plotted against the grand prince. My brother Ogodai confirmed the tale and suggested I approach Daniil Nikolaevich for details. But the details don't concern me at present. I wasn't allied with Koshkin then. What brings me here is Telepnev's statement that Koshkin met in private with Prince Andrei's majordomo last autumn. As a result, Telepnev and the grand princess distrust Koshkin. That *does* concern me, since it threatens to embroil me and my family in a mess not of my making."

"A serious charge," Nikolai said.

"Very serious, if the meeting means what Telepnev thinks it does," Alexei said. "But when I asked my father-in-law, in a roundabout way, he said he met with several people in an attempt to find out whether Prince Andrei was as sick as he claimed. Which was why Grand Princess Elena sent the envoys in the first place. What's suspicious about that?"

"So what brings you to us?" Daniil asked. "Don't you believe him?"

"I thought you might help me discover whether I should." Alexei leaned back, extending his feet until one touched the bulbous leg of the desk. "I don't want to condemn an innocent man, but as my father says, Telepnev's suspicion is enough to doom the lot of us, including you."

"He's right, son," Nikolai said. "You married his sister. He's wed to Koshkin's daughter. We're in this together, like it or not. If Koshkin backs Andrei, he will endanger our clan and Bulat's as well as his own. So our best hope is to prove his innocence—or, brutal as it sounds, to confirm his guilt so that we can turn him in."

Daniil sighed, then nodded. "Fair enough. I accept that we need to work together."

Not the most enthusiastic support, but Alexei decided to take Daniil's concession as a positive sign. "Then my first question is what caused Telepnev and Elena to misconstrue a meeting that appears innocuous. Koshkin's explanation makes sense to me. Maria says her father has not expressed support for Andrei." He held out a hand to Daniil, palm up. "You work with Telepnev. Can you explain it?"

"He remembers the past, I assume." Daniil's eyebrows came together, and he elaborated. "It's true that Koshkin has kept his nose clean since he returned from Vologda, but he's a sneaky son of a bitch who already got away with treason once. And the stakes here are sky-high. The Russian lands stand on the brink of civil war. If Andrei rebels, brothers will be fighting brothers, and I mean that quite literally. Telepnev doesn't want to take chances."

"Who might have more information, then?" Alexei asked. "Who went with Koshkin on that mission to Staritsa in the fall?"

"Prince Ilya Shuisky headed it," Daniil said. "Koshkin did the work. My cousin Grigory added to the body count, with the usual complement of junior servitors and guards. Any of them could have reported a private meeting. It would be their duty."

"Of course." Alexei stared at the window, which permitted barely a hint of light to pass through, and thought. "Could you ask your cousin what he knows? I've already talked with Koshkin, and Shuisky is a stranger to me."

Daniil nodded. "I can ask."

"Koshkin has not expressed a whiff of treachery, even in private?" Nikolai tapped the feather end of the quill against his sleeve. "I wonder ..."

"What, Papa?" Daniil asked.

Nikolai did not answer directly. Instead he stared at his son, then Alexei, from under his beetling brows. "I think you may have the right of it, Tsarevich. I've known Koshkin since he turned fifteen. He has a healthy respect for his own skin—and his own advantage. Staritsa can't stand against Moscow. Andrei lacks even a quarter of the resources his sister-in-law can command. Why would Koshkin risk his life to join a losing cause?"

"That's true," Daniil said. "The slightest hint that he plans to flee, and Elena will execute him without a qualm. I'm amazed she hasn't done so already."

"They're watching him, according to Telepnev," Alexei said. "To see if he leads them to others."

"And another thing." Nikolai dropped the quill on the desk before him and, like his son, crossed his arms. "Koshkin has a new wife. He doesn't care what happens to us—or even to your father, Tsarevich—but surely he wouldn't endanger her. You haven't told him what Telepnev said to you?"

"Not yet," Alexei said. "Telepnev spoke in confidence. If I break it, won't Koshkin confront him?"

"Probably," Nikolai said. "He didn't see you talking with Telepnev, I gather?"

"He may have." Alexei tapped a finger against the nearest candelabrum, casting his mind back to his wedding ceremony and the feast that followed. "If he did, he wasn't close enough to overhear the conversation. He certainly saw *Ata* and me arguing, but we did that in Tatar."

"I suggest you visit Koshkin again," Nikolai said. "Don't mention Telepnev. Ask general questions about Andrei and Elena, the possibility of conflict, and so on. You may get a sense of where he stands. It will tell us more than knowing who reported on the meeting in Staritsa, because only Koshkin knows whether he told you the truth about what happened there. The rest is speculation—dangerous but unproven."

"I can try," Alexei said. At worst, he'd discover nothing useful. "He'd have to be mad to admit that he plans to switch sides, though. And that worries me. I have a wife and two children in my care. How can I guard them from a danger posed by my own father-in-law? And if those in power suspect him, he *does* pose a danger, guilty or not."

"We too have families to protect," Daniil reminded him. "We understand. See what you can discover. Papa will watch him at court. I'll have a chance to observe him next week. Perhaps among the three of us we can figure out what's going on."

"Next week?" Alexei asked. The mysterious trip to the hidden destination.

Daniil hesitated, then shrugged. "Telepnev ordered me to keep silent. He doesn't want word to reach Staritsa before we even leave the Kremlin, but for the sake of our alliance I'll share the news with you. In confidence, if you please."

"Of course," Alexei said. "May I tell Maria?"

"Yes," Daniil said. "But swear her to secrecy for the next few days. On Monday Grand Princess Elena is sending another group of envoys to Prince Andrei, demanding that he travel to Moscow to swear allegiance to his nephew or risk being brought to her court in chains. As before, Prince Ilya Shuisky heads the mission, while your father-in-law gets the job of delivering Elena's ultimatum. My cousin Grigory goes along to demonstrate that Moscow has nobles to spare. I'm to command the escort, keep an eye on the lot of them, and report the whole when I return."

"The situation's heating up then. And Koshkin will have another opportunity to negotiate a change of allegiance." Alexei wrinkled his nose, considering. "That's why he's included, I assume. So those in power can identify his co-conspirators, if any."

"Watch Andrei too," Nikolai told his son. "I doubt he intends to oppose Elena, but he's upset the council by increasing the number of warriors on his lands. For defense, most like, but a man may attack out of desperation."

"I'll watch them both," Daniil said. "Andrei won't share his plans with me, because he knows we have sworn allegiance to Moscow. I'm not high enough in rank to challenge him face to face, but I can look for signs of anxiety versus confidence, preparations for war, and the like."

"And I'll visit my father-in-law before he leaves," Alexei said.

"Good," Nikolai said. "If you learn anything useful, let us know. Otherwise, we'll send a messenger when Daniil returns."

On that note the meeting ended. Alexei pondered what he'd learned the entire way home. He couldn't wait to talk the situation over with Maria, but in the end he did not: when he reached their estate, the sight of her white mare, saddled and bridled in the courtyard, reminded him that he had told his wife and sister-in-law their riding lessons would begin today.

"He wants me to wear these?" Maria held up the felt trousers that Tanya, the housekeeper appointed by Sumbeka, had carried in and laid on the bed. Lyuba—dressed in a smaller version of the same abominable garb, plus a linen shirt secured by a sash, several layers of long coat, a fur-trimmed hat worn skin side out, and leather gloves—skipped behind Tanya.

"Do hurry, Maria," Lyuba called. "I'm boiling here."

"You must be, silly girl," Maria said. "Why did you put everything on at once?"

"Timur said to rush, so I did." Lyuba issued this dictum as self-evident explanation, which in a sense it was. Her initial awe of Timur had grown during the daily experience of shared lessons, and except when he challenged her for control of the chess set, she tended to regard him as a godlike presence whose experience of the wider world so far exceeded hers that he need only command and she would obey. Maria had yet to decide whether the result heartened or appalled her. For sure, life was more pleasant when she need not monitor every exchange between Lyuba and Timur. Still, unabashed hero worship did seem undignified.

But she had bigger concerns this morning. Alexei had decreed that the riding lessons should begin, and Tanya (otherwise an excellent addition to the household, who had soon overcome Maria's halfhearted efforts to dislike her) had delivered these disreputable garments for her mistress to wear. "You can't be serious," Maria said. "Women don't wear trousers."

"They do to ride, Tsarevna," Tanya told her. "The saddle will chafe your thighs something dreadful if you don't." She tapped Lyuba's cheek. "You will roast, my child. Either remove the hat and gloves or go down to the courtyard. Tsarevich

Alexei and Prince Timur are there. They have a horse picked out for you."

Lyuba jumped up and down. "May I go, Maria?"

Her face glowed as if she stood by the fire. So many ridiculous layers. "Yes, go," Maria said. "Tell my husband I will join you soon."

Lyuba ran from the room. Maria looked at the trousers and sighed, then peeled off her robes down to her shift. With Tanya's help, she donned and secured the trousers and added the various layers the housekeeper supplied. By the time Tanya pronounced her ready, Maria wore as many clothes as her sister. The felt clasped her legs, and the combined effect of wraps and boots and outerwear raised her temperature until she imagined herself a hapless victim of Baba Yaga, thrust into the witch's lit oven. How would she walk, never mind ride?

"Wife," her husband yelled from below. "It's cold out here!"

Maria grimaced at her reflection in the brass mirror. Was obedience such a virtue?

"He's waiting, Tsarevna." Tanya gave a soft push from behind, as she might do with Lyuba. "Off you go, and don't worry. Your Kumai is a beautiful horse, and she has the prettiest temper I've ever seen. You'll be riding her in no time."

Maria turned to stare at her. "Kumai? That's the horse's name?"

"Your husband didn't tell you?" It was Tanya's turn to sound surprised. "Yes, Kumai. Firebird. Very appropriate. She is a creature of air and flame, that one."

Maria shook her head, not an easy thing to do in three layers of coats, then left without explanation. As she lumbered down the stairs, the name formed a kind of song in her head.

Kumai. Firebird. Phoenix. What had she expected? Naturally her husband would have picked that name.

✦

"Sit still," Alexei said. "There's no need to clutch the reins like that; they won't help you if you get into trouble. You guide the horse with your knees. Keep your heels down and your back straight, and you won't fall off."

His wife scowled at him. "My back *is* straight. In six layers of clothes I couldn't slouch if I tried."

"Look at me, Maria," Lyuba cried from the other side of the corral. "I'm riding!" Timur held her reins, and her pony had yet to move faster than a slow walk, but she showed no fear, and her upright posture revealed the advantages of having too few years under her belt to acquire habits she must unlearn.

"Good for you, Lyuba." Maria's voice matched the wintry day in temperature, but the child gave no evidence of hearing that.

Alexei grinned as he took the reins from his wife's hands. "She's young," he said. "It comes naturally to her. That's when we learned too, which makes it easier to teach her. Let me walk Kumai, and you concentrate on moving with the horse. If you're still uncomfortable after a few rounds, I'll take you up on Ajdar and let you become accustomed to the stance and the motion. This beauty can't bear the weight of us both."

Holding the reins loosely, he backed up a few steps in the direction of Lyuba and Timur. The mare followed him, eager not to stand in the cold. "Remember," he told Maria. "Heels down, back straight. Trust the horse. She's gentle; she has no desire to toss you off or hurt you." He laughed. "Not like Ajdar when I began training him. He was a dragon in truth!"

He stopped, realizing she might refuse to mount Ajdar if she thought the horse likely to throw them.

Maria stared at him, her lips parted. "Ajdar means 'dragon'?"

"In Persian, yes." *What on earth?* "Why do you look so startled? Dragon is a good name for a warhorse. He's well trained now, and if I put you on him, I will be there to control him. He will do you no harm."

"It's nothing," she said. "I should have guessed when I heard the name you gave the mare." For no reason he could detect, her lips curved at the corners, and she glanced at her hands, where only dim outlines of the henna paintings remained.

Then he understood. Dragon and phoenix—she had made the connection. And despite her unfamiliarity with horses and her unwarranted fear of the mare, she was here, learning to ride. Marital harmony might lie within their grasp after all.

Chapter 14

KOSHKIN THREW HIMSELF ONTO THE STRAW PALLET PRO-vided by the monks at St. Joseph of Volok's Monastery and allowed his attendant to pull off his boots. He was getting soft—worse, old. Once upon a time he could ride from dawn to dusk and emerge with no more than a few aches and pains. Yet here he was: three days in the saddle, two nights in a tent, and he had to strive to raise his head. A day's rest in Volok, then another two days before he reached Staritsa. The very thought kinked his spine. What would it be like when he turned fifty?

"Food," he groaned at the attendant, who bowed and scurried off, boots in hand. Koshkin considered calling him back. Suppose someone came in and found him unshod? As the oldest—if not the most prestigious—member of this mission he could not undercut the little credit he had earned by allowing visitors to discover him in a state of partial undress.

With his luck Prince Andrei, who held the town of Volok as well as his main seat of Staritsa, would himself appear at the door at the most embarrassing moment. Koshkin released a deep sigh and stretched spreadeagled on the bed, murmuring prayers to his guardian angel to preserve him from any such humiliation and suppressing the moan that rose to his throat in response to his aching legs and back. The straw ticking jabbed his ribs, and the pallet provided no more than two fingers' width protection from the planks that formed the floor.

Whatever happens, I will not become a monk. Imagine living in a hovel like this for the rest of my life!

A rap sounded at the door. Cursing under his breath, Koshkin pulled himself to a sitting position and wrapped his outer robe around his unbooted feet before calling, "Enter."

Three young men came in and sat side by side on the single bench that ringed the room. Prince Ilya Shuisky—the most elevated by birth but not more than twenty-five years old, short and plump, with light brown hair, pale blue eyes, and a bushy beard in which he took inordinate pride—was the member of the trio Koshkin disliked least (although the only one whose good opinion he valued).

The other two, Daniil Kolychev and his cousin Grigory, Koshkin could well have done without. More accurately, he could have done without Daniil—a rising star at twenty-one, whom Koshkin regarded as a spy for Ivan Telepnev and, through him, the grand princess; the boy's presence on this journey signaled nothing but trouble. Koshkin sensed Daniil's eyes on him wherever he went—assessing, judging, condemning.

Grigory, in contrast, had formed part of Koshkin's circle for decades. He was a known quantity: closest to Koshkin in age at thirty-four and by some accounts sympathetic to Prince Andrei's cause. Grigory exuded a bland amiability that caused him to glide through the Moscow court without drawing attention to himself. Koshkin didn't like him, exactly, but they got along well enough.

"We came to discuss how best to approach Prince Andrei," Prince Ilya said. "He will not, I think, react well to these renewed demands from the grand princess. He must guess that she harbors ill will toward him, whatever she says." Grigory Kolychev leaned forward, elbows on his knees—unlike Daniil, who lounged in a corner, his gaze intent.

"Does she?" Koshkin regarded Prince Ilya through narrowed eyes, trying to deduce what Shuisky was not saying. "Why should she, when Andrei poses no threat to her? If he attacks his nephews, the Moscow nobles will rally around her fast enough. Andrei will find himself in a Kremlin cell like his brother before he finishes issuing the call to his troops."

Take that, Daniil Kolychev! If you sought evidence against me, you did not get it, did you?

Daniil did not react, and Koshkin strove not to fidget under the boy's steady gaze. Whether it was Daniil's lithe strength or the quickness of intellect shared by neither his cousin nor Shuisky, Koshkin couldn't decide, but Daniil got under his skin without even trying.

Ignore him. Daniil would draw his conclusions and make his report no matter what. Koshkin addressed Shuisky once more. "When you say, 'how best to approach Prince Andrei,' what have you in mind? Our orders leave little room for maneuver. The grand princess wants her brother-in-law to present himself in Moscow, a demand he has already refused three times. She wants him to send his troops to Kolomna, a move that would leave him vulnerable to whatever action Moscow decides to take against him. So he won't agree to that either. Dipping our words in honey won't change his mind. He's not a child, to forget his own best interests in pursuit of a sweet."

Shuisky stroked his mustache, a habit he no doubt regarded as making him irresistible to the ladies but which in this company merely increased his resemblance to a pouter pigeon. "Tact, my dear Koshkin," he said.

As if Koshkin hadn't mastered the art of diplomacy before this young idiot strapped on his first coat of mail. "Tact." He heard the bite in his own voice. Careful, careful. "What form of *tact* do you suggest?"

A glance at Daniil revealed a grin, hastily concealed. Koshkin waited for a comment, but none came.

"Suppose we tell Andrei that riches await him in Moscow," Shuisky suggested in a pompous tone that left Koshkin staring longingly at the younger man's bushy beard, wishing he could pull it.

"Or that he can satisfy his sister-in-law with a gift?" Grigory Kolychev added.

"Do *you* think he can satisfy Elena with a gift?" Koshkin asked. If he must undertake a mission likely to doom him in his ruler's eyes, could she not at least have assigned him competent help? "And what of you, Daniil Nikolaevich, have you nothing to offer?"

Thus challenged, Daniil straightened. "I agree with you, Fyodor Mikhailovich. This visit is aimed at the Moscow nobles. Grand Princess Elena wants them to see that she's given Prince Andrei every chance. She must guess he won't comply. False promises will do no good. Go, deliver the message, and leave—then pray we don't get stuck carrying through on the threat. That's my counsel."

He added, as if it were an afterthought, "Although we might persuade him to offer her something: the dispatch of men to Kolomna, say. His refusal to go there started the conflict; perhaps a partial surrender would mend relations with Moscow."

He leaned back again and shrugged. "If you can convince him."

Prince Ilya and Grigory burst into speech, filling Koshkin's ears with variations on their proposals. He didn't listen. Instead he watched Daniil, restored to his position of quiet surveillance.

Hell. Like the boy and his family or not, one couldn't help respecting Daniil. He'd summarized their dilemma in a few short sentences, then offered a solution that might work, if only for long enough to get them out of their present hole.

God help him if his enemies had become better allies than his friends.

Maria sat among a gaggle of young women. This time she had brought her embroidery to court: the baby blanket that Alexei had admired. She had begun to expand its overlapping chains into leaves and join them to the golden flowers. The pearls and sequins that she applied to her cuffs and collars could choke a child, but the thread, if well maintained, would do no harm. More important for her current setting, her needlework offered a ready topic for conversation. Every noble girl learned to sew, and most non-noble girls too. Not all mastered the craft, but they knew how to appreciate work done well.

Aunt Theodosia had stayed at home today, saying that Maria had her introduction and did not require constant oversight. Armed with her embroidery needle and without the deterrence created by her aunt's formidable presence, Maria had attracted a circle of admirers. Many of the women present belonged to branches of her own large lineage; others had attended her wedding—or other weddings that had included her. Despite Russia's vast size its court was compact, and each person existed within a web of cousins close and distant. Maria still believed that charming the grand princess lay beyond her powers, but her ladies eagerly chattered about the details Sumbeka had asked her daughter-in-law to gather.

What she lacked was a means to separate truth from rumor—assuming the truth mattered. As Alexei had said, Papa posed a danger even if the grand princess's suspicions were false. But it might be useful to learn who at court bore ill will toward the Koshkin clan. Who wanted to "catch the cat," in the phrase she'd overheard during her previous visit?

Today's gathering was typical: a dozen members of the linked Koshkin, Zakharin, Kolychev, and Kobylin clans—fun to have around and likely to share whatever they knew. They had introduced into the group a Cheliadnin princess or two, less predictable but more promising targets because of their connection to Prince Ivan Telepnev and his sister, the royal nanny. Then a wrinkle in the usual weave appeared in the form of Princess Nadezhda, wife of Prince Ilya Shuisky—whom court gossip had traveling to Staritsa in the company of Maria's own father.

With Nadezhda's arrival Maria caught her first glimpse of a path ahead. With the messengers almost a week on the road the expedition to Staritsa was no longer a secret. And here was Princess Nadezhda, who had never before shown an interest in Maria, cooing over the beauty of the baby blanket. What could Maria ask that would get the princess talking?

At first the chatter barely sufficed to keep Maria awake. Discussing the relative merits of different preservation methods and the vagaries of servants bored her to tears. With a few carefully dropped phrases, she managed to redirect the women to clothes, babies, and husbands, but the tide of words remained relentlessly personal. Childhood illnesses, brocades and buttons, quirks of male behavior— she enjoyed the stories and contributed a few of her own (the war between Lyuba and Timur over the chess pieces provoked an avalanche of similar tales), but the embassy to Staritsa appeared to provoke no curiosity, not even the usual chit-chat about Prince Andrei.

What should I ask? What should I do?

Grand Princess Elena summoned her. Maria put away her embroidery and stood. A promising sign? An ill omen? The bland faces around her provided no clue. She moved forward, wary as a cat on the prowl.

Elena sat at the far side of the room in a high-backed chair lined with red velvet. It bore a distinct resemblance to a throne, although only the six-year-old grand prince was supposed to sit on a throne. Three women stood on her left, and three more to her right—including Solomonida Sheremeteva, whose dislike Sumbeka had ordered Maria to overcome.

Maria approached and bowed low, as if to a queen. Although her marriage to Alexei raised her rank close to (her father-in-law would say above) Elena's, she saw no point in irritating the grand princess by showing insufficient deference.

"Tsarevna." Elena greeted her in the same chilly voice as before. "Do you enjoy marriage to your tsarevich? These ladies have placed a wager on your answer. A handsome man, they tell me, and well respected in battle. But a Tatar. One hears such rumors—of harems and quarrels, poisons and plots. Entertain me, if you please. The same chatter, day after day, grows tedious." She waved a careless hand at the six, who turned as one to glower at Maria.

Thank you, Princess. Just what I need, a gaggle of women out for my blood!

Yet Elena had given her an opportunity. Amuse her, and some of those defenses might fall. What would entertain this hostile princess? She could not truly believe that Maria would share incriminating stories about her husband's family.

A thought occurred to her. She probed it quickly and found it good.

"My husband could tell you such tales, no doubt," she said mildly. "Alas, I cannot. But I do enjoy marriage to my tsarevich."

"Told you so." Solomonida patted the arm of a woman on the left. "Pay up!"

"Solomonida." The grand princess frowned, but her lips twitched.

Maria, encouraged, went on. "If you want entertainment, I will tell you of my little sister, who lives with us, and my stepson. He is only three years older than your son, but sometimes one would think him forty and at other times no more than four. Or perhaps you would rather hear of my trials learning to ride a horse."

Elena laughed. "A husband, a horse, and two children? You've wasted no time. I wonder if you've told me the truth, or what you thought would please me."

"*Would* it please you?" Maria asked, greatly daring. Perhaps too much deference was not the best approach to this prickly sovereign. "But yes, I told the truth. I have no reason to lie. And they are funny stories—especially the one about the horse."

"Tell me that one then, before we go into dinner."

Maria released a long breath and obeyed. In the hope of making herself as likable as possible, she emphasized her discomfort, the mannish clothes required of her, her awkwardness on the horse. She didn't talk about Alexei's patience in teaching her or the pride she experienced when he released the reins and let her ride free. Instead she compared herself unfavorably to Lyuba, so much quicker to respond to the lessons. In portraying herself as ridiculous, she hoped Elena would also see her as harmless.

For a while her strategy seemed to work. The grand princess smiled, then chuckled. Each sign of thaw on Elena's cold face strengthened Maria's hope that she might succeed in undermining the grand princess's massive defenses.

Yet throughout her talk she sensed the eyes of the six attendants burning into her. If the price for appeasing Elena was the enmity of her retainers, what had been gained?

🐎

Dinner brought another onslaught of food. Fish pies, fish stew, caviar, cabbage soup, bean soup—only the plain breads indicated that Lent still ruled the menu.

As before, Maria sat at a shorter table facing the one occupied by the grand princess, her attendants, and the young grand prince—released from his duties to eat with his mother. As a tsarevna she occupied the center place. Princess Nadezhda had taken the seat on her right.

So much attention from Nadezhda—unexpected and therefore interesting—suggested that hope was not lost. Maybe in this more restricted environment, where conversation took place one on one, Maria could learn whether the Staritsa assignment boded good or ill for the envoys. She was turning over suitable questions in her head when at the last moment Solomonida, who should have sat with the attendants, slipped onto the bench at Maria's left.

Maria permitted herself one silent complaint to the Mother of God.

Do I not already have a difficult task, trying to uncover damaging information that may not even exist? Must I also cope with a woman who dislikes me?

But Sumbeka had ordered her to befriend Solomonida. Be grateful, Maria told herself. She smiled at her cousin by former marriage and exchanged a few pleasantries. To her surprise, Solomonida responded in kind.

After a while Maria turned to Princess Nadezhda, who had just ended a conversation with the woman on her right. She could not ask outright what Nadezhda thought about her husband's current assignment (such a horrid man, who had pinched Maria's bottom at her own wedding!), but a simple expression of interest should not go amiss. She said softly, "I hear your husband and my father are traveling together."

Nadezhda turned her head sharply in Maria's direction. "Yes, God save them both. And for the second time, too. The journey of the condemned, Ilya tells me."

"Is it?" Maria strove to conceal her shock. Such bluntness was unexpected after such a dearth of plain speaking, despite the oddity of Nadezhda seeking her out. "But why condemned? Papa supports the grand prince."

"That's not what I hear in the grand princess's chambers," Nadezhda said. "Although I hope for your sake it's true. But he has now received two assignments guaranteed to end in failure. Why, unless he has upset those in power? Even someone as new to the court as you must understand that good intentions alone will not save a man." She stared straight into Maria's eyes, as if sending a message. "Or a woman." And having delivered her warning, if that's what it was, Nadezhda resumed her conversation with the noblewoman on her other side.

Stunned, Maria glanced across the room in time to intercept a raised eyebrow from Grand Princess Elena. The attendants chattered with one another. Maria could not hear what they said.

Journey of the condemned. Good intentions will not save a man—or a woman. What is Nadezhda trying to tell me?

Solomonida murmured in her ear. "If Prince Ilya is condemned, it's his own doing. I overheard him at your wedding, deep in conversation with Grigory Kolychev about the merits of siding with Staritsa. If one of them toys with treason, both do, and with the rumors flying about, it won't take much for them to pull your father down with them, no matter whom he supports." Under the table, she touched Maria's thigh. "Don't look at me. We have never been friends, but I care for my cousins. What affects you endangers them too."

Maria, reeling under the assault of conflicting information, longed for the meal to end so she could share what she'd learned. But with whom? Alexei? No, Sumbeka, who knew more about the Russian lands. Go there first, then seek out Alexei.

Solomonida introduced a discussion of embroidery patterns and drew Maria into the conversation. As she chattered about cross stitch and chain stitch, a single thought drummed in her head.

I have never felt so confused.

Alexei brushed the hair back from his forehead, tugged at the hem of his mail coat to straighten it, and angled the blade of his Turkish saber for best effect. He could have dispensed with the mail for this practice bout with Ruslan, since neither of them aimed to injure the other. And in the warmth of the room, a bare space stripped of furniture except for the padded benches along the walls, the armor added to his discomfort. He wore the coat because he would need it in battle, so compensating for its weight and inflexibility was an essential part of the exercise.

Ruslan copied his actions and his stance. From outside, the thrum of arrows hitting targets and the clatter of galloping hooves confirmed that the men did not slack in their practice.

"Ready?" Alexei asked. Ruslan nodded. They lunged at the same moment, and the curved blades clashed. They withdrew, and Alexei lunged again, touching the tip of his saber to Ruslan's chest, in the vicinity of his heart. Ruslan brought his blade up right away and knocked Alexei's aside.

"You'd be dead already," Alexei said.

Ruslan grinned and stepped back. "So I would. Cursed quick feet you have." Before Alexei had time to respond,

Ruslan lunged. This time his blade touched Alexei's mail, right above the liver. "Now you're worse than dead. Expiring drop by drop with no cure. Nothing to hope for but a mercy killing."

"Bloodthirsty ruffian," Alexei responded, without rancor. It was a game they'd played since they became friends in Crimea. He attacked once more, scoring a hit below Ruslan's collar bone before a parry deflected his blade to the upper arm. A quick feint, and Ruslan's riposte went high.

A few more rounds, and they were both breathing hard. Alexei dropped his blade, gasping. "A month off for my wedding," he said when he could speak. "And look at me, a wreck."

Ruslan slapped his shoulder. "Not quite. You 'killed' me three times." He propped his saber against the nearest sofa. "Sit. Catch your breath. Talk to me."

"About what?" Alexei dropped onto the sofa and rubbed the sweat from his eyes with a linen towel from a pile left by the servants. His wife's housekeeper had an uncanny ability to guess what any member of the family might need at any given moment.

Ruslan grabbed a towel of his own before collapsing on the bench nearest the windows. Afternoon sunlight turned the mica panes the color of lemons, but already Alexei saw the tinge of orange marking the approaching sunset. Would Maria return soon? She had reminded him this morning of the grand princess's summons but not told him what she expected to come of it.

A tinge of anticipation constricted his chest. It could not be that he yearned to see her. His happiness did not depend on a woman.

"Your father-in-law," Ruslan said. Alexei stared at him, puzzled, until he explained. "I said, 'Talk to me.' You asked, 'About what?' The answer is your father-in-law. You went to have a chat with him five days ago, and ever since you've been acting like a cross between a thunder cloud and an angry bumblebee. Unless it's your wife who has you so riled up."

"No, you got it the first time. It's her father." Alexei wiped his forehead once more, then balled up the towel and tossed it into a corner. "I went to his house on Saturday, as you said. Tried out the approach Nikolai Kolychev suggested—asking him about this crisis with Prince Andrei. At first it seemed to work. He relaxed enough to confirm that he had orders to travel to Staritsa. He didn't share details about the mission itself, but he probably had orders not to discuss it. I didn't tell him I'd already talked to Daniil."

"So what's getting under your skin?" Ruslan shifted position, resting his head on his hand.

Alexei studied his fingernails, questioning how much he could safely confide. "He went into a tirade," he said after a while. "He hates Grand Princess Elena. Blames her for the death of her brother-in-law Yuri, whom he supported. Believes she wants to do the same to the other brother, Andrei—well, everyone believes that. But not everyone froths at the mouth at the thought. And he went on and on about the stupidity of letting a child rule under the guidance of a woman, rather than an adult prince."

"So he's confirmed your suspicions." Ruslan had come to a full sitting position, booted feet on the sofa, elbows on his raised knees. "About his sentiments, at least. Isn't that what you wanted?"

"Not exactly. I still don't know if he plans to act on his beliefs." Alexei gripped his hands together until the knuckles showed white. "But the ranting alone could doom him if anyone else hears it. I left Crimea to get away from one family feud. Andrei, Elena—who's right? I neither know nor care. One will kill the other, just as Islam-Girei will plague his uncle until one of them dies. But I can see that Elena holds the power. The last thing I need is my father-in-law switching sides. My wife and her sister deserve better. And I didn't keep Timur here to put his head in a noose."

Ruslan regarded him with keen eyes. "You love her."

"Lyuba? Well, of course. She's a sweet child."

"No. Your Maria." Ruslan shook his head and grinned. "Who'd have thought it? A pretty spitfire, for sure, but no equal to some of the beauties you've had in tow. Even Guzel before camp life got to her."

Alexei scowled. "Maria has twice the brains of Guzel. No, ten times. The only smart thing Guzel ever did was give birth to Timur. And don't even mention Roxelana. Yes, I can see you were planning to, so shut your mouth."

The grin turned to a roar of laughter. "Alexei the Ice King, melted by a fiery Russian. It's too good to be true. Wait till I tell the men."

"Don't you dare!" Alexei leaped to his feet, but too late. Ruslan grabbed his saber and ran from the room.

Chapter 15

MARIA CLIMBED OUT OF HER SLEIGH, PUSHING ASIDE THE impediment created by bulky robes and clasping the coachman's hand to steady herself. Her mind roiled with the information she'd garnered during her dinner at the Kremlin. Despite their efforts, she and Alexei still did not know whether her father was plotting or falsely accused. But with each rumor they heard, the clearer it seemed that Papa's innocence or guilt didn't matter to those in power. Only to his family, God help them.

As she ascended the stairs, the sight of her husband's friend Ruslan in the center of a cluster of warriors, near the doorway to the wing of the house assigned to him by Alexei, distracted her. Their discussion, whatever it was, amused them mightily, to judge from the guffaws and shoulder slaps.

Men. Do they even understand themselves?

She entered her own part of the house, where another, louder distraction drove the chortling warriors from her head. Lyuba raced to greet her, trailed by Tanya with a shamefaced Timur in tow and a story of archery practice gone wrong, to the detriment of a prized porcelain vase.

Maria bit her tongue lest she speak her annoyance aloud. Wasn't it enough to have great matters cluttering up her mind? Must she also handle these petty children's problems?

"At least it wasn't a person," she told the miscreant. "Do you see now why we have the rule 'no archery indoors'?"

Timur nodded, his cheeks pink. "Sorry, Auntie."

"Off you go, then," she said. "You must confess to your father, as he's responsible for your uncle's vase. And don't forget again."

Timur retreated, hanging his head. One problem solved, for the moment.

Lyuba grabbed her sister's hand. "I telled him," she whispered. "But he wouldn't listen."

"Don't tattle, Lyuba." Maria tapped her sister's nose. "Where is your sampler?"

Lyuba had reached the midpoint of an elaborate tale regarding the sampler's unhappy fate when Tanya's swift bow alerted Maria to a new arrival. She turned to find her husband looking stormy. "Welcome home, wife," he said. "I expected you some time ago."

Maria blinked. Well, she need not hunt for him. But why the frown? Since their marriage, he had not once questioned her comings and goings, just as he rarely shared his own absences or the reason for them. She turned over potential wifely sins in her head and came up with none. On the contrary, had she not spent her entire day protecting the family's interests?

A spark of rebellion lit her heart. How dare he scowl at her!

"Maria's in trouble," Lyuba announced in a loud singsong. The little dance she put on suggested she loved this idea.

Alexei's stormy expression dissolved in laughter, dousing Maria's anger. "Away with you, repellent brat. Your sister is *not* in trouble." He administered a playful slap to Lyuba's backside, well padded with layers of robes. "Take her to the kitchens, Tanya, and send some food to my wife's sewing room. The sun's down, and I'm ravenous. Where is Timur?"

Tanya glanced at Maria before grabbing Lyuba's hand. "He'll explain presently," Maria said. "An accident with the bow. No one was hurt, but we'll have to replace a vase."

"Devil take him. After a thousand warnings. You told him to confess, I hope?" But he seemed to take Timur's misadventure in stride.

"Of course," Maria said.

"Good." Alexei clasped her elbow. "Come, I want to talk to you. Did you learn anything today?"

It was as if he'd read her mind. She gripped his hand where it lay on her arm. "Yes. I stopped first at your parents' house, to see if *Kaenana* had any ideas. We talked for quite a while— that's why I was late—but neither of us can figure out *what* I've discovered, only that it must be important." She stripped off her cloak and handed it to the nearest servant. "Let's see if you and I can do better."

Alexei followed his wife to her favorite room, where they sat side by side. He held her hands while she shared her experiences at court, stopping only when the tray of food arrived.

As after her last visit to the palace, she shook her head when he offered to fetch her a plate. "Only tea, please. You wouldn't believe how much they feed us there. I didn't touch half the dishes, yet I feel as if I could starve until Sunday without a pang. Help yourself."

Acknowledging her comment with a nod, he handed her a filled cup and examined the tray. A nice selection of finger foods, from which he chose half a dozen pieces and a bowl of dumplings in broth. He had no sooner returned to his wife's side than she launched into her tale once more, describing the antagonism she had encountered as she spoke with Grand

Princess Elena and her attendants. As she talked, he fixed his eyes on her face, watching each flicker of expression.

At the same time a second, unrelated stream of thoughts ran alongside the first. *Was* he falling in love with her? He didn't think so. But when she hadn't come home before sunset, he had worried that she might be in danger. And as he listened to her quick and clever narrative, applauded the way she had dodged an awkward question, appreciated each swift deduction and sharp observation, he admitted privately that his reaction to her went beyond an obligation to protect or even physical attraction. He definitely sensed a desire to cherish, a comfort and sense of equality that the sultry Roxelana—and even Guzel, the mother of his child—had not evoked.

Should he say something? No, it seemed too soon. To open his heart to any woman posed a threat he hesitated to face.

Maria reached what appeared to be the crux of her story: one Princess Nadezhda's obscure remarks. "She went out of her way to warn me that Papa's in trouble," Maria said, waving her hands in confusion. "But why? He has lain low since his return from exile, spends most of his time at home. Who attacks him in the grand princess's chambers?"

"Before we consider enemies, are you certain of your father's loyalties?" Alexei set aside his empty plate and picked up the bowl of broth, cradling it between his palms.

"I have no reason to doubt him." She sipped from her cup, frowning. "Why do you ask?"

Did she honestly not know? He repeated what he had said to Ruslan about her father's tirade, adding a summary of the conversation with Daniil and Nikolai Kolychev.

She listened, eyes fixed on his face, without interrupting. "You heard this at our wedding, and you didn't tell me—not even the last time we talked about Papa?" she asked when he reached the end.

He heard hurt in her voice, hastily suppressed. She covered her mouth with one hand as if she wished to call the words back. He took the hand in his and brushed his lips across her fingers.

"Sorry," she said. "Men's business, I'm sure."

"No, a bad habit," he told her. "My father discusses everything important with my stepmother except military campaigns, but I haven't had a woman I could trust with my affairs until now. Ruslan and I have served side by side for years, so I tend to go to him first." He squeezed her hand, then released it. "Although I did wonder whether you could see your father clearly. You're close to him, I think."

Her eyes widened, as if she couldn't believe he had delivered an implicit apology for something she took for granted. A small smile played around her mouth. His implied compliment had pleased her. "I don't have illusions about Papa," she said. "He's gotten himself in trouble before. But since he married Roxelana, he has attended court only to fulfill his service obligations."

As Nikolai Kolychev had also noted. It was worth a try then. "And you're sure he has no intention of switching sides?"

She spoke slowly, as if weighing each word. "Not completely, no. But since he met Roxelana, he's seemed so happy. He doesn't approve of child rule. He wanted the succession to go from adult brother to adult brother. Three years ago he came up with a wild scheme to get Prince Yuri out of jail and onto the throne. It ended with his exile, but he could have been executed. He fooled himself, Papa Nikolai said—"

Alexei quizzed her with his eyes, and she added, "Daniil's father. Nasan's father-in-law. I call him that so as not to confuse him with your father."

"I see," he said. "Continue."

"Papa Nikolai said my father convinced himself that the grand prince and his brother would come to no harm in their uncle Yuri's care. That Papa didn't like to dirty his hands. But I thought he'd learned his lesson. That he wouldn't take risks if they imperiled Roxelana." Her mouth twisted in a way Alexei couldn't interpret. "The rest of us he uses to serve his own ends, but her he truly loves."

Hearing currents he didn't understand, he patted her hand. "Your Papa Nikolai has a good head on those burly shoulders. He said the same to me—that a man doesn't marry for love one day and throw his life to the winds the next. And when I asked your father about the private meeting in Staritsa, he did have a plausible explanation. Except for his outburst, I have no reason to suspect him of treason. But I can see why the grand princess and Telepnev do. And so long as they do, your father poses a danger to us."

Maria left his side to pace about the room, her silk skirts swishing against the carpet. "Yes, he does. And we know the grand princess hasn't forgiven him. She jumped down my throat the first day she met me, demanding I swear to his loyalty. And what was I supposed to tell her: that he hates her guts but is too much in love to abandon Moscow? Of course I swore he would never waver in his allegiance."

Alexei smiled at that, but the danger of their situation soon sobered him again. "Telepnev hasn't forgiven your father either; that's clear. But if Koshkin hasn't done anything wrong, who's spreading tales to the contrary? His past indiscretions count against him, of course, but your Princess Nadezhda was speaking of current rumors. Who are his enemies? I assume he *has* enemies."

"By the score," she said with a sigh. "He loves to scheme, so he offends people without even trying, by clambering over them or threatening their position or just putting himself first."

"Curse him for a tricky, lying bastard." Alexei drummed his fingers against his bowl, then dropped it on the nearest side table. It hit hard but didn't break. How had he managed to ally himself with a man who loved to scheme? It wasn't as if he'd never encountered the type before. Islam-Girei's makeshift court in the grasslands north of Crimea drew more schemers than a banquet had dogs.

Disgusted with himself as much as his father-in-law, Alexei said the first thing that came into his head. "May the fleas of a thousand camels infest his armpits. *Ata* was right—and you can imagine how much he'll crow when I tell him that. I should have sought a different alliance from the beginning."

Maria produced a sound somewhere between a gasp and a sob. "What are you saying?"

Caught up in his own thoughts, Alexei didn't answer. He circled the room, brooding and swearing at the absent Koshkin as well as his own unsatisfactory parent. How could he have guessed that Bulat would offer support if asked? But because he'd failed to predict the unpredictable, here he was, stuck with a father-in-law who threatened to bring down his whole clan.

After three turns Maria interrupted his wrathful musings. "Will you stop?" she demanded. "You're talking about my *father*, not the devil incarnate. You don't know that he's done anything, and here you are cursing at him!"

Alexei whirled. Why had he believed she could talk about her beloved Papa dispassionately? He should have known better. Damn it, he *had* known better. "He's been disloyal in the past. Otherwise the story would carry no weight. You said so yourself."

"He was *not* disloyal. He served Prince Yuri before he moved to Moscow."

"And three years ago, when he tried to free Yuri? Was he loyal then?"

Maria blushed. "No."

"You see?" he snapped. "He abandoned them in turn. Yuri, then the grand prince, then Yuri again. And where will his loyalties lie tomorrow? He picks his ruler to serve his immediate interests. I'd kill a man as unprincipled as that."

"You admitted he had a good explanation. That he has enemies." She stamped a foot. "And who are you to talk about shifting loyalties? You abandoned your lord in Crimea. The two of you deserve each other!"

That hurt. He raised a hand, then dropped it when she cringed. Devil take her for a sharp-tongued bitch.

Yet she was right. He had abandoned his lord Islam-Girei under threat of death. That he regretted it changed nothing. And as a punishment he had been burdened with her father, whose oath of allegiance *meant* nothing. The flash of self-recognition stopped Alexei in his tracks.

Tempted to shake her, then storm out, he instead kicked the rug, causing her to make a dive for the embroidery frame as it teetered. Her beautiful baby blanket fell to the floor, and she picked it up, muttering words he couldn't hear.

"Look," he said through gritted teeth. "I understand. He's your father. You think well of him. Good for you. But his past behavior has destroyed any trust that those in power once felt toward him, and his present attitude toward Grand Princess Elena could get him hanged. Then what happens to Roxelana, to your brothers, to *you*? You suffer for his sins, that's what. The only way to stop disaster from happening is to prove his innocence beyond the shadow of a doubt. And how are we to do that? Even if I ask him flat out, he won't say, 'I plan to betray the grand prince by making a private arrangement with his uncle,' will he?"

"But you don't have to assume he will!"

"And you don't have to assume he won't!"

Koshkin's dupe or not, she had brains. So why did she stand there like a woman carved from rock, looking as if, given half a chance, she would toss him out the window and run? Did she love her cursed father *that* much?

More than me?

He thrust the thought savagely to the back of his mind. At least he'd had the sense not to reveal his feelings for her. "Well?"

She made a dash for the door. With a speed honed by years of war Alexei grabbed her around the waist as she passed and swung her around to face him. "Where are you going?" He swore in Tatar, not caring that she flinched at the sound. "Don't run from me! What are you, six?"

Maria, dragged against her husband's body, blinked back angry tears and stared at his chest. He had admitted their marriage meant nothing to him. He would have done better with a different alliance. A different *wife*. He'd had the nerve to look at her with impatience plastered on his face, yell at her, swear at her father. For a moment there she'd feared he would hit her, as so many husbands did and Alexei so far had not. He and Papa were two of a kind.

"Answer me!" Alexei's voice had a hard edge she seldom heard from him. She shuddered. "Running away, sulks? That's behavior I'd expect from Lyuba or Timur, not a grown woman."

"I *am* a grown woman!"

"Then act like one."

"Ooh," she said. Too angry for words, she pressed her fists against his unyielding torso. She wasn't ready to apologize. But she had to admit that he was right about one thing: running away was childish.

"Yes," she said, not bothering to conceal her reluctance. "That was wrong of me. But so is calling my father a scheming bastard."

"He is a scheming bastard," Alexei said. "You can't deny that his scheming endangers us."

The truth of his words nagged at her, but after his rejection she refused to give him the satisfaction of agreeing with him. So she said with as much firmness as she could muster, "Even scheming bastards can have enemies."

"Your father is his own worst enemy." Alexei bit off each syllable as if the words were appetizers from the sewing-room trestle.

The heat in his voice melted her anger like a late spring snowstorm, revealing the heartbreak beneath. She dropped her head on his shoulder, ordering herself not to cry, but the tears fell regardless. He patted her back, an awkward but welcome attempt at comfort. He didn't ask why she wept—one small mercy. How humiliating to have to explain how he'd hurt her!

When she pulled away, rubbing her cheeks with the back of her hand, Alexei said, "All right, let's try again. Suppose your father *is* innocent. Who wants to entrap him? No one would endanger a man's life and lineage for trivial reasons. Could the noblemen sent on this mission have a common enemy? Is that what your Princess Nadezhda meant when she called it 'the journey of the condemned'?"

He was meeting her halfway; she should respond in kind. To buy time, Maria walked to the sofa and arranged her skirts. A linen kerchief disposed of the remaining tears. She took deep breaths to calm herself. When she could match his dispassionate tone, she said, "Daniil's heading the escort. I doubt he has enemies—or is one. He dislikes Papa, but he hates conspiracies more. Given a chance, he'd punch Papa in the nose and enjoy doing it, but engage in deception? No, I can't see that."

Alexei joined her on the sofa, where she created a physical barrier between them, knees raised and arms crossed over her stomach. "I agree. Not Daniil. What of the others?"

She clasped her knees, thinking aloud. "His cousin Grigory may have enemies, although it seems unlikely. He tends not to draw attention to himself. Ilya Shuisky is the most likely target. Either he's a victim, as his wife suggests, or a traitor, as Solomonida believes. If Nadezhda is right, Ilya must have an enemy, but why would Ilya's enemy attack Papa?"

"We need more information. Both these men are strangers to me." Anger still flashed in Alexei's dark eyes, lingered in his grudging comments. She sensed he was humoring her, as if he saw their conversation as a contest for her loyalty between him and her father.

Although that would imply that he wanted her, and he had made it clear he did not. The tears wheeled like Tatar cavalry and threatened a renewed attack. She reached for her cup and sipped. The tea had cooled, emphasizing the grassy taste.

She answered his comment about needing more information. "And I would see them only at weddings, although I can pursue my acquaintance with their wives." Unshed tears dried her throat, and she sipped more of the tea.

"Do that. I will see what I can find out among the men." He glanced sideways at her, as if wondering how she would take his next suggestion. "You could approach Roxelana. I wouldn't confide in her, but your father might."

"She won't talk to me. She hates me."

"You'll have to stop by someday. We've been married a month." He reached out, easily breaching the barrier created by her knees, and brushed her cheek with his thumb. The gesture raised her dismal spirits by the width of a thread.

"I can try," she said, her voice unsteady. "Most likely she will hint and tease, because even if Papa did share his plans with her, she has no reason to tell me. I'd do better to go straight to him when he gets back."

He shook his head. "I'll talk to your father. He won't wrap me around his finger with stories about enemies."

There, it was out. He didn't believe her. Tempted again to run from the room, Maria bit her tongue and wrapped her arms once more around her knees. Let this hideous conversation end soon, she prayed.

"Visit Roxelana," Alexei said. It sounded like a command. "Tell her what you know. Even if she refuses to answer questions, you'll see how she reacts. If she's anxious, that's evidence of a sort."

It was a fool's errand, but he was her husband, whom she had sworn to obey. The words stuck in her throat. Then an idea occurred to her and she said, "I'll ask Nasan to come with me. Roxelana doesn't like her either, but she has less reason to feel jealous of your sister."

"Roxelana doesn't like any woman. But do what you can. I'll tackle your father as soon as he returns." He reached out again, caught her chin in his fingers, and kissed her hard on the mouth.

When he released her, she looked up to find his face relaxed, his eyes soft and warm, but she could manage no more than a trembling smile. "I will try."

Chapter 16

"MARIA!" NASAN TOOK HALF A DOZEN STEPS TOWARD HER visitor and stopped, waving her hand at the household pond, free of waterfowl and covered in ice. "Isn't this dreadful? I waddle like a duck. I remember watching the harem concubines and thinking I would never look like them, and here I am. I can't wait for this child to be born!"

Maria patted her swollen belly, as if checking its size. "You still have two months to go, poor thing."

"Ugh." Nasan took her guest's elbow and ushered her toward the stairs. "By then I will be rounder than I am tall, and Daniil will have worried me into a frenzy trying to wrap me in unspun wool. Come and greet Mama-in-law; she's doing much better today. You can tell us both your news."

Maria tugged gently, resisting her pull. "I came to persuade you to visit Roxelana with me. On the way back I'll stop to chat with Lady Natalya. Unless you think she'll be asleep then? If so, I can talk with her now."

Nasan stopped dead. "Visit Roxelana? Why?"

"My husband insists. I'll explain why on the way. But you can, can't you? You told me you would accept the housekeeper *Kaenana* sent."

Nasan narrowed her eyes at her visitor. *My husband insists?* That didn't sound like Maria. Well, the edge to her voice when she said it definitely did. Something must have happened, and this was her chance to find out what. It touched her, too, that Maria had come here. In the old days Nasan would have been the last person Maria would talk to.

"Yes, I can." Nasan gestured to the stairway. "Come up for a moment while I give orders and tell Mama-in-law where to find me if she needs me. And thank you so much for persuading me to agree to Sonya. She's a miracle worker."

"My Tanya too," Maria said, climbing the stairs, one hand on Nasan's back as if to catch her if she overbalanced. "But the true miracle worker is your mother." She blushed. "You know that, of course."

They had reached the top of the stairs. Nasan caught Maria's outstretched hand. "I do. I'm glad to hear you say it, though." Surprising a look of strain on Maria's face, she said, "What is it? Has something gone wrong?"

Maria stiffened. Nasan braced herself against attack, but Maria shuddered and put her hands over her face. "Oh, Nasan," she said in a voice Nasan strained to hear. "Your brother does not give a fig for me."

"I don't believe it." Nasan put her arms around her sister-in-law and guided her to a nearby window seat. "I thought the two of you were getting along well. What has he done?"

"He said it himself." Maria gulped, as if holding back sobs. "He should have chosen a different alliance, he told me. A different *bride*, that means."

Nasan patted her shoulder. "By the grandmothers, what's wrong with the man? Newborn lambs have more sense. I'm sure he didn't mean that."

Maria stared at her. "He did. He stormed around my sewing room calling Papa a tricky, lying bastard, then blurted it out." Tears ran down her cheeks, and Nasan tugged a square of cloth from her pouch and pressed it into Maria's hands.

It probably wouldn't be a good idea to point out that Koshkin *was* a tricky, lying bastard. "He didn't mean it," Nasan said instead. "He's worried that your father's troubles, whatever their cause, will endanger you and Lyuba. He wouldn't say something he knew would hurt you. He has excellent manners."

"But that's the problem, isn't it?" Maria wiped her cheeks and sniffed. "It's what he says when he's *not* remembering his manners that I believe."

Nasan laughed and patted one damp cheek. "It will be fine, I promise. Let's go cause Roxelana some trouble."

With Nasan at her side Maria managed to approach Roxelana with some equanimity. Alexei's comment still stung. What was wrong with her that her first husband rejected her, then her second? The first she didn't care about, but this one—she had done everything she could to please him, even mounting that dreadful horse!

Nasan's assurances rang in her head. Perhaps she *had* read more into Alexei's comment than he intended. As the carriage approached her father's house, Maria tried to focus on the task ahead.

But that task also held little appeal. As they mounted the stairs, the late morning sun beating on their veiled heads, Maria wished she had refused her husband's ridiculous demand.

Just getting in to see Roxelana proved a challenge. At first she claimed a need to oversee the household tasks, an assertion neither of her visitors believed for an instant.

"As if she doesn't make Mitka do all the work," Maria murmured as soon as the steward withdrew his ponderous bulk, leaving her and Nasan in the room where they had entertained Sumbeka and Firuza the day before the wedding. "Has she forgotten I used to *live* here?"

"Of course not. She wants us to know she has more important things on her mind than us." Nasan pulled Maria down beside her. "Tell me while we're waiting how we should approach her. She's not in a cooperative mood, for sure. What can we offer that might persuade her to talk?"

That was the problem, wasn't it? "Everything sounds like a threat. 'Your husband is suspected of treason. Your husband has enemies at court. Tell us what you know or watch him go down in flames, and you with him.' Would you open up to someone who said those things?"

Nasan shook her head. "I would not. And I don't have much to offer either. My husband plans to watch Koshkin when they reach Staritsa, but so far we have only reports of a meeting that your father explained away."

In whispers they discussed strategy for a while, discarding one option after another until Maria threw up her hands in despair. "We're wasting our time. She won't talk to us. Why should she?"

The door opened as if on cue, and Roxelana glided in, exuding a cloud of chypre and trailed by a servant with a tray of sweets and another bearing a steaming jug. More tea, Maria decided. She'd drunk so much of it since her wedding that she was learning to like it.

"Tsarevna Maria," Roxelana said in her usual purr. "And Tsarevna Irina. How delightful that you found time to visit, and how desolated am I that I kept you waiting. I had thought you both preoccupied with your households. I even wondered if you had fallen ill, and no one told me."

Nasan emitted a soft sound, like suppressed laughter. "Please," Roxelana added. "Don't get up."

"I can't." Nasan treated their reluctant hostess to a smile of extraordinary sweetness and tipped her head in Roxelana's direction. "Not without a cart and horse."

A manifest exaggeration, but Roxelana must have recognized a battle she could not win. "So unfortunate," she said, returning the salutation. "And you, Maria? Have the delights of marriage consumed every waking moment?"

"Forgive me, Stepmama." Maria rose and bowed. "I should have come to see you before now. The house, two children, a guest, and a new husband—I have indeed been busy, but that is no excuse. Of course, you would have been welcome at my home too."

Roxelana scowled. Nasan's mouth twitched, and Maria resumed her seat, her spirits rising with the knowledge that she had scored one point. The servant appeared in front of her with the tray, and Maria accepted a ginger-flavored biscuit on a napkin and a steaming cup that turned out to contain hot cider instead of Tatar tea. Well, cider tasted even better.

She opened the conversation by asking for news of her sister and brothers. Aided by Nasan, she lured Roxelana with snippets of court gossip and pretended interest in the tasks that had consumed her stepmother's attention for so long after their arrival. She avoided mention of Lyuba and, despite an involuntary flinch, succeeded in sidestepping an acerbic question about Alexei's health and stamina—intended, she assumed, to disconcert her with reminders of his past attachments. Only then did it seem advisable to edge toward her true purpose before Roxelana's obvious impatience ended the call. But what to say? Alexei had recommended voicing their suspicions, but wasn't the point of this visit that he assumed Roxelana already knew her husband's plans?

Then it came to her. So what if Alexei saw Papa as a traitor and a schemer? Roxelana might perceive the situation differently.

"We'd like to combine our forces," Maria said. "The court buzzes with tales of those likely to flee to Prince Andrei's side.

Alas, Papa's name often crops up among that group. And now he's traveled to Staritsa, twice. It's as if someone wants to lure him into making a mistake. We're very worried. I think he has an enemy who seeks to discredit him. Do you have any idea who that might be?"

Roxelana stilled, watchful as a plover in the reeds. "Fyodor Mikhailovich said nothing of this to me."

"He may not know," Nasan said. "These missions to Andrei are assignments he can't refuse. But does he talk about those he trusts and doesn't trust at court? Or about the men sent with him to Staritsa?"

"No, he does not." Roxelana, her face taut, rose from her chair. "I apologize, but you have not come at a good time. Another day?"

Interesting.

"Whenever you wish." Maria went to help Nasan off her bench, to support the story that she could not rise unaided. "Thank you for putting your tasks on hold for us."

Roxelana did not wait for their farewell. Instead she walked faster than Maria had ever seen her move, without a hint of the usual glide, and the door shut with a definite snap behind her.

"Too bad," Maria said. "I thought for sure that would get her talking. But she seems scared, as if she already knows he has an enemy." Her throat closed up, and she struggled to get the rest of her thought into words.

Nasan finished it for her. "Or that he does plan to switch sides."

Koshkin stepped across the threshold of Prince Andrei of Staritsa's reception room and bowed. After more than a week's wait, followed by long days spent in fruitless talks—including several private sessions between Prince Ilya Shuisky and the court chamberlain and not a few discussions involving Koshkin himself, not one of which had clarified the question of Andrei's intentions—the envoys had at last received permission to enter Andrei's royal presence.

At a word from the prince, Koshkin rose smoothly from his obeisance and spoke, keeping his voice steady as a general's in the drill yard. Long practice ensured mastery of the complicated protocol as it tripped from his tongue. "On behalf of Our Lord and Grand Prince Ivan Vasilyevich of All Russia and his mother, Our Lady and Grand Princess Elena Vasilyevna of All Russia, to Andrei Ivanovich, prince and lord of Staritsa, greetings. May you be of good health and good heart. We who are bound in service to the sovereign—" He gestured right, then left, at his traveling companions. "—Prince Ilya Petrovich Shuisky, Grigory Osipovich Kolychev and his cousin Daniil Nikolaevich, and I, Fyodor Mikhailovich Koshkin—carry a message from Moscow, to be delivered into the hands of Your Excellency."

Although the honor of leading the mission belonged by right to Prince Ilya, he had again yielded the duty of performing the opening salutations to Koshkin on the grounds of age and experience. A surprise, but a welcome one: these days Koshkin rejoiced at the smallest sign that their group's nominal head—a pompous young ass if Koshkin had ever beheld one—recognized the advantages of seniority. Or perhaps Shuisky wished to avoid the public flogging he would suffer if he omitted a single one of the juvenile grand prince's titles and possessions.

Either way Koshkin was, for the moment at least, in command. In response to a curt nod from Prince Andrei, Koshkin drew a tied scroll from his belt and held it out. One of the half-dozen noblemen who stood to either side of the prince's throne stepped forward and took the document. He passed it to a clerk, who unwrapped and perused it before bending to whisper the contents into Andrei's ear. Koshkin permitted himself a small sigh of relief. He had made it through his prescribed speech without incident.

While awaiting a response, he conducted a private survey of the room. He had not seen Andrei since last fall, when the prince had refused a military assignment, citing an illness that the court physician sent by Elena at Andrei's request had declared minor and Koshkin had been unable to confirm. Despite repeated demands, Andrei still insisted that he could neither serve nor travel to Moscow—thus setting up today's confrontation.

The prince's appearance supported the claims of the doctor over those of the self-proclaimed patient. Although Andrei had not risen from his seat since the envoys entered, Koshkin suspected that had more to do with the need to separate ruler from subject than princely incapacity. At forty-six Andrei had graying reddish hair, pale blue eyes sharp with intelligence, and the broad shoulders and chest one expected to find on a man who had spent his life in the saddle and at war. He sat straight on the throne, his voice sounded clear and strong, and his demeanor radiated controlled power. Yet the room, overheated by normal standards, did bear a faint sickly sweet odor of infection.

"Speak," Andrei ordered. "What brings you here on this fine spring day? Did you ride for a week solely to convey my charming sister-in-law's good wishes? How touching." His mouth quirked, as if he expected Koshkin to appreciate the unlikelihood of Elena's ever wishing her brother-in-law well.

And Koshkin did appreciate that point, but he knew better than to admit as much in this company. "Our sovereign *and his mother*," he said, underlining the true source of the order, "require your presence in Moscow forthwith. If you persist in this refusal to kiss the cross in fealty to your nephew, you risk having their armies escort you there in chains."

"Will nothing convince Elena that I am ill?" Andrei asked in a clear, carrying baritone that belied his claim even as he stated it. He pointed at his thigh, invisible beneath his fur-trimmed robe. "Six months this sore has plagued me, yet still she carps, although her husband died of just such an ailment. How can I ride when I cannot stand?"

Wishing himself already on the road home, Koshkin bowed once more and presented the next of his planned speeches. "It will end better for you, Prince, if you accompany us as far as the Kremlin. Allow the grand prince to see your wound for himself. He and his mother swear you need not fear for your safety. You have friends at court. They will not permit your relatives to harm you."

"I have *enemies* at court, whispering lies into Elena's ears." Andrei's brows drew together until he resembled the gloomy saint adorning the apocalyptic vision that covered the walls of the reception room. "Have you forgotten my brother Yuri, three years in chains? She finally managed to starve him to death last summer. You were once his man. Yet there you stand, Elena's lackey, seeking to deliver me into her hands!"

Koshkin blushed. His past service to Yuri would haunt him the rest of his days. His inability to place Yuri on the throne still rankled. But Andrei did not know about that. Or did he? The courts of Staritsa and Moscow enjoyed close ties, despite the current conflict. Members of the same noble lineages served at both, just as they had served Yuri while he still occupied the ancient principality of Dmitrov. One could not assume any secret would remain hidden.

Koshkin glared at Shuisky and the Kolychevs, standing silently by while he handled their joint assignment, until they murmured agreement with his assurances. Andrei's boyars bobbed their heads like puppets carried from town to town by peddlers. Did they support their prince's defiance? Koshkin could not guess.

"Tell my sister-in-law," Andrei repeated in the flat tone of a man accustomed from birth to command. "I do not travel until this sore heals. My sovereign cannot expect me to serve him from a stretcher, or even to attend him carried in on one. Elena overreaches. Royal widows should be neither seen nor heard."

Koshkin itched to agree, but prudence held him silent. Prudence and rage. With reluctance he admitted that Daniil Kolychev had read the situation accurately.

And had offered the most sensible compromise. Koshkin swore under his breath, considered alternatives, then bowed to the inevitable. Elena would be mad as a she-bear deprived of its cub if another mission ended in failure—and would no doubt take out her anger on those she considered responsible. So he said through gritted teeth, "Then send your men to Kolomna against the godless Tatars, as Moscow also commands. Kazan's villain of a khan sues for peace, then attacks again before the ink dries on the treaties. Contributing your men to the fight will reassure your sister-in-law that you wish no ill to her and her son."

A hiss of fury sounded from the assembled nobles. Andrei regarded the four envoys through narrowed eyes while Koshkin braced himself for another refusal. Nothing could have startled him more when Andrei raised a hand to silence his men and said, "I will consider it. Leave me while I discuss the matter with my counselors."

Another week passed, and Koshkin's party remained in Staritsa. While Andrei and his counselors argued the inevitability of surrender, Easter came and went, further delaying the envoys' departure. But at last Andrei summoned them once more. After so long a wait Koshkin watched in amazement as the prince dictated a summons to his men, requiring them to depart for Kolomna under the command of his majordomo.

Daniil copied the order in his own hand—another surprise—and, as soon as the ink dried, rolled it into a scroll and handed it to Koshkin. Not to Prince Ilya—Koshkin, with an effort, concealed the unworthy sense of satisfaction that simple gesture evoked. When Ilya grabbed the scroll away and snarled a correction at Daniil, who ignored him, Koshkin's satisfaction increased. Whether Daniil sought to communicate disapproval, disrespect, disinterest, or simple dislike, that small act of rebellion, in Koshkin's view, could not fail to heighten his own status relative to Shuisky's. Any conflict between others was, as the peasants said, grist for his mill.

Another round of courtesies, the reassignment of a half-dozen of Daniil's soldiers to verify that Andrei's troops left as ordered, and Koshkin and his companions were again in the saddle heading for Volok. His relief as they passed the fortress gates knew no bounds. He was going home, to Roxelana. Impatient to end his longer-than-expected absence, he rejoiced to see his horse headed in the right direction at last.

They rode two by two along the narrow, rutted road. Daniil, in charge of the escort, had insisted on taking the lead, so Koshkin rode at his side. Awkward, given their history of not getting along, but Koshkin had a burning desire to find out what Daniil planned to tell his master, Telepnev, when they reached Moscow.

But since he could not pose that question directly— Daniil would not admit that part of his job consisted of spying on the grand princess's envoys—Koshkin began with an expression of gratitude, often a sure means to loosen an adversary's tongue. "Thank you for your support back there, Daniil Nikolaevich."

Daniil jerked his head to the right, a question in his eyes, as if he had not expected conversation from that quarter. "When you gave me the scroll instead of Prince Ilya," Koshkin explained.

"Oh that," Daniil said. "Ilya rates himself too high. I like to remind him every so often that competence does more for a mission than lineage. Otherwise the strutting peacock becomes unbearable. You are the real head of this misbegotten enterprise." He looked Koshkin in the eye. "If anyone ran off to have private meetings with Andrei's chamberlain, it should have been you, don't you think? Or did you find out enough in your conversations with the Staritsa nobles?"

What does he mean by that?

Another question he doubted Daniil would answer. Koshkin took the opportunity to move to the subject that interested him most. "Not enough. They were tight-lipped about their prince's intentions and even his health. Of course, they see us as spies, so they don't want to talk. And what of you, watching quietly from corners? Is Andrei faking it, as his sister-in-law believes, or genuinely sick?"

"I don't know," Daniil said. "He seems sturdy enough. His voice is strong, and although he never rose from his chair, he was not in bed. Did he look ill to you?"

"Not that I could tell," Koshkin said. "Stronger than when I saw him last autumn, when the reek in the room would stop a destrier in full charge. Although I still caught a whiff of infection. If I had to guess, he either exaggerated his illness or has recovered from it, but who but a physician can say for sure?"

Daniil regarded him through the steady brown eyes that always made Koshkin think of a lion.

Am I the prey?

"I suppose what matters," Daniil said after a while, "is what you plan to tell the grand princess. She already fears and suspects him. Revealing him as a liar will sign his death warrant." His mouth tightened in a way that suggested he might not like that possibility. "If he hasn't signed it already."

Interesting. And a moment ago he had called the mission "misbegotten." Was Daniil not the unwavering supporter Koshkin had believed him to be?

"That would disturb you, Daniil Nikolaevich?" Koshkin kept his voice casual. Even lions can be lured to their destruction. "What do *you* plan to tell her?"

But Daniil's steady gaze did not falter. "The land needs stability, Fyodor Mikhailovich. If Prince Andrei threatens his nephews, those in power must act to protect them. Don't you agree?"

Damn the boy. Just damn him. Him and his father, always turning the tables on me. Now what will he report to Telepnev, causing trouble for me and my lineage? How do I get out of this with a whole skin?

"Of course," Koshkin said. With luck Daniil would not notice that he spoke through clenched teeth.

As soon as Koshkin decided he could safely withdraw, he slowed his horse to ride beside Prince Ilya, sending Grigory ahead on the pretext of not wanting to separate the cousins.

Grigory gave him a look that indicated profound disbelief but nonetheless kicked his mount forward. Koshkin drew up beside Shuisky and asked him, too, about Prince Andrei's health.

This time he pursued higher stakes than the contents of the mission reports. Ilya's requests to meet Prince Andrei's chamberlain alone struck Koshkin as suspect. Prince Ilya, so junior among his own lineage that he could never hope to attain top rank in Moscow, might see a switch of allegiance to Prince Andrei and the prospects for advancement in the Staritsa court as a sufficiently appealing prize. The private meetings gave Ilya a chance to negotiate the terms of such a switch.

After almost three weeks of observation Koshkin felt quite certain of one point: Shuisky was *not* a straight arrow like Daniil Kolychev. Shuisky took great pride in his ancient lineage. He was quick to take offense and slow to forgive. He itched for higher standing at court. All of which suggested that he might harbor schemes that left him vulnerable to manipulation.

Koshkin disliked the ugly word "blackmail."

Shuisky had not answered his question. "Do you believe Prince Andrei is sick?" Koshkin asked again. "As sick as he claims?"

"It is not for us to determine health or illness," Shuisky said with a sideways glance that hinted at dislike. "The grand princess's doctor has already declared the wound minor." He stopped, twisted his mustache, then added, "Although six months—if the illness in truth lingers, then it must be serious, whatever the doctor said."

A minuscule crack in the façade—it could mean nothing. "His oldest brother didn't last so long," Koshkin said, probing. "Three months at most. Perhaps I should have mentioned that. It might have shaken Andrei from his denial."

Shuisky turned his head then, astonishment visible in his eyes. "Causing him to admit his lies?" He scowled. "Young Kolychev doesn't have your best interests at heart. Remember that when he's handing you scrolls that should come to me. I can't imagine how you persuaded Andrei to comply, even in part, with Elena's demands, but that message we carry will only delay matters. Better to have let me lure Andrei to Moscow, end things one way or another. You grow old, Fyodor Mikhailovich. Exile has robbed you of your wits."

Arrogant puppy! I'm thirty-seven. Not in my dotage yet!

Koshkin bit down on his tongue, hard. The pain forced him to concentrate, to remember the costs of speaking his mind to this pompous youth. "Perhaps you're right," he said with false lightness. "But would Andrei have accepted the lure? He has good cause to fear imprisonment and death."

Shuisky glowered at the surrounding forest and did not answer.

Koshkin set out to soothe the young man's ruffled feathers by talking of the comforts of home, the delights of married life, and his hopes for a swift and hazard-free journey. Annoying or not, receptive to manipulation or not, Ilya did have one characteristic to recommend him. He didn't have the brains to cause serious trouble.

And given how many wolves circled Koshkin at present—including his precious son-in-law, possibly bent on coaxing Roxelana back to his bed—a stupid, preening puppet might be just what he needed.

Chapter 17

SIX DAYS LATER, IN THE AFTERNOON, ALEXEI KISSED HIS wife goodbye with the solemnity of a man heading into battle. Word of Koshkin's return had reached them not an hour earlier.

"Good luck," she said. "And don't look so grim. It's only Papa. Are you sure you don't want me to ride with you and distract Stepmama?" The expression on her face as she made this offer left him in no doubt that she would rather dig ditches with her bare hands.

"No need. You did your part already." The relief on her face made him smile. "I'll lead the charge. We agreed, did we not? I'm to attack before he has time to construct a defense."

"We did," Maria said. "Fly high then, my falcon, and return victorious."

He regarded her with his eyebrows drawn together. The light voice contrasted with an undercurrent he couldn't define but had sensed, almost like a barrier between them, since the day they had argued over her father. As if she no longer trusted him even when he held her in his arms.

Her love for Koshkin ran deep, deeper than he had suspected. He couldn't take back his words—and would not if he could, because his alliance with Koshkin chafed him more with each day that passed—but he did miss the closeness he had not fully appreciated until she pulled away.

Not knowing how to heal the wound with words, Alexei touched his hand to his heart, the way his warriors did when acknowledging an order, and left his wife in the foyer of the house. Once mounted, he glanced over his shoulder. Maria stood at the window watching him go, as if she cared for him despite the chill he at times sensed between them. Puzzled, he turned Ajdar toward the open gates and the muddy street beyond. The memory stayed with him as, trailed by his personal guard, he wended his way to his father-in-law's house a few streets away.

Koshkin greeted him with a harassed air, which Alexei wrote down to his father-in-law's month-long absence from Roxelana. A flash of remorse evaporated as he realized that Koshkin's frustrated desire might render him more malleable. He accepted a mug of beer but rationed his sips to keep his head clear.

"I apologize for my poor timing, Fyodor Mikhailovich," he said with a fine disregard for the truth. A show of courtesy never hurt. Under normal circumstances he would have engaged in the long preliminaries that Tatar social occasions required, but the impatience on Koshkin's face suggested that tactic might end with him thrown out, however politely, before he broached the topic that had brought him here. So he went straight for the jugular. "I'm sure you're anxious for time with your wife. I won't keep you long. How did your mission go? We have heard some strange rumors in Moscow."

Koshkin's scowl intensified. "Rumors?"

"Idle gossip, I feel certain." Alexei permitted himself one more sip of beer and crossed his right leg over his left. He calculated that since Koshkin had every reason not to confess that he toyed with the idea of betraying both his ruler and his family, the more confrontational the approach, the better. Shock might jar loose an admission that Koshkin would otherwise conceal. "That Grigory Kolychev might defect. That *you* plan to, because of your past allegiance to Prince Yuri. That you went to assess your odds of success if you backed Prince Andrei."

"By the saints!" Koshkin sprang to his feet. "How dare you accuse me of treason? And you my son-in-law!"

"Easy." Alexei raised his hands in a pacific gesture. "I didn't say *I* believed such calumny. I feel sure you can assess the odds as well as any man, and better than most. Whatever you think of Grand Princess Elena, you must know Andrei's is a losing cause. But whether you toy with disloyalty or not—and I'll believe you if you tell me you don't—Elena and her favorite distrust you. We need to discuss how to convince them to change their minds."

Seeing no hint of yielding in his father-in-law's tense frame, Alexei hardened his voice. Perhaps an even more direct statement was needed. "Understand that I place the safety of my wife and son—Lyuba too—above the concerns of any Russian prince. Our alliance, such as it is, does not include my suicide." To underline his point, he crossed his arms over his chest and returned his father-in-law's scowl in full measure.

Koshkin turned purple—with fury, no doubt—but he had no chance to reply before a sultry voice rich with the accents of the south interrupted them. "Dearest," Roxelana said from the doorway. While Alexei watched, appreciative as ever of her machinations, she crossed the room and wound her arms around her husband's neck. Only then did she turn and say, "And Tsarevich Alexei. Always a pleasure. I trust your wife is well?"

"As well as when you saw her two weeks ago," he said, allowing his lips to curve in acknowledgment of a fine performance. "Thank you for your concern. No need to ask how you fare: you are lovely as ever."

Roxelana preened. Koshkin frowned. Alexei considered his options. However much he wanted to push his father-in-law into confession, a discussion held in front of Roxelana wouldn't produce the information he sought even if the conversation had not already been heading full speed for the nether regions. So accepting temporary defeat, he stood and bowed. "I will not delay your reunion with my presence. I said what I came to say, and if you wish to discuss the matter further, you will find me at my estate tomorrow."

"Don't be silly, Tsarevich." Roxelana grabbed his elbow and, with startling strength for such a willowy young woman, maneuvered both him and her husband toward their seats. She settled Koshkin in his chair, cooing over him like an entire flock of turtle doves. Alexei, surrendering to unholy amusement at the expense of his better nature, seated himself opposite his father-in-law without waiting for an invitation. Roxelana sank onto a cushion at her husband's feet and fixed him with an adoring gaze, reminding Alexei of an illustration from one of his favorite books, a story about a young wife spinning tales out of a desperate desire to please her cranky old husband.

"Isn't this cozy?" she said. The glance she threw over her shoulder, filled with promise, almost shattered his self-control.

One man at a time, Roxelana!

By placing a hand over his mouth, he managed to hide his laughter long enough to turn the incipient roar into a discreet cough. When he looked at her again, he found her glaring at him. Good.

With Roxelana subdued—although if he knew her, not for long—Alexei concentrated his attention on his father-in-law. "You didn't tell me how the mission went," he reminded Koshkin. "Your choices affect me and my family, which is also yours. Don't you think I have a right to know? If only so I can help you?"

"Would you?" Koshkin asked. "Help me, that is. I wonder."

"I will, if it lies within my power," Alexei said. Ignoring his father-in-law's hostility, he kept his own voice level. "You sponsored me, gave me your daughter's hand. I pay my debts. But I will not aid you in destroying yourself, any more than I will destroy myself for you. What is happening?"

Out of the corner of his eye he saw Roxelana reach for her husband's hand. Fear tightened her mouth and widened her eyes. Koshkin patted her arm in a distracted manner, looking neither at her nor at Alexei but at the far wall.

Fascinating. Does he realize he's scaring her?

For the first time in years Alexei found himself sympathizing with Roxelana, so vulnerable to the schemes of men, devoid of family or even female friends who might support her.

He stashed the thought away to share later with Maria. "Fyodor Mikhailovich," he prompted. "What is happening?"

Koshkin's eyes focused again. "Nothing of importance," he said. "Prince Ilya Shuisky hasn't the brains to do serious harm. That pest Daniil Kolychev gathers information on me to share with his master, Telepnev. Grigory Kolychev walks, as ever, the middle path. And Prince Andrei refuses to travel to Moscow before the Day of Terrible Judgment—which if he keeps this up will arrive for him soon enough. I will not help him dig his own grave. So you see, nothing threatens our alliance."

Unbelievable. Alexei rose. "Nothing? When you don't trust me with the truth? You leave me no choice but to ask Daniil Kolychev what information he has gathered. Because if you're worried about him spying on you, you must be concealing *something.*"

And with that he left, furious, with a nod to them both. So much for taking his father-in-law by surprise.

Although in certain respects he thought he had done exactly that.

Koshkin could barely contain himself. As soon as the door closed behind his ungrateful son-in-law, he leaped to his feet and prowled the room, kicking tufted hassocks as he passed them. Roxelana trailed him at a discreet distance, twisting her hands together and looking distressed. He hoped her unhappiness reflected concern for him rather than her former lover, but tonight that possibility again seemed far from certain.

When he reached the window, he whirled on her. "Stop following me. You knew what he was like. Why didn't you warn me?"

Her distress faded into confusion. "Warn you about what?"

"Giving my daughter to that traitor!" Even as he hurled the statement at her, he admitted it was a bald-faced lie. Prince Vasily Shuisky had ordered him to find their latest Tatar recruit a bride, and what better choice than Koshkin's own daughter? Why let such a high-ranking match improve the status of someone else's lineage? He hadn't even met Roxelana until later.

His wife's mouth twitched, which did nothing to lessen his fury, but she did stop trailing him. "Alexei has ever been one to speak his mind," she said. "How do you think he ran into trouble with his father? I didn't meet him until years afterward, of course, but I've heard the story."

"Then you know more than I do. I asked him a dozen times what bad blood lay between him and Bulat, and he evaded me every time." He put his hands on his hips, half-hoping she would soothe him as she sometimes did.

Instead she glided to the chair Alexei had vacated and perched on the edge of the seat. "They argued. The details don't matter. Alexei, although no more than sixteen, refused to back down, so his father declared him dead to the clan." With her foot she tapped the chair opposite, where he had sat during the contentious interview just past. "Calm yourself, dearest. Alexei won't betray you."

"Then why is he listening to rumors? Slandering my name? Threatening to seek out Daniil Kolychev! He speaks of protecting my daughter as if she had no connection to me—of defending Lyuba, damn his arrogance. I should bring the child back here, just to remind him who her father *is*." He crossed the room and threw himself onto his chair, angling his right leg over the arm, but he didn't miss the alarm that flashed in his wife's eyes. Since Lyuba could not be the cause, his suspicions of Roxelana's feelings for Alexei flared anew.

"Don't do that." She reached out and patted his arm, and he jerked it away, determined not to give in to her cajolery. "The child is happy in her new home, Maria tells me. It would be unkind to uproot her once more. And I doubt Alexei concerns himself with the rearing of a girl, so you would disrupt her life to no purpose."

He grunted, unable to deny the truth of what she said. "I don't like his tone. I don't like the way he flirts with you. And I expected more appreciation from him of my efforts on his behalf. Paying his debts! Going behind my back! If he thinks I'll confide in him after such treatment, he is very much mistaken."

"Of course, dearest." Roxelana shimmied in her seat, then when he could no longer resist looking at her, left it to resume her place at his feet. "He will rue the day he opposed you. But in the meantime won't you confide in me? *Are* you planning to support Prince Andrei?"

The truth—that the only thing that stood between him and forswearing his allegiance to a haughty wench and her milk-fed brat was his conviction that the prince of Staritsa lacked sufficient ruthlessness to survive, never mind rule—trembled on the tip of his tongue. Roxelana was his wife. He owed her the truth. His choices, for better or worse, affected her life more deeply than even his children's or his son-in-law's.

But he still distrusted her. Suppose she and Alexei plotted against him, intending to renew their prior relationship even if it meant sacrificing his welfare? Koshkin had seen the longing glances his wife cast Alexei's way and the light that gleamed in Alexei's eyes when he looked at her, and no one could imagine that a chit like Maria, however dear to her father, could oust a beauty like Roxelana from a man's affections. He would share his thinking with neither of them. Not even with Maria, in case she passed along what he told her to her husband.

"As your beloved tsarevich pointed out before you joined us, Grand Princess Elena has her brother-in-law in a vise," he said. "If Andrei had the sense of a newborn pup, he would either flee the country or submit. Since he chooses instead to send foolish messages while trying to buy Elena off with half-measures, I would have to be an even bigger idiot than he is to put myself in the line of fire. I doubt he will last the month."

He stood and stalked to the door, avoiding her hands. "You can tell Alexei that when you see him. And now, excuse me. I intend to sleep alone tonight."

Alexei went straight to the Kolychevs' estate. He cared a good deal more about interrupting his sister's reunion with Daniil than delaying Koshkin's with Roxelana, but when he reached the house he found Daniil in deep discussion with his father. After a round of greetings he accepted their invitation to sit and relayed the gist of his unsatisfactory conversation with his father-in-law.

"I pushed him too hard," he admitted at the end. "I hoped his eagerness to get Roxelana alone would undercut some of those defenses he maintains so well. Instead I sent him into a fury. My besetting sin: I don't know when to hold my tongue."

Daniil grinned. "Me neither. Better forthright than duplicitous, I say. But in this case, I fear, he played chess better than you did."

"He knows more than he's saying?" Alexei rested a fist on his hand. A dyspeptic saint in the icon corner caught his eye. He knew how the holy man felt.

"For sure," Daniil said. "Even I know more than he's saying, so it's good you came here. In short, Prince Ilya had more than one private session with Prince Andrei's chamberlain. No one knows for sure what they talked about, but I doubt it was the state of their beards. Ilya's plotting something. The question is what."

"And Koshkin?" Alexei leaned forward, elbows on his knees, frowning. This news was not good. Even if Koshkin, damn his tricky soul, had not entangled himself in any developing conspiracy, his presence on the mission that gave rise to such a conspiracy would cast further shade on him and those associated with him.

"He talked with a lot of people," Daniil said with a quick lift of one shoulder. "When I asked, he said he wanted to know more about Prince Andrei's intentions and the state of his health."

"The same claim he made before." Alexei pondered the implications of that. "It's still plausible, don't you think?"

Daniil spread his hands in an "I suppose so" gesture. "I have no reason to doubt him. He didn't ask to speak to Prince Andrei or even the chamberlain or majordomo. Just held conversations with people around the court."

"And what of troop movements and such? You were planning to watch for those as well."

"I saw a lot of whispering in corners, not shared with us," Daniil said. "Conversations that ended abruptly as I approached, general tension—you know the kind of thing. I didn't see signs of an imminent attack: no stockpiles of weapons or armor. But Andrei did have a lot of warriors nearby, because when he agreed to send men to Kolomna, he had them to hand. Unless he countermanded the order the moment we left, he'll have many fewer now. I'm hoping that will suffice to allay Moscow's suspicions, but I wouldn't count on it."

"And my father-in-law did nothing to prevent Andrei dispatching his support?"

"On the contrary. I first suggested it as a possible compromise, but Koshkin was the one who proposed it to Andrei. I plan to tell Telepnev that, for what it's worth."

"Perhaps Maria was right, then, and her father has enemies who will twist whatever they can into evidence of guilt." Alexei pondered what he'd heard, but no matter which angle he viewed the information from, Koshkin still looked innocent. "In that case, we need to find out who they are and counteract the lies." He glanced at Nikolai, again sitting behind his desk, watching without speaking. "What do you think, Nikolai Borisovich?"

Nikolai steepled his fingers and stared over them, his blue eyes intent. "We have to move fast. This situation will spin out of control any day. Talk to Koshkin again. Tell him you believe in his innocence. See if *he* knows who his enemies are."

Alexei sighed. "I'll be amazed if he lets me in the door. But if he does, I'll do as you suggest."

Chapter 18

THE SUN HAD SENT ITS FIRST RAYS PAST THE HORIZON WHEN Alexei and his troop of forty armed men rode out of the Kremlin to intercept and escort back to Moscow, under guard, the latest envoy from Prince Andrei of Staritsa. As the highest-ranking officer present, Alexei led the detachment, although its mission struck him as quite mad. Try as he might, he could not imagine any way in which capturing Prince Andrei's emissaries could advance Grand Princess Elena's cause. Not more than ten days had passed since the return of Koshkin and his traveling companions to Moscow.

A short mission, less than a full day to the expected intersection point and back—or so Daniil had told him. This had been Daniil's force, and in most respects still was. Alexei had yet to see evidence that Daniil bore a grudge at being superseded as leader, but he watched for it.

For himself he welcomed the return to military duty, even so questionable a mission as this one. Used to spending most of each day riding, fighting, or training for future combat, he had found few outlets for his restless energy in the two and a half months since his wedding—however pleasant an interlude that had been.

At the same time, his unfamiliarity with Russian ways sent prickles of uncertainty down his spine. "Help me understand," he asked Daniil, riding at his right. "What's the point of arresting Prince Andrei's emissaries before discovering what they have to say? Does Elena think she can frighten her brother-in-law into compliance? I'd expect the exact opposite myself."

"So would I." Daniil looked uncomfortable. "Perhaps she wants to scare him into flight. Or signal that the time for negotiation is over. I got orders, not explanations. The higher-ups like to keep their reasoning to themselves."

Alexei pondered the bitterness in his companion's tone. Daniil didn't like the situation any more than Alexei himself did; that was obvious. But were their reasons the same? "What's bothering you?" he asked.

Daniil stared into the distance as he spoke. "I served under Andrei in Borovsk. He's a good commander, loyal and straightforward. If he threatens the grand prince, this confrontation is necessary. But I never saw evidence that Andrei wanted more power."

"He could become the hope of others without wanting power for himself," Alexei said. He had seen that often enough among the Tatar khans. Although he'd expected something different from Russia. Something better.

More fool him. Not for the first time, Alexei wondered what snake pit he had landed in because his rush to escape death in Crimea had blinded him to the dangers ahead.

"True," Daniil said. "And that thought keeps Elena up at night, I'm guessing. One can't entirely blame her. Her children's survival depends on her. But suppose she has created a crisis that would not exist without her fear?"

Alexei had no answer to that question. Most likely, Daniil didn't expect one. In silence they rode toward the town where they expected to find Prince Andrei's envoys.

Maria emerged from her carriage in the courtyard of the Sheremetev estate and studied the multistoried wooden house before lifting her skirts and placing a foot on the first step of the covered staircase. In response to Sumbeka's renewed order to befriend Solomonida, and aware that friendship would require an apology for past slights, Maria had concocted an excuse for her visit: the delivery of an embroidered kerchief for Solomonida's six-year-old daughter, Anna, and a request that Anna might be permitted to visit Lyuba, who despite her near-adoration of Timur yearned at times to play with someone guaranteed *not* to turn her dolls into warriors. Maria admitted to herself that she hated the thought of apologizing—never one of her strengths. But she would do what she must and hope that the excuse would make any plea for forgiveness unnecessary.

But as she climbed the staircase and performed her opening bows, Maria pondered her real purpose: to find out the truth, if any, of the information Solomonida had whispered in her ear during that dinner a few weeks ago. Three more visits to court had not lowered Grand Princess Elena's emotional barricades, and Maria's discreet inquiries among the ladies had failed to yield anything new. With Papa blocking Alexei at every turn—and why, if he was as innocent as he claimed?—and Roxelana as uncooperative as ever, Solomonida represented Maria's last best hope of discovering her father's true intentions in time to stop him from bringing disaster down on the heads of his entire lineage. Not to put too fine a point on it, she was desperate.

When she reached the top of the stairs, Solomonida ushered her into a pretty sitting room, bright with sunlight and warm. One servant took Maria's outer robe, and another appeared with refreshments. Maria, although not hungry so early in the day, accepted a piece of dark bread covered in smoked salmon and a cup of cherry juice. The fish—fresh and creamy, with a delicious salty bite offset by the dark rye—filled her mouth with a cool richness that the tart cherry juice only enhanced.

In response to her hostess's invitation she sat on a wooden settle, so much less comfortable than the cushioned sofas in her own house. Solomonida exclaimed over the kerchief and called Anna to appreciate its glories. A pretty blonde—she could hardly be otherwise, with two such light-haired parents—Anna managed a creditable bow and a gracious thank you that Maria had difficulty imagining emerging from her own small sister's mouth. Anna agreed readily to the idea of a girl her own age to play with and soon retreated to the far side of the room, where she tested the magical kerchief at various angles against the window.

With Anna disposed of, Maria moved on to inquiries as to her hostess's health and welfare. Solomonida responded in kind, and for a short while Maria believed that her reason for visiting had passed muster. Then Solomonida—with a glance at her daughter, still preoccupied with the kerchief, now dangling from a doll's beaded headdress—said quietly, "What really brings you here, Maria?"

Well, she had known this moment must come. Maria sighed. "I want to apologize for the way I've treated you," she said. "I was so unhappy in Lady Natalya's house that I couldn't see that others might be miserable too. You, for example, married to that awful Semyon. Losing your sons, one after another. I'm sorry for the barbs I sent your way. I would like to do better from now on."

Solomonida listened to this speech with her chin propped on her hand. Maria reached the end and stopped, uncertain of her next move. Make her bow and leave? Wait? Prepare for Solomonida's attack? But that would end any chance of gathering the information she needed.

She took a deep breath and forced herself to wait. How hurtful could a response be, in the end? But she turned over possible retorts in her head, just in case.

Solomonida sat in silent observation for what felt like an eternity before her face broke into a smile. "Well, you astonish me, Maria. I didn't think you had it in you to apologize. I forgive you. And I apologize too. I have to admit, I sent more than a few barbs in return. Will you forgive me?"

"I will." Maria extended a hand across the short distance that separated them. "Thank you. I look forward to being friends."

They talked for a while about neutral topics, until Maria mustered the courage to ask about the subject that most concerned her. "And since I am here, can you tell me more about Princess Nadezhda and her husband? I have learned nothing at court that could explain her strange warning to me that day at dinner. Is Prince Ilya a victim, as she hinted with her 'journey of the condemned' comment? Or a traitor, as his conversation with Grigory Kolychev indicates?"

"Princess Nadezhda says many things." In response to a quizzical glance Solomonida closed her hand around Maria's, squeezed briefly, then released. "You were new to the court, the daughter of a former exile, a man suspected of harboring treasonous thoughts. She spoke with care, in case you too had divided loyalties. But she wanted you to know about the rumors surrounding your father because she sympathizes with you. Like you, she has felt the lash of Elena's tongue, and at times she has been held to account because the men in her life played political games without considering anyone but themselves."

Maria turned the information over in her mind. She had not heard the warning as sympathy, but in retrospect she could see what Solomonida meant. It warmed her to think that both Solomonida and Nadezhda had reached out to help her despite past unpleasantnesses and simple unfamiliarity. "And 'the journey of the condemned'? Who are the condemned: those Elena suspects?"

"Rightly or wrongly. Yes, I think so."

Which cleared up one mystery, but … "Which means I still don't know whether Papa is a true suspect or a false one. Or who is slandering him, if he's innocent." Maria tried to contain her disappointment. Her high hopes for this visit seemed foolish in retrospect. What could Solomonida learn from Princess Nadezhda that Maria herself had not already deduced?

"Nor do I." Solomonida gently shook her head. "If I hear anything, I will stop by. With Anna, so no one will question my sudden desire to visit."

At the sound of her name Anna ran to her mother. The kerchief dangled from one hand, and she held a wooden horse on wheels in the other. "Look, Mama, Beauty likes her new blanket!" She draped the kerchief over the horse's back.

"I'd better go." Maria rose and touched a hand to the crown of Anna's head, then bent to kiss Solomonida on both cheeks. "Bring her soon to play with Lyuba. And a thousand thanks for your willingness to start anew."

"It was nothing." Solomonida also rose. "Thank you for visiting." She held out a hand to her daughter. "Come, Anna, let's say goodbye to our guest."

The scouts had done their job well. Alexei and his troops encountered Prince Andrei's emissaries where they expected to find them: in a village not half a day's ride from Moscow. The sun still stood far below its zenith when the encompassing woods opened onto a clearing, as the Russian forest tended to do, and the village appeared as if conjured by a giant.

Although the giant might, Alexei thought, have put a bit of planning into his design, for the location had nothing magical about it. A group of about thirty armed men—most of them nobles, to judge from the quality of their armor and horses—stood among a tangle of wooden huts, one rather larger than the rest. Alexei gave the prearranged signal, and the troops encircled their quarry. Pandemonium ensued among the captured emissaries as they recognized the threat the horsemen posed.

One large, stocky man of middle age, hair and beard a mix of gray and a brown that matched his eyes, let out a roar and rode the short distance that brought him face to face with Alexei. The leader, presumably.

"What's the meaning of this?" the man demanded.

"Your name?" Alexei asked.

"Prince Fyodor Dmitrievich Pronsky," the man announced with a sneer, emphasizing the "prince."

"*Tsarevich* Alexei Bulatovich," Alexei responded with a snap equal to Pronsky's own. "You act as Prince Andrei's chief emissary?"

"I do," Pronsky confirmed. The slight dip of his head acknowledged Alexei's higher standing. "And you?"

"Grand Princess Elena has ordered us to escort you to the Kremlin." Alexei saw no need to elaborate. Instead he indicated Daniil. "This is Daniil Nikolaevich Kolychev, who today serves as my second-in-command."

"Prince," Daniil said. Other than the usual bow, he too dispensed with courtesies. The armed guards showed that the time for polite exchanges had long since passed.

Pronsky glanced from one to the other, then appeared to accept that he and his men had no choice but to submit. "Very well," he said. "Let us ride to Moscow."

"You're joking." Koshkin turned from the window of his office in the Ambassadorial Chancellery and stared at Prince Ilya Shuisky, who stood, stroking the side of his mustache, about the length of a man's foot from the door. "Why would I do anything so stupid as to back Prince Andrei? He's bound to lose." As anyone but a dolt like you could see, he added silently.

"Andrei can draw a lot of support. You don't want to be on the wrong side of his victory." Prince Ilya's stolid expression gave him the look of a well-fed hunting dog. No one would believe he had rebellion on his mind. A less likely plotter Koshkin had yet to meet.

"I do not," Koshkin said, testing the ground beneath his feet. It felt more like quicksand than firm Russian soil. "But where will he find this support? He faces the entire power of the Muscovite armed forces, with only a handful of Staritsa nobles on whom he can rely. I know of no others, and I suspect you don't either."

Prince Ilya came into the room and gestured at a bench next to Koshkin's desk. "May I?"

"Of course." Koshkin took his seat, then watched his guest reposition the bench until it lay within an arm's reach. He waited until Ilya sank onto the seat and leaned forward before murmuring, "If you intend to speak in confidence, we might do better to move into the courtyard."

"I had forgotten." Ilya's pale eyes gleamed in the late afternoon sun. "You are an old hand at plotting. I can learn much from you."

Was that a compliment or an insult? "Not so," Koshkin lied. "My exile came about in response to unjustified suspicions, fomented by a criminal eager to save his own skin. You can't believe that I would have escaped knouting or imprisonment if I'd done the things I was accused of."

"Maybe not." How someone so sleek and round could look skeptical, Koshkin could not figure out, but skepticism clearly etched its lines around Ilya's cheeks and mouth. "But you won't insist that you prefer service to a woman—a foreigner!—surely."

A trap? A hint of shared distaste? "Elena has lived in Russia since infancy," he said, in the hope of drawing Prince Ilya out. "Her family came here from Lithuania, but she's no more foreign than you and I are."

Ilya waved away this objection with a sweep of his left hand, narrowly missing Koshkin's fur cap. "Do you deny arguing before the inner circle that we need an adult male to command the armies? My uncle Vasily remembers it well." Impatience tinged Ilya's voice, and Koshkin took heart. His gift for maneuvering, a subject of pride long stifled by his need for caution, stirred, calling him to take a chance, throw the knucklebones, get back in the game.

But he had much to lose from a poor choice, and everything he had learned so far indicated that Prince Andrei lacked the spine either to mount an uprising or to succeed if he did. He also had little reason to trust Prince Ilya's judgment. "I won't deny that," he said. "Half Moscow knows it. But I was talking about Prince Yuri, who expected to rule; although excluded from the day-to-day business of government, he had many opportunities to watch and learn. Andrei has never shown any interest beyond his small principality. The height of his ambition seems to lie in building churches for his wife to decorate with altar cloths. So I ask you again: where will he find this support you insist he has?"

Prince Ilya leaned forward, close enough that his bushy beard brushed Koshkin's shoulder. "From the Moscow nobles.

Many of them have reached the end of their tether. They share their concerns with me in private. Prince Telepnev and his Cheliadnin relatives grow mighty while the rest of us languish. Even the members of Grand Princess Elena's family can't hold their own against Cheliadnin ambitions. The more of us who stand together, the better our chances of success." He bent forward and murmured a series of highborn names into Koshkin's ear.

An impressive list, if true, but Koshkin needed more evidence before he pledged his life to Andrei's cause. "Your uncle maintains his position without difficulty," he observed. "So what pulls you to the rebel side?"

"Telepnev tightens the reins on my uncle too, despite his age," Ilya said. "When Uncle Vasily goes, do you think one of us will replace him as head of foreign affairs? Or will that post go to a Cheliadnin? I support Andrei because if he wins, I can expect the kind of post that suits my rank in *his* court. So could you."

The promise drew Koshkin. His eighteen months of clawing his way back to power—fixed in a single daring move. *Take a chance. Be bold!*

Yet he still hesitated. If he switched sides, he could not return to Moscow unless Andrei won. He must abandon Roxelana, because only a brute would force her to accompany him to a city that might fall under siege. Alexei would no doubt take her back under his protection, but then? Even the thought made his insides burn.

At the same time, he hated Elena. Hated her for ruining his plan three years ago to advance his lineage and save the Russian lands from the consequences of rule by a woman and a child. Hated her for his long exile, for the sneers and suspicion that had dogged his every step since his return, for the effort he must exert nonstop to lull her concerns. Hated her for being a woman who refused to keep to her God-decreed place by retiring to a convent or at least remaining in the background with her brats while the boyars ruled, as her husband had intended.

And his hatred paled next to that other yearning, bursting again into life after too long in the ashes. The thrill of playing for high stakes, of leading rather than following, of steering events to benefit not only himself and his lineage but the land as a whole. He refused to back a prince who couldn't win, but if the Moscow nobles deserted Elena?

The thought set the blood rushing in his veins. A better world, a better future, a better Russia—he *wanted* it. Wanted to live in it, wanted to take part in bringing it into being. For the first time since he had lied his way out of disaster three years ago, Koshkin felt alive in a way that surpassed even his passion for Roxelana.

Yet he had not forgotten the cost of his past failures. "I commit to nothing," he told Prince Ilya. "I will consider what you've said."

"Very well," Ilya replied. "But don't delay. As a token of my friendship let me reveal that your name comes up in every discussion of those Grand Princess Elena distrusts. Keep that in mind as you ponder your circumstances. You don't want to end up like Prince Andrei's emissaries."

Koshkin stared at him. "Prince Andrei's emissaries? Are you speaking in code? He has sent no one to Moscow since mid-March, and that envoy returned unscathed. We saw him during our last visit."

"More are on the way. They will arrive before sunset. Bearing a letter of complaint from their master about the treatment he has received. And the grand princess has prepared an appropriate reception for them, including dispatching your son-in-law to escort them hither. I'm surprised he didn't tell you." Ilya stroked his beard and grinned. "Wait too long, Fyodor Mikhailovich, and our sovereign lady will find a cell in the Kremlin towers for you. As I said, she already has your name on her list."

He'd underestimated Ilya. Not stupid after all. Dangerous, deceptive—worse than stupid. No matter how hard Koshkin pressed, Ilya refused to supply the source of his information. After a few rounds of stalling, he departed, grinning and stroking his mustache.

It took every shred of self-control Koshkin had not to kick the man's ample rear as he left.

Chapter 19

ALEXEI AND DANIIL DID REACH MOSCOW BY SUNSET. IN RE-
sponse to instructions sent by Prince Ivan Telepnev as they
passed through the Kremlin gates, the troop escorted Pronsky
and his men to the quarters normally reserved for their royal
master. As the door closed behind the emissaries from Staritsa,
palace guards raced in and took their place outside, weapons
at the ready, so intent on their mission that they shoved Alexei
and Daniil to one side.

Alexei slammed the man who'd shoved him against the
wall, gripping him by the throat. "Watch where you're going."

The guard, a rabbity little man with pale blue eyes and tufts
of dirty blond hair sticking out around his helmet, cringed.
"Sorry, Commander. That was an accident."

Alexei glowered at the fool as he released his grip.
"Understood. But what brings you here?"

"The grand princess has ordered us to keep Prince Pronsky
and his men under lock and key until she chooses to receive
them, when they will answer for their master's intransigence,"
a second guard said. This one looked as if he might have
half a brain. The leader, Alexei guessed.

"Complete your task then," Alexei told the second guard, who ducked his head with an alacrity that suggested he hoped to avoid offending this fierce Tatar commander. Good. It was the effect Alexei sought.

Seeing Daniil's combative stance, Alexei grabbed him by the elbow before he could protest. "Leave it," he said in Daniil's ear. "We've done our job. Let's report and go."

Daniil nodded, his expression grim, and the two of them led their small troop toward the stables. A brief report to Prince Telepnev, and the men were dismissed. Daniil and Alexei rode together out of the fortress, not speaking until they reached the marketplace, its stalls silent and deserted on this Thursday evening.

"I have no stake in this fight," Alexei said when it seemed safe to talk. "No understanding of it, in truth. You knew we were sent to capture them. What's got you so angry?"

Daniil directed a fearsome scowl between his horse's ears, then twisted to face Alexei. "They used me. I was the one who urged Koshkin to persuade Andrei to comply with Grand Princess Elena's last demand by sending his troops to Kolomna. I believed she'd back off if he showed a willingness to negotiate. Instead, she and Telepnev have decided to strip Andrei of his support, man by man if necessary, then go after him whatever he does or says. The unfairness of it infuriates me."

Alexei shrugged. "Isn't that what royalty does: use us?" His lord in Crimea certainly had, and without a moment's hesitation.

"I suppose," Daniil said. The glare he directed at the empty shopkeepers' stalls looked fit to set them ablaze. "We're in it now, though. Even if Elena changes her mind tomorrow, she can't undo the damage she's done by arresting those men."

"Right," Alexei said, his voice flat. "Andrei must retaliate or flee. Or submit, but if he intended to submit, he'd have done it already. I don't suppose it was ever likely that he would. What ruler's son will yield to a woman half his age, no matter how large a force she commands?"

"You're right," Daniil said. "Andrei will decide the next move. And we're nothing but pawns on the board."

The marketplace lay behind them. They entered the crisscrossing streets of the Kitaigorod, its brand-new brick wall a dim presence in the dark. Thinking about the heft of that brick, Alexei understood more than ever what Prince Andrei was up against in terms of his chances for survival. "But if you could choose?" he asked. "Would you defend the grand princess even though you don't approve of what she's doing?"

Daniil winced. "Yes. Because what's the alternative? My father and I swore allegiance to the grand prince, which, God help us, means allegiance to his mother as well. Elena pushed Andrei out of fear. If she'd left him alone, he probably would have spent the rest of his life in Staritsa, not bothering anyone. But once she made her demands and he defied her, she had to insist or lose the respect of her own nobles. Her position is precarious as it is. I don't like how she's handling the situation, but I can't ignore the fact that Andrei's victory would mean the death of the grand prince and his brother. So we stand with the grand prince."

Alexei nodded. Put like that, Daniil and his father made the only honorable choice. Had he himself not stood by his lord until that allegiance threatened his very survival? It was what a warrior did.

In truth, even now he wondered if he should have stuck it out to the end in Crimea, and not only when his wife threw his past sins in his face.

Although if he had, he would never have met Maria. And each day that passed underlined what a loss that would have been.

Early the next morning Koshkin rode at Grigory Kolychev's right along the same road he had already traversed twice—and at a much faster pace, because they had to reach the boundary of Prince Andrei's domain by nightfall.

When word had come yesterday evening that the grand princess had ordered Prince Andrei's emissaries placed under guard in the Kremlin, Koshkin realized he must flee. The envoys' confinement showed that Ilya did have the access to inside information that he claimed, and Ilya had insisted that Koshkin's arrest would soon follow. And much as he would miss his beautiful wife, Koshkin had stuck with his plan to leave Roxelana behind. She could not ride fast enough to escape pursuit, he could not take her into a war zone, and he could do her no good from a Kremlin cell. If he survived the current crisis, he would send for her.

For that and other reasons, Koshkin would have preferred to stay in Moscow. But since he had to leave, he decided to look forward. It would be good to again have the chance to fight for a cause he believed in. Prince Andrei might not equal his older brothers in strength or firmness, but he far exceeded his six-year-old nephew in ability. He would lead the armies to victory. He would command the respect of foreign leaders. And he had an heir to preserve the dynasty when he joined his ancestors—which, God willing, would not happen for a decade at least. He just needed some good advice, which Koshkin would be happy to provide.

"Did you tell anyone in Moscow that you meant to join Prince Andrei?" Grigory Kolychev interrupted these musings. "Ilya Shuisky, for example."

"I told my wife I had to flee to avoid arrest," Koshkin said. "Not where I intended to go. Safer for her not to know. Prince

Ilya will guess, I assume, but I saw no need to take him into my confidence. Let the others find out in due course. And you?"

Grigory raised a shoulder, as if shrugging off the question. "Likewise."

"Don't you trust Prince Ilya?" Koshkin asked, his curiosity genuine. His own suspicions tugged at him, although he could not identify a cause.

"Do you?"

"I can't say I do," Koshkin admitted after a pause. "But I couldn't stay in Moscow on the off chance he was lying. What did he tell you?"

"That the boyars doubted my loyalties. That the grand princess—or the council—would order my arrest at any moment. But I would have left anyway. What they did to Andrei's envoys stinks of corruption. It's an immoral court run by an immoral woman on behalf of a boy too young to hold the scepter. Whether Andrei wants the throne or not—and I believe he doesn't—the Russian lands need a man of integrity to rule them. And so I plan to tell him." Grigory's gloved hands gripped the reins hard, as if he clenched them around the grand princess's neck, and his horse shook its mane in protest. He gave no sign of noticing.

"My thoughts precisely," Koshkin said.

That ended conversation for a while. They rode steadily through the encircling woods, stopping only long enough to stretch their legs, grab a bite from their saddlebags, relieve themselves as needed, and rest the horses.

So far, Koshkin had heard no sounds of pursuit. Yet the urge to press on drove him. Sooner or later, someone would discover his flight from Moscow. Roxelana had no entrée into the government, let alone the palace, but suppose she had already thrown herself on Alexei's mercy? Of course, he would be in no hurry to get rid of her—Koshkin ignored the pang that thought caused—and his contacts with those in power did not far exceed Roxelana's own. Maria wouldn't turn her father in, but he wouldn't put it beyond the Kolychev clan to report a missing cousin.

Gospodi, that his future should depend on the will of principled idiots. Idiots who had long disliked him despite their family ties.

Later that day Nasan turned over supervision of the female servants to her housekeeper, told Pashka the steward to oversee the men, and ordered a small number of dishes and place settings laid out on a table in her mother-in-law's private sitting room. Since Lord Nikolai had left in the early morning for the Kremlin and Lady Natalya had elected to eat in her room, Nasan looked forward to a rare opportunity to share a midday meal with no one but her husband.

Alas, she and Daniil had just taken their places behind the trestle table when Pashka appeared, leading Alexei and Ruslan.

"Welcome." Nasan did not rise; at almost eight months with child, leaping to her feet had become a distant memory. But she did her best to infuse pleasure into her voice as she gestured at the table. "Please join us. I will send for additional place settings."

Alexei stepped forward and pressed his cheek against Nasan's, then pulled a small settle into place and sat. "I apologize, *sengel*, for this unannounced intrusion. We have news you need to hear." He held out a hand to Daniil, who leaned forward to shake it before resuming his seat. Ruslan also greeted Daniil before taking the remaining chair. The servants returned, performed their duties at the table, and distributed shallow lacquered bowls containing baked fish, noodles, wheat bread, and the first sorrel of the season.

Only after they left did Daniil reply. "News? What news?"

Alexei picked up a piece of bread, which he proceeded to tear into quarters. "Koshkin left at dawn," he said. "A few hours ahead of the grand princess's troops, who came to arrest him not long ago. Before they took Roxelana away with them, they told the steward that Koshkin went to Staritsa, based on information received—from whom, they did not say. The steward, thank God, had the wits to seek me out as soon as the troops left. Otherwise, I'd still know nothing about it." He threw the torn bread onto the fish. "Wherever Koshkin went, he'd better stay there. I'll have his guts for horse tack if he dares show his face here."

"But what did he do this time?" Nasan asked. "Oh, poor Maria!"

"Ass," Daniil chipped in, his voice furious. "I thought he had more sense. Has he been plotting behind our backs the whole time, then? And I watched him so carefully in Staritsa. May he break out in boils and develop the runs! What about his family?"

"Well, I don't know that he *deserved* arrest," Alexei said. "Maria insists he must have an enemy, and our failure to turn up anything incriminating suggests that he does. I don't blame him for running, either; I did the same thing myself. It's his not caring about his wife and children that has me riled. He left orders that his sons should live with his daughter Varvara, but that won't stop the authorities from throwing the boys in chains if they feel so inclined. I can look after his youngest daughter, but Roxelana's in custody already. Didn't Koshkin think about that?"

"And the tale affects you as well," Ruslan added.

"How?" Nasan asked.

Daniil spoke at the same time. "How so?"

"According to the grand princess's troops," Ruslan said, "as reported by the steward, Koshkin left with one of the Kolychev clan. Grigory Osipovich."

"My cousin." Daniil swore under his breath. "Then they probably *are* heading for Staritsa. He has long sympathized with Prince Andrei." He sat brooding for a while. "I'll talk to Papa. Damn Grigory. His behavior tarnishes our entire clan."

"And what of you?" Nasan asked her brother. "If troops came to arrest Koshkin, are you and Maria safe?"

"For the moment, I think, but my position could be compromised by association with him. I must speak with *Ata*. Today. He will rub my nose in the dirt, but there's no help for it. I'll admit that I made a mistake in choosing Koshkin as my sponsor and hope for the best." Alexei looked as if he had eaten meat left by scavengers on the steppe. "Curse all selfish bastards."

"That might work." Daniil sounded thoughtful. "If your father vouches for you, I mean. I doubt even Grand Princess Elena would contradict him."

Ruslan gave a snort, and Alexei's grim expression lightened. "Since he's twice her age and sees himself as Genghis reincarnate, I don't suppose she will. He won't hesitate to haul her over the coals if he thinks she's showing insufficient respect."

"In fact, he could become your biggest problem," Ruslan put in. "Suppose she throws *him* in jail to cool him down?"

That comment relieved the tension with an outburst of laughter. The conversation shifted to less fraught topics, and the food soon disappeared.

Alexei wasted no time in running his father to earth, eager to get the awkward conversation behind him as soon as possible. Talking with Bulat was difficult enough; imagining the potential for conflict made him itch, as if a pair of ant armies had decided to wage war with his skin as the battleground. He and Ruslan arrived at his parents' estate right after dinner.

Bulat was waiting for them in the room where they had met before the betrothal ceremony, with much the same expression on his face. Alexei's hackles rose before he had even crossed the threshold, but he reined in his temper. It annoyed him that two and a half months of marriage had left him in more of a supplicant's position than in the days before he had sealed his brand-new alliance with a bride, but the fault for that miscalculation did not lie with Bulat. And today he sought his father's support for his family, not for himself. He must keep that in mind no matter how hard his father's eyes or how angry and unforgiving his voice.

"Your patron has flown the coop, I hear." Bulat, as usual, went straight to the point. "I assume you want my help." He gestured at the benches that ran along one wall, and his two visitors sat.

Alexei leaned forward, elbows resting on his knees, so he could stare straight at his father. Best get this next sentence out of the way first, so they could move on to the business at hand. "You were right about Koshkin—and me. I should have come to you when I arrived from Crimea."

"Hmph." Bulat's face relaxed. The hawk's fierce glare shifted into something resembling intent watchfulness.

"But then it was my neck on the line," Alexei went on. "Now it's my wife's and my son's and her sister's." He held out his left arm, palm up, indicating Ruslan. "Ours too, but we are warriors. I came to ask if we can count on you to vouch for us. If not, I understand. But in that case I need to find a place of safety for those who depend on me. And if this royal squabble leads to bloodshed, then I also seek a guarantee that they will survive even if I don't."

Blunt to blunt—that approach worked best with Bulat. Alexei had planned his speech with that knowledge in mind: admit his fault, state his purpose, show courage and honor, leave his father a way out if his conscience did not permit him to fulfill the request. Learning to meet anger with reason rather than shouting had taken him more than a decade. He could only hope he had judged the present situation correctly.

Watching his father, for a hideous moment Alexei thought he had failed. He glanced at Ruslan, silent on his left, but his friend had fixed his eyes on Bulat. Alexei returned his attention to his father, who leaned back in his chair, not speaking, arms crossed over his chest, the same intent expression on his face. The sunlight filtering through the semitransparent window sparked glints in his gray hair, and dust motes dancing in the shaft formed a nimbus around his head, in stark contrast to the skeptical if not rejecting position of his arms and body.

"Will you fight under my command?" Bulat asked after a long and uncomfortable pause. "Both of you? Because there will be bloodshed. Either Andrei presents himself in Moscow as required, in which case the blood shed will be his, or we attack, with the usual prospects of injury and death. The generals have already made their plans. Your father-in-law has again backed the wrong prince."

"I know," Alexei said. "If the reports of his going to Staritsa are true—we have only the troops' word for that."

"It's confirmed," Bulat told him. "The generals sent scouts along the trail, but Koshkin and Kolychev had already reached Volok, so the scouts turned back."

"May all the demons of hell dance on his vitals," Alexei said. "He had to flee—I understand that—but why there? We argued the last time I saw him. He swore to me he had no plans to support Andrei. I told *him* that our alliance ended at the point where he endangered my family."

The hand that supported his chin clenched, and he saw his father's mouth tighten in response. He did not want to say what came next, but he had to. This was a test. He recognized that without being told. He could almost hear the words in Bulat's head. *Show me you've changed, that you can take orders as well as issue them. That you've grown up. Then I'll help you.*

It was a fair bargain. He was no longer sixteen. Time to give up childish resentment when the lives of real children were at stake. "And yes, I will fight under your command, if you vouch for me to the grand princess and help me protect those in my care." Alexei nodded at Ruslan. "My friend can speak for himself."

"I should be honored," Ruslan said. "Your reputation, Khan, inspires awe even in Crimea."

Smooth. Very smooth. Easy to see that Ruslan had not grown up under Bulat's harsh tutelage. But the words had an effect: Bulat's icy expression thawed; he even mustered a smile. The sight, so unexpected—Alexei last remembered seeing his father smile sometime around his own seventh birthday—provoked a flicker of warmth around his heart. Bulat, susceptible to flattery. Who would have guessed?

"Very well," Bulat said. "I will speak to the grand princess. Tell your wife that she and her sister have a home here if they need it. Your son is always welcome as a member of our lineage."

Alexei stood and bowed, hand over his heart. "Thank you, *Ata.* I appreciate your generosity of spirit."

And for the first time in years he meant it.

Chapter 20

MARIA'S SUMMONS TO COURT ARRIVED VIA THE MOUTH OF A gentry servitor not long after she had sent Lyuba and Timur to complete the lessons assigned to them by Father Job. Three days had passed since her father's flight from Moscow and Roxelana's arrest, and the summons from Grand Princess Elena boded ill. She questioned the man, but he repeated his message woodenly, revealing nothing of use.

The news could not be good. Rulers did not receive the wives and daughters of self-proclaimed traitors, which Papa, by choosing flight, had become. Why would Elena summon her if not to punish her for her father's sins? Alexei had assured her that his family would protect her and Lyuba no matter what, but he had not expected the grand princess to act so quickly. They could not flee to Sumbeka's house with Elena's man there at the door.

Since feigning death would not work—the servitor could swear she had received him standing—and no other excuse would serve, she agreed to accompany him to the Kremlin. She asked only for permission to change her clothes, which he granted. A quick command to Tanya saw him shown to a seat near the door, and Maria mounted the stairs, the housekeeper in her wake and the choicest of the epithets that Alexei had hurled at her absent father since they received the news of Papa's departure running through her brain.

Papa had abandoned them. To escape arrest, but that excuse just poured honey over a bitter gourd. He had saved his skin and left his family to suffer the consequences. He didn't care that he'd forced Alexei into an uncomfortable confrontation with his father, that Maria cringed at each knock on the door, or that Roxelana, whom he'd promised to love and protect, faced an uncertain future. No, he had slunk off with Grigory Kolychev, heading for Staritsa.

The refrain rang in her head as she climbed each new step, matching the angry rhythm of her feet, the drumming of her heels. *He doesn't care. He doesn't care. He doesn't care.* Then, in a twist that surprised her, *It's not my fault he doesn't care. He never wastes a thought on anyone besides himself.*

Her fingers tingled with the urge to smack him. Alexei had fled his lord in Crimea under similar circumstances, but he had had no family then. These days, he did whatever was necessary to protect those in his care. Not Papa! He had left his daughter to answer for his misdeeds before a sure-to-be livid grand princess.

What will happen to me? Will I be placed under arrest? Divorced and sent to a convent?

She wished Alexei was here, in the house. She needed his advice. Despite his limited familiarity with the Moscow court, his experience with difficult rulers far outweighed her own. But he had woken her at first light to say he had received orders from his father: something about calling up additional warriors for the coming campaign against Prince Andrei. He had promised to return by suppertime today. Until then she was on her own.

As she reached her room and, with Tanya's help, changed into robes more suitable to the grand princess's reception hall,

Maria turned over options in her mind. She could not refuse or delay. She could send a messenger to Sumbeka, but would that do any good? Only as Tanya draped a pearl-strewn collar over an outer gown the rich orange of the setting sun, with slits in the sleeves through which Maria's gold-embroidered tunic showed, did she remember that, thanks to two and a half months of lessons, she had the ability to write Alexei a note.

A flurry of commands, some hasty manipulation of pen and ink, and she had produced a short text close enough to legible for her purposes. *Summoned by Elena*, it said. *Back by supper. If not, look for me at the palace.—Kisses, M.*

Lamentably terse, she knew, but writing still challenged her, and the note conveyed enough information that its recipient could predict trouble. She handed the note to Tanya on her way out and asked her to give it to Alexei Bulatovich as soon as he returned.

The journey to the Kremlin, never long, seemed to fly on wings of anxiety and rage. The moment she stepped out of the closed carriage, Solomonida ran down the steps—not the ones Maria usually used but those previously pointed out to her as leading to the Faceted Palace, where ambassadors and other important (male) guests entered. Solomonida caught her arm and pulled her toward the Red Porch, which lined this side of the royal palace. The ever-present guards tried to block them at the door, but Solomonida waved them away. "She's with me," she announced with a regal self-confidence that the grand princess herself might have demonstrated.

Once they entered the main passageway, Solomonida pulled Maria aside. "It's going to be bad," she murmured. "Not fatal, but bad. And there's nothing I can do to stop it. So brace yourself. But when she's done with you, leave the chamber, then wait for me. There's something I must show you. Now follow me." And before Maria could comment, question, or protest, Solomonida lifted her robes in one hand and took off down the passageway at a speed a hare would envy.

Maria ran to keep up, but she could not catch Solomonida before the doors to the reception hall came into view. Her quarry spun on a red leather heel and pointed at the double doors, then slipped through a smaller portal and disappeared from Maria's line of sight. Her fears coalesced into one burning question.

What will happen to me?

Bad but not fatal, Solomonida had said. What did that mean? Arrest? Exile? Knouting?

Maria's pulse raced and her stomach whirled as she imagined herself captive or flogged. Seeing no alternative, she ignored her uncooperative body and forced her feet to propel her through the double doors.

At first the scene inside did not support her fears. Only ladies filled the room; even the usual quartet of honor guards had abandoned their posts. Her spirits rose—to the level of her ankles, if no more—as her fears receded.

Then she noticed how the women regarded her. Not one friendly face greeted her—except Solomonida, who had somehow arrived via a circuitous route and stood behind Grand Princess Elena's right shoulder. The others—friends, enemies, even relatives—stared at Maria as if they had never seen her before and never wanted to set eyes on her again. The woman scribe she had noticed on her first visit stood at her lectern, a pile of paper in front of her and a quill pen at the ready. Maria's brief glimpse of hope dove under the water and disappeared.

From her throne-like chair Elena stared with the lack of expression one might expect from the ice maiden in a fairy tale. When Maria glanced at her, she beckoned. Too terrified to speak, Maria stepped forward, knelt, and placed her forehead on the tiled floor. Not fatal, she repeated silently, as if it were a talisman. Not fatal.

"Rise," Elena said, and Maria stood.

"Maria Fyodorovna," Elena continued, her voice harsh. "You have disappointed us."

A titter swept around the assembled ladies, sounding like a flock of menacing birds.

"In what way, My Lady?" Maria pushed the words through her constricted throat. She could manage little more than a whisper, but Elena heard her.

"Your father has taken up arms against us." The answer—so stark, so cold—caused Maria's gorge to rise. "You promised us that he would do no such thing."

"I believed he would not, My Lady. He did not share his plans with me." Again she bowed to the ground. "Forgive me, Grand Princess. My husband and I are wholly committed to your cause. Alexei is the son of Bulat Khan, who has served you well."

More titters of skepticism and disdain sounded from among the assembled ladies, and Maria shuddered. In believing she had friends here, she had deluded herself. She understood that now. And she hated them—every privileged, *secure* insider laughing at her, rejecting her. Even her cousins, shame be upon them. She vowed never to speak to any of them again.

This time Elena did not command her to rise. Maria stared at the floor, willing it to open and swallow her up, but it remained solid, unyielding as the grand princess herself. In the absence of speech the scratching of the quill pen against the paper sounded loud, reminding her that her mortification was being recorded. The rustle of silk sleeves, the tap of Elena's fingers against the wood, the breeze from an open vent, the swish of a veil charged the room with an ominous energy, like a lightning bolt waiting to strike.

Arrest? Exile? Flogging? A convent?

The silence extended into infinity before Elena spoke. "Leave our court. Until we summon you again, you will not see the bright eyes of myself or my son. Perhaps your father duped you, as you say. Perhaps he did not. But you have disappointed us. Go."

Maria did not protest. There would be no point. And Solomonida was right. Bad, humiliating, horrible—but not fatal. She could survive this formal disgrace.

Assuming, that is, she could leave the room without sobbing. Under the stern gaze of fifty women Maria touched her forehead to the floor once more, then pushed herself to her feet and backed out of the reception hall. She did not once raise her eyes above her knees. Heartless snickers and chatter swirled around her ears, causing her to cringe with each step. And the unceasing scratch, scratch of the pen.

It took forever to reach the double doors, and by the time she got there her cheeks burned like the flame in a February furnace. Her hands and feet felt numb; her head pounded; her stomach ached worse than it now did each morning, when only dry bread would stay down; and her limbs trembled as if she had contracted an out-of-season fever. But somehow she made it, and when the doors at last closed behind her, Solomonida waited on the other side. Without a word she wrapped both arms around Maria. Their long-simmering feud, already on the mend, dissolved in a flood of tears.

When the weeping stopped, Maria followed the tug of Solomonida's hand through a bewildering series of rooms and up a staircase, ending in a small space that appeared to consist mostly of a large viewing area covered with a light curtain hanging from a set of copper rings.

Solomonida pressed a finger against her lips and walked toward the opening. Trying not to rustle her skirts, Maria followed. Through the curtain, translucent as her own gauze veil, she gazed into the room below, and her mouth dropped open. Hundreds of candles flickered and guttered, emitting a strong scent of beeswax and enough smoke to obscure, then reveal, those within. A boy about Lyuba's age—dressed in elaborate gold robes, a wide pearl collar, and a sable-trimmed cap of Tatar design—sat cross-legged on a decorated ivory throne: Grand Prince Ivan himself, looking as bored as any six-year-old trapped in the midst of an adult conclave would look. Maria gaped, stunned by the knowledge that she was staring into the main reception room of the Faceted Palace— the flower-decorated, icon-encrusted, gilded walls with their arched ceiling points meant it could be nothing else—at what the clamor of men's voices suggested was a meeting of the most prominent nobles of the realm.

She guessed that Solomonida had brought her here for a specific purpose. They could not move, let alone talk, without drawing the attention of those on the other side. But they could see and hear what went on below. And so long as they remained absolutely still, the curtain would obscure their faces and perhaps even their presence.

Not every voice or face was familiar, but Maria identified the main speakers without difficulty. Aunt Theodosia's husband, Uncle Mikhail, of course. Prince Ivan Telepnev, who had attended her wedding. Prince Vasily Shuisky had been at the wedding too, with his disgusting nephew Ilya the bottom pincher. And she could not mistake Nikolai Kolychev, her father-in-law for three years. The others—well, she'd have to hope they either said nothing important or someone called them by name.

She noticed that the men ignored Grand Prince Ivan except on one occasion when he tried to leave his throne; then Telepnev walked over, placed a hand on the boy's shoulder, and urged him to stillness. Every time she glanced at Ivan after that, he sat slouched in his chair, glowering and fidgeting. Maria, imagining Timur in Ivan's position, felt sorry for the little grand prince. A child had to learn the skills he would need as an adult, but it was difficult for someone so young to sit for hours in court robes while grown men discussed policy around him as if he were not present.

Solomonida had not brought them here to worry about the grand prince, however, so Maria thrust the boy from her mind and focused on the boyars, who were discussing the arrest of Prince Andrei's envoys. Nikolai Kolychev did not approve, and said so. Telepnev disagreed. "The grand princess ordered it," he said. "It was a necessary step. We are sending three holy men to bring Prince Andrei to his senses. The hostages will ensure that he takes our demands seriously, and I will have sufficient troops in position to enforce any agreement they reach. We cannot permit him to go on flouting the grand prince's authority. It sets a bad precedent."

Nikolai grumbled but did not persist. Another voice spoke up, one of those unfamiliar to Maria. "And what of Koshkin? Not to mention your own clansman Grigory, Nikolai Borisovich. Running off to Staritsa as if we were the enemy. Do we stand back and let them go?"

"Grigory has brothers in Andrei's service," Nikolai said. "If he has indeed defected, I will cast him out. But suppose he has not switched sides but instead left to urge his brothers to join us? As for Koshkin, he does not answer to me or I to him."

"Although his daughter married your son," the unknown speaker replied, his sneer audible. A short man with lank brown hair falling to his high collar, as if making up for its absence on the crown of his head, he made a dismissive gesture that sparked a flash of recall. Maria had seen him boring Papa to tears at the wedding, but she had forgotten his name.

"An arrangement we both later agreed had been a mistake," Nikolai said smoothly. "And long over, to boot."

"Enough squabbling." Prince Vasily Shuisky stepped forward, pushing the unknown speaker to one side. Maria concentrated her attention on him. Even a neophyte like herself knew that Prince Vasily had more influence than anyone at court except the grand princess and her favorite. The court ladies whispered that Telepnev wanted to push Shuisky aside and grab full power. True or not, the rumor received some support from the glare with which Shuisky regarded the favorite, who reacted by spreading his feet and crooking his elbows in a warlike stance.

"Koshkin left," Prince Vasily said, "because my nephew Prince Ilya told him he would face arrest if he stayed. Ilya wanted to flush out the traitors, and he succeeded."

Maria clapped a hand over her mouth to keep her gasp unheard.

That squirming beast Prince Ilya tricked Papa! Why?

She didn't believe Ilya had been flushing out traitors. Papa had ranted in private about the grand princess, true, but he had done that for years. He had sworn he didn't intend to support Prince Andrei, agreed that Andrei had no chance of success. He was *not* a traitor—until Prince Ilya frightened him with threats of arrest.

"How noble of Prince Ilya to undertake this effort on the crown's behalf." Telepnev looked as skeptical as he sounded. "But would it not have worked better for him to report his suspicions to those of us in a position to capture Koshkin and Kolychev *before* they fled?"

Interesting. Telepnev did not believe Prince Vasily either. And he was, without question, displeased.

Another quick glance revealed Prince Vasily shuffling his feet. "Alas, you speak truth," he said. "My nephew did not tell me what he had in mind. When I questioned him, he admitted that he lusted after Koshkin's wife. It angered him that another man had acquired such a prize—and boasted about it. In short, he carried a personal grudge against the man that clouded his judgment."

Roxelana? Ilya betrayed Papa to get his paws on Roxelana? Curse the day Papa brought her into our family!

"Indeed," Telepnev said, his voice dry. "If his lust and desire for revenge caused him to push Koshkin into flight, those emotions did more than cloud his judgment. They obliterated it."

Prince Vasily, his face taut with discomfort, acknowledged this comment with a small bow. "I believe he feared that Koshkin might again escape punishment. If his wife accompanied him into exile, my nephew would lose his chance with her."

Roxelana accompany a husband into exile? What a ridiculous thought!

Prince Vasily cleared his throat. "But thanks to Ilya's intervention you must admit that we now have no doubt about where Koshkin's loyalties lie."

"What of the woman?" Uncle Mikhail asked. "And do Koshkin and Kolychev retain their properties despite their treason?"

"No," Telepnev said. "Confiscate them. Our troops have already taken the woman into custody. Transfer her to Prince Vasily's estate. Let the Shuisky clan maintain her at its own expense to remind your nephew, Prince Vasily, not to meddle in the affairs of government. And if that is settled, let us adjourn. We have much to oversee before we meet again. Tomorrow at the same time?"

A chorus of yeses greeted this suggestion. The noblemen filed from the room, led by a small grand prince miraculously restored to life. As silence fell over the room, Maria turned toward Solomonida, who again touched a finger to her lips.

Chapter 21

LEAVING RUSLAN AT THE ENTRYWAY TO HIS OWN SECTION of the house, Alexei took the stairs two steps at a time, eager to see how Maria was doing. Despite his assurances that his family would protect her and her sister no matter what, she had wandered about the house in an uncharacteristic silence since hearing of her father's defection, as if crushed by the news. Only his own father's summons had gotten him up and on the road so early this morning despite an unexpected urge to stay and console her. Fortunately he had located the needed warriors without difficulty and kept his promise to return by supper. The position of the sun marked the time still as mid-afternoon. He hoped his early arrival would comfort her—encourage her, perhaps, to accept that he would not desert her as her father had done.

The first sign of trouble came when he ran into Tanya in the hallway leading to his wife's favorite room. The housekeeper was biting her lip and twisting a piece of paper in her hands, a far cry from her usual bustling, cheerful self.

"Sultan!" she cried, using his Tatar title, the moment he shut the outside door behind him. "I'm so glad you're back." She held out the paper. "A man came from the palace an hour or two ago and took our tsarevna off with him. She left this for you."

"Took her off with him?" Alexei didn't like the sound of that one bit. He grabbed the paper from the housekeeper's hand and perused it. "What did he want with her?"

"I don't know, Sultan," Tanya said. "He demanded she leave right away. She objected, but he refused to take no for an answer. He allowed her just enough time to change her clothes."

Disturbing news. In Alexei's experience royalty and its officials preferred the slow, deliberate path. They compelled diplomats and even their own nobles to kick their heels for weeks or months to emphasize the prestige of those who ruled and the powerlessness of those who served. Had his plan to protect his wife already failed?

He turned back to the paper in his hand. The writing had the careful rounded appearance of a child's, and the ink had smeared in several places. In the dim light he struggled to make out the words. "Come with me," he told Tanya after a while. Still wringing her hands, she followed him into Maria's sewing room.

The sunlight streaming through the clear panes revealed the message: *Summoned by Elena. Back by supper. If not, look for me at the palace.—Kisses, M.*

"Not terribly helpful, is it?" Alexei frowned at the simple lines. Still, it seemed that his wife expected to return. Perhaps he had overreacted.

He didn't believe it. "Where at the palace?" he asked Tanya. "It's a big place. I can't ride in and demand they fetch her."

When she held up her palms to express her inability to answer, he frowned at the note once more. "I can ask, I suppose."

"Yes, Sultan," Tanya said. "What should I do?"

"Prepare supper," he said. "And if my wife returns before I do, send a message at once."

He heard her assent but did not acknowledge it. He was already running down the stairs and calling for his men. The groom had not even had a chance to unsaddle Ajdar.

This time Prince Andrei deigned to receive Koshkin and Grigory Kolychev the morning after their arrival, in the same hall where he had met with them before and with the same complement of chamberlain and men-at-arms. Standing tall in his princely robes, Andrei wasted no time on preliminaries but went straight to the point. "What do you two want this time?"

A discouraging start. "We came to pledge our swords in your service, Prince." Koshkin bowed and, when Grigory stared dumbfounded at Andrei, nudged him in the ribs with an elbow until Grigory bowed as well. "Word has it that Grand Princess Elena intends to attack you, despite your attempt to appease her. Many of the Moscow nobles disapprove; we are only the first to abandon so vile an enterprise. The arrest of your envoys—"

"What!" Andrei said. "That bitch has arrested Pronsky and his men?"

"Yes, Prince. Word has it that she has confined them to your quarters in the Kremlin." Koshkin once more prodded his log of a companion until Grigory mumbled assent.

"The arrest has alarmed many," Koshkin went on, risking exaggeration for the sake of effect. "The Cheliadnins become over-mighty, and the others wonder who will suffer next." He did not mention the threat of his own arrest, still less that he had only Prince Ilya Shuisky's word for the Moscow nobles' support. Such details would not help his case.

"And I come to join my brethren," Grigory Kolychev put in. "I have long deplored your sister-in-law's treatment of you and your brother." He indicated Koshkin with a twist of his hand. "My friend Koshkin hesitates to remind you of his past service to Prince Yuri Ivanovich, but I know you have not forgotten it."

Koshkin cringed. Curse Grigory for his loquaciousness. Koshkin's past service to Andrei's older brother was the last thing he wanted Andrei to recall at this moment, given its unsatisfactory outcome. To turn Andrei's thoughts in another direction, Koshkin said, "We will do what we can for you, Prince, if you accept us into your service. But I suggest that you prepare for battle. Gather your men, develop strategy and tactics, decide whether you will advance or retreat." He bowed once more. "It would be my great honor to advise you. As a general I enjoyed considerable success."

"As did I," Andrei said. "Much good it did me—risking my neck to protect my nephew and his sorceress of a mother."

Grigory, devil take him, kept his mouth shut. The man spoke when he should stay quiet and turned into a very stone when speech was required. Even a second nudge to the ribs did not jar loose a word.

"That is why we came, Prince," Koshkin said when it became obvious he would receive no help from his companion. "To support you against the sorceress and her son. If you will be so gracious as to permit us."

An uncomfortable silence followed. Andrei regarded them steadily from under hooded lids and stroked the tip of his short, stylish beard. He beckoned to the court chamberlain, Gleb Glebovich Bogdanov, whom Koshkin remembered from a shared assignment in Smolensk, before Bogdanov received orders to present himself in Staritsa. They had not liked each other then, and Koshkin saw no reason to expect any improvement.

"What do you think, Gleb?" Andrei asked. "Shall we grant their request, even though Koshkin deserted my brother in his hour of need? Or shall we treat them as my charming sister-in-law chose to treat *my* envoys?"

Koshkin suppressed a curse. He should have guessed that Andrei might choose to retaliate in kind for the capture of his envoys, no matter that Koshkin bore no responsibility for the men's detention. Why did he never think far enough ahead?

Bogdanov stepped forward. "At this point, I trust no one who travels here from Moscow. I last saw these two persuading you to accede to Grand Princess Elena's demands. No doubt they spied for her as well. And Prince Ilya Shuisky warned me about them, Prince, when he met with me. I think we should imprison them until we have a chance to verify their story." His sneer as he dipped his head in Koshkin's direction justified Koshkin's worst expectations.

"Elena won't care," Koshkin told him. No point in concealing the whole truth now. "She wanted to arrest us both. And Prince Ilya was the one who urged us to join you!"

No one responded. If anything, the despicable Bogdanov's sneer intensified.

"Do it." Andrei waved a commanding hand at his guard. "Not a dungeon. Match the accommodations that, according to these two, now house my envoys. Let the grand princess's spies alert her that she's not the only one who can take hostages."

As the guards escorted Koshkin out, he groaned inwardly. At this rate, Moscow might seize Staritsa before he had the longed-for chance to exercise his political skills. In that case he'd end up worse than before.

When sounds of movement in the chamber below stopped, Solomonida tapped Maria on the shoulder and pointed in the direction from which they had entered. With extreme caution Maria sidled toward the first doorway, peered around the edge, then stepped through. Solomonida caught her elbow and pulled her toward the stairway. They ran down it as quickly and quietly as possible.

Fortunately no one had seen them enter or leave the small space. Their presence in this section of the palace might raise questions, but they were close enough to the women's quarters that discovery would not instantly brand them as engaged in some illicit activity.

Before Maria could continue to the next entryway, Solomonida pulled her in the opposite direction. "Don't speak," she whispered in Maria's ear. "Look like you know where you're going." Maria did her best to comply, although she had no idea where Solomonida was heading.

In silence the two women crossed one passageway, passing the double doors that opened onto the Faceted Palace on their left, and came out in another, much larger corridor with a pair of the usual white-clad guards at one end. Solomonida released Maria long enough to pull her veil, then Maria's, into place. Then she tucked her hand in the crook of Maria's arm, tipped her head sideways, and launched into a string of innocuous chatter, interspersed with girlish laughter, that made her sound as if she had no brains whatsoever.

Maria, catching her companion's intent if not its purpose, joined in, although she could not swear her remarks made sense. A difficult deception, with her heart pounding loud enough for the guards to hear and her stomach churning. But as they passed the guards, who looked down their aristocratic noses at two silly veiled females on their way out of the palace, she understood. Solomonida had made them not worth challenging.

Very clever. How many times, Maria wondered, had Solomonida used this trick, counting on others' willingness to underestimate her?

And who has underestimated her more than I?

The thought shamed her, but she had no time to dwell on it. Past the guards, down a stairway, and they emerged in the Annunciation Cathedral. The ranked saints on the exquisite iconostasis, their gold-rimmed frames encasing the finest work of Russia's master icon painters, seemed to reach out to her as she passed by. At last she and Solomonida emerged into the cool air of late afternoon. For the first time since the summons, normal breathing became possible.

"May the Holy Mother bless you!" Maria told Solomonida, who had abandoned her mindless giggling for full-throated laughter and a celebratory twirl. "I don't know how I would have survived that without you! What was that place?"

"Where Grand Princess Elena goes to observe the council meetings. We ladies-in-waiting often accompany her there."

Maria's pounding heart threatened to drop into her toes. "*Gospodi*, suppose she had decided to observe this one?"

"I knew she wouldn't. Not after that scene with you. And don't thank me yet," Solomonida said. "We still have to get you out of here so I can return to my duties. I pleaded a headache, but that means I have to find my way back to the room where they sent me to rest before the other ladies finish their dinner."

"Oh, but you must leave at once, then." Maria clasped Solomonida's hands. "And please say you will not go hungry because of me!"

"I will beg some soup and bread," Solomonida said. "Don't worry about me. But I can't walk off and leave you here. Where is your coachman?"

"At the house. The grand princess's courier brought me here." Maria thought quickly. She could *not* cause more trouble for Solomonida, who had already done so much. "If I can send a message," she said. "The priests will let me wait near the doors of the cathedral, surely."

"I don't think you'll have to." Solomonida, laughter audible in her voice, pointed to Maria's right. "That horseman looks rather familiar."

Maria spun on her heel and gasped. Of the many incredible events of the day, this one topped the lot. Her husband, riding Ajdar at a perilously fast clip for such a crowded setting, crossed the square between the cathedrals and halted at the barrier, so close to the pointed sticks she feared they would impale his horse. His personal bodyguard skidded to a stop behind him, milling around like a tiny horde. She turned back her veil so he would recognize her. He dismounted and held out a hand, the other gentling his mount.

Solomonida hugged her. "Problem solved."

"I can't thank you enough." Maria returned the hug with vigor. "We will talk soon, yes?"

"Yes," Solomonida said. "I will bring Anna to see you tomorrow. Don't keep your lord waiting."

Alexei did look impatient, or perhaps concerned. But he had come to fetch her. He had not left her to cope alone as Papa had done. Heartened by the thought, Maria hugged Solomonida once more and ran to the gate. As she stepped through, Alexei swung her sideways onto Ajdar's back, then mounted behind her. "How did you know I needed you?" she asked. "I'm so glad you came."

"How did I know?" He turned the horse with one hand on the reins and set it trotting toward the moat. The men fell into place around them. His right arm encircled her waist. "You left a note. Have you forgotten?"

She had forgotten. So much had happened since, his arrival seemed like a miracle.

He grinned at her surprise. "A cryptic note, I must say. You hinted you might be in trouble but not where in this monstrosity to look. So I decided to make a pest of myself throughout the Kremlin until somebody told me where to find you. Running into you wasn't part of the plan. Why did the grand princess summon you?"

"Oh, Alexei, it was dreadful!" At the memory the tears she had thought long shed gathered again at the back of her throat. "I wished I were *dead.*"

He kissed her cheek before dropping her veil into place. "Don't cry, sweetheart. I'm here, you're safe, and I much prefer you alive. Although that note of yours almost sent me to an early grave. Tell me what happened."

So Maria did, between sobs that abated as her tale proceeded. She was still talking when they reached the house. Alexei sent Lyuba and Timur to eat with Ruslan (an opportunity that caused them to leap for joy), so he could be alone with his wife, and they were halfway through supper before she remembered to ask about the task he had performed for his father.

As a prison the quarters assigned to Koshkin and Grigory Kolychev had much to recommend them. However hostile, Bogdanov had respected his royal master's orders, and other than the guards outside the door the connecting rooms in which he had ordered the visitors confined exemplified opulence and comfort. Crimson velvet hangings surrounded the bed Koshkin would occupy, whereas those in Grigory's room were the color of fir trees in winter. Otherwise the two chambers looked much the same: carpeted floors, painted walls, small-paned windows too high from the ground and narrow to facilitate escape, oak bed frames and chests, covered window seats, chair and table with writing supplies, candles both in sconces and arrayed atop the larger pieces of furniture, solid doors with metal locks and large keys removed at the moment of entry.

Even the food was enjoyable: rich borsht filled with chunks of beef and pork; wheat bread dark of crust and soft inside, with airy pockets where the soup lingered; a plate of sliced cucumbers brined with dill; brown ale spiced with the tangy flavor of hops and sweetened with honey to make it palatable.

All quite amenable, except for the lurking guards and the dullness of Koshkin's companion, who exclaimed nonstop about Prince Ilya's treachery, Bogdanov's arrogance, Prince Andrei's ingratitude, and the fecklessness of his own relatives, who had failed to speak up on his behalf. That said relatives had also not defended Koshkin seemed to trouble Grigory not one whit.

"I can't imagine what Prince Ilya was thinking either," Koshkin said in response to the umpteenth repetition of this particular complaint. "Andrei has reason to suspect anyone from Moscow. I hope he changes his mind, but I don't blame him for retaliating after his sister-in-law's attack on *his* envoys. As for Bogdanov, he thinks himself the equivalent of the emperor in Constantinople and always has. And who's to say your brothers know you're here? We need to convince Andrei that we have his best interests at heart. Then we can worry about the rest."

Grigory subsided into grumbling. Koshkin took the opportunity to check the walls for irregularities, although a secret passage was too much to hope for. If such things existed here, Andrei must know better than to confine unwanted guests in rooms that had them. They stood a better chance of bribing a guard—an option to keep in mind if attempts to secure their release by more straightforward means failed. Otherwise, Koshkin admitted—to himself if not to his dimwitted companion—the situation appeared dire. He couldn't return to Moscow without fear of arrest and execution, and he couldn't accept prolonged captivity in Staritsa, soon to become the target of Grand Princess Elena's rage.

His appetite lost, Koshkin abandoned what remained of his meal and prowled the room, searching for an escape route while pondering approaches that might convince Prince Andrei and his advisers that he and Grigory came in peace.

The search proved ineffective, and the ideas skittered uncooperatively at the back of his mind. Grigory's useless rehashing of their predicament continued, even though Koshkin ignored every infuriating word. He had circled their prison three times before his eye alighted on pen, paper, and ink.

He couldn't talk, but he could write. Pushing past Grigory, he said, "Go and whine in the other room. I have an idea that may save our necks."

"What?"

"I'll tell you when it works." Koshkin picked up the quill and examined it. It had a clean point. He drew a sheet of paper toward him, dipped the quill in the ink, and began.

Prince Andrei Ivanovich, he wrote, *I offered my service in good faith, whatever that blackguard Shuisky told you. And I have valuable information. Release me, and I will share with you my knowledge about your friends in Moscow.*

He avoided mentioning Grigory Kolychev. Let Grigory sit here as the lone hostage, bemoaning his fate, while Koshkin assumed the position of power that had so long eluded him. He risked everything on one calculated move. But when had he ever done otherwise?

"What are you saying to him?" Grigory dragged the paper from Koshkin's hands and held it up to the light, as if the letters formed some kind of talisman that he could absorb through his eyes. Koshkin had never exulted so much in the effort he had exerted to learn the alphabet's mystique.

"Why, what else would I say?" he asked, keeping his face and voice guileless. "That we left Moscow out of the pure desire to enter Andrei's service, and we beg that he will give us a second chance."

Grigory nodded and rather sheepishly put the paper in Koshkin's hands. A quick dusting of sand, a tap on the door, an explanation to the guard outside, a few coins changing hands, and the deed was done. Now he need only concoct a story to pour into Andrei's ears if the ruse worked.

His appetite restored, Koshkin returned to his supper. Nothing to do now but wait.

Chapter 22

Staritsa, Late April 1537

THE NEXT MORNING KOSHKIN AWOKE FILLED WITH ANTICI-
pation. How soon would he receive a response to his letter?
Surely Andrei could not refuse the lure laid out for him. Information about "friends" in Moscow—if Koshkin had to say
it himself (and he did, because no one else knew what he had
written), that approach had been inspired. A quick release, a
meeting with the prince, and Koshkin would have the influence for which he yearned. He could already taste the triumph.

The first setback to this pleasant dream came in the form
of surly guards carrying water and cloths for washing.

"Well," Koshkin demanded. "What says your prince? Do
we go free?"

The guards shuffled their feet as they crossed the room
and deposited their burden on a flat-topped chest. Koshkin
responded with his haughtiest stare. Perhaps the dolts were
mute. But as they clomped back to the doorway without lifting
their gaze from the floor, one of them mumbled, "Food next."

"Is that any way to address a nobleman?" Koshkin snapped,
but the dolts had left.

Without turning the key in the lock. Koshkin bolted for the
exit. He had crossed half the room when the door burst open

and a nobleman with a strong resemblance to Grigory strode in. Stopped in his tracks, Koshkin glowered. Could he slip past unnoticed?

No. The new arrival blocked the doorway. From the man's hair (ample), complexion (ruddy), and beard (bushy), combined with the length of his stride and the vigor with which he belted the word "brother," Koshkin assessed his age at around thirty. Boots of scarlet leather, felt trousers, long quilted coat, and a fur-trimmed hat suggested he either planned to ride or had come straight from the stables. Another amiable Kolychev idiot, he guessed.

Grigory howled with joy and embraced the newcomer. Koshkin interrupted what looked set to develop into a long exchange of apologies, compliments, and queries about family members. "Who are you?"

"Denis Osipovich." The man didn't even have the grace to turn his head.

"And what brings you here?" Koshkin strove to maintain his patience. Did these fools have nothing on their minds besides some cousin's this or aunt's that? "Has Andrei agreed to receive us?"

"Yes, yes," Denis said. "Not to receive you, but you are free to walk around the palace."

"And what changed his mind? The letter I sent?" It was like leading a foal around a paddock. Koshkin clenched and unclenched his hands to keep them away from Denis's throat.

As usual, Grigory was no help, distracting his brother with pointless comments instead of concentrating on the task at hand. Koshkin asked his question twice more before getting an offhand response.

"Couple of the Moscow men confirmed that Elena doesn't like you," Denis said. "That rumors have swirled for months that you planned to join Andrei. And since no one cares about you staying locked up here, you're free to go. Just don't poke your nose where you shouldn't or you'll find yourself in a real cell."

With that Denis hauled his brother Grigory off to pay his respects to the rest of their numerous family. Koshkin washed his face and hands, changed his robe for one more appropriate to a royal presentation, and left to pursue the meeting he craved. His concocted story of support for Prince Andrei among the Moscow nobles—adapted from the list of names that Prince Ilya Shuisky, the bastard, had mumbled into his ear during that fateful meeting a few days ago—lay coiled in the back of his brain, ready for use at the first opportunity.

Couriers from the Kremlin reached Bulat's house the day after Maria's formal disgrace. She knew because she was standing at the top of the stairs with her husband, about to go inside for the midday meal, when a Tatar messenger galloped into the courtyard. "Alexei Sultan," he shouted.

Alexei sent her a questioning glance, then leaned over the banister. "Here," he called. A flood of Tatar, too swift for Maria's limited skills to decipher, followed. She stood, hands twisting her sleeves, until the exchange ended in tones from her husband that even she recognized as a series of commands. He drew back, and the messenger rode away.

"What's happening?" She struggled to control her anxiety, without success. Her throat felt tight, and she heard the edge of fear in her voice.

"The muster." Alexei caressed her cheek. "That was my father's man conveying his orders. We march in four days. Grand Princess Elena and her advisers plan to send three of your most prestigious clerics to shame Prince Andrei into obedience, but this time they will back up their demands with steel. If Prince Andrei refuses to heed the monks and attempts to flee, we capture him and convey him to Moscow by force."

So the moment of separation was near. She had known it would happen: the presence of a highborn husband was a precious gift delimited by time. Boris's departure had invariably come as a relief. Not so Alexei's.

"Four days," she said, trying not to panic. "So soon. I hoped …" She couldn't finish the sentence. Despite Alexei's casual displays of affection, their passionate nights, his expressed desire to protect her and Lyuba, she could not fool herself into believing that her husband loved her. Sometimes, basking in the pleasure of his company, she thought otherwise, but too soon she sensed the barriers he raised against the world. Then the doubts crept in once more, and the whispering specters of her childhood warned her that no one valued her or ever would. Even her mother had deserted her, just as her father had lost whatever affection he had once felt for her mother when baby after endless baby robbed Mama of her looks and vitality.

Maria did not share these thoughts with her husband. Alexei had spent his life at war, like every other man of his rank. He must take its demands for granted. To hold him back with protestations that she wished he would stay with her would perplex or irritate him. Her mother had taught her that, too.

"Why, sweetheart." He bent and kissed her nose. "I do believe you'll miss me. But don't worry. I'm one of thousands, and I've survived many a campaign. I'll be back in Moscow interfering with your housekeeping before the servants have time to wipe the dust of my departure from the floors."

She reached for his hand and pressed it against her lips. "Yes, I will miss you."

He hugged her. "And I you, sweetheart. Does that surprise you?"

She nodded.

"Silly girl. Don't you know I care for you?" Without waiting for an answer—which Maria could not have given if she'd tried—he tugged her toward the dining hall. "Let's eat. Then I must visit my father. Come with me. That lovely horse of yours needs the exercise, and my stepmother will be delighted to see you."

"I'd like that," she said.

As they ate, his words sang like a chant in her ears. *I will miss you. I care for you.*

Did she dare believe?

I will miss you. I care for you. Silly girl, don't you know?

Maria shivered. Alexei caught her around the waist, pulled her close, whispered in her ear. "Are you cold? I can warm you up."

Silly girl, afraid to take the risk. Maria wavered, teetering on the edge of surrender before rallying enough to kiss his cheek. "When we get back from your parents'," she whispered in turn.

After all, she could count on only four more days.

Solomonida arrived with Anna in tow just as Maria and her family finished their meal. Lyuba and Anna stared at each other, shuffling their feet and looking uncomfortable, until Maria had the happy idea of introducing their dolls. Before long the two girls were giggling and chattering in a way that left Timur, arms crossed over his chest and foot tapping, quite left out.

"You can come with us, Timur," Alexei said. The boy's face lightened. "Go and tell the grooms to get the horses ready."

"Why don't you come too?" Maria asked Solomonida. "The girls will do fine here with Alina, and I would love you to meet my mother-in-law. I promised Alexei I would ride with him, but your coachman can follow us."

Solomonida agreed without hesitation, and Maria led her upstairs while she changed into her riding clothes. Solomonida exclaimed at the trousers but enthused over Maria's robes and pointed hat, with its gauze veil floating from the tip. "Why, you do look like a Tatar tsarevna in that outfit!" she said. "I wish I had such gorgeous clothes. Do you ride unveiled?"

Maria pulled the gauze over her face and tucked it into the high collar of her jacket. "Not in a crowd. I could, but I've worn the veil for so long it makes me uncomfortable to show my face on the street." She pulled the gauze free again and flipped it so that it fell down her back. "But if it inhibits my vision, then I don't wear it." She took Solomonida's arm. "Let's go."

Soon she was on Kumai, Alexei at her side—every moment with him made precious by his imminent departure, her thoughts aglow with the memory of his words. Timur rode between his father and Ruslan, his upright stance and beaming face revealing his pride at occupying the position of Alexei's second-in-command. Guards surrounded them, and from time to time Maria turned her head to check on Solomonida's carriage.

They soon covered the short distance to Bulat and Sumbeka's estate, and Maria found herself reluctant to dismount from Kumai after so short a time. "We'll take a longer road home," Alexei told her when she mentioned this. "The horses need the exercise—Ajdar, especially, if he is to carry me on campaign. You will have to make time to ride Kumai while I'm away, even if you restrict yourself to the courtyard."

"Lyuba will ride with me, I'm sure," Maria said. "And Timur."

Alexei helped Solomonida from her carriage, then escorted both women inside before leaving for the meeting with his father. Timur trotted at his side.

"*Gospodi*, but he is charming," Solomonida murmured when Alexei and his son turned a corner. "If Semyon had had one-quarter of his manners, how different my life would have been."

"I'm so sorry your father married you to that monster." Maria ushered Solomonida toward her mother-in-law's sitting room. "Come and meet my *kaenana*." Solomonida's eyebrows rose at the unfamiliar word, and Maria grinned. "Mother-in-law. She insists I use the Tatar term, and as you'll see, when she insists, one does not refuse." She opened the door, poked her head around the edge, and said, "Nasan!"

A cry of joy sounded. Maria pulled Solomonida forward and into the room. Palms pressed together, she bowed to her mother-in-law and introduced Solomonida, then crossed the room and touched her cheek first to Sumbeka's, then to her sister-in-law's. "I didn't expect to see you here," she told Nasan.

Solomonida bowed in turn. "Welcome," Sumbeka said. "I remember you from the wedding. Both weddings, in fact—my son's and my daughter's."

The words were courteous enough, but the constraint in Sumbeka's voice caught Maria's attention. Solomonida's husband had killed Sumbeka's younger son. They had not known that at Nasan's wedding, and of course Semyon had not attended Maria's, but so deep an injury could not heal in so short a time—or, perhaps, ever.

Solomonida must have heard the constraint too, because she hesitated before saying, "I grieve for your loss. Semyon was a hateful brute. I hope you understand I didn't support—or even know about—his quest for vengeance."

Sumbeka's lips trembled. "Thank you, my dear. He was indeed." She paused, then stretched one hand toward Nasan. "You are neighbors, I think."

"Yes, Tsaritsa," Solomonida said. "I didn't realize her name was Nasan, though. We always call her Irina." Maria saw her glance at Nasan. "If you prefer your birth name, I have no objection to using it."

"I do," Nasan said. "My in-laws insist on Irina, so we will continue to use it around them. Maria has made the change out of kindness, and I appreciate it."

Maria, watching Solomonida, noticed a tightening of her lips. So Solomonida still questioned Maria's capacity for kindness. Opening her mouth to snap a retort, Maria caught her mother-in-law's warning frown and stopped herself with a sigh. Her past left long shadows, it seemed.

Sumbeka rescued them from the awkward moment, urging her guests to sit, offering food and tea, asking questions and telling anecdotes with quicksilver charm. When they were settled on the corner sofas, she held out a hand to Maria. "I am glad you decided to visit me today, *kilen*. Otherwise I would have come to your house tomorrow. When the men leave, I want you and Lyuba—and Timur, of course—to stay here. Nasan will join us, with her mother-in-law, to free their husbands to perform their duties at court and on campaign. Then my husband and Lord Nikolai can assign one troop of men to guard us while the others go to war with Bulat, Alexei, and Daniil."

Maria blinked. *Stay here?*

"You especially are in danger," Sumbeka went on. "Your father's thoughtless behavior has already led to your stepmother's captivity, as well as to the confiscation of his urban estate. We cannot chance the government turning on you and your sister next. I hope those in power will refrain from attacking the families of men fighting for their cause, but if need be we can get you to a safe place until Alexei returns."

Maria's head reeled. She grasped at the first straw of sanity that presented itself. "If Alexei agrees, I will bring Lyuba and

Timur here, and thank you. What of my brothers, though? They were living in Papa's house until the morning he left." Rage at her father threatened to choke her. Thoughtlessness? Betrayal, rather. She clenched her hands at her sides. What she wouldn't give for a chance to shake some sense into Papa!

"We will make inquiries," Sumbeka promised. "They have gone to your sister's, my son told me. Can she protect them?"

"I don't know," Maria said. "She lives a considerable distance from Moscow, so I doubt anyone will bother the younger two. The older boys are in service, so if the grand prince summons them, they must report."

She shuddered. "Papa's flight has changed everything. I'm so angry with him for abandoning the rest of us this way. Why should my brothers or Roxelana suffer because Papa chose to flee? I don't like her, but he might have taken her with him instead of leaving her here. Although I'm furious with the grand princess as well. If she had not listened to Prince Ilya's lies and ordered Papa's arrest, he wouldn't have run away."

Another question remained unspoken: could Sumbeka keep her and Lyuba safe if the grand princess decreed otherwise? But she decided not to ask. If nothing else, she would feel less vulnerable here than at home.

"Prince Ilya's lies?" Nasan asked. "What lies?"

"That's right," Maria said. "You haven't heard this. It's why I came: to share what Solomonida and I learned at the palace yesterday."

"Yes, do tell us." Sumbeka poured more tea into her cup and Nasan's, then raised the pot in Maria's direction. When Maria tipped her cup to show that it remained half-full, her mother-in-law returned the pot to its tray. She did not offer more to Solomonida; perhaps she had noticed that her Russian guest had yet to sample so much as a sip. "My husband says the Shuisky princes have Roxelana in custody at their estate."

"That's what we heard, too." Maria related to Sumbeka and Nasan her experiences of the day before, beginning with her disgrace and ending with Alexei's arrival at the Kremlin, interspersed with cries of sympathy and outrage from her listeners and the occasional interjection from Solomonida.

As the tale reached its end, Sumbeka extended a hand to Solomonida. "We are much indebted to you," she said. This time, Maria heard genuine warmth in her mother-in-law's voice. "If you and your daughter need sanctuary, please do not hesitate to seek it here." Sumbeka's vivid face crinkled in laughter. "My husband left his harem in Kasimov, God be praised, and we have ample space."

"I thank you," Solomonida said with a fervency that suggested she had heard the implicit forgiveness for her husband's crimes. "My father requires constant care, and my younger sister does too much of it because of my service to the grand princess. So I had better stay with them and offer help when I can. But in an emergency I will throw the four of us on your mercy."

"Good," Sumbeka said with a brisk nod. "And now, darlings, we must weave our thoughts into a plan. When our men leave, how will we occupy ourselves?"

In the last week of April Bulat gathered his men and led them out of Moscow. Alexei rode at his right, Ruslan on Bulat's left. Although tradition required Tatar warriors to depart without regret, Alexei risked a backward glance before they reached the gates. Timur's doleful face showed at one window, and Alexei raised a hand to his son. The boy ached to accompany the troops, but Alexei had no intention of granting that wish before time left him no choice. He'd seen more than a few striplings lost to stray arrows and misdirected swords, not to mention their own untrammeled zeal.

At another window stood Maria, her face shuttered as if she fought back tears. To her he blew a kiss. It was good that she had agreed to stay with his stepmother and sister. The shock on her face when he admitted he would miss her still touched him. Had she truly not guessed that he loved her? When he returned, he must find a way to tell her how much she meant to him. His partial confession had already lessened the distance that had grown between them since the day they quarreled over her father. A welcome change.

He anticipated a short absence—a few weeks at most. A preparation for the longer campaigns to come. Alexei did not fear death, which lay in the hands of the Almighty, but he did wish for a swift and sound return. It became more likely with each passing day that he had got his wife with child. Given how long he had waited for a family of his own, what a tragedy it would be never to have a chance to love them!

To reach the forces on the western side, Bulat's troop had to pass through the outer walls, then cross the Moscow River twice, riding six abreast over wooden bridges. With two hundred men and three times as many horses, this initial passage consumed a considerable part of the morning, but at last they reached the Staritsa road. Ahead of them a long train of cavalry extended to the horizon. A rabble of infantry and artillery huddled to one side. Alexei saw neither Telepnev nor his cousin Nikita Obolensky, who together commanded the Muscovite forces. Presumably they headed the cavalcade.

Alexei turned his head to look, amid the mounted men carrying his father's nine-tail standard, for a small group riding under banners bearing the winged horse—as elegant and stylized as his brother's yet distinct; designed by Maria, then embroidered in scarlet against a white silk background by his stepmother's needlewomen. It had not occurred to him, on that day before his wedding, that he would ever again agree to fight at his father's side. But the banners marked a step along the road to his ultimate goal: a command of his own.

Bulat barked questions in Russian to the closest mounted nobleman. The answers appeared to suit him, for he ordered his own troops to join the end of the cavalry train. Alexei passed the order down the line and kicked his horse into motion. They were off.

Four days later, they stopped in Volok. There they would wait while the three holy men, dispatched with a smaller escort from their army, did their best to convince the errant Prince Andrei that his continued existence—and even the health of his soul—depended on full compliance with Moscow's demands.

Alexei hoped that the prince would at last see reason or, if he did not, that vengeance would be swift. Only four days from home, and he already missed his wife, his son, and his small sister-in-law.

More than a week passed before Koshkin's attempts to wangle a meeting with Prince Andrei bore fruit. Even then he could not evade the lowering presence of Bogdanov, who scoffed openly at Koshkin's manufactured list of names. "A bucket of lies," he said, while Andrei regarded Koshkin with a stare steely enough to pin Koshkin's feet to the floor. "Do you think we don't know who our friends are? Every clan has members on our side and on Elena's. Obolensky princes here, Obolensky princes there—if these Moscow nobles supported us, they would have ridden here, as you did. Who told you this nonsense anyway? Or did you invent it yourself?"

"Prince Ilya Shuisky told me," Koshkin said in the iciest tone he could manage. "Your friend, whose testimony against me you were so quick to believe."

"And you were so quick to deny." Andrei waved a lordly hand. "If Ilya knows such secrets as this and shares them so freely, then why should I assume he did not also tell me the truth about you?"

A dangerous road to go down. Koshkin sought to turn the conversation in a more profitable direction. "Prince, during my last mission here we urged you in good faith to dispatch your troops to Kolomna. We believed your sister-in-law would accept compliance as proof that you do not pose as much threat to her as she fears. But we were wrong. She will capture you if she can. If I can offer ideas that you can accept or reject at your pleasure, is that not sufficient reason to listen to me?"

Bogdanov stepped forward, his hand curled in a fist. "You would speak so to a prince of the blood? Curb your tongue!"

But Andrei straightened in his chair and held out a restraining arm. "Quiet, Gleb. Talking does no harm. I will listen to him." When Bogdanov retreated—still furious, judging from his expression—the prince spoke to Koshkin. "I know my options. I can fight a superior force and lose. I can flee, giving up my lands and my standing to live as a hanger-on at a foreign court—if Elena's troops don't stop me before I reach the border, in which case she can execute me for treason. Whether I fight or flee, many of my supporters will end up dead or injured, and my wife and son will suffer. I might also travel to Moscow and kiss the cross in fealty to my nephew, something I have already done more than once to no avail. And since my brother was arrested in Moscow within a week of *his* loyalty oath, then starved to death in a Kremlin jail, I'm sure you can understand why I don't choose to place my trust in Elena's word." From his place at Andrei's right shoulder

Bogdanov growled like an angry bear in response to this last comment.

"But there is one possibility you have not mentioned." Koshkin ignored the growl. For the first time since entering the room, he saw a path forward. "If your warriors agree to fight for you, they agree to die for you. To protect your wife and your son, you must not only take the battle to the enemy but win it. Call on every wavering noble you can find. Promise them rewards. Tip the balance in your favor by reminding them that your nephew cannot command an army or even receive a diplomat without his mother or her paramour at his side. But do it soon, Prince, because Elena was massing her forces when I left Moscow. You have no time to waste."

"I will consider what you have said." Andrei glanced over his shoulder at his fuming chamberlain. "And discuss it with Gleb Glebovich. Go. I will summon you if I wish to speak to you again."

Koshkin bowed to Andrei and left. Had he found words strong enough to push this dithering prince into action? If not, Koshkin was wasting *his* time. He should forget Andrei and plot his own escape before the Moscow troops arrived.

Still, Andrei might yet stop his procrastination. Koshkin would wait and see. For a few days, at least.

Events, not Koshkin's urging, pushed Prince Andrei into action. The day after their conversation a horseman galloped into Staritsa shouting that a Muscovite army lay camped at the edge of Andrei's lands, ready to block any effort to flee toward Lithuania. It was the first of May, exactly two weeks since Koshkin's arrival at Andrei's court, and the news threw the entire palace into confusion.

At dawn Koshkin packed his saddlebags, mounted his horse, and watched Andrei usher his princess and their three-year-old son into a closed carriage. Surrounded by his men, they set off for Torzhok, a town to the northeast, away from the advancing Muscovites.

Koshkin rode among the rear guard, his thoughts and emotions churning. Even without the hasty departure, unplanned and driven by fear, he doubted that Andrei could meld this motley crew of followers into a force capable of opposing his sister-in-law's far greater army. Yet for Koshkin to remain in Staritsa waiting for the Muscovites to take the city was unthinkable. Elena's troops would kill him on sight. Hence his decision to stick with Prince Andrei.

But only for the moment. Koshkin's already blighted hopes for victory plummeted as Andrei's forces pushed toward Torzhok, the exact opposite of the direction in which they should be heading. His thoughts turned ever more often to escape. Suppose he were to locate a foreign court and find a new path to his goal? Russia's neighbors, eager to exploit the weaknesses that arose from minority rule, would welcome his expertise.

An appealing prospect, yet still he hesitated. Could he say goodbye to his family, his estates—and, most important, every chance of reclaiming his beautiful wife?

Chapter 23

Moscow, May 1537

"WE SHOULD VISIT ROXELANA," SUMBEKA ANNOUNCED.

Maria exchanged incredulous glances with Nasan. Five days after their husbands' departure, the two of them had settled into a new routine under Sumbeka's tutelage: daily discussion of topics ranging from the history of foreign lands to the best methods of retaining a spouse's affections.

Maria loved the lessons more than she would have believed possible. Not only did they distract her from missing Alexei with an intensity that itself amazed her, but at times it seemed she had spent her whole life waiting to learn about the conflicting motives that drove other people. But visiting Roxelana? What did *that* have to do with anything? "Why?" she asked.

"Well, it is a kindness," Sumbeka said. "She remains your father's wife, and we should remind her captors that she does not stand alone. But visiting her also gives us an opportunity to assess how much damage your father's behavior has caused."

"Will Nadezhda receive us?" Maria turned questions over in her mind before settling on this most important one. "I don't know her well."

"Nor do I," Nasan said. "We chatted briefly at your wedding, but no more."

"She can hardly refuse a tsaritsa and two tsarevnas, but I also sent a messenger to your friend Solomonida, asking her to smooth our path." Sumbeka rose and walked to the window as a clatter sounded from the courtyard. "And here she is."

The words had hardly left her mouth when Solomonida, dressed as if for court in sky-blue silk and pearls, rushed into the room and kissed each woman in turn on both cheeks. "Let's go," she declared. "I can't wait to get started."

"Wait." Sumbeka gestured her to sit. "Let's make a short list of our questions. I will ask Roxelana how the Shuisky family is treating her. That's the most obvious reason for us to visit, and the answer will tell us something about how those in power see her (and us). I doubt anyone believes she urged her husband to flee, so her arrest sends a signal to him and to others plotting to switch sides. Don't try it, or your family will suffer."

"Prince Ilya has rid himself of Papa. Is he satisfied now that he has a chance to woo Roxelana? I'd like to know whether he will leave us alone from now on." Maria wrinkled her nose. "Would he tell his wife, though?"

"I'll try to find out whether Nadezhda has picked up information from her husband about plans to punish other members of Maria's family," Solomonida said. "The Shuiskys won't dare go after Tsarevich Alexei because of his relationship to Bulat Khan, but what of her brothers and brother-in-law? They have not backed Koshkin, but loyalty alone may not protect them."

"And I will encourage Princess Nadezhda to share how she feels about her husband's behavior," Nasan said. "She can't be happy having him in close proximity to Roxelana, whatever the circumstances."

"An understatement." Sumbeka laughed, and the others joined in. "Very well. We have a plan. Let us depart. God willing, we will learn something useful."

And with that the four women set out.

The Shuisky estate looked much like the Kolychevs' house, Maria decided, but grander, with more outbuildings and a larger yard. Located inside the Kremlin, as the homes of only the most prominent noble families still were, it sat within its own log enclosure a short distance to the left of the main thoroughfare that Maria had traveled for her audiences with Grand Princess Elena. She repressed a shudder of remembered humiliation as the carriage passed through the Kremlin gates, and Solomonida, sitting next to her, clasped her hand and murmured reassurance.

Princess Nadezhda received them inside the terem, the women's quarters on the third floor, with Roxelana at her side. If captivity disagreed with their southern beauty, she showed no evidence of it. She appeared as sleek and comfortable as ever, although tension hummed between her and Princess Nadezhda.

Maria understood *that*. Most women saw Roxelana as a threat, and Nadezhda had every reason to fear that sultry presence in her home.

After kissing her stepmother's rose-scented cheek and bowing to Princess Nadezhda, whose skeptical eyebrow contrasted with her welcoming remarks, Maria stepped back and let Sumbeka take the lead. Not only did she hold precedence in rank and age, but of the various questions they had prepared hers required the least explanation. That three family members (if you did not know the whole story of their relationship) might inquire after Roxelana's health seemed natural.

Solomonida settled next to Nadezhda and engaged her in friendly and harmless chit-chat about the goings-on at court, homing in on the question of Prince Andrei's support, whether it might be expected to increase, and the risks taken by those who toyed with changing sides. Nasan clustered with them.

"I trust they are treating you well," Sumbeka said, taking her seat next to Roxelana. "Are you in good spirits?"

"Well enough." Roxelana looked wary but less frightened than the last time Maria had seen her. "I am free to move around, as you see, so long as I do not leave the house. I have my own room and a servant to take care of my needs. Prince Ilya, in particular, could not have done more to make me feel *quite* at home."

She compressed her lips as she finished the last sentence, and Maria narrowed her eyes. Given Ilya's desire for Roxelana, Maria had taken it for granted that he would make advances to her stepmother. She had not considered the possibility that her stepmother might not welcome the chance to extend her dominion over another male admirer. Yet the distaste in Roxelana's voice made that conclusion inescapable.

And she was completely in Ilya's power. Suppose he had taken her by force?

But how to ask with Princess Nadezhda sitting right there? Maria struggled to find the right phrasing. While she pondered potential approaches, Sumbeka—on the surface oblivious to the undercurrents in the room, although Maria didn't believe that for an instant—briefed Roxelana on what they had learned of Koshkin's flight, the plot against him, and the messages sent by Bulat. Nasan's conversation with Solomonida and Nadezhda continued, but Maria focused on her stepmother, trusting the others to pass along whatever they learned.

At last she saw an opening. Sumbeka completed her tale, avoiding both Alexei's name and any direct reference to Prince

Ilya with an aplomb Maria could not help but envy. Silence descended on their half of the room. Maria leaned forward and took Roxelana's hand, ignoring the flinch that provoked and speaking not much above a whisper. "I hope your jailer realizes you have a family concerned about your welfare. It would distress me to think he might take advantage of you. I feel certain that news would distress Bulat Khan as well, not to mention Papa."

Sumbeka murmured agreement. Roxelana's eyes widened in what Maria read as astonishment. "Your father has made his choice and must live with it, but Bulat Khan's concern, should he choose to express it, might indeed"—she hesitated, as if searching for the right words, then finished her sentence— "cause Prince Ilya to take a less *personal* interest in my well-being."

Maria expressed her comprehension with a nod. "We will speak to the khan."

"How thoughtful. I hope Prince Ilya will listen," Roxelana said with studied indifference.

As if drawn by her husband's name, Princess Nadezhda turned her head toward their threesome, studying them with her head tilted to one side. Maria saw anger in the princess's gray eyes and the rigid cast of her narrow shoulders. Cutting across Solomonida's attempt to introduce the subject of Maria's brothers, Nadezhda snapped, "You have guessed then, Tsarevna, why my husband brought her here? How?"

Maria glanced at her stepmother, then her mother-in-law, seeking inspiration. The rage behind the question set her cheeks aflame. It would be so easy to respond in kind.

Don't. Offer her respect. Sympathy, if I can manage it.

Nadezhda must know what her husband was like, but better not to accuse him to her face. "My stepmother has an extraordinary appeal to men," Maria said, feeling her way, sure whatever words came from her mouth would be the wrong ones. "She arouses their lust without effort. My father, for example, dotes on her."

Roxelana snorted. Maria ignored her. "It wouldn't surprise me to learn that Prince Ilya read too much into Papa's flight. My father will return for her as soon as possible."

"That will be difficult," Nadezhda said, her voice shifting from hot to cold. "As you must realize. He stands accused of treason, and should he fall into the wrong hands, your stepmother will find herself a widow confined to a convent."

Roxelana gasped. Maria clutched her sleeves as the reality of Nadezhda's words sank in. Papa captured and executed. It wasn't news that those in power saw her father's flight to Staritsa as treason, but to hear his fate laid out in such stark terms horrified her beyond the point of speech.

Nadezhda continued. "Unless that disgusting animal I married begs to keep your stepmother here. I don't believe I deserve that particular form of humiliation. And if it's true that she doesn't want him, then it will benefit us both for her to go. So tell your father to keep his distance. Once this crisis passes its peak, I will throw myself on Elena's mercy and plead for your stepmother's release. If I do it now, she will not listen; she may even order some less palatable arrangement."

"That's generous of you," Maria said.

"Most generous," Sumbeka agreed. Her beautiful dark eyes exuded warmth, and she smiled. "And most clever. You eliminate your rival and place her in your debt at the same time. As the chief wife of a harem I applaud your grasp of the essentials."

Nadezhda produced a sound somewhere between a chuckle and a sigh. "Yes, you understand. I have two sons with this wretched man. I can't divorce him, even if that option were easy to obtain. I must guard my boys' interests as well as my own."

"But what of the moment?" Nasan directed a speculative gaze at Roxelana. "Forgive me, but did you really push him away? I watched you at work on my brother."

"I *did*." Roxelana jumped to her feet, hands clenched at her sides, her anger for once unmistakable. "How dare you judge me? You know nothing about me. I hate you! You're all so sanctimonious, just because you happen to belong to the right families!"

Sumbeka caught the nearest clenched fist in her own. "Then tell us. Help us understand."

Nadezhda reached out and clasped Roxelana's other hand. "Yes, tell us. I can't control my husband, damn his lecherous soul for eternity, but there may be something I can do."

Maria, Solomonida, and Nasan added their pleas. Roxelana stood, sputtering, for a moment, then collapsed onto her chair. Maria saw the glimmer of tears in her stepmother's eyes. First anger, now sorrow—it was more emotion than she had glimpsed from Roxelana in the nine months since they met.

"My father sold me when I was six." Roxelana's voice shook. "To a man older than himself, older than your father."

"Six?" Maria asked, stunned. "That's Lyuba's age. It's an abomination!" In a flash of insight, she understood Roxelana's lack of empathy for Lyuba. The sight of a happy child must sting like salt in a wound. The other women echoed her statements.

"But common," Roxelana said. "Men sell their daughters to provide for their sons. That master waited five years before claiming his rights, but then he made up for lost time. After a few months he sold me to another. By the time Bahadur Bey bought me at sixteen, I had had four owners, each worse than the one before. I learned a great deal about what men like; everything else was secondary. Bahadur was kind, and his son easy to manipulate, but their desires were the same. Alexei was the first man I chose for myself. I thought he was different. Better."

She glared at Maria, although the tears spoke of something else. "I loved him until I realized he too saw me only as a body he could possess. Your father promised to support me, and I rewarded him in the way all men crave. But I hate this life, shut up alone in my house as if immured in a cave. And I do *not* have to sleep with Prince Ilya. So I won't." She kicked a nearby cushion as if it were a stand-in for the prince.

Maria didn't believe every detail. She had seen Roxelana flirting with Alexei long after she claimed her "love" had ended. Yet such a terrible history couldn't fail to evoke sympathy. No wonder Roxelana made the most of her appeal to men. What other means of support did she have?

"Did you tell my husband this?" Nadezhda paced the room, muttering imprecations against her spouse.

"No," Roxelana said. "I reminded him of my wedding vows, told him I had no desire for him. He didn't listen, and he is too large to fight off." Her voice broke. "It is not my first rape, but I had hoped never to endure that again." Her eyes flashed as she shook her head to clear the tears. "Your father has much to answer for, Maria."

"So does Prince Ilya," Maria said. "For Papa's flight, as well as the attack on you. But how do we help you today?"

Nadezhda returned to her seat. "We must find a way to remove her from the house. No one on the estate can stand against my husband's orders, and his uncle has chosen to turn a blind eye to this affair."

"Could she stay with the priest and his wife?" Solomonida asked. "My sister would take her in, but without the council's agreement I fear that would not last."

Nadezhda frowned. "The priest, too, owes his living to the Shuisky clan. But he is a man of God, and the Church doesn't tolerate rape, even by the mighty. It could work. If naught else, he would make a great fuss. Ilya could no longer perform his evil deeds in secret. But he could transfer her back to the house."

Nasan, who had been staring as if transfixed at the window, rose and addressed her mother in Tatar too rapid and fluent for Maria to follow. Sumbeka nodded, her expression vivid and alert.

Roxelana leaned forward. For the first time since their arrival, Maria saw hope in her stepmother's eyes and realized that Roxelana had understood every word. But what had Nasan come up with?

"Send one of the servants at once," Sumbeka, returning to Russian, told her daughter. "It is the perfect solution. I should have thought of it myself." Eight months gone with child, Nasan could not run, but she moved with impressive speed for the door. Another exchange in Tatar took place with whomever stood on the other side, followed by the sound of departing boots.

"What's going on?" Nadezhda demanded as Nasan recrossed the floor.

Sumbeka's queenly beauty only enhanced her smile. "My steward will send a quartet of female warriors, fully armed, with instructions to protect Roxelana day and night."

"*Female* warriors?" Nadezhda could not look more astonished if she tried, as did Solomonida. Maria also experienced shock, although she should not. Not after seeing her sister-in-law in action.

"They guard the harem," Sumbeka said. "For obvious reasons male warriors would not do. Most of the concubines remain in Kasimov, as do most of the guards. Still, we have a few to spare. And they report not to your husband but to me, as the khan's chief wife. I assure you, Prince Ilya will not succeed in intimidating them."

Roxelana burst into tears and, more amazing still, hugged Sumbeka. "Thank you, thank you. A million times thank you."

"Holy Mother, who ever heard of such a thing?" Nadezhda started to laugh. "Oh, the joy of imagining Ilya's face when he sees them. What shall I tell him when he demands to know where they come from?"

"Why, that they are a gift from Bulat Khan." Sumbeka patted Nadezhda's hand. "A gesture of good will to alleviate the strain on your clan caused by our family member's incarceration. Do mention that the khan would be *most* unhappy if they failed in their task. They will stay as long as Roxelana does and not one day more. So the sooner the council chooses to release her, the sooner he will see their backs. And with that settled, what can we do for you?"

Nadezhda smiled and shook her head. "You have done everything I could wish for. I will speak to Grand Princess Elena as soon as I see the slightest chance of success."

Andrei and his force reached Torzhok by evening. An amazing push, as an army could normally travel less than half that fast. While Koshkin huddled in the outer ring around the prince's cooking fire with Grigory Kolychev and his brother, their presence tolerated but their opinions not sought, Andrei and his advisers hammered out a plan: go to Novgorod, Moscow's ancient rival, twelve days' journey to the northwest. He dispatched a courier bearing a call to arms aimed at the gentry of Novgorod, reminding them that the grand prince could not rule alone and promising rewards for those who heeded his summons. With the decision made and servants arriving with platters of food, Andrei retreated into his tent to join his family, his inner circle piling in behind him.

"Come on." Grigory Kolychev threw a friendly arm across Koshkin's shoulders. "Let's go and eat with Denis. You don't want to tag along with those dullards."

"They might say something important," Koshkin noted as he accepted being dragged away to a more distant campfire.

"Not likely. Not with us around." Grigory laughed. "Lord, have you ever seen such a botched enterprise as this? I'm tempted to take my chances back in Moscow. I had no idea Ilya Shuisky was such a lying bastard. He could have made up the whole story of our arrest."

Koshkin grunted. "He fooled me too. But for what reason?" When Grigory did not reply, Koshkin changed the subject. "This latest scheme seems less botched to me. If the Novgorod gentry responds, it might work." He didn't point out that he had urged the plan on Andrei two days ago.

"*If* they respond," Grigory grumbled.

They had reached the campfire. Saddle-sore and weary, Koshkin crouched on a fallen log and accepted a bowl of beef stew, redolent with garlic and green onions, from Denis's servant. "Will you stay with Andrei?" he asked Grigory.

"Oh, I suppose. Gotta keep an eye on this oaf. He's spoiling for a fight." Grigory slapped the arm of his brother, who dropped onto the log beside them carrying a loaf of rye bread.

Denis broke off pieces of the bread and handed them to Koshkin and Grigory. "If you mean I'd rather fight than run, yes. Wouldn't you?"

Grigory shrugged. "I didn't flee Moscow to play the rabbit to Elena's fox throughout the Russian north, so yes. Even though we have family on the other side. What of you, Koshkin? Any second thoughts?"

Pondering his answer, Koshkin sampled the stew, earthy peasant fare but excellent, and sank his teeth into bread solid enough to stop an advancing army. Fresh though, with a crisp outer crust, and it softened in the gravy. "Thank you for the food. It's delicious. On Andrei, no second thoughts. I'm here. I can't go home. But can Andrei succeed? I do wonder about that."

Denis looked sideways at his brother. "You have sharper wits than Grigory if you understand that you're stuck here."

Grigory swore at him, but his brother only grinned. "Do you honestly think Andrei will fail?" Denis asked Koshkin.

"Depends how many gentry answer the call." Koshkin did not mention his half-formed plans to seek refuge abroad. "Andrei's right: the Russian lands need a grown man to rule them. But he can't win without a stronger force. That's why he's running."

The conversation turned to more congenial topics. As night fell, Grigory Kolychev offered space in his tent, and Koshkin accepted with unspoken mental apologies for the scorn he had so often heaped in private on Grigory's amiable head. The apologies turned to effusive thanks after a drizzle began not long after sunset. A horse blanket could not equal a tent when it came to protection against the rain.

Yet sleep brought no rest. Roxelana haunted his dreams. Visions of her on their wedding night mingled with the sounds of her laughter as she twirled in Alexei's arms, flirted with every man that passed. When he reproached her, she tripped him so that he fell headlong into a river. Floundering, he reached for her, calling her name, but she continued to dance, silk skirts swirling about her.

He woke in full dark, listening to the trickle of raindrops as they slid down the side of the tent, the drip-drip of saturated cloth wetting his forehead. The horse blanket folded under his head lay damp against his cheek. No wonder he dreamed of rivers.

He should not have left his wife in Moscow. They could have fled to Lithuania together. He had given up, abandoned her to another. He might never see her again.

The thought made him want to weep.

The next day the army rested, but it soon moved north, taking a more reasonable two days to travel the same distance as during that first mad scramble. Amid the hills where the mighty Volga flowed little wider than a stream, Andrei and his forces waited for the men of Novgorod to answer his call.

They did not. Koshkin, again standing with Denis and Grigory, regarded the few arrivals with disdain. "I count less than thirty," he said. "Pitiful. If he can't do better than that, why head toward Novgorod at all?"

"I doubt we will," Denis said. "Didn't you hear? Novgorod's closed its gates. Threw up a damned palisade around the Trading Quarter. Yellow-bellied merchants don't dare take a stand against Moscow."

"Can you blame them?" On every side Koshkin saw groups of warriors debating their options with raised hands and voices. "After what the present grand prince's grandsire did to them?"

"They deserved it," Grigory growled. "Traitorous beasts."

Which seemed vastly unfair, when that previous grand prince had laid waste to Novgorod with fire and sword in response to what many regarded as a made-up conspiracy, but Koshkin saw no need to argue a distant past. "That doesn't help Andrei, though, does it? Without men and a base of operations, his odds of success are nil." Grigory and Denis grumbled, and Koshkin grabbed the opportunity to take a walk around the camp.

He didn't like what he saw. The debates among Andrei's fighters had turned into disputes. Shouts led to blows, and squabbles turned violent. That night more supporters slipped into the forest, heading who knew where, strengthening Koshkin's sense that only a dolt would stay.

As he considered when would be the best time to leave, a courier galloped in, demanding to see Prince Andrei in person. Soon the news spread throughout the camp. The men dispatched to Kolomna had learned of Moscow's campaign against their master, sneaked off without permission, and ridden hell for leather to join him. By tomorrow they would reach Novyi Berezai, less than two days' march away, back in the direction from which Andrei's forces had come.

Koshkin again weighed the odds. Images of his house, Roxelana, his children plagued him. Could he turn his back on that life and entrust his future to strangers? It was too much to ask of any man!

Yet Andrei had wasted a week when he could have taken the opposing forces by surprise, and the men arriving from Kolomna stood high in his regard. They, not Koshkin, would benefit from the renegade Andrei's success, if any. Better for Koshkin to establish himself abroad, then search for another road back to Muscovy.

At last he had a clear goal. But the route to that goal lay to the north, because the grand princess's troops barred the main road to Lithuania and the west. So although Koshkin intended to leave Andrei at the first opportunity, that time was not yet.

Andrei's forces, Koshkin still in their midst, got on the road right after sunrise.

At noon on the fourth day of May, Alexei stood with his father and Ruslan at one edge of the camp that had housed the

Muscovite forces since they reached Volok. Men were striking tents as the prominent clerics packed their remonstrances in their saddlebags and turned their horses homeward. "Why are they leaving?" Alexei asked his father. By virtue of rank and seniority, Bulat had the answer to most questions.

"Andrei has fled Staritsa." Bulat scowled at the troops as if their quarry's flight somehow reflected on them. More likely, he disliked the news he had to relay. "Put his wife and son in a carriage and run off with every man he could muster. Telepnev thinks they're heading for Novgorod. Spies came in last night with word that Andrei has issued a call for support from the Novgorod gentry."

"Will he get it?" Ruslan appeared more curious than concerned.

Bulat jerked his chin in the direction of Telepnev's cousin, supervising a good half of the warriors as they mounted their horses. Amid the throng Alexei caught sight of a golden-brown head atop a tall frame: Daniil Kolychev. "I doubt it," Bulat said. "The people of Novgorod remember their last flirtation with disloyalty. It ended badly. But Prince Nikita will prevent any backsliding."

"And our mission?" Alexei raised a hand in the direction of the distant Daniil, who responded in kind.

Bulat's face was grim. "To prevent civil war. The very thing Elena fears and has done so much to provoke." He sighed, and for a moment the fierce autocrat looked like a tired old man. "That's why the clerics are heading home. The time for negotiation has passed. The only solution left is to capture Andrei before he can mount a serious opposition."

"He's a good general, Daniil says. We'll have to move fast." Alexei watched the milling troops. "I'd better say goodbye, for Nasan's sake."

Bulat nodded acquiescence. "Don't dawdle. Telepnev will call for our departure at any moment."

Alexei acknowledged the command and swung onto his saddle. As he rode toward Prince Nikita's troops as fast as the terrain and the crowd would allow, he marked the moment in his mind.

One day, God willing, I will tell this story to my grandchildren.

Daniil had his force lined up by the time Alexei reached him, and Daniil himself already sat high on the back of the large black gelding he favored. "I'm glad you rode over," he told Alexei. "If you get back and I don't, tell your sister I love her." He brushed a stray lock of hair off his forehead. "And keep an eye on my child, will you?"

"Of course," Alexei said. "And you will do the same for me?"

"I will." Daniil clasped Alexei's hand. "May God go with you."

"And with you." Alexei gripped Daniil's hand in turn. "May we both see home again." He watched Daniil ride off, but the column had not passed the Volok gates before a roar from Bulat had him turning his horse to rejoin his father. The hunt was on.

Before long, the cousins and their troops would surround their quarry. Andrei would have to choose between submission and death.

Chapter 24

KOSHKIN MADE HIS MOVE TWELVE DAYS LATER. ANDREI'S forces, doubled in size with the return of his majordomo and his cavalry, had resumed their march to the northwest. For a week and a half Koshkin stayed with the army, camping with Grigory Kolychev, supplementing their meager food supplies with goods purchased on the road or hunted near the end of each day.

It was a miserable existence. Koshkin missed his wife, his home, the life he had left behind. One day he would fight for what he had lost, but to do that, he must first survive this crisis.

His sense of what lay beyond the Livonian border was hazy. He had never traveled outside the Russian lands. Yet he needed a safe haven, and he had skills and knowledge to offer in exchange. From Livonia he could make his way southwest to Lithuania, where the elite spoke Russian and the Orthodox Church had not entirely lost ground to the Catholic Poles. He aimed for a place in a noble household, even the government—as an adviser, perhaps. He had met many envoys during his years in the military and the Foreign Office. He had connections, some of whom would remember him. He could parlay those old friendships into a basis for future success. He hoped.

At the intersection of roads leading to Novgorod and another ancient town, Staraia Russa, Koshkin saw his chance. Less than one day's march away, the advance scouts announced, camped the vanguard of Telepnev's army. Novgorod, already an unlikely source of support, had opened its gates to Telepnev's cousin Nikita. Continue along the current path, and Telepnev and his cousin would spring their trap, ending Andrei's bid for freedom—and, more important, Koshkin's. He had not ridden so far and risked so much to lose his life in service to a prince whose indecision and bumbling had proven him unworthy of such a sacrifice.

A hurried conference among the leaders ensued. Koshkin did not wait to learn the outcome. Andrei could not continue on to Novgorod, therefore he must turn toward Staraia Russa. Which meant that Koshkin needed to race well ahead of Andrei's army. Because the moment Telepnev and his cousin learned of their quarry's change of plans, Koshkin's chances of crossing the border would vanish.

He did not take time to say goodbye. Better that the Kolychevs, however amiable, have no news of his departure that they might feel tempted to share.

The hill sloped upward, and the huts in the wretched hamlet above huddled into their wooden frames. A sluggish green stream flowed across the base of the hill, and the ever-present trees pressed against the edges of an open area barely large enough to contain the enemy troops clustered at the top. "Have you ever seen a less appealing battleground?" Alexei grumbled to Ruslan. "Give me the open steppe any day."

Bulat, riding half a length ahead, turned his mount sideways. "Yes, that field looks damp. Bad for the horses even if we had the advantage of height, which we don't."

"I could send a scouting party into the woods. See if there's another way up." Alexei squinted at the forest, trying to calculate how much undergrowth and shrubbery might bar the riders' way before concluding that from this vantage point the effort was a lost cause.

"We can expect worse mud among the trees," Bulat pointed out. "Less sunshine to dry out the mess."

"I don't like the idea of taking the horses through that stream, though," Ruslan said. "It's too shallow for them to swim, so they may founder in the mire. And if they don't, we have to get them up the other bank before we can tackle the hill. One good cavalry charge from above, and the entire troop will fall over itself getting into formation."

"Right." Bulat gazed at the hill as if assessing his options. "We need a way around." He gestured at Alexei. "Take your scouting party up river. See if you can find a place to cross that won't put us in their direct line of sight. No attack until I give the word, though. Understood?"

"Understood." Alexei wheeled his horse and called to his personal guard. If he moved fast, he would be out of hearing range before the urge to remind his father that he was no longer sixteen overwhelmed his self-control.

The strangely verdant stream indeed narrowed to a point where even the most skittish, least surefooted pony could jump it without difficulty. Better, a rutted road that at least appeared to head in the right direction lay on the other side. Alexei dispatched his fastest rider with the news and took his scouting party across, in search of water that looked as if the horses could drink it without collapsing where they stood. A small copse with a handy brook proved suitable, and he dismounted, handing Ajdar's reins to one of his men and lounging against a tree to await the arrival of his father's troops.

He was back in the saddle by the time Bulat arrived. The crossing, the copse, and the road won him a grunt of approval from his unyielding sire. Alexei grinned at Ruslan, whose raised eyebrows indicated that his experience with his own father might not have prepared him for Bulat's acerbic approach to parenting, and fell into line once more. "May I send the scouts ahead, *Ata?*" Alexei asked. "To see where this road leads?"

"Do," Bulat said, and Alexei relayed the order.

One bridge crossed. He decided to push his luck. "What's the plan? Do we wait for Telepnev or surround them while we can?" The Tatars had ridden ahead—splitting from the vanguard when word reached the commander that Andrei's forces had turned toward Staraia Russa. The vanguard followed on foot, and Telepnev's main army could not be more than a few hours behind.

"Depends," Bulat said. "I sent messengers. If the army is nearby and the situation looks stable, we wait. If we can take them, we do."

Alexei, about to push for the second option, bit his tongue. No doubt his father would make the same call himself when they reached the village. This campaign was a test: he had to prove he'd put the past behind him, take orders on occasion. Only then would his father treat him as a true second-in-command. "Yes, *Ata*," he said. They rode in silence down the road.

After a while a cluster of one-room huts signaled that the hamlet lay straight ahead. From this angle the presence of Andrei's forces could be deduced only from the large number of spare mounts happily cropping grass in their makeshift corrals. Bulat ordered his men into the forest and sent Alexei ahead with a small contingent to search for signs of Telepnev's approaching forces and Ruslan with another dozen or so warriors to assess the lay of the land.

Alexei had traveled far enough to see the waving banners and gleaming helmets of the approaching vanguard when the unmistakable snap of bowstrings sent him and his men careening toward the hamlet.

Bulat? Ruslan?

Ruslan galloped toward him from the far side of the village, a group of unknown Russians close behind. His men, twisted in their saddles, shot a steady stream of arrows at the pursuing enemy. Bulat's force emerged from the woods and spread out, sending more arrows into the Russian warriors, whose howls of rage intermingled with shrieks of pain. Alexei jerked his head toward his own men, releasing them to join the fray. At the same time he pushed forward, taking a position at his father's side.

"The vanguard's not far down the road." He pulled his curved saber from its scabbard. There were enough arrows flying around, and too many Tatars between him and the enemy for him to add to the number. "Andrei's men don't know what they've taken on."

"Go," Bulat said. "Find Buturlin and tell him the wasp's out of its nest."

With a nod Alexei kneed Ajdar, turning the horse in search of Buturlin, the Russian general commanding the vanguard.

Something flashed in the corner of his eye. On instinct he raised his shield at an angle over his father's head, blocking the sun.

"What?" Bulat roared. "I gave you an order!"

Alexei turned the shield. A tufted shaft protruded from the center, right where Bulat's forehead would have been.

He tugged the arrow loose and, inclining his head and shoulders, handed it to his father. "And I shall obey it,

Commander," he said, then left to do just that, Bulat's shocked gratitude a welcome ringing in his ears.

The skirmish ended in a standoff as the grand prince's main force arrived from the south, more or less at the same time as a contingent from the north that included Daniil Kolychev. Alexei clasped his brother-in-law's hand in greeting, amazed at the warmth he felt at the sight of a man whom only a few months ago he would have sworn he didn't like. He could blame his change of heart on the sense of comradeship created by war—except that this misbegotten campaign hardly qualified. Even the enemy seemed reluctant to fight.

Although Daniil had a blood-stained cloth wrapped around the upper part of his left arm. "What's that?" Alexei asked.

Daniil touched the bandage. "A scratch." He nodded at the forces arrayed on the other side. "Got it from a cousin of mine. That big brute in the middle, near Prince Andrei. His name is Denis, and he'd better pray to his patron saint that my mother never hears about this."

Alexei had no difficulty identifying the brute in question. "Your cousin attacked you?"

"Skirmish." Daniil scowled in the direction of Andrei's troops. "As we were riding in. Miserable lot, aren't they? Most of them are relatives of someone on our side. I don't mind Denis so much: he was assigned to Andrei as part of his military service. He didn't switch sides like Grigory and your father-in-law. I'd as soon not have to kill him—or let him kill me."

"It's an ugly business," Alexei agreed. "Tell me what brings you here. I thought you were investing Novgorod to keep Andrei out."

"We did. The Novgorodians greeted us with open arms. The last thing they want is to give the government in Moscow another excuse to raze their city to the ground. Andrei should have figured that out for himself."

"Is everyone riding south then?"

"No, just our contingent." Daniil indicated the rest of his troops, mounted nearby. "This insurrection needs to end here, today. Best if Andrei believes he has no place to run. I pity him, to tell the truth. I always liked him. But the quarrel between him and Elena has gone too far for either side to draw back. Prince Nikita decided he could spare us for the coming battle."

"There may not be one," Alexei told him. "Telepnev is negotiating, my father says. And Prince Andrei's men don't look like they're yearning for a fight."

"More like beggars searching for a place to hide," Daniil said. Andrei's men stood in a cluster as their master and his majordomo negotiated with Prince Ivan Telepnev, representing the underage and absent grand prince.

"And those represent about half the number Andrei started with." Stragglers had stumbled into the grand princely camp night after night since the campaign began. "I don't see my father-in-law among them, but he never struck me as a diehard loyalist."

"Koshkin?" The astonishment in Daniil's voice was unmistakable. "He's loyal to himself. His clan, maybe. No one else."

"So where is he?"

But Daniil had no answer.

Maria laid the latest missive from her husband out on the fret-work table in her mother-in-law's sitting room. For the moment she was alone. Sumbeka and Nasan had gone to visit Natalya in the rooms assigned to her when she first came from her own home, leaving Maria with her letter, received this very morning.

She traced the firm dark lines with her index finger, not to sound them out—she had memorized the sentences already—but as if by doing so she could touch the hand that had penned them. "We ride north in the morning," Alexei had written. "For better or worse, this mission will end soon. Expect me back at your side before long. I miss you, dear heart."

Her finger stopped, hovering over the last sentence. He had been safe when he wrote this, but was he still? As he rode north, the time between letters stretched. From Novgorod even the fastest courier could not reach Moscow in less than a week. A week in which she could become a widow, her unborn infant fatherless, without knowing what she had lost.

And what of Papa? Even if Alexei survived unscathed, would the troops capture her father?

If I must lose one of them, let it not be Alexei!

The prayer formed unbidden in her head, and Maria clapped her hand over her mouth as if she'd spoken it aloud, adding a muttered plea for forgiveness to the Most Pure Mother of God, Protectress of Women. Her other hand pressed against her belly, for to wish ill to another could unleash evil spirits on her baby, and the Mother of God oversaw childbirth too. Eyes closed, she made the sign of the cross three times.

A sharp cry interrupted her moment of penitence. Thrusting the scroll into the small purse that dangled near her waist, Maria ran toward the source of the sound, then stopped, confused, outside the room assigned to Lady Natalya. The cry had not been repeated, but she heard a flurry of voices within.

Could retribution have come so soon and her careless, wicked thought have brought about the death of Lady Natalya?

But then she would hear keening. Maria swallowed, hard, then pressed her hand against the door. It swung open under her touch.

Natalya stood in one corner, supporting herself with a hand on the windowsill. Sumbeka and Nasan, elbows linked, faced her. The three of them talked over one another, their words a cooing rush like doves in a cote. In the open area between them a puddle of liquid spread.

"What happened?" Maria raised her voice to a pitch she might use to sing, cutting through the overlapping phrases like a sword through caviar.

Sumbeka turned her head, her face alight with an expression Maria could not read. Delight, tension? It could be either or both. "Ah, there you are, *kilen*. Call Jamil. We have a mess to clean up."

"But what happened?" Maria repeated.

Nasan stepped around her mother. "My water broke," she said, her joy unmistakable. "It's started."

Chapter 25

Northwest Russia, May 1537

ONE ADVANTAGE OF SPENDING SO MUCH TIME IN THE SAD-
dle, Koshkin discovered, was that his stamina had improved to
the point where he could match the prowess of his early years
in the cavalry. A day brought him to Staraia Russa with no sign
of either Andrei's troops or the grand prince's army to cause
him distress.

To proceed further, he needed a guide. An evening in a
tavern that also boasted a room where travelers could, for a
small fee, spend the night proved a godsend in more ways than
one. The sturdy merchant who shared the room—an affable
man of middle age and florid complexion, about as tall as
Koshkin but twice as large around—gave his name as Kuzma
and his destination as Pskov, the next stage of Koshkin's
journey.

"I'm headed for the monastery at Pechory," Koshkin said.
"I've never traveled these roads, so I need someone to show
me the way. It won't take you more than an extra day or two,
and I'll reward you handsomely. Help me obtain food, clothing,
and places to stay, and I'll cover your expenses as well as my
own." He did not mention his plan to flee the country, which

would endanger the merchant if he abetted the attempt and himself if the man chose instead to report him.

"Thinking of becoming a monk, are you?" Kuzma patted his ample belly and gave a hearty guffaw. "Not a life that would suit me. Although they say some of those monks live as well as nobles like you."

"No, a pilgrimage, to thank the Lord God for His many blessings." Nobles like you. He should not travel so obviously as a man of high birth. "If you agree, your first task will be to find me garb more suitable to a pilgrim. I left my home in haste, without considering that my clothes did not befit a penitent."

"No difficulty there, Lord. And I'll accept your offer. Times are hard for honest men these days." Kuzma dropped onto the straw pallet laid out for him and dragged off his boots. "What do I call you?"

"Fyodor Mikhailov," Koshkin said, giving a name close enough to his own to avoid awkward moments of confusion but sufficiently common to prevent instant identification. "And thank you."

"Think nothing of it, Fyodor Mikhailov. I'll have a set of robes for you in the morning. It's but three days to Pskov, and one more to Pechory." Kuzma lay back on the pallet and soon fell into snoring.

Koshkin did not sleep so easily. The need to guard his possessions from potential thieves nagged at him, although he resolved that problem by putting the saddlebag containing his clothes and money under his head. It was the danger of his position—the possibility of capture followed by a slow, painful, and dishonorable death—that kept him awake.

Escape was paramount. And escape required him to reach Pechory, where a healthy bribe delivered into the right hands should see him across the river—so small he did not know its name, yet so momentous in the passage it offered to another world.

In that other world he could craft a future. And one day he would return.

Three weeks of pursuit, camping outdoors over skimpy fires, a skirmish or two resulting in few injuries and fewer deaths, and Prince Andrei's abortive rebellion ended in negotiations that lasted no more than a day. Alexei listened dumbstruck to the news that the prince had agreed to travel to Moscow under a safe conduct guaranteed by Telepnev and to perform the oath of allegiance to his nephew that if given freely in September or even January might have averted the whole sorry mess. Andrei's men would accompany him to show their good faith.

"Are we supposed to believe they aren't going to ensure that Telepnev remembers the terms of the deal?" Alexei said to Ruslan and Daniil, who stood beside him looking as stunned at the news as he felt.

"Of course they are." Daniil scowled at the ranks of Staritsa servitors. "But what of themselves? I have too many cousins among that crowd for comfort, and even if Andrei's safe conduct applies to them, who's to say they will not lose their homes or suffer some other punishment?"

Alexei acknowledged the justice of this complaint with a nod. "I still don't see my father-in-law, though. Do you?"

"That surprises you?" Ruslan peered about, as if searching under a bed for the absent Koshkin. "From what I hear, that cat always lands on his feet."

"And has nine lives," Daniil said. "Yes, I'm sure he ran off at the first sign of trouble." He gestured at the huddle of noblemen. "Leaving my cousin Grigory to take the blame. I'll go and talk to him, shall I?"

"Please," Alexei said. "I'd like to know what to tell my wife. Should we come with you?"

"No need." Daniil crossed the muddy field, giving the leaders a wide berth, and after a brief exchange with the warriors standing guard joined a group of men who somewhat resembled him, including the brute who had slashed his arm. Alexei watched, trying to deduce from their stance what Daniil might be saying and hearing, then gave up and fell into conversation with Ruslan.

They didn't have to wait long before Daniil returned. "Koshkin left my cousins at Zaitsevo, without a word of thanks after eating their food and sharing Grigory's tent ever since they left Staritsa. Stands to reason they can't find a kind word to say about him, but the point of his departure tells us …" His voice trailed off, as if he had to work out what it did tell them.

"Tells us what?" Alexei and Ruslan asked together.

"Zaitsevo marks a crossroads," Daniil said. "Staraia Russa in one direction, Novgorod in another, and Moscow to the south. He wouldn't have gone to Novgorod, because Prince Nikita is there, and he'd have to pass the Muscovite vanguard to get there."

"And he wouldn't go south," Ruslan said. "Not directly, anyway. He was fleeing Moscow."

"Staraia Russa, then," Alexei said. "As a way station, if nothing else. But why? What's in Staraia Russa?"

Daniil slapped his whip against his trouser legs. "The road to Livonia," he said after a pause.

Alexei twitched his own whip. "Do we chase him? I'd rather not."

"No point," Daniil said. "He's three days ahead of us, if not more. And we're speculating. We don't *know* he's fled to Livonia. He could have family in Staraia Russa or friends in

Pskov. Or have made a grand circle and headed northwest instead. We'd be wasting our time. Not to mention that I have a wife about to give birth. I'm for Moscow, unless Telepnev issues orders to the contrary."

"Same here. If I have to tell Maria her father may have fled the country, I prefer to do it in person." Alexei did not add, "And I am eager to see her." Ruslan would only make fun of him again for falling in love with his wife.

But it was true: he missed Maria's fire, her shy caresses, her quick comprehension and insightful responses, even her occasional sharp tongue. He couldn't wait to see her, and when he did, he would tell her how he felt about her.

At Sumbeka's and Natalya's direction Maria walked her sister-in-law about the bathing room—taking turns with Solomonida and with Tanya, who had temporarily abandoned her duties as Maria's housekeeper to take part in this vital event for Nasan, whose personal servant Tanya had once been. How exactly Tanya had heard that her former charge had gone into labor, Maria did not ask. Her household and Sumbeka's, intertwined from the beginning, had long-established ties that she saw no reason to probe, especially at a moment as sensitive as this one. A woman giving birth, a child in the moment of its arrival—these times of transition brought danger in the form of malevolent spirits. It was best not to speak about what was happening, except in code. Someone in Sumbeka's household must have whispered such a code in Tanya's ear, and she had responded.

Every door and shutter stood open, and the women had loosened Nasan's clothing and even unbraided her hair to encourage the child to emerge promptly from the womb rather than remain locked inside. As a result, a pleasant May breeze offset the sweltering heat of the bathing room.

Lyuba was not present. Sumbeka had sent her off with Solomonida's daughter, Anna—invited for the occasion—and a servant to watch over them, with instructions to take part in some odd ritual that had Natalya muttering under her breath about paganism but Sumbeka swore must be observed if the child were not to have its soul stolen and eaten by a monstrous demon.

"I will observe your customs if you observe mine." Sumbeka dangled before Natalya's face a triangular fabric pocket embroidered with talismans and stuffed with a prayer blessed by Father Job. "We agree that we must prevent any attack of the Evil Eye, do we not?"

"Very well," Natalya said after a pause. "I suppose it can't hurt." But she crossed herself surreptitiously as soon as Sumbeka turned back to her daughter. Maria suppressed a smile and helped Nasan make her way over the tiles once more.

Maria had attended births before. Her mother's nonstop pregnancies—yielding seven living children, several stillbirths, and three who did not see their second birthday—had not, could not have, all taken place before her eldest daughter reached an age when the grandmothers and aunts encouraged her to learn about childbirth. But this time the reality of bringing life into the world had a special resonance for her. Before this year ended, if her luck held, she would find herself in a bathing area like this one, attended by her mother-in-law and (she hoped) former mother-in-law, walked by Tanya and Nasan, her breathing heavy and her muscles taut, like Nasan's as she staggered about the room under Maria's guiding hand. If she bore a son, Alexei and his family would honor her for the rest of her life.

As she stepped back and let Solomonida take over, Maria caught a glimpse of her fingers, dark with the ink from her husband's letter. *I miss you, dear heart.* Perhaps she didn't need to bear a son for him to honor her. Alexei was different from Papa in many ways. Why not this one, too?

She looked up to see Solomonida easing Nasan onto the bench, holding her in a sitting position by wrapping both arms around her from behind. Sumbeka placed the prayer pocket on her daughter's swollen abdomen. It wouldn't be long now.

Nasan, at last delivered of the beloved burden that had consumed her for the last nine months, lay naked and blissful in warm water piped in from the cisterns concealed behind the tiled walls and beneath the floor. With the pain over and her infant son delivered into the arms of his two deliriously happy grandmothers, busy outdoing each other in counting his fingers and toes, Nasan could relax. It seemed sinful to rejoice that the royal family's troubles had led to her son making his appearance in this lush, inviting world that was his birthright, but Nasan did rejoice. Every familiar ritual and gesture added to her contentment.

She remembered less than a year ago attending Grusha in the bathhouse as she, a former Kolychev slave fallen on hard times, delivered her child. That had been exciting too, the dark and Grusha's obvious pain notwithstanding. Despite that experience, Nasan had not imagined how much labor hurt; her mother insisted no one did, even after the first time, until it happened again. Nasan didn't believe that—surely every burning, excruciating moment had stamped itself into her brain—although Natalya agreed with Sumbeka. But true or false, it didn't matter, because she lay in a bath perfumed with rose petals, the pain had faded to a horrible memory, and only a slight discomfort remained.

"Out you come, Tsarevna," Tanya said.

Nasan opened an eye to see her former maid holding out a large, soft towel. "Do I have to?" An infant wail sounded from beyond the cluster of grandmothers.

Tanya laughed. "Don't you want to greet your son, Tsarevna? He will not feed yet, most likely, but you can hear that he would like to snuggle with his mama. Let me dry you off, and we'll get the pair of you into a nice, soft, clean bed. I'll stay with you until he falls asleep, then put him in his cradle to keep him safe." She handed Nasan a cup redolent of cinnamon. "To cleanse the insides." Nasan drained the liquid, savoring the sweet spicy taste, then handed the cup back.

Drawn by the idea of greeting her son, she dragged herself out of the bath and allowed Tanya to dry her, sprinkle powdered garlic on her abdomen and private parts to remove the lingering impurities of childbirth, bind her loins with a soft cloth to catch any bleeding, and help her into a cotton robe as delicate as silk. Maria carried the swaddled bundle that held Daniil's son and placed the baby in Nasan's outstretched arms. She stared, transfixed.

It was real. *He* was real. She—Nasan of the sword and bow, the Golden Lynx, the despair of her mother—had given birth to this gorgeous boy. She lifted him so that a bent head allowed her to inhale his infant smell, clean cloths with a hint of soap. She whispered words of prayer in his ears, in Arabic and in Russian, because his father was not present to bless him and invoke divine protection. And she touched his tiny nose, since almost every part of him except his face lay encased in bands of cloth.

Watch over him, Grandmothers. He is your descendant, even though he has a Russian family too.

Jasmine-scented air caressed her cheek, and she knew the spirits accepted him.

"What will you name him?" Natalya asked.

"Daniil and I discussed it before he left." Nasan, cradling the baby in one arm, reached for Natalya with the other. "He wants to call him Boris, after his brother."

Natalya's eyes filled with tears. Maria sighed but did not protest. Nasan understood Maria's mixed feelings, but assuaging Natalya's grief for her dead son took precedence.

Natalya bent over the baby and kissed his cheek. "Many years, Boris Daniilovich. May God grant you many years."

"*Amin*," Nasan said, hearing her mother echo the phrase, then remembered that Christians did things differently. "God grant us all many years."

"And bring back our husbands soon," Sumbeka said.

"Yes indeed," Nasan and Maria chorused.

"Shall we send a message?" Nasan asked her mother. "They can't leave until they have permission, but Daniil will want to know that his son is safely born."

"Of course," Sumbeka said. "Tanya, take her to her room so that she and the little one can sleep, and Maria and I will take care of the messages."

For once, even Natalya didn't grumble about there being no need to write. Instead she said, "And I will send a servant, with your permission, to alert his grandfather in the Kremlin."

"Absolutely," Sumbeka said. "If the grand prince permits, ask Nikolai Borisovich to join us for dinner."

Chapter 26

THE TROOPS REACHED MOSCOW ON THE LAST DAY OF MAY. Although Alexei, riding at his father's side, juggled a constantly shifting blend of anticipation and relief—anticipation at the thought of returning to Maria and his son, relief that none among Bulat's forces had suffered so much as a stubbed toe— he could not ignore the cloud of gloom that hung over Prince Andrei and his followers as they limped into the Kremlin. Whatever they had hoped to attain—the throne, concessions, or simply the right to live in peace—had not come to pass. Their grand flight had tumbled to earth in the most ignominious fashion, leaving them dependent on the good will of an anxious and angry grand princess and the word of her favorite subordinate.

The crowds that lined the streets muttered and eddied as the cavalcade rode past. Faces sullen as those of the Staritsa notables mouthed phrases that reached Alexei's ears only as disconnected fragments, but the mood of glum dissatisfaction raised the hair along his arms. Whether the populace grumbled at the returning warriors or at the prince of Staritsa and his men, Alexei could not tell, but the atmosphere left him longing for clean air and warm, scented water. He couldn't wait to reach the citadel, deliver their reluctant "guests," and hear the words of dismissal that would release him to reclaim his wife from his father's house.

And that pleasurable prospect threatened to explode in his hands as well, because she would not welcome the news he brought. Her beloved father's disappearance made it ever more likely that he had fled the country, leaving his children and his second wife to suffer whatever retribution Grand Princess Elena chose to inflict on them.

Alexei's hands tightened on the reins until Ajdar sidled and nipped at the animal next to him. Alexei forced himself to relax, to focus on essential tasks. His father-in-law's desertion made him the effective head of the family. His brothers-in-law, raw youths, lacked the experience to guard themselves, never mind younger siblings and women. So far he had ensured the safety of Maria, Lyuba, and Timur, but his responsibilities extended beyond his immediate family. Even Roxelana had a right to protection in the absence of her traitorous husband. Something must be done about her captivity too.

But those tasks could wait. His nearest and dearest came first.

And he would reach them soon. He must be only streets away from his parents' home.

Alexei wanted to see his wife, the sooner the better. But he was not nearly as sure that she would be glad to see him.

"How beautifully you sing," Nasan told Maria, who sat rocking Baby Borya, not yet a week old, in her arms and crooning a lullaby. The four women, with Lyuba and Timur, had gathered after dinner, as they did almost every afternoon, in the rooms that Nasan shared with her mother-in-law.

The infant gave every evidence of agreement. His eyes pressed tight shut, he pursed his mouth as if nursing, waving his fists. The rest of him, wrapped in a blanket provided by Maria as a baby gift, lay relaxed in her hold. "You're going to be a natural at this when it's your turn."

Maria blushed, as she did every time Nasan mentioned babies or birth. "Lots of practice," she said. "I had six brothers and sisters, remember, as well as others who …" She stopped in mid-sentence, and Nasan understood why. It was bad luck to mention death in the presence of an infant, especially one as yet unprotected by baptism. She and *Ana* had entrusted Borya to God's benevolent care, whispered prayers in his ears every chance they got, and bedecked him in amulets against the Evil Eye. Still, one couldn't be too careful where unclean spirits were concerned.

Natalya's voice cut across the haunting lullaby. "Is it not time to find the child a wet nurse?"

Nasan sighed. Since Borya's birth, Natalya and Sumbeka had enlivened their days with a contest over which grandmother knew more about infants and therefore stood the best chance of winning Borya's heart. That Nasan, encouraged by her mother, chose to feed Borya herself had become one of their favorite reasons to battle.

"Not yet," Sumbeka said. "I don't expect my daughter to feed her son for two years like a peasant. We will find him a milk mother, so that he may have milk brothers to support him as he grows. But it's early days yet. To care for a baby oneself for a few months has many benefits: the mother heals faster, she learns to love the child and he her, our grandson will grow stronger and sicken less, and my daughter will enjoy a longer time between infants. I don't know why God has ordained that it should be so, but I have seen the effects for myself."

"Don't we need as many infants as possible? Enough of them join the angels before they walk as it is," Natalya grumbled.

But Nasan, her attention caught by the arrested expression on Maria's face, stopped listening to this variation on a conversation she had heard at least a dozen times and settled next to her sister-in-law. "What is it?" she murmured.

"Is that true?" Maria asked in the same quiet tone. "What your mother said about nursing women delaying their next child?"

"I think so," Nasan said. "That is, in the harem it's hard to tell, because except for *Ana*, *Ata* does not favor any one woman. And when I left Kasimov, I had not often attended births, so I didn't pay much attention to such things. But I trust my mother's judgment. Why?"

"Mama was always with child or recently delivered." Maria rubbed her hands as if the memory pained her. "It wore her out. I want to give my husband sons, but not so many that I can't care for those I have. If feeding my babies makes that possible, I will scandalize everyone and enjoy doing it!"

Nasan laughed, softly, so the feuding grandmothers would not notice. "You *will* enjoy it, I think. It's very pleasant." She touched the baby's tummy. "I feel so close to him when he feeds." Borya wriggled, somehow thrusting one arm outside the blanket. His nose wrinkled, and Nasan ran her finger down it, tucking the arm into place.

"So much the better," Maria said as she picked up the tune once more.

Maria rocked the baby and sang. Nasan moved to sit on the floor with Lyuba and Timur, showing them, with the help of Timur's toy warriors, how one could shoot an arrow from horseback. Natalya abandoned her complaints in favor of a question about one of the foods served at dinner, and she and

Sumbeka set aside their differences in chatter about household matters. A peaceful domestic scene, Nasan thought.

The hum of men's voices brought her to her feet. Several men, speaking Russian. In her mother's house people spoke Russian only occasionally, when addressing Maria or Natalya. Which meant ...

Nasan ran for the door and pulled it open. "Husband," she cried as she saw the visitors. "Come and meet your son!"

Maria leaped to her feet, startling Borya into a wail of protest. Nasan ran back and collected the howling infant. "My brother's here as well," she said before whirling to present the baby to Daniil, who stood in the doorway, his face alight with joy. He held out his arms, and Nasan placed Borya in them, standing on tiptoe and balancing with her hands on his shoulders while they kissed. They moved aside, and Alexei and Bulat came in together.

Maria started toward them, but Lyuba and Timur forestalled her, bowing jerkily to Bulat before hurling themselves at Alexei. He went down on one knee and caught a child in each arm. "Did you think me lost?" His clear tenor cut across their clamor. "Never."

"We did, we did!" Lyuba said as she kissed his cheek. "We were so scared. You were gone for *ages!*"

"Ages? It was hardly a month." He released them, twisting his wrists this way and that. "You see, not a scratch. Tamest campaign I've ever been on." He touched Lyuba's nose with his left hand and clasped Timur's shoulder with his right. "But I missed you two. What have you been up to while I was away?"

"It was exciting. We had a baby." Lyuba jumped up and down. "I am an *apa!*" She pointed at Sumbeka, as if to indicate the awesome status conferred by this miracle on her small self.

Timur gave her a shove. "Auntie Nasan had a baby, goose. Not us."

"I know that," Lyuba said, shoving him back. Alexei quickly intervened, pushing them apart.

"No name calling, Timur," he said. "And behave, both of you." Across the top of the children's heads Alexei sent Maria a smile that melted her insides, then rose to his feet. "Go and say hello to Ruslan while I greet my wife. Then you may show me this marvelous baby."

Maria rushed forward, and he wrapped an arm around her waist, treating her to a fervent kiss. "I'm so glad you aren't hurt," she said. "I missed you."

"No one was hurt. A scratch here and there. Except for a few unlucky souls on the other side. We surprised them." He tightened his arms around her, and she pressed against him. He liked that, she saw. His hand caressed her cheek, and he made no effort to release her. "In the end Prince Andrei surrendered without a fight."

"It's good to have you home." The sight of him filled her with simple bliss.

The hubbub of greetings and congratulations drowned his next words. Lyuba tugged at his robes, reminding him of his promise to let her show him her new nephew. Timur waved a toy warrior, demanding to share what he'd learned from Nasan. Maria kept an arm around her husband's waist as they crossed the room. The men greeted and admired Borya, thoroughly awake but no longer crying. Even Bulat relaxed his usual stern demeanor. "You've done well, my daughter," he announced, tousling the hair of his older grandson. "You'll look after your cousin, will you, young Timur?"

Timur, visibly awed by this profound responsibility, managed a nod. "Yes, *Babai*." He looked around the room as if seeking inspiration until Bulat let him go.

The conversation became general as those returning exchanged news with those who had remained in Moscow. The visit to Roxelana and the story of Prince Ilya's plotting astonished the men; the women drank in the tale of Prince Andrei's abortive rebellion, including the unrest that had greeted the warriors as they approached the city.

Maria waited on tenterhooks for someone to mention her father, while the men seemed to talk of everything but. She clasped her hands together, biting her tongue. They must know. No, they could not know. But whatever Papa had done, she wanted to hear about it. Or had he died, and the men feared to tell her lest they destroy the happiness of their homecoming?

No one was hurt, Alexei said. Except for a few on the other side. But Papa, driven by that devil Prince Ilya, *had* joined the other side.

At last Sumbeka said, "And what of Fyodor Koshkin? Did he indeed join the uprising? We have had no word of him here."

Silence fell. As if by prearrangement Daniil and Bulat turned toward Alexei, who looked uncomfortable. Maria's nerves, already taut, endured another turn of the winch. She was not going to like the news. Her husband's face told her that.

"He was in Staritsa," Alexei said, his voice flat. "That much we determined. Where he is now, I have no idea. Daniil's cousin Grigory said Koshkin left before the end. Most likely he has fled the country, leaving the rest of us to pay the price for his dishonor." His mouth twisted in a bitter curve. "I should have found a different sponsor."

Maria gasped, dragged herself free of him, and smacked his chest. "You said it again!" Tears stung her cheeks. His astonished gaze added to her fury. "I hate you," she spat at him. "After everything I've done to please you, how dare you say you want a different wife?"

"Wait." Alexei reached for her, but she couldn't stand to listen to him for one more instant. It had been bad enough the last time, when they were alone, but here he'd humiliated her in front of everyone. It was unbearable.

"Maria!" Natalya cried. "Don't treat your God-given husband with such disrespect!"

Maria ignored her too. Without another word she ran for the door. The last thing she heard was Natalya saying, "*Bozhe moi*, that girl will be the death of me, I swear."

And Sumbeka's response: "Really? I would have smacked him myself."

"Go after her." Sumbeka gave Alexei a shove, not unlike the one Timur had given Lyuba. "And do try not to be an idiot this time."

Alexei shook his head quickly to clear it. "What's wrong with her? What did I do?"

Nasan crossed the room and took her baby from Natalya's arms. "Honestly," she said to her mother-in-law. "Men!" When Natalya chuckled, Nasan turned to her brother. "You insulted her, *aby*, and not for the first time."

"Insulted her? I didn't insult her." Hadn't he guessed Maria would hate hearing what he had to say about her father? He'd gone out of his way to make the telling as easy on her as possible. But he couldn't keep the truth secret forever. She had to face it, whether she liked it or not.

"Unbelievable," Nasan told the infant. "He doesn't know." Borya scrunched up his face as if he agreed, then burped. Milky bubbles formed around his lips.

Alexei scowled at them. *And now riddles?*

Sumbeka caught his elbow and shook it. "Son, Koshkin sealed your alliance with Maria's hand. If you had picked a different ally, would you have married her? Of course not. And whether you meant to or not, you just told everyone"—she swept her free hand in an arc encompassing the room—"that you wished you hadn't. That's what she heard, in any case. Now go after her and make it right before I lose patience with you. And by the Sainted Miriam (may she rest in glory), think before you speak."

By the time Maria reached her sleeping chamber, tears blurred her sight. Her husband had said it again. He should have found another sponsor. He didn't want her.

The disgust in his voice erased the memory of his ardent kiss, the endearments in his letters. He'd repudiated her in front of the whole family. Suppose Sumbeka and Nasan supported him? Maria's fears from before the wedding revived, and she again felt herself alone among women whose values were foreign to her. Humiliation burned her cheeks and brought the acrid taste of bile to her tongue.

She hated him. No, she loved him, a man who cared nothing for her. She would never forgive him. Never.

Angels of God, take me away from here!

God's angels did not appear. On the contrary. "There you are," Alexei said from the doorway. He sounded grim. She did not acknowledge his presence.

She heard his feet crossing the tiles, the chink of mail, the snap of the closing door. Then he stood close enough that she inhaled the lingering sandalwood of his clothes. "Look at me," he said.

She would not look at him. Tensing her shoulders, she huddled on the sofa, her cheek pressed against the window frame. When he bent and caught her by the elbows, she sprang to her feet, ready to fight him off. Instead he pulled her into a long kiss.

Maria jerked in his hold. *What is he doing?*

His mouth softened against hers, and his tongue and hands caressed her. Sensation overwhelmed her resistance, and she relaxed in his arms. If this was to be the last kiss she received from him, she wanted to enjoy every bit of it. His arms supported her. His hands roamed over her body. His lips brushed cheeks damp with tears. She pressed against him, willing the embrace to continue, to deepen, to push every treacherous, fearful thought from her head. For a while it almost worked.

He drew back and touched his thumb to her face. "I'm sorry. I didn't intend to make you cry. I missed you. Every day, every hour."

Maria stared at him. He'd missed her. Every day, every hour. Was he deranged enough to believe she would swallow that after twice hearing what he really thought?

Should she lie, say she cried from relief at seeing him safe?

But he would break her heart whatever she said. Why not spare them both?

"I should have known better." She looked straight into his eyes as she fought the urge to sob as well as her own craven desire to avoid this confrontation. "You told me before. You wish you had chosen another alliance. Another *bride*. Now that Papa has committed treason, you can divorce me if you wish. You can have the wife you want."

Her words dangled in the air like a flock of tiny nooses, but Maria experienced an odd sense of calm. A soft fog surrounded her, quelling the urge to weep. She straightened her shoulders. There, it was out.

Through the mist she noted the shock on his face. He hadn't expected her to admit the truth. But whatever happened next, even if she hated it, she was ready.

Only she wasn't. Grabbing her around the waist and pulling her with him, Alexei dropped onto the sofa as if hit by a cannonball, then dragged her onto his lap. "*That's* what you think of me? Your swine of a father runs for the hills, so you expect me to turn you in like an ill-mannered horse and throw you and your sister to the wolves? What have I ever done to deserve an accusation like that?"

His anger did not touch her. The fog surrounding her numbed every emotion. "You said you wanted another alliance," she repeated, wooden as one of Lyuba's dolls.

His tense face relaxed, and he stroked her cheek. "Yes, my sister and stepmother said I insulted you. They ripped up at me, the pair of them. But you misunderstood."

The women hadn't betrayed her. A tiny ray of light penetrated the protective fog.

Alexei was talking. She tried to listen, hoping she hadn't missed anything important.

"I didn't mean you," he said. He spoke with the quiet patience he normally reserved for the children, and she wondered how many times he'd repeated the same words and she hadn't heard them. "Only your father, bastard that he is. It never occurred to me that you thought I wanted a different marriage." With his thumb he caressed her cheek once more. "I love you, *kaderle*. I hoped you felt the same."

Wait. Did I hear that correctly?

"You what?" A tingle of life ran through her veins.

He acted as if she hadn't spoken, compressing his lips and staring at the floor. "Stupid, I suppose. My own mother walked away and never looked back. Why should my wife want to stay? I will free you if you wish."

The sound of his pain tumbled Maria back into reality. She threw her arms around his neck, saying the first words that came into her head, not caring whether they fit together or not. "Alexei, no, she didn't. I do love you. I've missed you horribly. Couldn't you tell from my letters? And I'm going to have your child!"

He stared at her, his eyes blank. "What do you mean, 'she didn't'? She absolutely did. My mother left Bulat's horde when I was seven. I never saw her again."

The agony in his voice, for once unguarded, demanded an immediate response. She kissed him, then pressed her palm against his cheek to anchor him to adulthood, to the present. "She didn't *leave*, dearest. Sumbeka told me. Your mother died. That's why you didn't see her again. But she loved you more than anyone. You were her joy."

With a strangled sound he buried his face in her hair. She shared the story, then hugged him close, murmuring words of comfort.

Her fears dissolved in the late afternoon sun.

"I could throttle him." Alexei set Maria aside and paced the floor. Flexing and releasing his hands, he imagined putting them around his father's neck and squeezing. "How could he do that? Kill my mother, keep it secret, *banish* me because he saw something of her in me? It's barbaric!"

He raged on for some time, swearing at Bulat, reliving memories of those early years of exile. Despite his descent from Genghis Khan, he'd lived no better than a beggar, forced to work his way up in his lord's esteem. Maria listened, not interrupting, her eyes fixed on his face, as he talked about how it felt to be sixteen years old—homeless, nameless, bereft of clan and ancestors.

"But how did you survive?" she asked when his anger ebbed and he could hear her.

"Ildar Shirin took me in. The head of my father's council. To spite *Ata*, I think—they disagreed about many things, including how to raise their sons—but out of kindness too. Ildar sent me to his relatives in Crimea, where I met Islam-Girei and Ruslan. Without the three of them ..." He left the sentence unfinished. Maria held out a hand, and with a heavy sigh he walked toward her. His mail shirt clanked as he sat, and he recalled only then that he was still dressed for war. He rested his elbows on his thighs. "I would have become a roving *kazak*, I suppose—a man without a lord, fighting for anyone who would feed me."

The memories brought a lump to his throat. He couldn't bring himself to tell her that even in Islam-Girei's camp he had often lived by what he could scrounge. It took years to work his way back to the position into which he'd been born, only to watch his lord's mad fears explode his efforts into nothingness after more than a decade of devoted service.

She seemed distressed enough, a small frown creasing her brow. "You look worried, dear heart," he said. "Have I bored you to tears with my ramblings?"

"Of course not." She widened her eyes at the very idea, and warmth toward her flooded him anew. "I've waited since our wedding for you to share your past with me. I want to hear every word. It's only ... would you tell Timur, under similar circumstances? Would you let a woman live who killed babies in their cradles? I don't think you would. Please understand: I hate your father for banishing you, and I grieve for how you suffered. But what your mother did was also terrible."

Tempted to snap at her, he stopped. *Would* he tell his son that the father he loved had executed the mother he loved for murdering his half-brother? Who could impose such knowledge on a child? "You're right. I wouldn't. If Guzel had ever forced me into such a bitter choice, I would have taken the same path as my parents. At first. And in truth I don't regret the life I've led. It was often lonely, but it also forced me to become my own man, not just my father's heir. And it brought me to you."

She clasped his hand in both of hers and kissed it. "I meant to ask you this. Will you take Timur to visit his mother?"

"Yes, but not alone. When you're more comfortable on horseback, we will go as a family. Even Lyuba: she will love being an *apa* to my brother's twins!"

Maria laughed, and he pulled her close. She rested her cheek against the hollow of his shoulder. Only then did he recall what she'd said earlier. She loved him, and she bore his child. When he ran his hand over her belly, he sensed no change, then realized it wouldn't happen yet. It only felt as if he had waited for her half his life. Their marriage had lasted less than four months.

"You weren't supposed to tell me till the summer," he said, rubbing her stomach so she would know he was teasing. "Now what am I to do? I just got back from a war—a pathetic excuse for a war and a damned nuisance, but a war nonetheless—and here's my wife with child."

Maria giggled, a soft girlish sound he hadn't heard in far too long. "Remember you became a Christian?" she suggested. "We don't have that prohibition—not so early, anyway. But you did hear me. I wondered if you had."

"Hmm," he said. "I could manage that. If I also heard you say you loved me. You did admit it? I didn't make that up?"

She pulled back enough to kiss him. "I did. As did you. I won't let you forget. And what was that you called me?"

"*Kaderle?* It means 'beloved.' Darling, dear, precious—pick whichever one you like." He tightened his hold.

"I like them all," she said. "Welcome home, *kaderle*. You stayed away far too long. Now let's get rid of that armor, shall we?"

Chapter 27

THE THREE DAYS TO PSKOV TURNED INTO A WEEK, DUE TO an onslaught of bad weather that required Koshkin and Kuzma to shelter in one barn after another, huddled among the scanty remains of last year's hay. But heading into June the peasants had other things on their minds besides strangers squatting in their outbuildings: plowing, sowing, hoeing, weeding, and many tasks to do with farm animals that Koshkin could not name and had not the slightest interest in. So long as he exercised caution, let his northern companion do the talking, and rode as hard and as far as the mud wallows that passed for roads permitted, saving the barns for impassable days and impossible nights, he could keep himself fed and moving without attracting unwanted attention.

At last he reached Pskov. The massive stone walls—raised against the very German knights on whose mercy Koshkin, thanks to Prince Ilya and his machinations, planned to cast himself—offered protection and relief. Failing a safe harbor, he would settle for a good meal, a set of dry clothes, and a bed that did not stink of the barnyard. He sent Kuzma into the town for supplies and waited in a copse across the river from the menacing white stone fortress with its wooden elf-hat towers.

Kuzma did not return for some time, and when he did, he brought food and clothing, but also a glum face and a disheveled appearance. "Won't do, Lord," he said as he dropped the bread and homespun robes at Koshkin's feet.

"What won't do?" Koshkin moved the pile of clothing away from the damp grass and brushed dirt off the bread. Beggars could not be choosers, as the saying went, but honestly!

"Entering Pskov, Lord." Kuzma scratched his beard and squinted his eyes, as if searching for words. "I made it out with my skin, but it was a close call. The townsfolk are grabbing any stranger they see."

"Holy Mother, why?" Koshkin started, almost dropping the chunk of bread he'd raised halfway to his mouth.

"That Prince Andrei." Kuzma waved his own loaf in emphasis. "The one who's been causing trouble for months—seems he's surrendered to the grand prince. The Muscovites are looking for his supporters. Locals don't want any suspicions about which side they're on, so they're capturing and turning in any visitors. Let the troops figure out whom to keep; that's their view. The men at the tavern told me that, so I took the hint and made a run for it. Couple of the townsfolk chased me even so."

"You did well." Koshkin dug in his purse and handed over a few small copper coins. "We'll stay here for the night, then press on to Pechory in the morning. What else did you learn about this Andrei business?" Kuzma moved into a long tale about Andrei's capture while Koshkin munched bread and thought.

He'd made the right decision. He'd seen Andrei's weakness and fled at the right moment. Otherwise he too would be heading to Moscow in chains. He could only hope that Kuzma failed to realize that he was aiding one of Andrei's fugitives.

At times Koshkin wondered what his guide made of him. He'd withheld his real name, not spoken except to issue orders, offered no private information other than his lie about the pilgrimage to Pechory. Yet a man in noble dress, speaking with Muscovite "a" sounds in place of the full northern "o," and arriving in Staraia Russa at the very moment when the forces of Staritsa and Moscow converged must raise a few questions in Kuzma's mind. Perhaps the man thought he harbored a deserter from the Muscovite army. Perhaps he didn't care, so long as the job paid well.

Or perhaps he planned to milk the situation for as long as he could, then turn Koshkin in. That prospect kept Koshkin up at night, especially the night they spent outside Pskov. It wouldn't take much for Kuzma to alert the guard.

Although the good citizens of Pskov had chased Kuzma too …

Koshkin couldn't wait to reach the border. Indeed, he had to fight the temptation to leap for his saddle and ride. So far north, the June sky remained light enough to ride even at midnight. But the horses needed rest, as did their riders, so he gritted his teeth and waited.

Dawn saw them back on the road, Koshkin still in his undistinguished townsman's clothing. Knowledge that the Muscovite troops sought stragglers imparted a humming, anxious energy to this last leg of the journey. Pechory lay but one good day's ride away, although the muddy ruts that passed for roads challenged the horses.

Throughout those endless hours Koshkin said a sad farewell to his wife and children, on whose ungrateful behalf he had risked so much. Did any of them appreciate his sacrifice? He doubted it.

Well, let them see how well they did under the leadership of a cocky Tatar sultan preoccupied with their stepmother. By the time Koshkin established himself in a new government, a new land, and could return, his family would be glad to welcome him home.

The danger from Muscovite troops forced him to revise his initial plan—to seek shelter among the monks while his guide arranged for transport across the small river that stood between him and the German knights. Suppose a conscientious abbot or zealous novice thwarted his escape after he had traveled so far? Better to swim his long-suffering horse across the river himself if he couldn't find a fisherman or a ford.

As evening closed in, he caught sight of the star-scattered sky-blue domes that marked his arrival at Pechory. On the riverbank he saw fishermen in small boats, some on rafts, tying their craft for the night. Tension tightened his gut. So close.

He could pay Kuzma now, approach the fishermen himself, but where would the man spend the night except at the monastery? The moment for concealment had passed.

"Kuzma," he said. "Find me a man with a raft."

"Not a pilgrimage then?" the merchant asked. "One of Andrei's men, I suppose."

When Koshkin hesitated, struggling to express his complex reality in the terms most likely to win Kuzma's support, the merchant held up a hand. "Don't answer. Can't say what I don't know. But understand that I've no love for the Muscovites. My family hails from Novgorod. I grew up on tales of what the grand prince's forces did to my city. My granddad drowned in the river, a pike through his heart. My granny threw herself through a hole in the ice after they raped her and burned the house over her head. My father hid in the cellar next door, but as an old man he insisted he could still hear the screams."

Koshkin, shocked beyond words, watched his guide walk toward the riverbank. Here, so close to his destination, the tale underlined the narrowness of his own escape, the perils he faced if he could not complete this final stage.

While Kuzma searched, Koshkin took refuge under the walls surrounding the monastery to avoid unwanted attention from the monks. He forced dry bread and cheese down his throat, washed them down with weak kvass, and checked his saddlebags.

Before long Kuzma returned with a dull but sturdy fisherman, accepted the promised payment, and left. Koshkin followed him with his eyes as the merchant circled the monastery and approached the main gates. Would Kuzma keep his word?

He had reached the crisis point. He could not afford a moment's delay. The Lord had shown extraordinary mercy so far, and he must hope that divine favor would extend until he crossed the river.

"Help me get this horse on the raft," Koshkin ordered, and the stolid fisherman moved forward to grasp the reins.

"Nice beast," the man said.

Koshkin froze. Would the quality of his horse give him away? "A gift from a former master," he said, imitating the merchant's mode of speech. "A bit skittish. A steppe pony would suit me better, but who says no to a free horse?"

The fisherman laughed at that. "Agreed. C'mon then, horse, and none of your fidgets. Fine feathers won't help you here."

The horse responded, after a moment's unrest that made Koshkin wonder if he might not do better to hire a new mount when he reached Neuhausen. But his stash of coins had dwindled considerably since his departure from Moscow. He sent a prayer of thanks heavenward when the horse at last sidled onto the raft.

The fisherman poled off, and as the soft glow of sunset lit sparks on the star-spattered cupolas Koshkin watched his motherland recede against the horizon. Ahead, steep banks and solid German engineering marked the boundary between his old life and the new. He had intelligence and skills, a knowledge of diplomacy, good blood in his veins, and recent experience of government. God willing, he could put this fiasco behind him and rebuild his life. The Lithuanians could not be so different: they were men, after all.

But would he ever see Russia again?

"Roxelana did *what?*" Maria handed Solomonida a plate of *chek-chek*, a specialty of her cook's. The white porcelain with its lively blue ducks created a backdrop against which the small fried dough balls seemed to swim in their honey pond. She held up a brass ewer. "Tea? Or shall I send for juice instead?"

"I'll try the tea," Solomonida said. "It's an odd taste, but better than adding more sweet to that honey."

In the background Lyuba and Anna were serving *chek-chek* and tea to their dolls, "helping" them by eating the sweets themselves. Timur had gone off with his father to do boy things, and Maria rejoiced when Solomonida and her daughter arrived. Alexei's return had brought them back to their own home, and as much as she enjoyed his company and the familiar surroundings, she would miss her daily interactions with other women. She could visit whenever she liked, but it was not quite the same, especially with Nasan and Natalya also restored to their own house.

Her hostess duties complete, Maria poured herself a cup of tea and sat next to her guest. "Tell me again," she said. "Last I heard, Roxelana was in custody at the Shuisky house. How can she be on her way to Lithuania?"

Solomonida burst out laughing. "Honestly, Maria, can't you guess? Princess Nadezhda!" She bit into a *chek-chek*. "Oh, these are good. I'll rue the day I discovered them."

"Princess Nadezhda?" Maria puzzled over that one. True, the princess had promised to help when last they met, but so soon? "She spoke to the grand princess?"

"Exactly," Solomonida said. "Begging her to get your stepmother out of her house."

"And the grand princess agreed?" Maria tasted the *chek-chek* and found them excellent, as always.

"After Nadezhda told her the whole," Solomonida replied. "Prince Ilya should have controlled his lust. It's one thing to imprison an enemy's wife and confiscate his property, but quite another to subject a fellow woman to unwanted and sinful advances, especially if doing so angers one of your closest ladies. Elena understands that as well as any of us."

Maria nodded. "I suppose. Why Lithuania, though? And how is she getting there?"

"Well, there's no point in forcing her to stay here." Solomonida gently waved her tea cup in the air, then took an experimental sip. "She isn't Russian, and she has no home to go back to. Her traitor husband has disappeared, so they can't use her as a lure. Nadezhda arranged for her to travel with a group of merchants; one sight of Roxelana, and they agreed. More surprising is that she did too."

"Maybe not." Maria thought of her stepmother. "Surprising, I mean. If she's given up on marriage, as she indicated she had, she'll find better opportunities in the western lands. She came here only to be with Alexei, although he says he didn't invite her and now he's definitely broken with her. So why would she stay?"

"No more worries for you *or* Princess Nadezhda," Solomonida said. "You'll have your beautiful husband all to yourself. I expect Elena will rescind your disgrace soon, and you can go back to court. Not yet, though. She's still raging over Prince Andrei challenging her. Doesn't matter that she's the one who pushed him to it. Even Telepnev's not immune. Did you hear?" She bit into a *chek-chek* with vigor.

Maria set her plate aside in favor of the tea. The intense sweetness of the honey, however delicious, demanded a fresh taste to counteract it. "I did. Papa Nikolai's livid. Elena revoked the safe conduct, chastised her favorite for offering it, threw Andrei and his supporters in jail. Thirty men sentenced to hang, including Grigory Kolychev. Papa Nikolai will offer surety for him (he's mad about that as well), but I doubt it will work."

"Not a chance." Solomonida, too, set her plate aside. "Elena wants to make an example of the thirty that no future rebel can ignore. Your father's lucky he escaped. Otherwise he'd find himself at the end of a rope as well."

Maria shuddered. Solomonida spoke the truth. "That beast Prince Ilya," she said. "I've never believed that Papa intended from the beginning to betray the grand prince. If Ilya hadn't lusted after my stepmother, my family would still be together. I swear, he'll pay for that if it's the last thing I do." She touched the medallion of the dark-haired Mother of God that hung from her neck. "Poor Papa. I remember my wedding. He was so happy with Roxelana. Even though it made my skin crawl at the time, it's sad to see love broken. Especially now that I know how happy a marriage can be."

For a moment Solomonida stared into her cup without speaking. Then she said slowly, as if picking the words one by one, "I suspect we haven't seen the last of your father. Perhaps marital bliss has escaped him, but he reminds me of a phoenix: he burns to ashes, only to revive and return."

Maria gazed at her hands. The henna had long since faded, yet she recalled the designs that Roxelana had painted there—

was it only four months ago? Phoenix and dragon, dragon and phoenix, joined eternally in marital harmony. How strange to think that she had tumbled into love with a man she had not chosen, carried his child, won his heart in return, while her father had lost the bride of his passion.

A wicked thought occurred to her. "Suppose he and Roxelana cross paths in Lithuania?"

Solomonida picked up her plate once more. "Now *that* is a meeting I would like to see!"

Right after Solomonida and Anna left, Alexei arrived to sweep Maria off to his parents' house. "My sister will be there," he said. "With that infant you adore. Not to mention his grandparents and Daniil. A regular family conclave. We'll take Lyuba and Timur as well. They can play in the courtyard while the rest of us discuss the political situation. Don't pretend you aren't interested. I know you better than that."

"I'm not trying to pretend." Maria did her best to look outraged, but he laughed at her. "Of course I'll come with you. But you won't convince me that Lady Natalya wants to be part of any political conversation."

"Well, she can look after the baby if she doesn't." He shrugged as if this were the most idiotic choice a woman could make.

"And *Kaenana* would love that, wouldn't she? In her own house! Are we riding?" He nodded. "Then let me change my clothes and fetch Lyuba, and we'll be on our way."

They met in the courtyard a short time later. Alexei lifted Lyuba onto her horse, then helped Maria onto Kumai's back before mounting Ajdar, fidgeting nearby. "He's frisky today," Alexei said. "Ready?"

They set off, two by two with the children in front so the adults could keep an eye on them. The ever-present guards surrounded them. The sun brushed Maria's cheeks; a soft breeze kept the heat under control. The steady gait of the mare moving beneath her, her husband's strong and loving presence, the baby growing inside her, the prospect of family, the joy of shared interests, the sparkling potential of a rich and exciting future among people who valued her for more than her ability to conceive (although they valued that too)—even with the looming clouds caused by Prince Andrei's rebellion, her father's flight, and Grand Princess Elena's rage, Maria treasured this lovely day.

Inside the gates that guarded Bulat and Sumbeka's estate, warriors mingled with servants rushing to perform this domestic task or that. Alexei took Kumai's reins in one hand and pushed through the throng to the base of the stairs before dismounting, lifting Maria down, and turning to search for the children. Thanks to Ruslan's guidance they appeared right behind him. Two members of the escort took charge of the horses, and the family, plus Ruslan, ascended the stairs.

The scene inside made Maria want to laugh. Someone— Sumbeka? Nasan?—had unwrapped Baby Borya. The infant, clad only in a fresh cloth, lay kicking blissfully on a blanket in the middle of the floor. What made it funny was Natalya, who hovered in the background like a clucking hen, her hands waving in the air as if she could hardly contain herself from reaching for the child. Meanwhile Sumbeka had positioned herself between Natalya and the baby like a physical barrier, while Nasan knelt on the blanket beside her son tickling his feet and cooing at him. "But his limbs," Natalya was saying as Maria came through the door. "They won't grow straight unless you keep them tied. How often have I told you that, daughter?"

"They will," Sumbeka said in a firm tone that suggested she had made this point several times already. "I have seen dozens of babies—even more than you because of the harem—and I swear that if we feed the child well and let him lie in the sun and kick his darling feet and wave his sweet hands, he will grow straight as a poplar. That's why I keep telling you to let his mother nurse him." She gestured at Alexei, who had come forward to greet her, Timur in tow. "Look at these two. Their mothers did the same, and they turned out fine."

The argument continued without a pause. Maria hugged her mother-in-law, kissed Lady Natalya, then took Lyuba's hand and went to sit beside Nasan on the rug. She pressed her cheek against Nasan's and touched the baby's perfect toes. She so hoped her own child would come out like this one. He was gorgeous, but she couldn't say that aloud for fear of the Evil Eye. "He loves this," she said instead. "A shame to keep him tied up from dawn to dusk."

"Yes," Nasan said, but Maria heard a note in her sister-in-law's voice that suggested distraction. She glanced to her right, and Nasan put her hands on Maria's shoulders, studying her. Maria raised her eyebrows but received no response at first to her unspoken question.

Then Nasan said, "I don't believe it."

"What?"

Nasan smiled, a warm, embracing smile that lit her dark eyes and enhanced every exquisite feature of her face. "You are happy," she said in a voice tinged with awe. "For the first time in the years I've known you, you look truly happy. How that pleases me!"

"Yes," Maria admitted, blushing. "It turns out I like being a Tatar wife after all."

Fire and water, earth and air—balanced and entwined in the eternal cosmic dance. The spirit world should rejoice, but harmony lies out of reach. The crime of double fratricide weakens the center, generating ripples of energy strong enough to shatter a shaman's drum. Revenge, betrayal, distrust, ambition: the sins of the past stalk the present, and wolves gather from the four corners of the world, threatening the Russian lands.

Historical Note

IN THE WEST THE PHOENIX SYMBOLIZES IMMORTALITY: A bird every so often consumed by fire only to rise from its own ashes. But along the Silk Roads the phoenix, which bears many names and takes many forms, has richer and more complex associations than immortality alone. From the Indian Garuda to Fenghuang of China, Kumai, Huma, Firebird, and the other variations of the Turkic, Persian, and Russian lands the phoenix symbolizes virtue, aspiration, constancy, good fortune, and—most appealing for the present story—happiness. In relation with the dragon, itself a multifaceted symbol of everything from long life to stormy weather, the phoenix is Yin to the dragon's Yang, fire to water, the source of marital harmony blending passion and prosperity. In China the phoenix takes two forms: Fenghuang, the golden phoenix associated with the center, and the Vermilion Bird, linked to the south and to fire. The latter seemed a better match for Maria, whose snappy comebacks seldom fail to land her in trouble.

For those encountering Nasan, Daniil, and their extended family for the first time, a note on the Tatar words sprinkled throughout the book. Most of them express relationships, which Tatars even today often use in preference to names (the custom, now largely confined to older women, of showing respect by avoiding a husband's name is an extension of this practice). The terms given here—*ata* (father), *ana* (mother), *aby* (uncle or older brother), *ené* (younger brother), *sengel* (younger sister, with the "g" as in song), *apa* (aunt or older sister), *babai* (grandfather), *kilen* (daughter-in-law), and *kaenana* (mother-in-law)—may not be exactly those common in the sixteenth century, but they are close. Alexei should call his stepmother *uti ana*, rather than mother, but that seemed to introduce an unnecessary complication. The correct address in Russian, even in the 1530s, for a khan's daughter or daughter-in-law was *tsarevna*, just as *khan* was translated as *tsar*, *khatun* as *tsaritsa*, and *sultan* as *tsarevich*.

The "rebellion" or "uprising" (always given in quotes in the historical literature because of the circumstances surrounding the brief confrontation) led by Prince Andrei of Staritsa, the uncle of the young grand prince who grew up to become Ivan IV the Terrible, did happen much as detailed here, although historians argue about the motives driving both sides in the conflict and even about some of the timing, since surviving sources tend toward the tendentious and many crucial details remain unclear. I have swapped in my own characters for their historical counterparts as needed and have selected from the different narratives available the versions that best serve the needs of my story. And although I have done my best to discover what the Kremlin looked like in the 1530s and how court protocol operated at that time, I have had to make up many of the details because accurate information is often simply not available. For example, the gallery overlooking the main reception area in the Faceted Palace definitely existed in the seventeenth century, but its presence in the sixteenth remains less certain. My thanks to Ann Kleimola and Claudia Jensen for investigating the question on my behalf.

I owe a special debt to M. M. Bentsianov for his research into the makeup of Prince Andrei's Staritsa court and to V. V. Shaposhnik not only for his detailed reconstruction of the events leading up to and beyond the Staritsa conflict but for his calculation of distances and speeds that make it possible to estimate how long, say, an army would require to get from Staritsa to Novgorod or Kolomna in 1537. My estimates of dates and side journeys such as Koshkin's flight are based on his figures. I owe an even deeper debt to M. M. Krom, whose in-depth analysis of the troubled regency of Elena Glinskaya has enriched this book and its predecessors; Russell E. Martin for sharing his study of Muscovite royal weddings and in general responding with prompt and erudite answers to my questions; Catherine Merridale for her richly informative *Red Fortress: History and Illusion in the Kremlin*; Daniel H. Kaiser for his research on childbirth in Muscovy; and Ann Kleimola, again, for reading *The Vermilion Bird* and two of its predecessors for historical errors. On the Tatar sultans who entered Muscovite service, both those who converted and those who did not, I have found invaluable the work of A. V. Beliakov, Craig Gayan Kennedy, Janet Martin, and Donald Ostrowski. None of these fine scholars, nor any of the others whose works I consulted, is in any way responsible for the fictional use I have made of their findings.

NASAN'S FAMILY

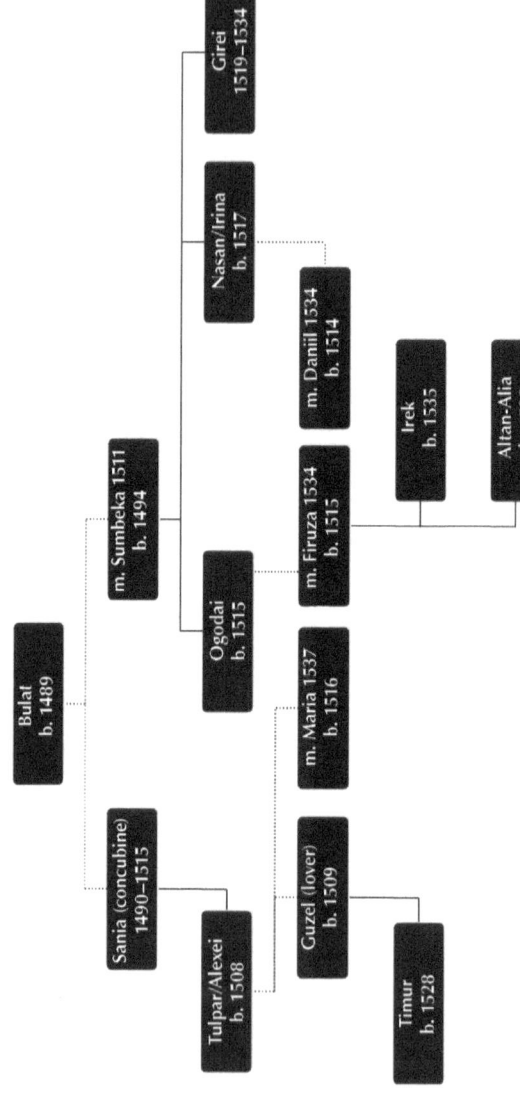

Dotted lines indicate marriages and romantic relationships; solid lines indicate parent/child links.
Most couples had additional children who died before birth or in infancy; Bulat also has wives and concubines not listed by name.

KOLYCHEV CLAN

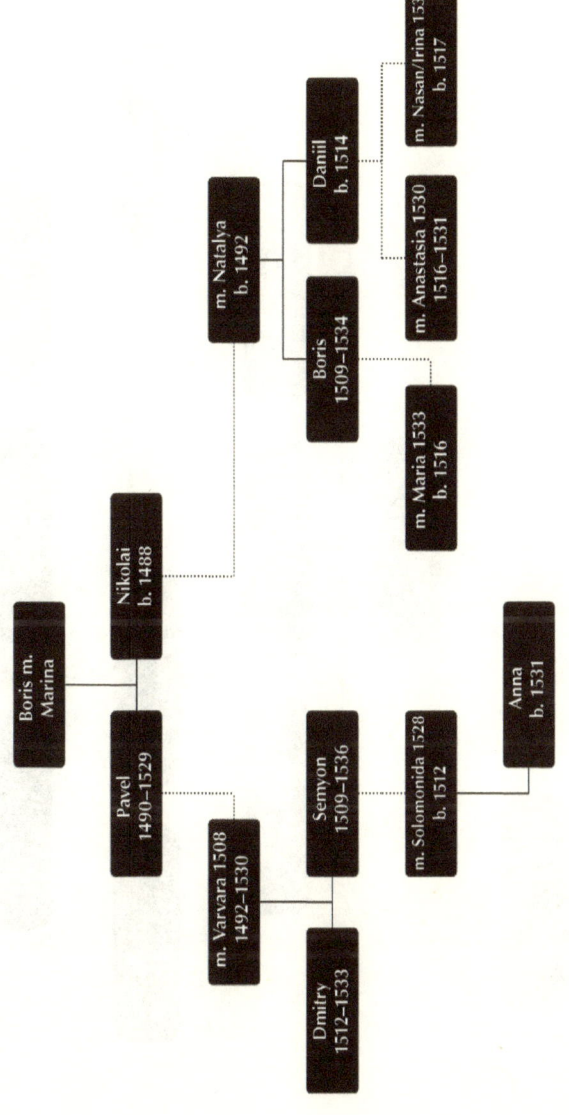

SELECTED MEMBERS OF THE HOUSE OF MOSCOW, 1440–1537

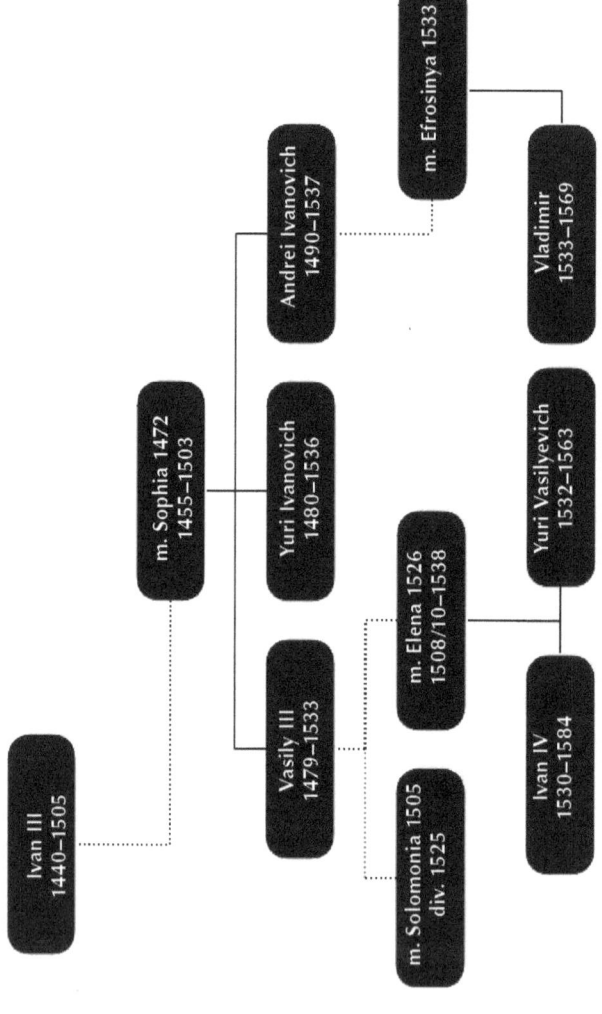

Acknowledgments

IN ADDITION TO THE SCHOLARS MENTIONED IN THE HIS-
torical Note, I tip my hat here to my invaluable writers' group,
now entering its tenth year. Ariadne Apostolou and Courtney J.
Hall, I can't imagine writing a book without you!

I thank the other members of Five Directions Press for
their contributions to our joint enterprise, as well as Diana
Holquist, herself an author, for friendship and emotional
support. Gabrielle Mathieu of Five Directions Press and Liza
Perrat of Triskele Books read the penultimate draft, and *The
Vermilion Bird* is richer for their comments. I owe a great debt
to you both.

To my husband and son—and, of course, the cats, who
purred encouragingly at all the right moments—words cannot
express my gratitude. Warm and heartfelt thanks also go to all
my readers. I hope you consider *The Vermilion Bird* a worthy
addition to the series.

The Author

AS A CHILD C. P. LESLEY THOUGHT EVERYONE MADE UP stories while falling asleep. It never occurred to her that anyone would pay her for them, and for a long time she was right—no one would. But after years of producing horrible prose, reading books about novel writing, and pestering hapless fellow writers and friends to read her drafts, some of the advice stuck, and she finished *The Not Exactly Scarlet Pimpernel*, then *The Golden Lynx* and its sequels—*The Winged Horse*, *The Swan Princess*, and *The Vermilion Bird*.

She is currently working on the last of the five directions, *The Shattered Drum* (Legends 5: Center), which explores the consequences of Grand Princess Elena's ascendancy over her brothers-in-law.

When not thinking up new ways to torture her characters, she edits other people's manuscripts, reads voraciously, maintains her website, and practices classical ballet—an interest reflected in *Desert Flower* and *Kingdom of the Shades* (Tarkei Chronicles 1 and 2). She also hosts New Books in Historical Fiction, a channel in the New Books Network. You can find out more about her and her books at www.cplesley.com.

Forthcoming in 2018

C. P. Lesley, *The Shattered Drum*
(Legends of the Five Directions 5: Center)

Moscow, December 1537

NASAN BLEW AIR ACROSS HER BABY'S TUMMY AND GIGGLED as he waved both chubby hands in the air. Boris, known as Borya within the family, had reached the ripe age of seven months. With his father's honey brown eyes and her dark hair he looked fit to become a sturdy and handsome boy, but she didn't share that opinion out loud, lest she attract the attention of dangerous spirits. In case even the thought could draw unwanted attention, she murmured a short prayer in her son's ear. His baby scent, floral soap mixed with a hint of milk, filled her nostrils.

But as she released him to sit on the rug, his face crumpled. He grabbed his right cheek with one hand and batted her away with the other. Concerned, she touched his forehead and found it warm and damp. "What's wrong with him?" she asked his wet nurse, Zhenya. Since birth Borya had been a placid child, not given even to such small outbursts as this.

"He's teething, Tsarevna." Zhenya crossed the room and crouched next to the baby. "He didn't sleep well last night or feed well this morning. No doubt his gums hurt."

"But he feels hot," Nasan argued. "He should not feel hot, even if he's teething. Suppose it's something else?"

Zhenya patted the baby's cheek, and he pushed her hand away as well. His outraged howls rose in volume.

Her husband's voice cut across the child's cries. "Time to go," Daniil said. "It won't do to arrive late for a royal funeral—especially this one, which will harbor more serpents than chickens. Let's not offer ourselves as prey."

Alerted by the edge in his voice, Nasan turned to study him. Resplendent in robes that matched her own, black velvet trimmed in gold, the snow-laden sky behind his head no match for his tawny good looks, he never failed to provoke a shiver of desire.

But her child needed her. She pressed her hand against Borya's forehead once more. "He's ill," she said. "I should stay with him."

"He's teething, Tsarevna," Zhenya repeated. "He will be right as rain by the morning, I promise. Or if not then, as soon as the tooth breaks through."

"You don't know that," Nasan snapped. "Babies get sick even when they're teething."

"And besides," Daniil interjected, "I'm sorry, but we *must* go. The funeral procession will start within the hour. Unless one of us dies before then, we have no acceptable excuse for staying away. Even if Zhenya is wrong, you'll be back with Borya soon enough. Come."

Nasan bit back the retort that hovered on her tongue and studied her baby.

Was Zhenya right? Nasan had seen plenty of babies in her father's harem, and teething did show itself in various signs, including a slight fever. Borya had reached the age when teeth should begin to appear. Her medical books insisted that no harm came from it. Her touch revealed an uncharacteristic warmth, not a child burning up; he might recover even before she returned.

But she had also seen slight fevers escalate at terrifying speed. And this was her *baby*, her precious son, not a child in a medical book. She didn't want to move so much as a step until she felt certain nothing more ailed him than his first tooth.

Yet she could not stay. As Daniil had pointed out, the highest families in the land must attend any burial service for a royal prince—even one callously murdered by his sister-in-law, who seemed set on covering up that inconvenient reality, known to the entire court. Some duties a khan's daughter could neither skip nor postpone, no matter how little she welcomed them.

"*Ana* will be back soon, Borya," she told him in Tatar. He was still too young to respond or even understand, but she wanted him to learn the languages of both his parents. With one last snuggle she handed him to Zhenya. "Send for me at once if he seems sicker," she said before crossing the room to join Daniil.

"It's teething," Zhenya said once more. "He will do fine. But of course we will send a message if there is need."

As if it mattered, Nasan thought bitterly. She could not depart in the middle of this wretched ceremony even if Borya stood at death's door.

Yet the assurance comforted her a little. Enough that she refrained from snapping at her husband when he caught her round the waist. "What happened to my warrior princess?" he asked. "Tell me she is not wholly submerged in Mama!"

"Don't tease," she said. "If he is only teething, then I will not worry. But infants sicken so fast."

"Make no mistake." He kissed her. "I too worry about our son. I will bring you home as soon as possible. Agreed?"

"Yes." She allowed herself a small sigh of relief that he had abandoned his question about the warrior princess, which she no longer knew how to answer. How to explain the conflicting demands that tugged at her heart? Without her archery and her riding and her swordsmanship, she would become like any other Russian lady of the house. Daniil, too, deserved as much attention as she could give him before war and government duties again called him away. Yet Borya changed and grew with each passing day, and she hated the thought of missing his first smile, his first word, his first attempt to sit or crawl or stand. She loved them both beyond bounds, her husband and her son. She could never choose one over the other.

God willing, I will never have to.

http://www.fivedirectionspress.com/the-shattered-drum

MORE BY THIS AUTHOR

The Not Exactly Scarlet Pimpernel

Legends of the Five Directions
The Golden Lynx (1: West)
The Winged Horse (2: East)
The Swan Princess (3: North)
The Vermilion Bird (4: South)

Tarkei Chronicles
Desert Flower
Kingdom of the Shades

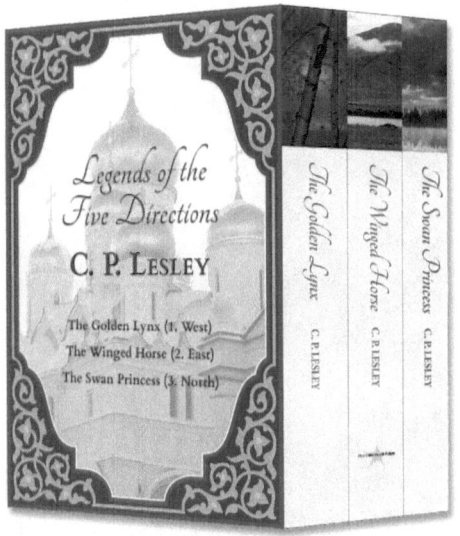

WHO IS THE GOLDEN LYNX?

This question drives the first book in Legends of the Five Directions, a series that will sweep you to the distant world of sixteenth-century Russia, amid the descendants of Genghis Khan and courts that could teach the Borgias a thing or two about political ambition, assassination, and chicanery. Follow Nasan and her kinsfolk as they struggle for power, honor, identity, and love across the steppe and through the vast forests of the Russian North.

"A richly depicted, exciting adventure set amongst the Tatars of 16th-century Central Russia. Fans of historical romance will find this a delight."
                    —Yangsze Choo, author of the acclaimed novel *The Ghost Bride*

Kindle box set of Legends 1–3 available July 2018.

http://www.fivedirectionspress.com/boxsets

Have you ever wanted to rewrite your favorite novel—fix the heroine's mistakes, win the hero's heart? Nina Pennington does. She is overjoyed when she lands the plum role as the heroine of *The Scarlet Pimpernel* in a class assignment based on a computer game.

Nina knows she can win—until she realizes her one chance for success requires an alliance with her least-favorite fellow grad student, cast as the Scarlet Pimpernel himself.

The game challenges Nina in ways she never anticipated, and that least-favorite fellow grad student starts looking better by the minute. But then, she has always had a soft spot for the swashbuckling Scarlet Pimpernel.

Now Nina has to choose: win the game, or take a chance on love?

http://www.fivedirectionspress.com/not-exactly-scarlet-pimpernel